Only If Threatened

A Mystery

KATHRYN A. IMLER

FOREST PARK PRESS
FORT WAYNE, IN

www. kathrynimler.com

This is a work of fiction. Names, characters, places, and incidents are either the product of the author's imagination or are used fictitiously. The author's use of places or businesses is not intended to change the entirely fictional character of the work. In all other respects, any resemblance to person living or dead, businesses, companies, events, or locales is entirely coincidental.

ISBN: 978-0-9979723-0-6

CHAPTER
ONE

Twelve-year-old Simon Webster closed his book, looked up and out on quiet Apple Street. "I think maybe murder."

He sat with two younger siblings on the steps of their front porch in pools of sunlight like frogs on lily pads eyeing a fly.

It was early morning, early summer. They were free from school. Free to do whatever they chose.

Sarah, eleven, lifted her pen from a notebook, tapped it at her lower lip. "Murder is good," she said, "but it can be so ... grisly."

"Gross," said nine-year-old Ann, adjusting the pink-rimmed glasses jutting forth from her short, blunt-cut dark hair.

"What about robbery?" offered Sarah. "Maybe that fits our neighborhood better."

Collectively, they regarded their street, beginning to stir up and down the line of old, mostly well-kept houses: the nurse next door waving as she loaded the back of her van, the man across the street watering his lawn; a guy rolling out his motorcycle.

The three on the porch turned back to their books and notebooks.

They had a lot of options to consider.

At the other end of the block, Libby Kinder stood in her front yard. The June air was sweet and fresh all around. Nearby sat Dash, her miniature Dachshund-terrier mix, waiting.

A slight lift in the land let Libby's corner lot rise slightly above the rest, giving her duplex a perch-like overview of the neighborhood.

For twenty years she had lived here and admired that view: the row of mostly American Foursquares, sturdy two- and three-story boxes interrupted occasionally by a Cape Cod or Workman's bungalow.

Any one of them might offer arched doorways, six-over-one windows, or gabled roofs. No matter the design, they all resided neatly on a street edged by sidewalks and curbs; its park strips full of trees, now leafy and green.

Libby loved standing there, day or night, just to watch. Sometimes the street was wild with activity, sometimes serene like this morning.

Today she was there early because she had promised to pass out fliers for Apple Street's annual block party planning meeting. For many, the block party was a much-anticipated event. Kids looked forward to bike parades and chalk-drawing competitions on the closed-off street. Adults gathered for a day of catching up with friends they otherwise only passed briefly as each dashed off to their separate outings. It was a day of homemade food and simple games, of neighbors being together for an end-of-summer celebration.

Libby needed to make the rounds soon—up thirteen houses on one side, down thirteen on the other—before too many people were out. People she would be happy to chat with otherwise when she did not have her other work waiting.

She started north with Dash in tow. The little Montgomery girls weren't out to tease, so her first drop was easy.

She would have crossed the open grass to the next house, but that was not allowed. She would have let an obedient Dash walk by her side untethered, but that was truly unwise. People had been reported to the police for the former; Libby herself turned in for the latter.

One did not mess with Mrs. Thorne.

Granted, dogs were supposed to be on a leash. The city law didn't irritate Libby so much as its being tapped by a neighbor who never balanced her formal and rigid complaints with any neighborly pleasantries.

Best guess was that Mrs. Thorne was in her eighties. She lived alone in a plain gray house. Regardless of the weather, she wore blue sweatpants and matching windbreaker. How often she had her coif of lacquered white hair done was uncertain, for it never deviated from that tight look.

Any Thorne family resided out-of-state and visited rarely. Conflicting stories about a husband who'd left her or died, children sent away to school or who'd run away from home, money inherited or darkly acquired all gave her a mysterious quality.

The woman kept to herself unless moved to action or comment.

Like someone putting something in her mailbox.

"Good thing that dog's on a leash."

Libby jumped as Mrs. Thorne showed up behind the screen in the front door just as Libby slipped a block party flier into the box mounted on the porch pillar.

"Leash laws, you know."

Adjusting to Mrs. Thorne's sudden gauzy appearance, Libby smiled and prepared to sound congenial.

Catholic upbringing, parents hellbent on kindness, and lots of opportunities to practice with squabbling siblings in her youth had given Libby plenty of practice. But as with many of those early lessons, permanent success was illusive. Snide was still just as likely to pop out of her mouth.

By actuarial tables, fifty-something Libby Kinder was young. But she was not oblivious to the aging process. Physically, she tried to stay fit. Mentally, she read and did crossword puzzles. Controlling her temper and occasional acerbity was on shakier ground. She lived alone and loved it. But with no spouse or roommate reminding her of her foibles or calling her out for being snide, she felt continually prone to become a waspish old lady.

That's how they got in novels, the old ladies—Miss Havisham, Mrs. Danvers. Miss Priesmeyer.

This last one hadn't made it into any books; she was a character from Libby's childhood. A bossy old woman who yelled for quiet all summer, through every kickball game, game of tag or hide-and-seek—to stay off her grass! Boys and girls alike were too loud, too dirty, too sassy.

And so it did not come naturally for Libby to be nice to Mrs. Thorne after all that oppression by Miss Priesmeyer. She forced a chipper, "How are you today?"

Mrs. Thorne was not won over. "At least your dog's not a barker like that thing next door. Or those howling beasts across the street. What's that you're putting in my mailbox?"

"Fliers about the block party."

It was difficult to make out more than hazy movements of Mrs. Thorne through the screen, as if she was an informant purposely staying in the shadows.

"When's that lady next door having her baby?"

"End of the summer."

Mrs. Thorne didn't snort, but her tone had the same effect. "Must have gotten pregnant over the winter. Dogs barking. Children screeching. Now wailing babies. When's that block party?"

"In August as usual. There are some dates you can vote on listed in the flier. Plus, when the general planning meet—"

"Going to close the street again? Everyone running around wild? Leaving toys and balls and bikes all over the place. Trampling my grass."

"That's the plan" was what Libby wanted to say. Instead she choked out, "It's only once a year." She felt like Bob Cratchit pleading with Scrooge for Christmas Day off. "The kids have such a good time. And it's good to connect with neighbors."

Mrs. Thorne argued her case no more, but in keeping with her character, gave an updated version of "Bah, humbug" and disappeared.

The cheerful twittering of birds lightened Libby's mood after the encounter with Mrs. Thorne and she moved on. House after house, flier after flier, observing how things were on Apple Street.

Early summer in the Midwest meant repairs after the winter. One house had loose boards on the steps, another needed painting. Here and there gardens came to life, tidy from work done in the fall or like the Two Sue's, midblock, with raised beds still in disarray.

Toward the end of the west side of the block, the slight rise in terrain that started on Libby's property tapered off and came level with the houses. The Webster kids lived at this end, and Libby was prepared to run into them sitting out front as they often were.

Libby thought of them as the Happy Trio. They were always together, always full of energy. And plans. Always full of plans. They might be building a tree house or learning Morse Code.

But they were nowhere around.

Libby dropped off a flier and wondered what they would be up to this summer.

A motorcycle revved. She crossed the street behind the bike's roar and it sped away.

Once Libby started down the east side of the street and the motorcycle din had faded, she heard the brief flourish of a cello. Then the morning quiet returned.

She delivered fliers to the motorcyclist's place, then the cellist's, noting the latest changes he'd made already this spring: royal blue shutters on the white house, new brass light fixtures, and an antique railing to enclose the small porch.

Next door, elderly Mae O'Malley was undoubtedly having her coffee, unfazed by the cello concert or the motorcycle racket. Mae had done little to renovate her little house. A nephew in a nearby town managed basic upkeep; a caregiver, in and out during weekdays, managed Mae's personal needs.

For Libby, Mae was easy to be nice to. She was both feisty and dear. She had a quirky sense of humor and proudly claimed the title of spinster. Libby didn't think in those terms, but Mae's situation did occasionally cause Libby to further imagine how she herself might end up. Libby dropped a flier into Mae's mail slot and wondered which neighbor or nephew would watch over her as she aged.

One house down she stepped around a haphazard pile of newly cut rosebush canes and had to hang on tight to Dash's leash to keep him from tangling up in them. She ducked to miss a pole of dangling bird feeders and dodged a wheelbarrow of compost to reach the mailbox.

A gap in a low hedge allowed her a pass to next door, where, in contrast, the sidewalk glistened, hosed down, sprayed spotless; the lawn lining it with not a blade of grass out of place.

On down the block.

"Boy, you don't dawdle, do you?"

Libby swung around to the man rushing towards her. Jonah Pemberton, at just under six feet, stood half a head taller than Libby. A slender sixty-year-old, Jonah was a long-time Apple Street resident, widower, and branch manager of the library at the end of the block. Dash gave him a quick sniff and allowed him to continue.

"Only a few minutes ago you were over talking to Mrs. Thorne." Jonah lowered his voice. "Did she say anything more about my car leaking oil on the street over there?"

Libby mocked her friend, lowering her own voice. "Didn't come up."

"What are you passing out?"

"Block party fliers. Pinning down the date. And a reminder about the general planning meeting."

"Oh, good. Looking forward to that. Been working on my own event." He beamed with a self-congratulatory grin. "You'll love it. It's really clever.

But mostly I was hoping I could get you to add my flier to your stops."

He held up a stack of yellow papers and spoke with a sense of urgency. "I have to be at work, and I wanted to get these out today. I'm already behind with them."

Jonah Pemberton would help almost anyone with almost anything. He'd given Libby a ride when her car battery died; helped with research at the library for one of her peskier grant-writing projects. And was always on hand after storms of any kind—snow or a summer gale.

Those were his best features.

He could, however, be annoying, assuming everyone had the time and inclination to be on call for him in return. Often for things less than critical.

While Libby had been on the receiving end of his aid several times, his "urgent" requests had been dropped on her more than once. Today, she begged off.

"I'm almost finished, Jonah. And I have work, too."

"At home," he slipped in, as if she was the most fortunate soul alive not to have to leave her house for employment.

"I'm sure it can wait until this afternoon," she countered. "It's a beautiful day." She smiled. "The walk will do you good. Besides, I've already been around once."

Urgency shifted to cajoling with a boyish tone Jonah could strike that was disarming. "See. You've already broken in the path. Please? I'll get stuck talking to people and never get to work."

This could be correct. Libby was more facile at getting out of casual conversations but chatting and time could slip away from Jonah. As it must have done already this morning.

While Libby wasn't falling for his line, she could be tricked by what seemed a reasonable plea. Underscored by some of that Catholic guilt about being nice.

Sensing Libby's hesitation, Jonah pushed his yellow fliers at her.

"Oh, no," she said, sighing as she read the banner line across the top.

"Jonah, all this does is get everyone on the block up in arms."

"It's an important issue, and I think this year we can really make some headway. If we get the information out. As soon as possible."

"The people who are going to fertilize their lawns and spray pesticides are going to keep doing it. We've been through this before. Those who don't like the stuff, won't use it. The rest don't really care. Much less feel like butting in on what their neighbors do."

The activist laced his plea. "Somebody has to keep bringing it up, Libby. All that poison running off into the sewers, into rivers, the parks. The stuff's killing my bees—"

"You know I'm on your side, Jonah. But people think of their yards as their kingdoms. For the last ten years the association has taken a hands-off position."

"I have more allies on that council this year. Even Mr. Randall seemed to listen to me."

Libby scoffed. "Was that before or after he had the lawncare company spray? You're crazy if you think he'll change. A green lawn is a perfect lawn, and a perfect lawn keeps property values up." She held the fliers out for return. "Save your paper, Jonah. Save a tree."

"It's on recycled library scrap. Please?" He pushed the stack back at her. "Come on," he added with a coy smile. "I'm not asking you to march in Washington. It's a short walk around the block with Dash. We all have to do our part. Think how good it will be when you do walk Dash. No deadly chemicals."

And he was off.

Dash had heard his name and the word *walk* enough times to be ready for as much flier delivering as he could be in on.

Libby looked down at her eager pet. She thought of her own concerns, of sidestepping lawns with little flags indicating they had been sprayed and cautioning every living thing to stay off; thought of all the pets, all the kids playing on the grass.

For the rest of the block, Libby put two fliers in each mailbox, two seemingly insignificant pieces of paper: one meant to draw neighbors together, the other likely to have the opposite effect.

Near the end of that side, Libby tiptoed up onto the last porch, assuming the teens inside were sleeping until noon on a day with no school. Their mother was probably already off to her job, and their father, who worked the night shift, was probably not yet—

Suddenly—ferocious barking!

Rocky and Punk, two beagles, snarled and howled at the window, flipping and tossing the sheer curtains as they frantically over-jumped each other from atop the couch in the front room. Dash responded in kind, his own bark ferocious and insistent, even given his miniature status.

Libby was startled, although the dogs were no surprise. They let loose like this for any trespass of their territory, and even with a large pane of glass keeping them at bay, the outburst was always a little scary. Libby slapped the fliers in the mailbox and picked up Dash to stop his end of the commotion.

"Shut up!" came a blasting male voice that hushed the indoor dogs immediately and called them away from the window.

The night shift was obviously over.

When set down, Dash did a half snort, half sneeze, expressing his disdain for the beagles' outlandish behavior and to assert his position of being in full command of the situation. Libby crossed the street with him and made quick strides back up and down and the block.

At the end of her deliveries Libby stood on her porch, satisfied with a task completed. Like the others, she looked forward to the block party and felt a twinge of excitement for having officially set plans in motion.

Making the rounds had also brought to mind the variety of characters who resided on Apple Street—different generations and lifestyles, manners and attitudes.

One of Libby's sisters lived on a small farm an hour north of the city.

Both single and in their fifties, they sometimes discussed whether it might not be beneficial for them to move in together.

When the time came.

This invariably set up a debate about who had the more desirable living situation: city mouse or country mouse.

"When the time comes," Libby would say, "I want stores close; neighbors and friends nearby to talk to. To bring me soup when I'm sick. Help shovel my walk. You should move into town with me."

"I don't need soup or help," her sister would say. "Besides, all that help comes with noise—people, kids, dogs, traffic."

"You're such a cranky old lady."

"You can't even see the stars," her sister would say. "Besides, cities are dangerous. Crime everywhere. Don't dare go out alone, day or night."

Libby, who loved people and kids and dogs, who never hesitated to take Dash out late or walk to the nearby park alone, would get defensive. "Apple Street is both wonderful and safe. "Crime," she would scoff. "This is the best place to live and grow old."

Namita Green knew about crime. The only child of an American father and Indian mother, she had been raised in Chicago, a city sometimes seemingly under siege. The neighborhood of her youth had been spared until recently it, too, was beginning to deteriorate. After high school, Namita had bounced around the States, going to university and working until she landed a job in bucolic northeast Indiana at a vocational college and found safe harbor in a nearby upstairs apartment at the end of a block on Apple Street.

One clear, warm, June Friday evening, thirty-year-old Namita left her second-floor windows open to the season's fresh air and retired early. By 10 p.m., the ragtag rock band of kids finished practicing. The Blue Donuts met in the garage of a house across the street and were all young enough that their parents could still make them be home at a reasonable hour.

Fortunately, the garage faced the alley behind their house, so the sound wasn't that invasive out front.

Except on clear nights.

The final bangs on a drum and twangs of guitar only roused Namita slightly. Lying next to her, her greyhound rescue dog, Paji, momentarily alert and attentive, was patted back to sleep.

The only other nighttime noise was usually the bounces of a basketball from guys who showed up occasionally at the elementary school yard across the side street at 1 or 2 a.m. They didn't talk or play music or even stay long, but in the dead silence of the night, the thunk of their basketball, followed by a direct hit through a basket made of kid-proof metal chains, sent a rattle out over the black air like a visit from Jacob Marley.

Saturday morning, it was Namita's landlady, Libby Kinder, who discovered the real source of this particular 2 a.m. racket.

It was Namita who reacted. "Shit."

Libby and Namita stood on the quiet side street and stared at the driver's side window of Namita's car.

Well, what was left of it.

Just outside the back entrance that Libby used, Libby's car was parked only a few feet from Namita's. Untouched.

The gaping hole in Namita's window was a different story.

"Must be why Dash barked," said Libby. "I figured it was just the basketball guys. By the time I got up to see, no one was around. Looks like they took a baseball bat to it. All the glass is on the inside." Libby peered in. "Probably rummaging for money. Sure is a mess."

"No," said Namita. "That's how it looked before."

"Oh," said Libby.

"Glad I kept my phone with me."

"Nothing stolen? That you can tell?" asked Libby. "Thought I'd better not touch anything till the police checked it out."

It was still early. Birds were awake, but not much else going on. Libby looked up and down, trying to find any clues about who or what had visited the night before. The tranquil side street had always seemed a bonus, no houses or neighbors, little traffic when school was out. Today, its isolation made her feel a little vulnerable.

Namita folded her arms and hugged herself as if chilled. "People are right. You feel violated."

Namita was Libby's renter, but after living upstairs for several years, she had also become a friend. Her plight brought out a protective streak in the landlady. "Is there anything I can do?"

Namita surveyed the intersection behind her. "I'm going back to parking out front."

"I highly suggest you stay by our house. Or Mrs. Thorne will not be happy."

"She's not happy anyway," grumbled Namita. "At least she can't turn my car in for leaking oil."

Libby suggested the driveway out back. "I know your car doesn't fit in my tiny garage, but you'd be off the street. Hardly visible behind the lilac bush. And not a target for the baseballs that come flying over here from the school."

Namita sighed, thinking of the inconvenience. "I'm too lazy to walk around from the front. I'll be okay." She scrolled and flicked at her phone to find a number for the police. "Who do you think did this?"

Libby had read enough murder mysteries to have a slew of possible answers at her fingertips.

They were all creepy.

"Probably just some kids bored being out of school."

Namita was less sanguine. "Probably initiation for some doped-up gang."

Libby grimaced. Whatever the explanation turned out to be, she knew she would not be telling her sister up on the farm about it.

CHAPTER TWO

"Maybe Monster Man!"

Sunday morning, ninety-two-year-old Mae O'Malley sat across from Libby.

Other days of the week claimed other colored sweaters, but on Sundays, Mae wore rose. The deep pink complimented her translucent skin, giving her a glow and setting off gray eyes behind wire-rimmed glasses. Her cotton ball of white hair was cut more for convenience than style.

Libby had stopped in for a visit after Mass as she often did. The two women had just said a brief prayer, making Mae's exclamation about a monster a bit of a non-sequitur. Some might have figured it was dementia speaking. While Libby granted that might be a partial explanation, Mae's love of the obtuse clouded such a firm diagnosis.

Libby realized she had mentioned Namita's car window and so Monster Man wasn't so out of sync. It had been the go-to explanation for unexplainable neighborhood events for years.

"You don't have to worry," said Libby. "Nothing stolen and no one hurt. Police think it was probably a random event. Said they'd keep an eye on the area."

"I suppose that'll have to do," said Mae cheerily. "I'm glad you came this morning. Weekends take forever." She dipped her head in a coy way. "You didn't bring any Communion wine, did you?"

Libby laughed. "No, I didn't. It's a little early, isn't it?"

"Too early for sun tea, too. I just put my jar out. No wine; no whining. Let's have a cup of coffee."

Libby found Mae's unconventional patter charming, and genuinely liked the older woman. There was also something homey about being with her. Libby's mother and last of her parents had passed away a few years earlier, and Libby still missed her. Especially on Sunday mornings when they'd had bacon and eggs together regularly after church. It was always a bittersweet visit with Mae, to be reminded of those other Sunday mornings.

Libby fixed two cups of coffee. When days got warmer, she and Mae would sit outside on the porch, facing Mae's back yard. For now, they took the room next to that.

They settled into worn and comfortable chairs. And gossiped. About the neighborhood—more about Namita's window. About sports—Mae loved baseball. About flowers—Mae's prized African violets, blooming throughout the house on doilied tables.

At one point, Mae got up for some magazine clipping. Libby watched her cross the room and tried to calculate how tall the woman was. Four feet? A little more if she stood up straight. Elfin by any standard. Small and wiry; both flinty and vulnerable.

A loud knock at the back door startled them both.

Mae shot a glance at Libby. "Monster Man!"

"Sunday morning—are you expecting anyone?" Libby asked, rising.

But Mae beat Libby to the door and, pulling aside the curtain on the small window next to it, declared, "It's the nut." She smiled impishly. "Bread."

Mae unbolted two locks to let Paul Paterson in. "Good morning, ladies," he said. Paul was taller than either woman, mid-forties, and had a freshness about him. Crisp blue shirt, the scent of light cologne. He tucked a pair of creamy leather work gloves under his arm and handed Mae a loaf. Nut bread.

"Sorry, Mae," said Paul. "Didn't know you had company."

"Not a problem," Libby said quickly. "I've already been here a while. Not staying."

"No, no," he said. "Glad Mae has someone else to entertain. I'm afraid I'm a nuisance sometimes."

Paul, too, liked his elderly neighbor. Besides her crazy sense of humor, she was kind. His own mother, living in New Jersey, didn't offer much of a connection. Not only had she withheld financial and emotional support in times when it had been sorely needed, but she had been a disappointing grandparent to his only child, Geoff. So unlike the beloved grandmother Paul had experienced. Mae came close. And whether she liked them with nuts or not, Mae graciously accepted his steady flow of sweet breads.

"Did you see Monster Man out there?" Mae asked.

Paul looked puzzled. "Um, uh … should I have?"

Libby shook her head. "An Apple Street myth."

Mae crooked her finger up at Paul. "He comes at night."

She then offered him a cup of coffee, which he declined. "Where's that lad of yours?"

Paul smiled. "Sleeping like the dead. Stayed up all night like we all did when we were teenagers. I'll call him shortly." Paul pulled out his gloves. "Doing a little garden cleanup first. Thought I'd water your flowers. Maybe give mine a shot while I'm at it."

"You can have the water," said Mae, adding, "I don't have any money."

Libby and Paul exchanged looks and shrugged. Paul laughed heartily. "I don't want any money."

"Well," said Mae, "you can have the water. Thank you for doing my flowers."

Paul tipped his head. "You are welcome."

Mae bolted the door behind him. "The nut."

Libby left shortly thereafter and found Paul out front, soaking the window box Mae's caregiver had planted with yellow and purple petunias and neon green sweet potato vines that were just beginning to cascade over the edge. "Hope you don't mind," Libby said as she held up a portion of wrapper nut bread. "Mae shared."

"Not at all. Enjoy it while you pour over those grants. That's what Mae says you do, right?

"That's right."

"They'd have to compensate me well for that much brain work. I like to read, writing, not so much. You must be good to be able to make a living at it."

"It can be challenging."

Paul pulled Mae's hose out of Libby's way and stepped over to a row of blue delphinium along the side of his house. He had heard about Namita's window. "Kind of unusual for this neighborhood, isn't it?" he asked. "Any chance it's this Monster Man creature?"

"He's more like Big Foot," said Libby. "More of a phantom. Not prone to smashing in car windows."

"I've only been here two years, but even in that time, nothing like this seems to have happened." Paul repositioned the hose to spray a bed of white phlox. "Just a little unsettling."

The comment gave Libby pause. She looked at Paul, tall and sturdy. Who was a little unsettled.

Hardly reassuring. Definitely not being passed on to the country mouse.

The body was quite beautiful.

It was so small.

Libby had heard about the custom: the telling of the bees. When a head of the household died, someone was sent to let the bees know so they wouldn't be alarmed and could mourn properly. She wondered if the telling was done the other way around, that when a bee died, the head of the house was informed so the house could mourn properly.

After coffee with Mae, Libby had come out to sit on her front porch with Dash and the Sunday *New York Times* crossword puzzle. Dash tucked himself toward the back in the strongest patch of sun, while Libby busied herself toward the front. Only the big blue spruce that spiked up three stories separated her from the neighbors, which, at the moment, included one old barking lab and two squealing little girls.

"Hey, Miss Libby! Whatcha looking at?"

The two Montgomery girls slipped around the tall fir tree. At nine, Nikki was the older one. Grandpa Nicholas had begat son Nick who had begat daughter Nikki. Some variation of the family name had been settled on the first-born child, male or female, from the time of its conception. On the other hand, Honey Montgomery had begun life named after no one. By the time an official name was decided on, the little girl had been generically called Honey for so long, Honey was the only name she answered to.

Honey's name did not correspond with the black ringlets of her hair or the deep brown complexion she'd inherited from her Jamaican mother, but it did perfectly fit her sweet disposition.

Normally.

"I wanna see." Honey pushed in behind her sister who, from Honey's perspective, was hogging the view.

"It's just an old dead bee," declared Nikki. After one quick look, just as quickly she blasted back through the underside of the blue spruce and left Honey standing in rapt contemplation.

"It's beautiful, isn't it?" said Libby.

The bee was completely intact. Wings spreading out from the thorax glistened in the sun like story-book angel wings. Perfect legs, slightly curled, black and hairy against the banded ochre and brown body, still looked furry and full. Soft to the touch, which Honey affirmed after Libby assured her the bee would not sting.

"Only if threatened," said Libby. "They're usually too busy gathering nectar from flowers."

"What's *frettened*?"

"Threatened," explained Libby. "If they think somebody might hurt them."

Honey bent in close over the small body in Libby's hand and whispered, "I would never hurt you."

The tenderness touched Libby, but before she could make any remark, Honey dropped down in a squat. "How's comes it's dead?"

"I don't know," said Libby.

"It doesn't look smooshed like somebody killeded it. Maybe it fell off a flower."

Libby smiled. The insect did look as if it had just stopped and lay down.

"Maybe it ate something bad," Honey suggested.

Libby turned the lifeless bee over in her hand. "I hope not."

"Honey!" A call came from the other side of the blue spruce. "Don't bother Miss Libby."

Camille Montgomery pulled back her own black curls and shifted uncomfortably on the porch swing. She could see Nikki, business-like and more inclined to her father's sun-sensitive skin, returned from next door and fully into chalk drawing on the sidewalk. Camille could not see, but heard, Honey jabbering with Libby next door.

Camille considered getting a pillow, blaming her discomfort on the hard, wooden swing slats. This pregnancy had been different from the beginning. She usually attributed it to the possibility of having a boy. At six months, she still didn't know the sex and was happy to keep the surprise until the baby made its appearance.

The suspense was driving her husband a little crazy, wanting a boy so badly. Wanting to know, yet not wanting to know, if the news was disappointing. The girls had cycled through phases of wanting a brother, wanting another sister, but mostly hoping for a kitten.

Out of the blue, their old black lab, Major, roused and began barking. He lumbered to the edge of the porch that ran across the front of the house. The dog's gait was lazy, but his bark, deep and energetic, contradicted his age. At the same time, Honey skipped back into Camille's view and plopped down next to Nikki.

"Get away, Honey!"

"Don't push me.

"Go find your own place!"

"I can draw here if I want to!"

"Mom, make Honey move—"

"Mom—"

"Stop it!"

It wasn't a loud shout, but, like Major's bark, deep and insistent.

And it wasn't Camille's.

Nick Montgomery stood in shirt and tie just outside the front door. The girls stopped immediately; Major needed one more sharp command and got it.

The Montgomery girls thought their father was a giant, more because of his position of power than any physical attribute. He was actually of average height but had a strong upper body that could hoist them effortlessly up onto his shoulders and carry them endlessly with ease.

"Be good while I'm gone," he said. "Take care of your mother."

Nick glanced over at his wife, then the kids, and smiled. "Maybe you girls can get the living room picked up. And don't just throw your bikes down on the sidewalk like that. Now, come say goodbye to Daddy."

Honey was the first up the porch steps. Nick caught her at the waist. Honey giggled and squealed as her giant hoisted her high. Within seconds she was airborne. Nikki was next in line.

"Sounds like a party over here," said Libby, appearing from behind the blue spruce with Dash.

"Nick's going out of town," said Camille. "Just our regular raucous farewell."

"Dash!" shrieked Honey, jumping off the porch. She ran and threw herself onto her knees in the grass to make direct eye contact with the little dog. "Oh, Dash!"

Dash barked in shared excitement and let Honey rub him all over as if she were toweling him dry after a bath. "What a good little dog you are," Honey crooned, "Oh, Dashy."

Major started barking again toward the other side of the house.

"Stop it!" said Nick. "What the heck is over there?"

"It's nothing," said Camille lightly. "Just Major. He's old."

Honey bounced back up onto the porch to Major's defense, hugging him profusely.

"Probably one of the rabbits that shows up in my yard," offered Libby.

Under his breath, Nick offered his own theory. "Probably the old bird next door."

"What bird?" Honey asked, crossing to lean into Camille's lap.

Camille smoothed Honey's hair. "Daddy's just teasing. Go move your bikes with Nikki and draw me a nice flower."

"Thorny old bird, that's who," added Nick with a glare in the direction of the plain gray house.

"Hey, Libby. You going to be around in case Camille needs anything?"

"Right next door."

"Great. Thanks." Nick turned to Camille. "I'm going in to finish packing."

"I'll be in in a minute."

After Nick left, Camille bent forward and half whispered to Libby. "Did Namita's car really get broken into?"

Libby moved closer to the porch railing. "Yeah. Why?"

"Oh, dear. Wait till Nick finds out." Camille's shoulders slumped with her sigh. "Here we find this lovely neighborhood. He's always worried when he's gone. Sure there's someone or something dangerous out there that he has to protect us from."

Worried. Dangerous.

Not very reassuring.

The country mouse wouldn't hear of this either.

CHAPTER
THREE

It didn't help that the block party meeting at the library several nights later raised more apprehension. It was supposed to be a pleasant reconnecting of neighbors after being separated by winter days inside.

It was not.

First of all, a miserable downpour set a miserable tone. Those who walked, even with umbrellas, were drenched; those who took a car were miffed to have to drive fifty yards to a meeting.

Second, people were prickly about recent occurrences.

Libby's casual remark about Namita's car window prompted the Two Sues to bring up their raised vegetable beds. Not in spring disarray as Libby had figured.

"Yes, busted on purpose," said Sue W., as differentiated from her partner, Sue G.

"I thought the boards were just warped from the winter," said Libby.

"Only thing warped was in someone's mind." It was a rare flash of irritation from Sue G., a person more committed to growing organic vegetables in the four raised beds out front of their house than to antagonizing anyone enough to elicit such damage.

Libby's flash was less rare. "That's just mean. Not right!"

Turned out a truck tire had also been slashed.

Jonah Pemberton's rosebush mutilated. "Came out one morning. Found it all chopped up."

No one expressed Namita's feeling of being violated. The more common reaction was more like Libby's: anger.

"Where the heck are the police when you need them?" asked Jonah.

Nick Montgomery had his own gripe. "They come soon enough when Mrs. Thorne turns in a dog not on a leash the minute it steps outside."

"Or barks," added Cindy Sparks, the curtain-pawing beagles' mom. Several voiced loud agreement on this point.

Then more.

"Here," added Cindy, passing an envelope across the table to Jonah. "Came to my house by mistake."

Sue W. rose up. "Hey, did you get the wrong mail? Me, too!"

Three others, including Libby, noted they had either gotten someone else's mail or someone else had gotten theirs.

"What's wrong with the mail carrier?" asked Sue W. "He's been great for years. All of a sudden he can't find our house?"

The mood of dissent gave Jonah an opening to crank up his campaign against using lawn chemicals.

"Not this again." Eighty-year-old Mr. Randall muttered under his breath. "Why don't you just move, Pemberton."

"And get out of your hair about this? You'd like that, wouldn't you?"

"Yes, I would."

"There's just no need for all that poison," Jonah said, championing his cause. "Grass grows fine without it."

"So do weeds," said Mr. Randall.

Jonah was ready. "Who cares? It's all green once you mow it. You might as well sprinkle atrazine right on your food. Skip hosing it down the drain to the rivers."

Mr. Randall had lived next door to Jonah for years. On Apple Street even longer. His lifelong passion had been preserving historical sites in and around the city. Nothing was more important to him than his own property and its appearance. Even at this age, he was sharp and fit, still put in five hours a day working from home on the computer, the rest of the time tending his yard. He could be funny and helpful. Or stubborn and sarcastic.

The more Jonah sputtered on, the calmer Mr. Randall became. Which infuriated Jonah.

"It's killing the honeybees," Jonah said.

"Honey is overrated," said Mr. Randall.

"That's not the point," said Sue G.

Jonah's voice rose. "If the bees die off—I'm not talking flowers here. Who do you think pollinates all those fruits and vegetables? Apples, nuts, tomatoes? Bees, that's who!"

Mr. Randall pushed aside a lock of his soft white hair and eyed his ranting neighbor. He cracked a wry smile. "I see your moral high horse is saddled up and ready to go for the summer."

"And quit chopping off my peach tree limbs."

"Quit letting them hang over into my yard to drop all that sloppy fruit."

It was one snarky exchange too many, and Cindy Sparks, as chairperson of the Block Party Committee, reigned in the discussion. She had teenagers who could be contrary, so her skills were sharply honed.

"Tone it down, Jonah," she said calmly. "We got the flier; we got your message. Now. I've tallied the votes for the date, and it looks like Saturday, August 25 is best for the majority."

Cindy then began to dole out assignments as if they were household chores.

"Sue W. How about you get the permit to close the street?"

In the end, Paul Paterson offered his yard as a place to set up food tables and grills; Mr. Randall agreed to have his front porch available for the evening talent show, which Libby confirmed she would direct again.

Once logistics were out of the way, the chairwoman steered talk to the lighter topic of planning activities for the big day. The Happy Trio's parents would host the traditional bicycle decorating contest and parade. Other standard offerings of face painting, street chalk drawing competition, the adult egg toss, and setting up the fire pit area were quickly commissioned.

People making suggestions for new events hardly had a chance before Jonah excitedly laid out his plans for an academic scavenger hunt. He had old books lined up from the library, quiz questions prepared, and thoughts about prizes. What he needed were people to assist. "Book-oriented people," as Jonah put it.

The condescending tone didn't help.

When no one jumped at the chance to be part of an educational game instead of something fun, Cindy stepped in once more.

"Paul," she said, "you're a librarian, too. Libby, you're a grant writer. And how about your renter upstairs? Doesn't she do something with research? Jonah, how many helpers do you need?"

"Four."

"Francie. You're a nurse. That takes brains. You're on."

The block party was not meant to be a life-altering experience, so none of the assigned persons put up much fuss. Cindy cut off any more of Jonah's lobbying for his event by negotiating a meeting at his home the following Saturday morning. He agreed, promising coffee and donuts as enticement.

Appeasement reached.

It was the end of the day, end of everyone's energy and patience.

End of the meeting.

Things had started out prickly, but by the end, the atmosphere was more friendly, everyone having eventually come together for the common good.

Plans for the block party on Apple Street were set in motion. They would be part of the conversation and buzz all summer.

What no one realized was that something else had already been set in motion.

Something more prickly, something much darker than anyone could have planned on.

CHAPTER
FOUR

As usual, Francie had tried to pack in too many things. She'd gotten up early to send her husband off fishing, but the extra time had slipped by with emptying the dishwasher and putting away toys from the grandchildren's visit. Even at the last minute, she rushed to lay out what she needed later to help update summer tetanus shot records at the clinic.

She looked longingly at her untouched cup of coffee and reminded herself that Jonah had promised both hot coffee and donuts.

Paul found doing laundry calming. Even in the cramped communal facilities at the old apartment it had been relaxing to match socks, fold t-shirts, and be distracted from other concerns.

The move to Apple Street had been good for other reasons. The house was nearer his job at the library, nearer other teens Geoff could hang out with. And farther away from the oppressive meddling of his ex. Her confrontations had become unbearable lately. Instead of lots of small nagging episodes, she poured all her fury into bigger and longer harangues about his supposed incompetence as a father.

Paul didn't really want to go to Jonah's for the meeting this morning, but he'd said he would go. Besides, Geoff was still sleeping.

Namita milled about on the front porch, waiting for Libby. Next door, Major barked sporadically until Nick yelled at him several times, then called the dog inside.

Namita's foot bumped several plastic containers of wilting herbs, which sat close to two flats of drooping impatiens. The flowers, noted for their ability to withstand neglect, were definitely being put to the test. A twinge of guilt hit her. She had every intention of planting all of them in permanent pots and window boxes but so far had not managed to do so.

The hose lay coiled next to the bottom step. She pulled at it, turned it on, and proceeded to give everything a good soaking.

Namita wasn't exactly sure what this Saturday morning meeting was for. Something about an academic scavenger hunt for the summer block party. Jonah Pemberton could have some lame and convoluted ideas, but he was a librarian, and Namita, who ran the college's Reference and Technology Center, thought this might be one of his more interesting proposals.

What she was sure of was that his offer of coffee and donuts was a point in his favor.

"I'm here." Libby came around from the back of the house. "Cute skirt," she said, admiring Namita's ankle-length sunflower print. Namita was tall like her father and dark-skinned like her mother. Libby, shorter and paler, in conventional jeans, plain top, and sweater, envied the way clothes looked on her renter and the flare she had for putting unusual pieces together.

"Thanks," said Namita. "Feels good to be in summery cotton clothes again. She turned off the hose. "Nice to have Saturday off, too."

Libby gave a playful grin. "How about your Friday night? Didn't go very late."

"Let's just say I'm getting faster at recognizing incompatibility."

Libby's grin faded. "Bummer. Sorry. How about the dinner?"

"Dinner was good. The date? Even my friends thought he was a little full of himself." Namita brushed aside further comment. "Where's that coffee you promised?"

From the other end of the block, Francie waved.

The Happy Trio, mounted on bikes, flew out from behind Francie and called ahead, "Hey, Libby! Hey, Namita!"

Simon, Sarah, and Ann pulled up as if they were on horses and had just ridden into an old western town.

"Hi, kids," said Libby. "What's up?"

Ann, the youngest, stood with her bike cradled between her legs, switching the handlebars from palm to palm. "We have a secret club this summer."

Libby laughed. "Is it still a secret if I know about it?"

Simon looked at one sister, then the other. He raised his eyebrows, seemingly signaling a message. "It's not a secret that we have a club. It's that we do ... secret things."

"You kids are out early," said Francie, coming up behind them. "As bad as my grandbabies when they sleep over. Not much sleeping going on in the morning."

Sarah elbowed her brother. He looked around furtively. "We can't ... stay here," he said.

Libby followed Simon's glances and saw nothing. "Why?"

The three children rolled their eyes toward the gray house they were all standing in front of.

"Mrs. Thorne," they whispered.

Ann leaned in over her bike. "She doesn't like us ... loitering."

The trio hopped on their bikes and rode off.

"Those kids," said Francie. "Always cooking something up. They seem so... precocious. Kind of in their own world."

"They are smart," added Namita.

"Oh, I don't disagree. I don't mean I dislike them at all. And I think they like me," said Francie. "At least that's what they said. No," she corrected herself. "They said they're glad I live next door to them." She rolled her eyes toward the gray house. "And not Mrs. Thorne."

"We'd better move on," said Namita.

"No loitering," whispered Libby.

As they crossed the street, Paul appeared from his side yard two houses north of Jonah's and joined the women. They fell in together and agreed that the one thing they were ready to scavenge for was that tantalizing offer of hot coffee.

The four stood on Jonah's porch and debated which was better: cake or yeast donuts. Raspberry jelly-filled were foremost in Francie's mind

Libby rang the doorbell a second time.

"He's probably out picking up the donuts," said Libby. "I'll see if his car is in the garage."

The back yard was all Jonah: more bird feeders; cobs of corn jutting out from tree trunks for squirrels; a peach tree with several grafting sites underway. Butterfly bushes backed by a row of tall arborvitaes lined the north side, separating his place from Mae O'Malley's. A lower row of unkempt yews edged Mr. Randall's on the other side.

Mr. Randall's yard was tidy to the extreme, with walkways edged, shapes of flower beds clearly defined. By comparison, Jonah's yard looked unstructured and natural, if not a little on the wild side.

Midyard, Libby was drawn to the soft hum coming from a white beehive. She'd read that a bee's hum was not really a vocal utterance but the vibration, the singing of their wings. It was a charming sound, as if from another time, and she took a moment to watch the magical flight of the golden insects circling in warm shafts of sunlight. She wondered how hard it was to raise bees.

As she walked down the stone path toward the garage at the back of the yard, the morning sun angling in from the east let Libby see that the garage door in the alley was open.

Out front, an impatient and caffeine-deprived Francie thought Libby was taking way too long and marched around to the back.

She's the one who screamed.

Some people's garages look like garden store displays—everything labeled and categorized; floors swept immaculate, like a room addition to the house.

Not Jonah's.

His was a jumble of Midwest seasons—winter snow shovels, fall rakes, summertime mowers, spring hedge trimmers, and a slew of all-purpose extension cords, half-looped on wall pegs or slung over bags of bird seed. Stacks of old magazines and boxes of books led to a workbench littered with tools and oil cans, manuals and mismatched gloves. It was a wonder Francie saw anything.

There in the middle of the all the clutter was Libby on the floor of the garage.   Kneeling over Jonah Pemberton.

Paul and Namita crowded in behind Francie.

As a nurse, Francie quickly recognized a critical situation and just as quickly put aside emotional reactions to respond. She did not ask what happened but dropped to Libby's side and went to pull back the shoulders and head of the scavenger hunt chairman.

"Don't!" Libby stopped her.

By then Francie could feel Jonah's cold arms, bare and exposed below his short-sleeved summer shirt, and she understood there wasn't anything she, in any capacity—nurse, neighbor, friend—could do for him.

"I've already moved him too much," said Libby. She knew that in all the murder mysteries nothing, especially dead bodies, should be moved.

And in the movies, music would have led up to, then underscored, the scene.

But this wasn't the movies. Instead of music, there was a moment of profound stillness, an unnatural and absolute absence of sound.

Paul and Namita stared at the dead man. Francie stared at Libby. Libby stared back. It was as if they had all been told to strike a tableau and hold it for one unbreathing moment.

Again, as if on cue, they broke from their stilted pose.

Paul, his hands sweaty, began swallowing hard—because even an empty stomach could throw something up—backed away, and turned to keep it all down.

Francie saw him, noticed Namita's face quickly losing color, and grabbed lawn chairs from the chaos for both of them.

Libby had caught the same topsy-turvy wave of nausea and leaned against the garage door jamb, taking in breaths, trying to go from shallow to deep by force of will.

Namita was the first to speak. "Stroke?"

"Heart attack?" offered Paul.

Libby and Francie answered succinctly together. "Neither."

Libby searched the nurse's eyes for confirmation. "You saw his neck?"

"And his face," Francie added.

Namita collected her wits. "We need to call the police."

Before anyone moved to do anything else, "Hey! What's going on over there?!" came a voice from the other side of Jonah's tall arborvitae bushes.

The group in the garage visibly flinched in one unified jerk. Francie mouthed "Randall."

"Mae thought she heard somebody scream," he shouted.

Libby looked around at the others. They all shrugged their shoulders and made faces of indecision. Finally, Libby spoke, trying to sound casual. "Mr. Randall? It's Libby Kinder. Jonah's had an accident. But the police are coming to… to take care of it… of him. Tell Mae it's all right. Stay with her a second. We'll tell you about it later."

CHAPTER
FIVE

It did not take long for the police to arrive. In fact, the four neighbors at the scene said they wished it had taken longer, because by the time they found their voices and began asking each other questions, they were separated and led off to different areas.

They had been asked to give a brief synopsis of what had occurred, but that was it. Now they stood on the periphery and followed the police actions as the procedural chapter unfolded: yellow crime scene tape laced around the garage and yard; the alley made off-limits from either end. Black duffel bags with forensic equipment carried in. Officers at the edges, huddling with occasional comments, nodding with implied commands; one or two officials allowed in close to examine the body.

And pictures. A camera clicking, clicking, clicking from every angle.

Namita, Paul, and Francie suddenly felt a loneliness, a sense of abandonment in their sequester. They had come to Jonah's house for a meeting about a harmless block party scavenger hunt. They had come together, found a dead body together, and determined a course of action together. Together, they could have kept observing each other and judging the appropriateness of their reactions by those observations. Alone, without such guidance, they felt unsteady.

To Libby, things did not seem real yet. It was a summer Saturday morning; she was in long pants and in the sun but wished for a jacket. A blanket, maybe. She was standing in a familiar alley with an unfamiliar police officer. Yesterday, Jonah Pemberton was alive. Today, he was dead.

She could hear a camera clicking not far away but knew no reminder would be necessary. She could, and would for a long time, picture the whole scene.

It was true that she had had some previous experience with police investigations.

Mostly she had read way too many murder mysteries.

She knew exactly what happened next.

Detective Mark Grass had been on the police force in this medium-sized city for over thirty years. He had been a homicide detective for more than half of that, not because of any stellar rise in the department, not any singular skill, but because he was a decent, conscientious worker.

Had the department dispatch called a few minutes later Saturday morning, Grass would have been on the way with his wife to a teenage son's summer league baseball tournament. Instead, he was crossing a bridge that took him in the opposite direction—not west where the city had spread, but east over one of the three small rivers running through town—driving down a tree-lined street of old, but restored houses. Most were large enough to have been turned into stately duplexes and other multi-dwelling residences.

The street curved to accommodate the pond of one of the city's parks. At the gardens on the far side, he turned on to Old Orchard Boulevard, making an abrupt shift from busy city route to quiet neighborhood way.

Grass thought his wife would appreciate the historic charm, the expansive lawns, all the flowering trees. All the trees in general. His own home was nice, but devoid of this kind of foliage. Devoid of leaves to rake in the fall and so much to mow, too, he thought. Still, Old Orchard had an enviable, classy feel to it.

It was not the kind of venue a homicide detective was called to often.

He made a quick glance at the small notebook open on the passenger seat next to him. Apple Street. Yes. He'd been there before. Interviewed someone involved in a difficult case. A murder. The house number didn't sound the same.

Had Grass been the only one parking at Jonah Pemberton's residence, he would not, in his unmarked car, have aroused any suspicion. But the three blue-and-cream patrol cars that preceded him had brought out local mowers of lawns, sweepers of sidewalks, and sitters on porches.

A few brave and curious neighbors had gathered in pods on the park strip directly in front of the house being visited, but so far, they had collected little information beyond what Mr. Randall had intimated after tracking down the scream Mae O'Malley had heard: Jonah Pemberton had had an accident. Bad enough that the police had been summoned.

One of the officers standing guard, slightly out of earshot of the pools of neighbors, spoke quietly to the detective as he approached the victim's house. "At first we thought it might be another Mrs. Thorne call. She's this old lady down the block who has downtown on speed dial. You know? Dogs not on a leash, people parking in her spot; noisy kids, noisy dogs, noisy motorcycles."

The detective nodded. "Heard about her. I didn't realize she lived on this block, too."

The officer looked puzzled. "Too?"

His superior waved it off. "Where's the body?"

Grass was a calm investigator. He believed in facts, believed he had good people around him to provide those facts, and that there were really very few confounding homicides.

He had been told that the body of a man, sixty-ish, had been found in his garage after not answering the door when some neighbors arrived for a meeting. The initial report was that he had either been strangled or had his throat cut.

Grass was also methodical, persistent, and patient to a point. Today, he didn't conjecture, anticipate, or dream up potential scenarios as he walked around to the back yard, then on into the alley. His plan was to hear the basics, question the witnesses, get the lab work underway. Still in khakis and a plaid shirt, he might possibly make it to the last few innings of his son's baseball game.

"Where are they?" Grass asked.

"One here; one in the alley. Two in the yard next door." The young female officer led Grass a short distance down the alley to the neighbor's. "When the victim did not come to the door, one of them, female, came looking and found him. Pretty much just as you saw him, according to this lady. She said they knew he was dead and tried not to move anything because she knew that's what they say not to do in the movies."

Grass took in an audible, exasperated breath. "Everybody's a crime expert."

"She did have the lingo down."

"Which one is she?"

The officer pointed to a woman who turned at the sound of their voices. Grass observed her: mid-fifties, same as he; athletic-looking, probably already walked or ran this morning—not the same as he; hair beginning to gray, eyes that were a little too observant, too quick to catch mistakes …

The officer said, "Her name is—"

"Kinder," finished the detective. "Libby Kinder."

In a quiet Midwest city of over 200,000, how many homicide detectives can there be, wondered Libby.

Obviously not so many.

She turned at the mention of her name and immediately recognized Detective Mark Grass. Several emotions collided as he walked toward her. Her past experience brought to mind his efficiency. Also, his obstinacy. But the present, with its shock of seeing her friend Jonah—harmed that way, lifeless—had taken its toll. A feeling of vulnerability was creeping in, and the sight of someone, anyone, familiar and with the authority to take charge was not such a bad thing.

"Hello, Detective Grass."

"Ms. Kinder. Looks like you're someone I need to talk to."

"Looks like."

They sat at a patio table on the deck in Mr. Randall's back yard where Grass took notes in a small black notebook while Libby explained about the scavenger hunt meeting, about Jonah not coming to the door, her going to look for him, her finding him.

"I figured he might have been out for the donuts he'd promised, but his car was still in the driveway."

"Did it seem odd for him to be out here, knowing he had this meeting?" asked Grass.

"Jonah lives by himself," said Libby. "Keeps his own hours. He's a putterer—works in his yard, tinkers with things in the garage. It didn't surprise me that he might have gotten up early and lost track of time."

"Or worked late?"

Libby recalled how cold Jonah's arm felt. "Yes, I suppose. Or worked late."

"You said the garage door was wide open. Would it be normal for someone to be in the alley, exposed like that? At night?"

The question sounded like something Libby's sister on the farm would say. "Alleys are safe around here," she said defensively. "People get along. It was a relatively warm Friday night. He could have been taking out the garbage. Talking to somebody."

Grass did not make any comment. Noted but did not react to her bit of pique.

Libby relaxed. After a steady line of factual and guided inquiries, Grass sat back in his chair. "Tell me about finding the body."

Suddenly Libby's recollection of the factual went squishy. Concentrating, telling events in her own time, slowed their sequence. Her senses crystallized, details got couched in emotion, making everything twice as graphic.

"I didn't see him at first. Car in the driveway. Sun coming in. Birds. Then I saw him kind of slumped there. His back to me. I pulled at his shoulder. To see if I could help."

Libby's mouth went dry. She couldn't tell if the words wouldn't come out because she was gagging at the image she recalled or because at that moment she had no vocabulary to describe it.

Grass did not rush her.

"Neck," she finally got out, and touched her own to demonstrate. "Red marks. Splotchy. Here. Above the collar." She shook her head and put her hand briefly over her mouth, then took it away and said plainly, "I knew he was dead. Because of the eyes. Wide open. And gone. He looked … gone."

She accepted the offer of a bottle of water from the officer standing behind her whom she had not noticed before. First, she took a good, deep breath of air. The worst was over.

She took a sip of water. "The others came. Francie screamed. Not big. More of a screech. She's a nurse, so she collected herself pretty quickly. Started to help. But she saw … how things were. I said not to move him because, you know, that's what they say, the police say, not to move anything. I was pretty sure, but Francie confirmed that Jonah was dead. I know it takes a while for rigor mortis to set in. Francie thought he might have been dead a couple hours. Maybe even overnight like you said."

Libby now drank bigger swallows of the water, welcoming it as if she'd just run a race and was completely dehydrated.

"Did you notice anything, near the body or there in the garage, that looked out of place?" Grass asked.

"Boy," she said with a nervous laugh, "that's asking a lot. Doesn't take much to see that Jonah is not the tidiest person." In her mind she rummaged around the image of the space Grass was asking about. So much stuff. Made her want to go home and clean out her own garage. And the basement. "Some of the papers on the floor might have been recently disturbed."

"How so?"

"There were some yellow fliers about using lawn chemicals I'd helped him pass out about a week ago. A booklet or something, thicker, sharper, that I knelt on when I got down to see."

Grass consulted his notes. "I understand there were four of you who came for this meeting. Who are they?"

"Just neighbors.

"Everyone know each other? Been in the neighborhood for long?"

"I've been here twenty years," said Libby. "Jonah was here before that. Francie. Ellison, too. Paul Paterson moved in a year or two ago. Namita Green has rented my upstairs apartment for a couple years."

"You said Pemberton lived alone. No family?"

"One daughter in Arizona. Charlotte. His wife died several years ago. Cancer. Two or three grandchildren."

"Do you happen to have a way to get hold of the daughter?"

The photo of a cute, towhead child came up in Libby's memory. A little girl who had lost her mother at a young age, and now would have to deal with the shocking and terrible news about her father.

"Yes," she said sadly, "I can get you a number."

"What about Pemberton's work?"

"Manager at the Riley branch library up here on Oak Avenue."

"Any outside interests, clubs, organizations?"

Libby realized she knew more about Jonah than she had thought. She explained that he was a member of nearby St. Lucy's Catholic Church. He liked to travel; seemed to take one big trip a year. Europe. England. Usually on a tour—footsteps of St. Paul, WWII battlefields, historic sites. And Arizona occasionally to visit his grandchildren. "He was a good father, especially after his wife died. Nice to Mae, the elderly woman next door. Generally, a good neighbor."

Grass continued with what Libby felt were the standard questions she'd read about in her mysteries. "When did you last see the victim?" he asked.

"The block party meeting, a couple nights ago. At the library."

"Where were you last night?"

Back to the facts. This was easy, thought Libby. "Went to a friend's for a movie in the next block. Walked home around nine with my dog. Heard the kids and their band at the other end of the block practicing. Till ten. Didn't see anything unusual when I came home. Didn't talk to anybody. Oh, said goodnight to Namita, my renter upstairs, when she came in around nine thirty. Watched a little TV. Went to bed. Home this morning till Namita and I came down here for the meeting at nine."

Grass looked at Libby and smiled. "Ah. Logical and thorough. It all comes back to me."

It all came back to Libby as well, the last time they'd been in an investigative situation. She was never quite sure when he was making statements. Or mocking her.

Grass caught the skepticism as Libby eyed him. "No, no," he reassured her. "Just hoping you'll work with me this time. Be on the right side looking for the truth."

"I *was* on the right side," she said, with a smart of irritation. "I was after the truth, too!"

Logical and thorough and that flare of temper, thought Grass. Yes, it all came back to him.

Libby swirled the water in her glass. Nothing made her less cooperative than what she perceived as a dig. On the other hand, she knew her anger could jump to high voltage readings in a flash. She sipped some water slowly. She'd had a rough time today. Just breathe.

"Sorry," said Grass. "Didn't mean for us to get off on the wrong foot."

Libby ran her fingers around the rim of the bottle. "I'm sorry, too."

Grass could not avoid acknowledging Libby's potential assets as a witness. Feeling the ship had been righted, he aimed at encouraging cooperation. "You do have good powers of observation.

"Thank you."

He pressed on. "Nothing unusual last night? Or this morning? Anything about this morning stand out to you?"

"You mean besides those eyes?" She hadn't meant to be flip, and the image of Jonah's eyes made her immediately regret her irreverent response. "Are his eyes like that because he was choked?" She asked, sincerely curious.

"Don't know for sure yet."

Grass looked at his notebook. After a long pause, looked seriously at Libby. "What do you think happened here?"

Libby gave the question full consideration.

"I think it was no accident," she said. "And no, I can't think of anyone who would do this. Sorry," she added quickly. "I've read so many mysteries. I keep anticipating your questions. I'm expecting you to ask if he had any enemies."

Grass refrained from rolling his eyes. "I am," he said. "Did he?"

Libby concentrated. Did she know anyone who would actually kill Jonah Pemberton?

"Jonah could be annoying," she started. "He had some pet issues, like the environment, not wanting people to use pesticides and fertilizers. He could be a bit of a nag about it. But he'd been harping on that for years. Don't know why all of a sudden somebody would get this whipped up about it. Is that what you think happened?"

"Keeping an open mind. Could have been someone he knew or a random event. Or anything in between."

Grass tapped his thumb on the edge of his notebook. "Thank you," he said. He hated giving the cliché to Libby, but it came out of his mouth as a matter of course. "Don't go anywhere in case we need to follow up on any of this. Call if something occurs to you that we might need to know."

CHAPTER
SIX

Namita Green wasn't a nervous person by nature. In fact, she spent her days anticipating and answering people's questions at the college. This would be her second police interview in a week. Of course, talking about a broken car window and finding a dead body weren't quite in the same category.

Grass watched the peasant skirt approach. He regarded it only insofar as he thought women seemed to have more clothing options than men. His wife had a closet full of skirts and pants and dresses, tunics and blouses and t-shirts. Men wore slacks and shirts; dress or casual.

Namita scooped her long skirt beneath her and sat across from the detective in khakis and cotton shirt at the patio table. She had expected a more suit-and-tie kind of guy, but it was summer and Saturday. Just as death had shown up unexpectedly in her life, perhaps it had done the same in his.

She moved into her mode of answering questions; he into that of asking them. Where did she live?

In an apartment above Libby Kinder for the last five years. She was single.

How well did she know Jonah Pemberton?

Hardly at all. A little from the library. She didn't often walk down this way, more likely to take her dog towards the park in the other direction.

Did she walk last night?

She did. Alone. She'd worked until six, gone on a blind date and dinner with friends till nine or nine thirty. Sat outside on the upstairs airing porch and read till midnight. Walked the dog this morning. Walked with Libby to the meeting.

She didn't see Libby last night?"

Well, yes and no. Libby's TV was on when she came home; she and her landlady exchanged greetings through the curtained, glass-paneled door that separates their apartment entrances.

Where did she walk?

Just around the block—down Apple, over, then back up Old Orchard and home. Didn't see or hear anything unusual.

Grass paused. "Nothing?"

"Not unusual," she said. "The neighborhood kids' band was still playing. So that's about all anyone can hear. Neighborhood code makes them quit by ten." Namita leaned in for emphasis. "Strongly enforced by one of our old ladies, so it wasn't ten yet." She leaned back. "I didn't see anything out of the ordinary either. And I *was* looking."

Grass glanced up from his notebook. "How do you mean?"

"My car was vandalized not long ago. Window smashed in. I've been more on the alert than normal."

"When was this?" asked Grass.

"Last Saturday night."

"Did you report it?"

"Yes."

Grass nodded to the officer standing behind Namita. "Pull that for me." He turned back to Namita and asked about the events of the morning.

She laid out the same scene Libby had. Described waiting out front. Going around back with Paul after hearing a scream.

"Francie and Libby were kind of bent over Jonah, who was slumped on the floor. I couldn't see much more than that. Libby kept warning us away. 'Stay back, stay back,' she kept saying. It didn't take an expert. I mean, I've never seen a dead person who wasn't in a casket before, but from what I could see, Jonah looked dead."

For a moment, the image returned to Namita, and she had to take a minute to collect herself. This was definitely not her usual vein of resource assistance.

Grass waited. Then prodded, "What did you do next?"

Namita looked at him blankly, her answering mechanism still on pause. "Nothing," she said.

Her faculties returned. "Oh. We called the police."

When Paul Paterson approached, Grass tried to determine if he was naturally pale or still recovering from the shock. Lean, he looked to be around six feet tall, probably somewhere in his forties. Smartly dressed for a Saturday morning—pressed slacks, fashionable shirt—but then Grass knew some people, male and female, who, even at their grubbiest, looked as if they were going out somewhere nice for lunch.

As with Namita, Paul was used to assisting people at the library. He prided himself on a normally unflappable manner, keeping a calm outer appearance, no matter how challenging the person's requests or attitude might be. This morning's scream, the body, the police were putting that to the test. However, once the detective began the interview, Paul found that being questioned on specifics helped him revert to his customary composure.

"Are you a neighbor as well?" asked Grass.

"Yes," he said, pointing past Jonah's and Mae's houses. "I live two doors down."

Yes, he had come for the scavenger hunt meeting scheduled for nine. He recounted what those before him had: meeting out front, Libby going out back, a scream, then all joining her and seeing the body.

"Did you notice anything unusual about the body—where it was? How it was situated?"

Paul shook his head. "To be honest, I didn't get a very close look. I was the last one to go in behind Libby's renter. By then Libby was telling everybody to stay back and not touch anything. Francie said he was dead. She's a nurse, so I figured she knew. I didn't really care to get any closer."

"Where were you last night? From about five on?"

"I worked at the library until—"

Grass followed a small thread. "You work at the library? Which one?"

Paul nodded in the direction of Oak Avenue that crossed Apple Street on the north end of the block. "Riley."

Grass checked his notes. "The same as Pemberton?"

"Yes."

"Did you work with him last night?"

"I did."

Grass flipped to a clean notebook page. "When did you last see him?"

Paul thought through the sequence. "I worked until nine. Jonah was off at six, but he often sticks around. I'm not sure exactly when he left. Seven? Maybe later? When Jonah stays like that he usually just sits in his office. Out of sight."

"Did you have any unusual conversations yesterday? How did he seem?"

Paul shrugged. "Normal. He didn't say anything special to me. Didn't seem different than he usually is."

"And how is that?"

"Jonah runs a tight ship. The library is an efficient place. I've worked in other branches. At Riley, everyone knows their job, and everyone does it. Sometimes he's a little ... demanding, anal about some things, like having all the pencils sharpened every morning, strict work break times, that sort of thing, but he's the boss. As I said, it's an efficient place." Paul looked across Mr. Randall's bushes toward Jonah's wilderness. "I'm always surprised his yard is such a ... less efficient place."

"And do people get along? The staff at the library?"

"Yes," said Paul. After a second thought, he added, "Of course, normal interactions when people have a stressful day or there are things going on in our personal lives, but I think we work well together generally speaking."

"Anything ever that could push someone to this point?"

Paul thought a moment before he said, "Not that I know of."

Grass switched gears. "Lot of activity at the library last night?"

It was the first that any real color came to Paul's face, along with a brief, wry smile. "This time of year? Warm weather, kids just out of school? Things are quite slow at a library on a Friday night."

"I can imagine," said Grass, knowing it was not a place either of his teens would be hanging out. "You left the library at nine. What did you do then?"

"I walked home. I have a fifteen-year-old son who my ex-wife had dropped off earlier for the weekend. He was at some friends' house down the block. When Geoff, my son, got home, we ordered pizza. He played video games. I put in some laundry. We watched a movie till I fell asleep. He was still watching it when I went on to bed around eleven. I got up this morning, showered and dressed for this meeting."

Paul checked his watch and chuckled. "Kid's probably still sleeping."

Grass chuckled, too. His Friday night had been similar: falling asleep while his night-owl sons watched movies or played video games in their basement. Had there not been a morning baseball game, his sons, like Paul's, would still be in bed.

"Understood," said Grass. "I have two sons the same age. Is Geoff your only child?"

"Now," said Paul registering only a slight hint of emotion. "Geoff was a twin. The other child died at birth."

As a professional, Grass took death in stride on a regular basis. But as a father, the devastation that would come with the death of a child did not escape him.

"But that was a long time ago," said Paul. He smiled. "Geoff is enough to keep my busy."

Grass did not comment further but returned to his routine questions about seeing or hearing anything unusual in the neighborhood, especially the night before.

"Mostly quiet. Well, the band kids were playing for a while at the other end of the block."

"Must be loud," suggested Grass.

Paul shrugged, not seeming perturbed. "They're kids."

The detective gathered his thoughts as he looked around Mr. Randall's manicured back yard. Everything trim, swept clean; grass as green as a golf course. Again, enviable, thought Grass, but again, more work than he wanted.

He turned back to Paul. "Seems like your library staff may have been some of the last to see Jonah Pemberton alive. Will the other folks who worked last night be in today?"

"Library's not open on Saturdays in the summer."

Paul obliged the detective by giving him pertinent names and contact numbers that he pulled up on his phone, but as he stood to go, something did come to mind. "We've had some vandalism in the neighborhood recently. One of the other witnesses here, Namita, had her car broken into or at least the window smashed in. Jonah had some rosebushes hacked up. Some other things, too."

"Yes," said Grass, standing up. "She told us about the widow. We'll check into the other complaints."

"Maybe the same person or group killed Jonah," offered Paul with a lift of expectation in his voice.

The thought had already crossed Grass's mind. "Did Jonah keep anything valuable that you know of in his garage?"

Paul smiled. "Jonah kept a lot of things in his garage. Hard to tell."

Grass knew what Paul meant. The detective had his own cluttered garage to contend with, and the thought of it kept him from piling on the dead man. So did the ring of Paul's cell phone.

"That's my son. Are you finished with me here?"

Grass nodded. Paul agreed to stay close to home and to let the detective know if he thought of anything else.

Paul checked his text message. "Not a problem," he said. "Looks like I'll be busy making French toast."

Nursing instructor Francie Ellison, a confident African American woman in jeans and a t-shirt declaring *Grandmothers Rule*, took a seat at the patio table Grass motioned to before he joined her.

Francie assumed her clinical demeanor as she outlined clearly and thoroughly the events of the morning, matching those relayed by the other three witnesses. She knew Jonah was dead as soon as she saw his pallor and felt his exposed extremities for body temperature. Her educated guess was that morbidity had set in several hours before, that Jonah had possibly been accosted the previous night as opposed to sometime this morning.

"Libby had already assessed that Jonah had been strangled. She indicated that there were neck wounds, at least in the posterior, and described the protruding eyes that would correspond with such an attack. I didn't need to examine the body any further, and we knew not to move anything." For a moment, Francie dropped her formal discourse and said in an almost playful way, "As Libby reminded me, that's what they caution you about in the movies."

Grass let the comment slide. He did not need to embolden another amateur sleuth. He was, however, impressed by the professional observations Francie Ellison had made. Between her and Libby Kinder, they might give him as much as half his forensic team. "Notice anything else?"

Francie hesitated, thinking. "There's an awful lot of ... stuff in that garage."

Finally, she shook her head. "Sorry. Nothing stands out."

"How about last night? I was told you're all neighbors. How close do you live?"

"Across the street and a few houses down. North. I spent most of yesterday—now wait." She furrowed her brows and searched her memory. "I was in the front yard putting toys ... what time was that? Close to eight thirty. I did see Jonah fussing with some bushes out front at his house. Like clearing them away. Or ... I don't know. It was too far away for me to see exactly. Must not have been anything unusual. I hardly remembered it."

Grass picked up another small thread. "You say it was around eight thirty. How do you figure that? Were you going out for the evening or—"

The professional medical person melted away as Francie gave a direct, no-nonsense retort. "Detective, I took care of three young grandbabies yesterday, and I am no spring chicken. They got picked up at 8:15 p.m., fifteen minutes later than the assigned time of 8 p.m. I spent fifteen more minutes rounding up their toys, told my husband to open a can a soup if he was hungry, that I was going to soak in the tub, which I and a romance novel did till my eyes began to close on their own. I was in bed and asleep by nine, if I even made it that far. Dead," she said forcibly, "as a doornail."

She clasped her hand to her mouth. "Oh, dear! I didn't mean that!"

CHAPTER
SEVEN

Simon, Sarah, and Ann Webster leaned against their bikes and watched the adults gathered across the street until Mrs. Thorne came out and shooed them away. Nick Montgomery joined the Two Sues and walked over with a couple from the far end of the block. Al Sparks, shouter at beagles, met up with them as they converged on the edge of Jonah Pemberton's front yard.

Mr. Randall, alerted by Mae, had been told only that Jonah had had an accident, that the police were needed. This gave him top billing as informant and the main source of what little was really known.

It did not keep them from conjecture. Heart attack? Stroke? A broken hip?

"My wife said a bunch of local yokels was there for some block party meeting," said Al in a gravelly voice. He sipped at a mug of coffee as he stood in his sleeveless muscle shirt and jeans, the muscles having been earned on third shift at a car manufacturing plant.

Mr. Randall concurred. "That's about when Mae heard someone scream and called me."

Nick surveyed the street before letting out a skeptical harrumph. "I don't see any ambulance. It's almost eleven."

"It was out back in the alley," said Mr. Randall.

"But no siren. No rush."

It took a moment for the meaning of this to sink in.

Sue G. finally said it out loud. "Sounds like more than a stroke or heart attack."

There was dead silence.

It was quiet in the alley as well. No noise, also no breeze; the sun warming things up. Grass stood in a patch of shade and stood with his notebook, surrounded by his team.

"Preliminaries point to strangulation." Grass turned to an officer across from him. "How does that square with the body location?"

The officer, glad he'd switched to his short-sleeved navy-blue uniform that morning said, "The garage is a mess, but doesn't look like there was more than a brief struggle in the area where the body ended up. Doesn't appear to have been dragged there either. The mess looks standard, on-going, not like it's been recently trashed or rummaged through. A little hard to separate that action from just a cluttered garage, but I would say if something was taken, it was either out in the open or its whereabouts already known.

"Your one witness was correct," he continued. "Yellow fliers about not using pesticides were on the floor next to the body along with an operating manual for a snow blower and some travel brochures. They didn't have any oil stains on them, so it appears they may have fallen more recently than the soiled newspapers and catalogs, but no telling when they might have landed there."

Grass turned to the uniform to his right. She lifted sunglasses and perched them on top of her head, then consulted her own notes. "Time of death tentatively set between nine and eleven or twelve last night. Choked from behind with something like a cord. Possibly a utility cord. Several hanging in the garage. All sent to the lab. Wound across the posterior was irregular, wavy or like dots and dashes. Did not find anything that might leave a corresponding mark. Victim probably surprised. No defensive wounds on hands to indicate there was time to grab at the perp. Lab may find something under the nails. Killer had some strength, but it didn't take an inordinate amount to kill this man. Deceased is slight, and a surprise attack could have made things quick."

"Did that rundown on the vandalisms in the vicinity come in?" asked Grass.

A third officer handed Grass a sheet. "Relatively tame stuff. Slashed tire, car window smashed, raised garden beds messed up. Maybe other things no one has reported, since they don't seem that lethal."

"May be lethal now," said Grass. "Who checked the house?"

Another officer reported nothing unusual. Nothing ransacked or grossly disturbed. "A few dishes in the sink. We scoped the yard. Guy was busy: garden, compost pile; beehive, bird feeders, corn for squirrels. Still looking, but nothing in the immediate yard or alley useful so far." He looked at Grass. "How about the humans?"

"Nothing unusual there either," Grass admitted. "Four unlucky neighbors over for a Saturday morning meeting. Find a dead body. Know enough not to move it or mess up the site. Last to see him alive so far was the nurse who saw him out front around eight thirty. Before that, would have been someone from the library up here where he worked."

Grass folded his notebook. "I'm getting the number for the deceased's family. I've got names and contact information for the library coworkers—only three now since I interviewed one of them already. Talk to the neighbors, both sides out front and on the other side of the alley. Keep your eyes open for anything that could have been used as a weapon. Listen for any vandalism that might not have been reported."

The detective pointed his notebook at a young male officer with curly brown hair barely under control. "Dylan. You've got a way with women. See if you can get any more out of the nice old lady next door. She heard the nurse's scream this morning but sounded a little confused about last night. You might also drop in on—who's the one you say calls and complains all the time?"

A small chorus nailed her. "Mrs. Thorne. 1911 Apple."

"Any questions?"

The four witnesses had plenty of questions. The police had turned them loose all at the same time, and as they were reunited leaving Jonah's back yard, the questions tumbled out: what had they been asked? what had they answered?

Having been in each other's company for the finding of Jonah's body, there was little new information to that piece. Instead, they focused on the night before. Paul told of ordering pizza and doing laundry; Francie of picking up toys and seeing Jonah in his yard. Namita remarked about hearing the band on her walk; Libby about the movie she'd seen.

Out front, the uncomfortable silence of the gathered neighbors was broken by the appearance of four of their own. Inundated with questions, the witnesses reported that they had been cautioned to say little until labs were run and other inquiries made. They could, however, disclose the most crucial piece of news: Jonah Pemberton was dead.

Stunned silence.

Disbelief.

Questions with no answers

"Not so good for property values, eh, Randall?" poked Al.

Sue G. gave a pained look. "Come on. Not appropriate."

Although said humorously, there was a slight edge to Mr. Randall's response to Al. "Neither is that dead truck out front. You're lucky you have neighbors nicer than me not turning you in."

"Everybody's nicer than you," said Al.

"At least I'm quiet. Not like all that racket banging out of your garage while you're off at work."

Al laughed. "You're just old."

Mr. Randall snorted. "Isn't it past your bedtime, Sparks?"

Most of the neighbors were accustomed to the trading of barbs between these two. It could go on. And it could get nasty.

Libby tried to step in. To lighten things. "You might as well stay up, Al. The police are checking in with everybody in the neighborhood."

They stood in a close clump, as if they were billiard balls, racked and set on the lawn, held together by their concern, even more by curiosity. Suddenly they were being told the police were on their way with questions. With implications. With accusations. It was like someone shooting the first ball smack into the group for the break.

On the spot, people found a reason to get home, citing ballgames and groceries and generic plans.

They all had plans and scattered accordingly.

Al was the first to peel off and start down the street with little fanfare or farewell. Others followed, muttering goodbyes, promising to see you later, but all taking the most direct path to their own houses.

"Well," said Namita as she and Libby walked home. "Not exactly the morning I had figured. Never did get any coffee. Hey, how was your interview with the detective? Isn't he the one you had friction with that other time?"

"Yeah. He was the one. I don't know. The whole thing felt surreal."

"Yes. Yes, it did. Does. You didn't yell at him, did you?"

"No. I ... challenged him once. Regretted that. Then I was flip. It was mostly about finding Jonah." Libby swallowed. "That was awful."

"A dead person," said Namita. "Right here."

"All the neighbors waiting for the gory details. Seemed natural and gross at the same time."

"Is this how it is in all those mysteries you read?" asked Namita.

Libby thought for a moment. "No," she said. "This was quieter."

Namita squinted one eye against the sun. "I have a feeling things will liven up when the police come knocking at the door. I think of myself as emotionally steady in a crisis, but this was totally different. Like every word was being judged. I know you're innocent until proven guilty, but guilty kept flashing across my mind."

She glanced at Libby. Was it distress? Or wariness? "Are you okay?"

Gently, Namita rubbed her palm across Libby's shoulders. "Too many books and movies?"

"Too much experience."

Namita gave a final pat to Libby's back with no other comment and went in.

Libby stayed on the porch and looked down the street. Except for the police cars left at the curb in the middle of the block, everything appeared outwardly the same as it had first thing that morning. But Namita had captured the core of it: there was a dead person. Right here.

The phrase "O death, where is thy sting?" came to Libby. Here's the sting, she thought. Pricking the hearts and lives of those left behind.

She couldn't see it, but she knew people had been affected.

Couldn't see Paul's hand shaking as he flipped French toast. Francie's extra-long hug when her husband returned. Namita's impromptu phone call to her parents. Mae's strong cup of tea.

Inside the house, Libby sat on her couch. Dash nestled in close, stealing furtive glances, alert to gauging his mistress's disquiet.

But it was BabyCakes, Libby's huge black panther-like cat who landed noiselessly on her lap and gazed into Libby's apprehensive eyes. Who let Libby knead the fur of his neck as she processed the recent events.

The loss. The sadness.

Death had visited Libby in most of the ordinary situations—the passing of beloved parents, pets, colleagues. all initiating her to loss and grief. Once, when a good friend had died under suspicious circumstances, grief had mingled with confusion and set loose a burning need in Libby to understand how such a horrific thing could happen. As a result, she had begun to question, be wary of, even close friends. In return, there had been blame, mistrust, accusations.

And something else.

After C.S. Lewis' wife died, he wrote, "I didn't know death felt so much like fear."

Fear, thought Libby. It hasn't emerged here yet. Here on quiet and pleasant Apple Street.

Maybe because another word—not death—but another word had not yet been spoken. A word that would set everything off.

Murder.

CHAPTER
EIGHT

"They all seemed shocked to realize it was murder."

At 4 p.m. later that Saturday afternoon, Grass stood with several police officers in front of the Sparks residence. Eight members of the Blue Donuts band had played music until 10 p.m. the night before, the now-confirmed night of the murder of Jonah Pemberton.

The kids and their parents waited inside for the detective who would question them, who would try to learn more than he had from Pemberton's co-workers—an older woman, a younger one, and a male security guard.

No one at the Riley Library had sensed any problem with Jonah Friday night or in the days preceding the murder; nothing about work, nothing about family. He seemed to be looking forward to the meeting Saturday morning, which he had talked about for most of the previous week.

Jonah's shift had ended at six, but he'd been in and out of his office till he left around seven thirty.

Grass noted the timing information and added the three new people his list. He didn't dwell on them much, knowing that the roster of people Jonah Pemberton was associated with was certain to expand long before Grass could start crossing most of them off.

He leaned against the shade side of an old pickup truck. "What's the report on the neighborhood?"

The officer removed her sunglasses. "Nothing. Nada. Zippo on physical evidence. Or maybe that depends on how you view it. *Everyone* in a three-block radius, probably three-mile radius, has a power cord, extension cord, rope, or some kind of twine. Lab's in the process of going through them for marks or some evidence that they might be connected to the murder.

"Neighbors, just like your library staff, were shocked that such a thing could happen in their own back yards, so to speak. Alibis for almost everyone or waived for the elderly and infirm. As for their opinion of the deceased—"

Here the officer read from her notes. "Friendly, normally laid back, packrat, didn't always mow his grass in a timely fashion according to some; helpful, cleared debris with everybody after storms, shoveled neighbors' snow, etc. He could be annoying about certain kicks he was on. Nagged people about using chemicals on their lawns but would also go on about public education or political issues. This never seemed to amount to much, certainly nothing to explain how he ended up the way he did."

The officer turned the page. "Except a Mrs. Thorne, who, I might add, did not fall prey to the charms of Officer Jones here."

Officer Jones pushed his unruly brown hair from his forehead and shrugged. His partner went on. "Although it's true Miss O'Malley, or Mae as she prefers to be called, offered him a drink. Iced tea. Mrs. Thorne, on the other hand, was happy to point out that Mr. Pemberton constantly parked in *her* space in front of *her* house, that his car left oil spots there, that it was none of his business if she used fertilizer, and that she was allergic to bees and hated honey."

"In my defense," Jones offered, "I did find another lady who saw the deceased in his front yard about eight thirty last evening. Same time as your nurse said she saw him. Talked to a pizza delivery kid who came about an hour later to the Paterson house but who saw nothing unusual."

Grass folded his arms. His gaze went one way up the block, across, and down the other side. "So," he summarized, "library staff sees Pemberton leave the library around seven thirty. Two neighbors see him out front of his house an hour later. The only other activity we have from last night, other than a man being strangled in his garage in the alley, is this kid band playing until ten. In the same alley."

The solarium of Libby's house was mostly three walls of half windows. To the west, they showed the back yard, its garden and garage; ones on the south overlooked the school playground across the side street; in the front, they gave view to Apple Street. In winter, sun poured in to make it the warmest, coziest room in the house. By August, it was avoided as the hottest.

Today, the temperature was irrelevant.

Libby hunkered down in a blue-and-white gingham-covered chair and tried to keep her head below the window line, her eyes glued on Detective Grass and his team congregating directly across the street.

Next door, Major barked at the edge of the porch until Nick Montgomery came out and pulled the dog into the house. He couldn't miss the bunch of cops at Sparks', couldn't keep from wondering what this meant after the discovery of Jonah Pemberton's body that morning.

Mrs. Thorne watched the police, too, from her side window.

Mr. Randall, carrying his white canister of weed killer, kept one eye on the officers at the end of the block as he sprayed the cement line in front of his property, then the unkempt cracks by Jonah's.

How many other neighbors—tense, scared, or merely curious—were watching was hard to tell. Were they riding by on bikes for exercise or for a better look? Walking the dog at an unaccustomed time? Pretending to get something from the car?

Whatever the case, they were all paying attention.

And waiting.

As the detective and his officer reached the Sparks porch, two beagles at the window went nuts. The barking was quickly subdued by a short, gruff shout from within.

Immediately after that, Cindy Sparks greeted Grass and Jones and led them through the dining room. A table with dog toys, books, piles of mail and magazines pushed to one side appeared to Grass like a rush clean-up job on a Saturday afternoon. A missed pair of sneakers under a chair looked only too familiar to a parent with teens with a penchant for leaving things where they dropped. He wondered how the baseball tournament was going after his son's team had won games that morning.

Grass and Jones were guided toward a room which sounded like a school carnival, low-toned adult voices counterpointed by high-pitched squeals of yakking kids. As the two investigators entered the room, the chatter abruptly ceased. Everyone dashed and jockeyed for a seat as if the tune for musical chairs had stopped.

The room was crowded. Adults stood against the wall behind the couch or off to the side. On the couch itself or the floor below, kids sat, hunched together, perhaps more for security than lack of space. Grass counted seven teens, judging their ages to run roughly from thirteen to fifteen—three girls: Heather, Morgan, and Tiffany; four boys: Harry, Darius, Javier, and Manny. As professed band kids, Grass had thought they might show up wearing all black, with crazy makeup or shaved heads.

Not so. Mostly jeans, some leggings and tights; tops and tees that everyone in that age group seemed to own. Grass was told three played guitar, one, drums; there was a lead singer, the rest backup singers or helpers on tech.

Grass sat in the straight-back chair provided and waited for a modicum of calm to settle in.

He adopted a casual tone. "I understand Mr. Pemberton came down to your practice last night."

Silence.

"Is that correct?"

Into the vacuum, an emboldened father blurted out, "You know, Jonah Pemberton was an old fart. Just came down to harass the kids."

Other parents mumbled in agreement.

"Did you ever speak to him?" Grass asked.

"I did," said a mother in the corner. "I said something to him last year. At the library. Said I was sorry the music bothered him, but they were just kids, and it was only one night a week. He gave a little speech about respect. When he started in on society's moral decay, I let it go. It just seemed like an axe he was going to keep grinding."

"Did you ever call the police?"

"We're a good neighborhood," said Al Sparks. "We don't call the police." He was standing beside what must have been his daughter. His own hair, where he wasn't going bald, bore traces of red roots which connected him to the girl next to him.

Her hair was striking, naturally red and thick, worn down and long, around a face with flawless pale skin. Grass thought his son would pick her out as attractive, although the term he'd use would be utterly foreign to his father.

Al went on, his words coming out short and croaky. "There's no real need. We get along. Or we leave people alone."

"I understand," said Grass calmly.

"Our kids are good kids," a mother said.

While Grass expected his sons to be forthright and honest, as a parent, he knew he, too, would be defensive if he thought they needed defending, needed a protector.

"Mr. Pemberton was killed," he said. "It was a brutal murder. I don't say this to frighten you, but so you understand how serious this is and how important it is that you be truthful."

He leaned forward and rested his elbows on his knees, cupping his hands lightly into each other, and tried to not sound patronizing as he addressed the children, yes, children still, in the room. They looked terrified.

"Please," he said. "Tell me about last night."

Even as the light faded, the Grass boys continued to play catch on the front lawn. Their detective father sat and watched. Appreciating their skills. Mystified by their growth spurts since starting high school. Savoring their juvenile teasing.

After the boys went in, Grass stayed.

He waved at a neighbor out for a walk. Thought about mowing the next day, grateful not to have an immense yard.

After lightning bugs appeared, he stayed.

Finally, he took his chair to the garage.

In the dark, he thought about different kids, who played in a band. About a different garage.

And about a murder down the alley behind Apple Street.

It was creepier than she thought it would be. Dark. No moon.

It was late, and it was eerily quiet.

The first lightning bugs of summer had dotted the early evening at the end of a very long, sad day and had shown brighter as the night's shade deepened and made them more visible.

Libby had been sitting on her small back deck as light slipped away, thinking.

Thinking.

Thinking about police questions, about her own questions.

She was, by nature, curious. Analytical. Figuring things out was part of the murder mysteries she was drawn to.

But tonight, she was mostly thinking about a neighbor who, for all his eccentricities, she called a friend.

Jonah.

When a lightning bug had landed on Libby's hand, she had watched it crawl noiselessly, unafraid, across her palm, pulsing its glow over her lifelines.

It was watching the gentle, vulnerable insect that had prompted her to go down the black alley.

There were streetlights at either end, but none in the middle; no light by the place where a most ungentle thing had happened.

She didn't plan to be there long. Too creepy.

She looked around and, seeing no one, ducked under the crime scene tape strung across the entrance to the back yard. Creepy and forbidden.

The box was white and easy to find, even in the dark. At first, it seemed empty, no expected buzz of activity.

She leaned in and hearing the very lowest hum of midnight bees, whispered, "Don't be alarmed. I've come to tell you that Jonah … has died." She hadn't thought it would be so difficult. "Someone will take care of you," she said.

In the quiet, the day's emotions rushed at her in a way she was not prepared for. "I'm so sorry."

CHAPTER NINE

"These are the ones from the store."

Namita crouched to eye level of the half dozen small children around her. "And here," she said dramatically, "are the ones I made. Very, very early this morning."

She smiled at how adorable the kids looked this morning, finally out of heavy winter garb, dressed in spring colors, with little embroidered sweaters or miniature adult polo shirts.

A child's hand hovered over the proffered plate of donuts, finally deciding on one

of the perfectly shaped, uniformly dusted.

"Probably a wise decision," Namita said.

While only the purchased donuts disappeared, Namita was still pleased with her contribution to Sunday's hospitality hour at the Unitarian Universalist Church.

One of the children's mothers smiled. "Should we add 'can make homemade donuts' to your dating profile?"

Namita looked down at the remaining lopsided specimens. "Not just yet."

It was almost noon when Namita drove home. She was tired from her early morning cooking venture and dreaded the mess from it that awaited her. She yawned. The wave of loneliness that had started in the night re-emerged.

She felt slightly ungrateful. She had just come from the church community that provided so much in her life—an anchor for her soul and spirituality, an outlet for her interest in social justice, a stable home base of friends.

What it hadn't yielded was a boyfriend.

Barreling toward her mid-thirties, Namita was more and more frustrated at her progress in this area. She had been fixed up, joined online dating services, played team sports she wasn't particularly good at, and volunteered all over the place with the hope that one of these activities might put her in touch with someone who would join her in sickness and in health, in good times and bad.

Not far behind this was the longing to have a child. A warm, cuddly babe in arms.

And so, she dated.

She dated kind men, interesting men; boring men, self-centered ones; ones good at conversation and at giving foot massages. But none of them had stuck or stuck around. These days she hated the search itself because it made her feel a little ... perhaps sometimes ... that it might be her problem. Something lacking in her.

It was an unpleasant thing to consider.

And so, today, she did not.

After all, there, out front reading the paper as Namita pulled up to the house, was her landlady, Libby. Not searching. Not disappointed.

Not lacking.

Brumous. Dark and gloomy.

It was sunny on the porch, but Libby wondered if brumous wasn't a more apt description for the day after a murder. From where she sat, Apple Street looked deserted. Was nobody out because it was Sunday and they were busy elsewhere? Or because they were frightened and cautious?

Brumous. On second thought, it was a nice sounding word. It also gave her the "r" for *farl*, a small cake.

She laid aside her pen and the Sunday crossword puzzle, then kissed Dash on the top of his warm head to celebrate her minimal victory. And to feel connected to something alive and breathing. She stood, arched her back, and closed her eyes against the sun and the brumous thoughts stewing beneath the surface.

As she reached to pat the dirt around the base of fledgling coleus plants, burgundy red, edged in gold, showing off in two cobalt blue pots on either side of the porch, she looked over at Namita's flats of parched impatiens, wondering if they had any future.

"Don't water them," called Namita, coming up the steps. "I'll get them. Need to deal with the aftermath of the donut project upstairs first." She yawned. "I was up so early, I may have to take a nap before I get to gardening."

Namita tugged at the strap of her green gingham sundress.

Libby had already changed out of her church clothes into shorts and a cotton blouse. "How was hospitality hour?"

"Good. Want a donut?"

Libby looked at the plate of leftovers. "I'll pass."

Namita shrugged. "A wise decision. How was singing?"

"Nice. Nice to have something … normal to do this morning. Predictable."

"Hey, Namita! Hey, Libby!" shouted the Happy Trio, bike riding toward the two women.

"Speaking of predictable," said Namita.

"I was just wondering," said Libby, "who might be out. Yesterday being anything but normal."

"Here. Give them the donuts." Namita yawned again, waved at the kids, and went in.

At the sidewalk, Sarah dismounted and dropped a proper kickstand; Ann merely dropped her whole bike on the ground. The girls helped themselves to donuts and took turns cooing and petting a tail-wagging Dash. Simon straddled his bike, looking pensive.

Libby thought about being twelve, being full of big notions, private and serious.

Simon was direct. "Did you really find Mr. Pemberton?"

"Yes," Libby said simply.

Simon seemed to weigh his next question, as if he really wanted to know but was uncertain how much to ask.

"Was he already dead?"

At the word *dead*, Sarah and Ann's attention to Dash fell off. "Were you all by yourself?" whispered Ann, her eyes big, magnified behind her glasses.

"Yes," said Libby.

Sarah was less dramatic but no less serious. "Was is scary?"

Brumous, thought Libby. "It was such a surprise," she said out loud. "Later, when I realized what had happened, I was a little scared." She stroked Dash's velvety ears. "And sad. Poor Mr. Pemberton."

"Poor Mr. Pemberton," Ann repeated in Libby's exact tone and went back to rubbing the dog's back. "He never yelled at us," she said in a wistful way as if she regretted missing such an event.

"That's because he thought we were studious." said Sarah. "And went to the library a lot."

"He yelled at the Blue Donuts Friday night," said Simon.

"Friday night?" said Libby, suddenly more alert.

"Yes. The night of you-know-what," said Ann.

Sarah brushed the reference aside. "He didn't really yell. Just went down and said not to play so loud. No biggie. He did that all the time."

"Not all the time," Simon corrected.

Libby looked over at the Sparks house. "Must be why the police were there yesterday. Checking that out."

"We wanted to go over," said Ann, "but our parents made us promise to keep on our block."

"Stay together. Don't go far," recited Sarah.

"Come on," said Simon.

Onto bikes and off they went.

Down their block.

Staying together.

CHAPTER
TEN

The lobby at the Holiday Inn did its best to resemble a real living room. A couch and two chairs faced a fireplace, unused in the early summer. A bouquet of fresh flowers brightened the corner of a polished wood end table.

It was still a hotel lobby.

Charlotte Pemberton Chase walked towards Detective Grass; he in work attire, she in sandals and loose-fitting top and slacks, Arizona evident in her sun-streaked hair, which was pulled back casually. Or perhaps hurriedly.

Grass couldn't decide if the circles under Jonah Pemberton's daughter's eyes were from taking the 1 a.m. flight Saturday night or grief.

There was little new for him to report except to reassure her that the attack had probably been a surprise and over quickly. The reassurance did not seem to soothe the young woman, who had to stop often to wipe her eyes. She told Grass the last she'd seen her father was when he'd come for Easter several weeks earlier. Church, church holidays, family were all important to him.

"I think it was that way even more after my mom died," Charlotte said. "Cancer. Ten years ago. I was in college, and he was left alone. I grew up on Apple Street, so there were neighbors, friends, but …. When my kids came along, he was overjoyed. They were an easy excuse for us to get together, mostly him coming out to Arizona."

She blew her nose. "My grandparents—his parents—are both gone. So is his only brother, who was in the service, but he was mostly a Christmas card at best. I'm an only child. Maybe all that set up his keen connection to my kids. He's crazy about them. Was. Always spoiling them."

Pause. Deep sighs.

Charlotte waited to be asked something else, having run out of steam to initiate more on her own.

Grass picked up the slack. "Did your father have any hobbies outside of work and church? And family?"

"Most of the things he liked to do, he did by himself—working in the garden, raising bees. In the winter he read a lot. Took a big trip once in a while."

"Any special friends?"

She shook her head while thinking and came up with no one but generic acquaintances.

"How about enemies?"

"Enemies? I thought you said it was probably a random act."

"There have been some minor neighborhood incidents that lean that way. Still, we need to consider all the angles. Just asking if there was anyone who might not have seemed particularly fond of your father."

There was a slight hesitation in Charlotte's answer—a wrinkled up nose—that prompted Grass to press her. "Is that look because he had enemies and you either do or do not know them, or that he wasn't the enemy-arousing type?"

Charlotte smiled for the first time. Then laughed. "It's just that *enemy* is so strong. My father was … quirky. Contradictory. Intelligent and helpful, but he had a quirky side. He worked at a library full of books, had access to them every day, but still felt a need to collect them. Hoard them is more accurate. He was tight. Frugal, he'd say. Dented soup cans, expired dates on his meat, but he'd waste gas driving all over town to find these so-called bargains. There were times he'd get hung up on some issue and bug you day and night about it."

"Like pesticides?"

"Oh, gee. Don't tell me he's back on that kick? Don't get me wrong," Charlotte said. "I agree with him, but I don't need to keep hearing that my kids are all going to have leukemia or birth defects showing up by the time they go to school. My father could be self-righteous, preachy. And yes, he could be quite annoying about it."

A shriek broke into the sedate mood of the hotel lobby. "I did it! I did it! Mom! I jumped off the diving board!"

A child of seven, her scraggly hair dripping over the edge of the over-sized hotel towel she was wrapped in, threw herself at Charlotte's knees.

"What a brave girl!" said Charlotte, hugging the excited swimmer. Charlotte turned to see her other child in the arms of her husband. Grass stood for Charlotte's introductions, which made the diving-board champion go shy, pulling her towel to her eyes and hiding most of her flushed face.

Charlotte eased the towel down and spoke soothingly. "He's just here to talk about Grampa."

The towel was gripped tight. "I love Grampa Jonah. He throws me up high in the water. And gives me books."

Charlotte cast her eyes to the ceiling. "Yes, millions of books."

Talking about Grampa Jonah brought his granddaughter out of her shell. "He's going to take me on a train. To the Grand Canyon. The *Eiffo* Tower. Machu Picchu. The train in Machu Picchu goes up the mountain. You can walk, but the train is faster. It's in the book he gave me."

The other child was not interested in these impending travels and began fussing for its own attention. Charlotte quieted the baby, then suggested peanut butter and crackers in the room, along with dry clothes. Her husband took the cue and ushered all but Charlotte away.

"Just a few more questions," Grass said, "and you can join the peanut butter-and-cracker crowd." He sat again and waited until Charlotte did the same. "We'll want you to go through the garage to see if you think anything was taken."

Jonah's daughter looked as if she'd been asked to walk up the mountain to Machu Picchu. "Oh, God. I always knew this day would come."

Grass prepared to take down possible vandal incentives. "Did your father keep a lot of valuables around?"

"My father kept a lot of stuff around," she said. "Valuables? Hardly. That I know of. He had the normal big TV, computer paraphernalia. In the garage, mostly things for the yard, bee-keeping equipment. Tools, I suppose. Was any of it stolen?"

"All the obvious things you mentioned are still there as far as we can tell. But that's why we need you to look. How about money? Did he keep any kind of cash on hand?"

"Doesn't sound like him."

Charlotte sighed again. The burden of another responsibility now added to her grief. She did not want to go through her childhood home or garage. She did not want to visit a place that had meaning and memories, not touched for a long time, and now was going to have very new and painful ones.

"Once you check things out," Grass was saying, "you and your family will be permitted in the house. If you'd rather be there than in a hotel. Or for something like a funeral dinner."

Charlotte was suddenly overwhelmed. She stared vacantly at the irrelevant fireplace, the couch and chairs and flowers. As impersonal as it may have seemed, its fake hominess was almost more bearable than facing what was real.

A heavy heart settled on Libby Sunday evening. She barely had any energy left to keep distracting her thoughts from the murder.

A sunny day had turned cloudy, threatening rain, and she came into the living room to turn on a light. To brush the cat. To—what is that dog barking at?!

Standing in her front yard was Major. Barking.

A healthy wind banged the open gate next door.

Libby tugged Major by his collar, latched the old pooch in the Montgomery back yard, and started around to inform them.

"Yes, you'd better get that dog off the street!" squawked Mrs. Thorne, materializing from behind the pillar on her porch.

The shout competed with the gunning of Mr. Motorcycle's bike in the next block, tearing in their direction.

The old lady snapped again loudly. "Next thing, I'll be calling Protective Services for that child roaming loose."

Libby turned in the direction of Mrs. Thorne's beady stare.

And froze.

Honey Montgomery, half hidden by a parked car, was beginning to step into the street.

On the opposite side, Paul Paterson looked up from his flowers.

Libby cupped her hands to call out a warning, but the roar of the advancing motorcycle, the wind blowing in every direction.

Honey stepped out.

Libby's breathing stopped.

She clamped her eyes shut in horror.

She did not see the motorcycle swerve.

In dodging the big man in the street, it had dodged the small child.

By the time Libby looked and rushed to the situation, Mr. Motorcycle had circled back, confirmed that everyone was safe, and gone on.

Although Paul was trying to reassure Honey, she squirmed in the arms of the unfamiliar person holding her.

"Thank God you were out here," Libby said, her heart pumping, partly from the scare, partly from her sprint down the street.

"Me, too," said Paul, also catching his breath. "There's so little traffic on Apple Street that kids don't know how dangerous it can be. My son's out here skateboarding all the time. It's not fair to the cars. Or motorcycles."

Honey continued to squirm, and Paul passed the child over to Libby. "I think she's okay."

"I am okay. I can walk," demanded Honey and twisted until Libby set her down. "Honey, thank Mr. Paterson for helping you," said Libby, "and promise you'll never run out into the street like that."

"Glad you were out here," said Paul. "I wasn't sure which house she belongs to, and I didn't see anyone out. I was pretty sure she didn't belong to Mrs. Thorne."

"Good guess."

They turned in the direction of the gray house, the porch now empty, the phantom having vanished.

Libby thanked Paul again, took Honey's hand, and started for home.

The sky was darkening. A few raindrops spotted the sidewalk. "What are you doing out here all alone, Honey?" asked Libby.

"Helping."

"Helping? Helping who?"

"Mommy. Mommy fall down."

A new layer of fear struck Libby—Major roaming free. Honey on the loose.

Libby took in the Montgomery house: no Nikki bossing Honey around; no Camille or Daddy Nick on the porch, hovering over the girls.

For the second time that evening, Honey was scooped up roughly by an adult.

The front door was open. Inside was silent. On a coffee table in the living room was a cup of unaccompanied tea, coloring books with no one coloring.

"Camille?" Libby set Honey down and raced through the uninhabited rooms on the first floor. "Camille?!"

Finally, Nikki appeared on the landing, halfway up the uncarpeted wood stairs. "Mommy fell," she said nervously.

"Libby?" A thin voice called from the second floor. "I'm up here."

Libby took the steps two at a time, turned and brushed past Nikki to find Camille, sitting near the top, looking shaken and disoriented.

"I think I blacked out for a minute. I slipped and landed hard on my tailbone."

"She wasn't moving," said Nikki, the panic still visible in her eyes. "I told Honey, go get help."

Honey pushed through to inform everyone that she had done as told. "Nobody was home. Miss 'horne said, 'Go. Home.' But I went for help. There was a man 'cross the street." She reached her arms for a hug from Camille, who gave it tentatively.

Libby eased Honey aside. "Nikki," she asked, "do you have an ice pack?"

A nod of assent. Libby motioned her off to get it. Honey trailed after her sister. "I can help."

"Can you move?" asked Libby. "Do you think you broke anything? What about the baby? Should I call an ambulance?"

Camille smiled. Libby was relieved to see that some of Camille's coloring was returning.

"I think the baby is fine," she said.

Camille took stock, flexing her arms and wrists, swiveling gently left and right. "I think I'm fine, too." She reached behind and along her lower back. "I think I'll be a little sore. My wrist is bruised where I tried to catch myself."

There was a low rumble of thunder.

Camille looked at the lifeless stained-glass window on the landing and gave a small laugh. "That's why it's so dark. I thought I might have been out longer than I was."

Nikki and Honey returned with ice packs. Camille stood and convinced everyone that she did not need an ambulance, did not need to call Francie, but that she would call Nick, scheduled to be back by noon the next day.

Outside, Major was barking again. Libby brought him in for the night and got Camille situated in bed. The girls brought all the pillows in the house to fluff behind their mother's back and to accommodate them— two extra occupants, who apparently often slept with Mommy when Daddy was gone.

Not long after, Libby left.

Camille lay on the bed. Breathed in and out. Slowly.

She leaned over to kiss each sleeping child. The movement hurt. She sat upright and adjusted the ice packs to ease the pain in her lower back. "The baby's fine," she whispered to herself. "Baby's fine."

The wind blew in window-rattling gusts, and she was glad the glow from the night light could be seen from her room.

Paul changed the sheets on his son's bed. It was therapeutic to have something physical to do after the scare with the little neighbor girl running into the street.

In the last ten years, there were very few times Paul had prepared the house for Geoff—getting in food, lining up activities, stocking up on favorite movies and video games—that he didn't feel some sadness that these times were just visits. Never permanent, never having Geoff in the casualness of time, but only—always—pre-arranged, marks on the calendar instead of days just free and continuous.

Sometimes Paul felt as if he lived in a perpetual scare, as if his own child might run into the street and no father would be there to protect or rescue him.

BabyCakes had hidden under the bed from the sound of the wind, but Libby coaxed him out with the creak of the refrigerator door opening and a tiny puddle of cream on the kitchen floor. She picked the cat up with hands under his armpits and let his full, long black torso hang, relaxed now and at ease. She kissed his face and eyes, then slid her palm down to support his rear and pull him up close, tucked into her arms.

"Don't ever run into the street, Baby," she whispered, as much to comfort herself as the cat. "Stay inside where you are safe and warm and spoiled rotten."

CHAPTER
ELEVEN

Fog and drizzle made opening the library an eerie undertaking when 8 a.m. Monday morning rolled around. J'az shrieked as Bin came up behind her at the back entrance, causing Bin herself to jump.

In her late sixties and a bit stocky, Bin got her name because her job for twenty years had been to empty the drop box bin full of books or materials that arrived overnight.

Her co-worker, J'az, in her late thirties, was taller than Bin by actual height and by several more inches of fluffy curls from a wig rising above her head and flowing halfway down her back. Today it was a cloud of purple.

"Sorry," said Bin. "Walt let me off at the street, and I walked around back alone."

"I forget how short you are," said J'az. "Easy to come in under the radar. Especially in this fog." She unlocked the door. They both hesitated. Only the damp and dreary outside persuaded them to go in.

"Seems like ages since Friday night."

"Even longer since Saturday afternoon," said Bin, slipping out of a wet raincoat as J'az deactivated the alarm.

"I still can't believe it." J'az brushed off her puff of hair, glistening with the mist she'd come in from. "I was with the girls at a soccer game when the police caught up with me. There I am, handing out juice drinks at the same time I'm hearing about this gruesome Jonah thing. Terrible. Just terrible."

The main room of the James Whitcomb Riley Library was unlit and gloomy until Bin flipped on lights, forcing it into life. "I was at the store," she said. "Glad Walt was home when they came to the house. So awful. Poor Jonah. Just standing in the garage and choked like that or whatever."

One shivered, the other reflexively did the same.

The death of their boss was shocking and not without sadness, but the women had the place to get up and running for the public coming in at ten. They were librarians, with a natural tendency to thrive on information, used to starting their days sharing news, local or international. Or personal.

"What did you say when they asked if Jonah had any enemies?" asked Bin.

J'az poked at her hair. "I certainly didn't say how miffed we were about the stingy way he assigned vacation times."

"J'az!" Bin said with a gasp. Then she laughed. "Or not letting us have stools to sit on behind the desk. No sitting on duty."

"Eagle-eyeing our timecards but keeping his own flexible schedule."

"Him and Paul," said Bin. "If I hear one more single dad excuse for being late, I'm gonna scream. Must have hit a nerve for Jonah."

"Men sticking together—that's the nerve."

"So much for respect for the dead."

"Oh, I'm just kidding," said J'az. "Kind of. Remember when I was looking for a used car? He did all that research. Wrote up all the options. Compared consumer reports on them all. For sure, Jonah could make me mad and irritate me no end like everybody else in this building, but nothing to murder the man over."

The word *murder* stopped the conversation as if car brakes had been slammed on. Slammed on when something unforeseen jumps in a person's path.

J'az moved to switch on the copier and began sharpening pencils. Bin retrieved the container she was named after and began checking in returned books and movies at the front desk. J'az left to get the green money pouch of petty cash from the back office. The day began to feel ordinary again as they went through their routine tasks.

Until.

Until J'az unzipped the green money pouch. "Hmmm." She pulled out a handful of bills, counted them off as she placed ones, fives, tens, and twenties in the cash drawer.

"What?" said Bin. "What *hmmm?*"

J'az looked again, rummaging every corner of the pouch. "That other envelope, the one with the big wad of library fines Jonah's been collecting." She turned the pouch upside down. "It's not here."

"Maybe it's in his desk somewhere," Bin offered. "It was white, wasn't it?"

"Yes." J'az ducked back into Jonah's office. "A big long white business envelope folded over that he kept inside the green pouch. The Book Fee Fortune."

Bin stacked all the checked in non-fiction books on a library cart. "I can't believe he had over $5,000."

"What do you expect? He's been amassing it for half a year," said J'az from the back. She returned empty-handed. "When we find it," she declared, "I am going to count it and turn it in. Stupid to have that much money lying around. It's a stupid game, seeing how much he can squirrel away. Not like it's his."

"I'm surprised downtown doesn't catch on," said Bin.

"Always sending that small amount to make it look like we collected something probably helped. He had some weird way of getting around the master printout. Creative bookkeeping, no doubt. It'll all be paperless soon."

Bin nodded. "I'm sure when they find out, they'll drag us kicking and screaming into the 21st Century. Downtown must think we have the best patrons in town—in the world. Hardly ever losing books or turning in things late for a fee."

Bin examined the green pouch herself. "That's what this little extra bit is in here for, right?"

"$24.50. Yes, I assume so. Last week was pretty slow. That's probably accurate."

J'az stood, her nose wrinkling with concern. "It's really not here."

Bin went back to sorting. She brightened. "Maybe he finally got wise and took it in himself."

J'az brightened as well.

But the phone call to Accounting did not alleviate their concerns.

Panic set in.

$5,000's worth.

They recalled that the alarm had been set and working when they came in, but they checked the windows and doors for a break-in, nonetheless. They rummaged through Jonah's desk and rooted all along the shelves under the front counter.

Nothing.

J'az sighed heavily. "Should we call the police?"

Bin hesitated. "Can we wait and see if it shows up? Maybe Paul or Louis knows where it is."

A good thought. Bought them time.

In that time, they both realized that these were the kind of concerns they would normally have handed over to Jonah. He was the boss. He was the one who made these decisions, dealt with these problems.

But Jonah was no longer there.

Even though a foggy morning had made the kitchen cooler, the sun was now out and heating things up. Libby was glad she had opted for baking one quick pan of brownies rather than several sheets of cookies. Being frugal with money and natural resources meant her oven would soon go dark for the summer except for an emergency.

Loading up a box with her goodies and some books for later, Libby walked towards Jonah's house, expecting to meet his daughter, Charlotte, at her childhood home. But it wasn't Charlotte coming down the front walk.

"Brownies?" said Detective Grass with raised eyebrows. "If I remember correctly, you don't indulge in a lot of sweets."

The reference made Libby bristle a little, Grass having tricked her once before in a different and more dangerous situation. He was making light of it now, but she hadn't forgotten the seriousness of it.

"I wasn't expecting you," she said, "or I'd have made some healthy muffins."

Grass smiled at Libby's nimble comeback to the reference.

For a moment, each considered another edgy exchange.

The temptation passed.

Instead, they both said, "What brings you here?"

"I'm meeting Charlotte," Libby said first. "She wanted to start going through her Dad's things, and the kids would be along. Not sure what Jonah might have on hand for kid food, so I brought some snacks. Apples," she said pointedly, "besides the brownies. She also asked if I'd help pick out funeral music."

"Forgot," said Grass, recalling more of their former connection. "You sing. Will the funeral be at St. Hedwig's?"

"No. Jonah belonged at St. Lucy's over this way. They'll let me cantor for the Mass. How about you? Find out what happened here yet?"

Now Grass bristled. Just like her to stick in the *yet*.

"We were leaning toward this being a random crime," he said.

"Like our random neighborhood vandal?"

"That was the leaning. We've had a … complication. Could change that theory."

A possible new piece of the mystery. Libby abandon all thought of brownies, apples, even being on guard verbally. "So," she said. "What's up?"

Grass told her about the missing library fine money and the travel brochures found on the garage floor.

She vaguely recalled hitting something clunky when she'd knelt by Jonah's body. She rested her box of treats on her hip. "I don't get the connection."

"The amount missing," explained Grass, "is almost exactly the amount for two plane and tour tickets for one of the trips circled. He'd even discussed taking his granddaughter on that specific one. More than two thousand dollars each."

Libby's eyes popped open wide. "They collect that much in fines at a dinky library like Riley?"

"Are you kidding? My wife and kids could have their own wing at our branch for the fines I've paid. Late fees, lost books."

"Guess I'm too cheap. Drives me crazy to have to pay." She switched the snack box to her other hip. "But wait. Did you track down tickets? Or just find the money?"

"Neither."

Libby squinted in puzzlement. "Then how do you know Jonah actually took it?"

Her mind began to spin out options. "Maybe the money was just stolen from the library. Maybe the theft wasn't even related."

"No evidence of a break-in."

"Hmm. An inside job."

Grass resisted rolling his eyes. "The staff does admit the pouch that holds the money just sits on a shelf behind the desk during the day. Not watched or guarded very closely.

Libby's shoulders dropped in disappointment. "Back to your random vandal."

"According to everyone, Pemberton was strangely obsessed with these fines, always adding them up, bragging about how much he'd collected. Done it lots of times. Set some goal and then tracked how long it took to reach it."

"What about an accounting office?" asked Libby. "Surely there's some sort of record-keeping firm for the whole system."

"Seems the library has only recently been setting up a less human system, but it hasn't been fully implemented, or they haven't plugged all the loopholes."

"If the money isn't locked away, couldn't almost anyone, staff or patron or bozo off the street, have taken it with little notice?"

"Staff says Pemberton was the last to handle the pouch. Locked it up for the day Friday night before he left. Even though all the staff can get into the safe, each swore they hadn't done so, nor had they seen anyone else get in there."

"What did Louis have to say?"

"Louis?"

"The security guard."

"He backed up everybody's statements. And we did check on him. Seems reliable."

Libby lit up. "Maybe they were all in on it together!"

The minute she said it, Libby rolled her own eyes. "Besides, hardly fits with the group I know up there."

She shifted her box again.

"Here," offered Grass. "Let's sit on the porch. Looks like your box is getting heavy. No offense to your brownies."

Libby was too interested in the missing money to be offended. She set her box down and the two took seats on weathered Adirondack chairs.

Libby squinted again in concentration. "Seems odd Jonah would make such a public deal out of how much he was collecting and then steal it."

"To be honest," Grass said, "this guy seems a little odd all the way around. I think if anyone else had stolen this money, he'd have thrown a royal fit. As of Friday night, that had not happened."

"And no one got in or was in the library over the weekend? Neither staff nor bozo?"

"No one."

"So. You think Jonah took it." Libby tried to square this with the man she knew. "But why?" she pressed. "He wasn't poor, that I could tell. Wasn't rich, but comfortable. I suppose we all could have some private debts. He never complained about any. Okay, he thought the cost of postage stamps was outrageous; car batteries, too, and they don't last. But thousands of dollars? That seems out of his range. To me. I know he's crazy about his grandkids. I can see him saving up for a trip, going on the trip—but not stealing for the trip."

"You're not alone. That's how the daughter sees it. Of course, it's how a daughter might."

"Not likely he only had a month to live? Or suddenly went bankrupt, or lost money gambling?"

Grass shook his head. "Not that we've found. Just a kooky old guy having this dream trip in mind, seeing the money, and taking the chance. The temptation just too great.

"He'd left work," Grass went on. "My theory is he had it with him. Staff said there'd been no fines added Friday night. Things were slow. Jonah had everything put away, so no one would have been wise to the cash walking right out of there with him."

Libby paused, thinking it through.

"Okay," she finally allowed. "Let's say Jonah took the money. Maybe had it out in the open in the garage? With the travel brochure he was looking at. Maybe actually counting the money, which he seems to have liked to do. Random Vandal comes along. Hits the jackpot."

Libby played out the scene in her head, imagining what might have followed, the results of which she had come upon the next morning. She swallowed and looked up, out over the front yard, and for a moment, was silent.

"I don't think so," she said.

Grass found this exasperatingly blunt—the tone, the confidence. The fly in the ointment of his theory. "Why?"

Like those first lightning bugs, blinking on, then blinking off before they could be chased down and caught, snippets of facts and unresolved lines of reasoning flickered across Libby's mind.

She folded her hands across her lap, firmly interlocking her fingers. "I don't know."

"What doesn't fit?" Grass hoped she would not drift over into women's intuition.

"It doesn't feel right."

Grass knew Libby was too smart to dismiss. She could be analytical and reasonable and rational.

Silently, he grit his teeth. She could also be a pain in the neck.

"They're in the back yard giving Dad's bees clean water. They'll love the brownies. Thanks." Charlotte stood at the Pemberton kitchen window, overlooking her children; a scribbled inventory list on the counter.

Libby had known Charlotte since birth. Had babysat for her. Had watched her be sad at her mother's death and watched her now be sad at her father's.

"I took almost everything I wanted after Mom died," Charlotte said. "I've put aside a few other keepsakes. Picked out some mementos of Grampa for the girls."

Libby found herself empathizing. Not with Charlotte, the one deciding what to keep and what to throw or give away.

But with Jonah.

Libby's plans were simple: Live in her house on Apple Street for as long as she could. Then either transplant her life to the farmhouse with her sister or entice her sister to move to town. Nursing home if necessary.

But her possessions. She was single with no children. What if, as with Jonah, death came like a thief in the night? If she had no time to have Dash and BabyCakes provided for? If there was no one who really knew what was important or sacred?

"What am I going to do with all this stuff?" asked Charlotte, her arms lifted to take in the whole room, the house, the property.

Libby gave a sympathetic smile and suggested something she herself had contemplated. "An auction?"

Charlotte picked up a jar with no lid and a mug with no handle. "Maybe a dumpster."

They both laughed, pulled out the brownies and apples, and agreed there was no rush to put Jonah's house in order. It was too early into grief to know what was important or sacred.

They switched gears and sat to pick out hymns for the funeral Mass. Having sung at many such services, Libby had a long list of options. Charlotte named a few contemporary favorites; Jonah had traditional ones he'd already spoken of. It was an easy task to accommodate each and put them in a proper order. At one point, Libby suggested Psalm 23, a standard choice for the Responsorial Psalm, *The Lord is my Shepherd/There is nothing I shall want.*"

Charlotte stopped.

She looked away.

Then turned back and blurted out, "They think my father stole money from the library!" Her eyes filled with tears. Her words hit a plaintive note. "I don't believe it. He would never have stolen anything. Especially so much money. Not even for the kids."

The look on her face turned to fear. "What if he died with such a grave sin on his soul? Oh, Libby. What would God do?"

Libby had had a lot of discussions with and about God. She did not necessarily feel the heavenly rules and regulations covered the compassion she thought might be called for in this instance. If Jonah was in such a predicament with his Maker, it was between the two of them. For Charlotte, the only theological comfort Libby had to offer was her belief that, in the end, yes, God was just, but also kind and merciful.

She found Psalm 103 and gave it to Charlotte to read:

> He pardons all your iniquities,
> And comforts your sorrows,
> Redeems your life from destruction
> And crowns you with his kindness.

> Merciful, merciful,
> And gracious is our God;
> Slow to anger, abounding in kindness.

"Yes," said Charlotte softly, "let's sing that one."

Libby collected her planning sheets and hymnals and placed them for the return trip in her empty box.

Charlotte thanked Libby several times, grateful for her help and her friendship, both now and for so many times in the past.

After a long embrace at the door, Charlotte stepped back and said, "I heard you out front talking to the detective." She fidgeted with the door lock. "You have to convince him that my father would never take that money. Please, Libby. It has to be somebody else. I just know it."

Libby looked at the young woman, her eyes red and beginning to tear up again. The emotion was contagious.

In the end, Libby promised nothing, but reassured Charlotte she would try.

It was easy to do this, because Libby also refused to believe the accusations about Jonah.

She wanted almost as badly to prove it.

On Thursday, Libby arrived early at St. Lucy's Catholic Church, a modern, hexagonal building with an open-thrust altar as opposed to the more traditional cathedral-like proscenium of her own St. Hedwig's; her *Ave Maria* to be accompanied by a shiny black piano as opposed to St. Hedwig's lofty pipe organ.

After a short practice, she stood in a black summer sheath and heels, waiting for the final prayers to be said over the coffin in the rear of the church.

She could see that it was a modest crowd, maybe sixty people. They were seated in clusters by categories that seemingly reflected Jonah's life: family—his daughter, her husband, and the two beloved grandchildren; colleagues from the library—J'az, Bin, Paul, Louis; neighbors from up and down Apple Street—the Montgomerys, the Randalls, the parents and their Happy Trio, Francie and her husband, the Two Sues, the Lagunas. There was a small group of parishioners and two dozen or so people Libby didn't recognize.

The Mass got underway. During the homily, Libby glanced at Charlotte. Raised Catholic and seemingly still practicing, Charlotte would take solace in the belief of an afterlife, of her father merely passing from one form into another, his soul going on for eternity. There would be little comfort, however, if that same Catholic background made her think he might be facing that future anywhere but in heaven.

As the judgment of Jonah Pemberton was being laid out in another realm, Libby found herself imploring the all-knowing God of mercy and compassion of whom she sang to let her in on anything that would help clear the man's name in this one.

CHAPTER
TWELVE

Like dominoes on paper, the chain of perfectly drawn boxes down the side of Libby's yellow legal pad had edges in common, then extended in one direction or turned in another.

Doodles.

Libby was a big believer in doodling. Especially when she was stewing about something.

Like proving Jonah Pemberton innocent of stealing a boatload of cash from the local library.

Since the funeral, Libby had been making lists of how to go about this: who to talk to, what to ask, how else to unearth evidence in his favor. Nothing lent itself to doodling like making lists.

At the moment, Dash was in the other room; BabyCakes next to her, his face planted into a cushion, snoring like a human.

Libby stared out the window.

She hummed *Frere Jacques* to BabyCakes.

She made another row of boxes on the legal pad page, now more decorated with doodles than any kind of clear plan.

Like everyone else, Libby had been forced to go on with her life, distracted by things like writing grants for the small local university which employed her.

She hoped today's interruption would be different.

Today she was scheduled to hold her first practice for the block party music and talent show.

At the library. Scene of the stolen fines and potential source of tips for mitigating the case against Jonah.

Libby's grandfather clock chimed.

She got up, gave a light pat to the cat's haunches; a carrot to Dash. She stuffed a book bag with her legal pad and pens, went out the back door, through the yard, through the wrought iron gate, and across the cement driveway.

First stop was next door to let Major out. As long as the old dog got his treat, he didn't seem to miss his family, gone for the day to one of Indiana's summer festivals.

Back in the alley, Libby began to hum.

Libby liked alleys.

She understood they were an indulgence of property, but they were a part of the charm of her hundred-year-old neighborhood.

Granted, some alleys were well-kept; others, rougher and more cluttered. Libby's was a mix, with asphalt-patched potholes and garbage containers, clumps of overgrown bushes. Occasionally a completely neglected yard.

Even so, there was an orderliness imposed by a crisp row of telephone poles and the uniform green of border hedges—privet, yew, and lilac, like Libby's heirloom lavender ones.

Generally speaking, Libby did not see the disheveled parts of her alley. This afternoon she hummed and looked over white picket fences onto neat patios ready for summer. She admired newly planted vegetable gardens and flowerbeds teeming with June phlox; trellises of climbing purple clematis or pink roses.

Not for the first time, Libby imagined her alley a cozy road through an old English hamlet, like St. Mary Meade, where villagers walked and greeted neighbors and gossiped.

Which brought her back to crimes and murders happening in quaint neighborhoods, to her doodles and lists and the goal at hand.

By the end of the alley, Libby was getting warm. She crossed Oak Avenue, a moderately busy street, lined with small local businesses: a tiny grocery, neighborhood bar, a bakery; a meat market, yarn shop, plumbers, and several diners. Like the houses on Apple Street, most buildings were a hundred years old, so sturdily built of red or yellow brick that contemporary concerns merely repainted the interiors, added a new sign or awning, and were good to go.

Directly in front of Libby, next door to the library, was Betty's Sweet Shoppe. Wood floors, glass cases of hand-dipped chocolates and penny candy. But Betty's was most famous for stocking thirty-four kinds of licorice. Black licorice.

There's a camp that likes only fruit flavors, but Libby had inherited a black-licorice-loving gene from her mother. Once in a while, she splurged on a quarter pound of All-Sorts that she would tuck away in its white paper bag and sneak it into the library to accompany a delicious afternoon read.

Not today.

No time with a rehearsal and sleuthing looming.

The James Whitcomb Riley Branch Library was not a large building, one-story brick. Recent renovations had pushed it back from the street, leaving a grassy area and small parking lot. An overhang above the entrance gave welcomed shade this warm afternoon. It covered the box drop slot, a bike rack, and black metal bench, where two kids sat reading.

"Where's Sarah?" asked Libby.

Simon looked up, but Ann beat him to the answer. "Orthodontist." She made a face and pronounced her sister's appointment, "Grisly."

"She's gonna need braces," Simon said, not unkindly. "She has teeth coming in like a vampire."

"Wow. I hadn't noticed," was all Libby could think to say. "What are you reading?"

Simon showed the cover of his book. *Crimes from Baker Street.*

"Sherlock Holmes," Libby said with delight. "One of my favorites. Are you here for the block party show practice?

"Oh, yes," said Ann.

Libby turned and addressed the kids milling around as she moved toward the door. "Why don't you all wait out here? I'm not going to start quite yet."

The library vestibule was an open gathering area. It had drinking fountains, a phone, and wall-sized bulletin board with notices of library events, lost dogs, and neighborhood news.

To the left, past restrooms, was a meeting room large enough to accommodate craft time for youngsters, book clubs for teens, tax preparation help for seniors—and rehearsals for block party musical shows.

Once inside, the first thing that caught Libby's eye was a yellow flier on the bulletin board proclaiming the evils of lawn pesticides and fertilizers.

The second was the long red hair. And the admiring look on the boy gazing at it.

A waft of cool air invigorated Libby. So did seeing these two teens, hopefully come for practice. Heather Sparks was the lead singer in the Blue Donuts band. She had a strong, clear voice and wasn't timid about using it.

Harry, the admiring boy, was a bit gawky at this stage, but dependable and happy to help in any way, especially with technical gadgets like speakers and electrical connections.

"How was freshman year?" Libby asked, coming up behind the two.

"Awesome!" declared Heather.

Harry shrugged his thin shoulders and looked at the floor.

Typical. The highs and lows of high schoolers, thought Libby. In an hour their moods could be completely reversed.

Heather chattered on. "Are we going to dance more this year? I've been checking out hip hop, and this winter I took a class in Zum-ba!" The last word was split into two dramatic syllables and highlighted by Heather's hands fluttering as if she were shaking tambourines.

"Sounds fun," said Libby. "We can talk about it later."

She passed through glass doors into the main room. The information and checkout desk was the hub to the right; ahead, a circle of computers, all in use. Beyond, children bounced around the picture book section, while older patrons browsed the rows of bookshelves.

Watching over all this from the copying machine just inside the doorway was the security guard, his navy uniform hardly standing out against his black skin. The uniform was starched and properly creased along the sleeves as if this were his first day of work, not one in his eleventh year. Yellow embroidered letters on the pocket called him *Louis*.

As did Libby.

"Hey, Louis. Looks like everything is under control. Considering."

"You got that right, Ms. Kinder. Especially considering." He replied in a voice so clear and deep it could have been that of a TV newscaster. Far from it, Louis was a retired foundry worker. His body was a brick, compact. Not much taller than Libby's 5'4", he watched over all the happenings at the Riley branch library with easy brown eyes that in no way prepared a person for the strength of his grip.

Louis folded his arms and looked at Libby with a sly grin. "Eighteen minutes."

"No-o-o-o," she said, dragging out her disbelief. The competition was for the completion time of the Sunday *New York Times* crossword puzzle, although Louis claimed the Saturday one was really the harder of the two and that solving the puzzle in eighteen minutes was not a record. He'd heard someone had done it in four.

Even though Libby preferred lounging over the puzzle all Sunday afternoon and cared more for the mental diversion than speed, she did often check the clock, knowing that Louis, at home with his wife after church, was methodically slamming through clue after clue, filling in square after square, across and down, with record-breaking speed.

"You got that corner with thirty-six and thirty-seven?" she asked.

"*Interloper*. Needed all those vowels."

"What was the Greek contest?"

"*Agon*."

Libby gave up. "Obscure."

"*Tenebrific*?"

Libby laughed. "Not another word for *obscure*, I'm saying *agon* is obscure. You're just faster, and I'm happy to declare defeat. Again. Agon.

Libby was comfortable with Louis. But as she stood there burning to ask questions from her many doodled-up lists, she was also concerned it might be too soon after Jonah's death. Co-workers can become like family, and Libby was sensitive to their having lost someone who'd been with them for a long time.

She determined to adopt a reverent tone. Before she got anything out, Louis spoke in his own low and serious voice. Decidedly not reverent.

"Hear about the stolen money? The purloined loot?" he asked, his glee barely masked.

Libby's wariness quickly fell away. "I did. And I am definitely curious."

Louis gave a knowing smile. "I bet you are."

A mischievous grin showed up on Libby's face. "Okay," she said. "Let me in on it. What do you know about the money?"

Louis folded his arms and began as if he were reading from the first page of a long Victorian novel. "Jonah Pemberton was part P.T. Barnum, part Bonnie and Clyde. Part Matthew, the Bible's tax collector. For years he'd amass small fortunes in library fines from the James Whitcomb Riley coffers. Amass them. Then tally them. Repeatedly and publicly."

The backstory continued. "It was a diversion at first. Every day the accounting, the fanfare when a big tab was settled. Everyone enthralled as the amount rose. But it was unwise to herald it so often. Not to mention leaving the money pouch sitting out on his desk or laying on the shelf up front there."

"All seems a little risky, doesn't it?" asked Libby,

He shrugged. "My warnings went unheeded. I did try to keep an eye on the pouch."

"So," mused Libby, "anybody could have … purloined the loot."

"Could have, but—" Louis put his finger alongside his nose like a warning from St. Nick. "—not without Jonah knowing it. *Tout de suite.*"

"And he never indicated this?"

"Correct."

"No mention of money missing Friday night?"

"Correct."

"It sounded like Jonah left before everyone else. Were you busy?"

"Pardon the terminology," said Louis, "but things were inordinately *dead* that evening. A Friday. Nice warm weather. Everybody who could be outdoors was outdoors. Not a soul in the library after about 6 p.m."

"Except staff."

"Correct."

"And Jonah was gone."

Louis smiled. "Now I didn't say that."

Libby scrunched up her face. "I'm confused."

Louis returned to his character analysis. "Jonah Pemberton came with a wide parsimonious streak. He may have been off the clock, but he and his skin-flinty ways often stayed on in his office to surf the web. Doesn't subscribe at home."

Libby looked over at the front desk. Behind it were two doorways leading to two rooms. "Jonah's office?" she asked.

"On the right." Louis nodded toward the other. "Staff's on the left.

Practically interchangeable. Unless Jonah was on a rare lengthy phone call, his door was always open. Staff might roam in and out for supplies or privacy when neither was available in the room next to it."

Libby turned to a clean mental page. "Then what time did Jonah leave?"

"We figured around seven thirty."

Libby tried to soften the way her next question might come out. "I don't mean this to sound like an accusation, but if Jonah left at seven thirty and you closed at nine, didn't that leave a lot of time anyone else—not Jonah—*could* have taken the money?"

Louis closed his eyes slightly and inhaled deeply, as if testing the bouquet of a fine wine. "Ah," he said, letting out a long sigh, "ratiocination at its best."

Libby smiled at the compliment.

Louis opened his eyes, the lexical swoon over. "Your logic is correct, Libby. However, I remind you that not a soul came into the library after 6 p.m. Furthermore, no matter what, even on dead nights like that, all remaining staff, in compliance with Pemberton's Rules of Order, stays out front—is required to stay out front at your post so we all see each other practically the whole time. Oh, someone probably goes to the restroom or gets a drink, which I think Bin did, but not for any extensive period. And restrooms are out in the hall, nowhere near the money pouch."

Louis then ticked off what he had undoubtedly already outlined for the police. "We all saw each other leave at the same time of closing. Paul had his son to get home to. J'az was picked up by friends for a night on the town." Here Louis injected old-fashioned parental concern. "I know it's unpatriotic, but a deployed husband is no help to her raising those two little babies." He completed the scene. "I waited in the parking lot outside for Bin's husband to fetch her. I did not go back in."

"But you, or any of them, *could* have. Could have come back later. Or even sometime over the weekend, right?"

Louis was adamant. "Once the night or weekend alarm is locked in, a person with an employee badge can enter—their branch only—but they must punch in their unique personal code to get out. Should they leave without doing so, the alarm is activated. Whose exit code is used, and time of departure is all recorded. After the four of us were out Friday night, no one—according to the police and the record—violated the premises until Monday morning."

Heather Sparks tapped at the glass door a few feet from Libby and did another gyration with her interpretive Zumba dance around the flushed, but obviously appreciative, Harry.

"Coming," mouthed Libby. She turned back to Louis. "First practice of the block party show."

"You are a brave woman, Miss Libby." He nodded toward the modern dance demonstration. "You do know you're dealing with young love there?"

Libby did not change the smile she'd put on for the two teens. "I do. And if you would be kind enough to open the meeting room door for practice, I will take their more primitive display of affection out of the public eye."

The library meeting room was L-shaped, with a small area that then turned and opened into a larger square space that could be set up with tables and chairs in any configuration needed. Or cleared totally for a rehearsal.

Libby's block on Apple Street was busy with children. Twenty-two showed up, ranging in age from five to sixteen.

The first practice could have more appropriately been called an organizational check-in. Parents who had brought young children volunteered to take down names and contact information. It was agreed that practices would be Tuesdays and Thursdays from 4 to 6 p.m. That would allow for misses due to the myriad competing summer activities and family vacations.

Every child would be in the program. How they all might be divided into manageable sections of some sort was the other goal of the day.

Libby invited each child to sing either *Happy Birthday* or *Twinkle, Twinkle, Little Star*, and to follow a few simple steps—to the left so many, to the right so many, with a little turn. Outwardly, the "audition" was to see how well they carried a tune and moved, but mostly it was to see how carefully they listened to, and remembered, instructions.

It was hardly Broadway.

Libby's primary goal, always, was that the block party show be a fun group pastime, running throughout the summer, but also a chance for a little of the performing arts to seep into lives otherwise often spent in front of some screen.

The kids' artistic abilities varied widely, but Libby was not disappointed or concerned. Part of what she enjoyed was the challenge this presented, of finding material that suited the group at hand. There was also the fact that her expectations were quite modest.

Performers ranged in age from five to sixteen. Their abilities varied, but Libby was not disappointed. She herself had a strong and decent voice, although her dancing skills were unexceptional. Overall, her expectations for the block party production were modest.

Not so, her small troupe. They were abuzz with excitement and ideas. The girls were ready to learn all of Heather's dance routines; several boys with jerking arms and heads like wooden marionettes or strumming air guitars to mimic the moves of their favorite bands.

Only the five- and six-year-olds were content with *Twinkle, Twinkle*.

After two riotous hours, Libby finally shooed everyone out. Left in the quiet, she studied her list of names, consulted attached notes about height and age and skill, and mulled over possible combinations. And song suggestions made by almost every human being there.

Nothing made Libby feel older faster than being dropped into the lexicon of contemporary popular music. She tried to keep up, conferred with nieces and nephews, listened for the latest hits, but it was never enough to yield familiarity with more than two or three songs from the top of the charts. If that's what they still called it.

Tucked away in a corner of the meeting room, Libby let her brain work to come up with songs that might appeal to the kids but still be something she and the rest of the block party audience would recognize as music. Lyrics that were neither indecipherable nor profane. *Frère Jacques*? Who was she kidding?

"Sometimes it's worse when it's a grandchild. Experience tells you more things can go wrong."

The voice of Bin, mid-conversation at the back of the meeting room, slowly seeped into Libby's music-planning consciousness, which was beginning to be overrun by another doodling binge on her sheet of audition notes.

"I'd be a wreck for any kind of operation," Bin went on, "but this...."

The male voice responding to Bin was Paul's. "I passed out when Geoff had wisdom teeth pulled. Just sending him into surgery. I couldn't bear it."

"After losing one already, I can—oh!" Bin gasped, suddenly coming upon Libby. "I'm sorry. We thought you'd left. There's an Alzheimer's support group in here at seven thirty tonight, and we were going to set up the room. We can come—"

"No, no. Not a problem," said Libby, gathering her lists and outlines. I'm more than finished."

"Looks like you had a good turnout," said Bin.

"I did. We'll see how long the interest lasts, but yes, a good first showing." Libby turned to Paul. "We need to get your son in on this."

"Good idea," he said. "Last year he didn't know many kids, but now he's connected with the Lagunas and some others. I'll make sure I have him that weekend. Did a date ever get set?"

Libby slipped the last of her papers into her bookbag. "August 25th. There were kind of a lot of … other things going on when we were finalizing it."

Paul gave a knowing, somber nod. "Agreed."

Libby wondered again whether there had been any change in the dynamics of the library staff. A boss in charge for years—murdered. A huge amount of money—stolen. Besides the grief, was there also some suspicion of each other?

Encouraged by Louis's ease with the topic earlier, Libby decided to wade into the matter with these two.

"How are you guys doing here?" she asked. "With ... everything?"

Bin shrugged lightly. "Okay. Glad the police have quit coming in." She looked at Paul. "Now that they seem pretty certain that Jonah took the fines money. And that somebody killed him for it. I guess things are getting back to normal."

Libby pressed on. "Does all that seem plausible to you? Jonah stealing the money?"

"Jonah doing anything seems plausible," said Bin, with a hint of sarcasm.

"Who else would take it?" asked Paul.

"I don't know," said Libby. "Seems like that pouch was an easy target for just about anyone."

"Not like we didn't tell him. He was a fool about this," concluded Paul.

"Louis said nobody came into the library that night. After Jonah left, it was just the staff," said Libby, being careful with her wording.

Bin didn't hear careful. "You sound like the detective," she said defensively. She gave a loud sniff. "Yes. *Just the staff.*"

Paul was less combative. "But we were all together out front the rest of that night."

"Just like Jonah beat into us," said Bin. She rattled off what Louis had mockingly called Pemberton's Rules of Order. "Everyone out front. At your post. No reading, no playing online games or surfing the web."

Libby couldn't help but laugh at Bin's recitation and how much she sounded like Jonah. "Let me get out of your hair here," she said. "Unless you want help setting up?"

"We can manage," said Paul.

Bin relaxed and smiled. "It's either this or standing at our posts. This'll give me some exercise. But, thanks."

Before she left, Libby stopped to run things off at the copier out front. Even with a meeting pending, the main room was relatively empty. It was only Thursday, but she could easily imagine how empty the place would be on a warm Friday night.

Louis joined her. "How goes the show?"

"Lots of kids, lots of interest." She sighed. "Lots of energy."

Pushing the start button, Libby let the machine *ka-swish, ka-swish* through thirty copies. "Sounds like Bin's grandchild is having some kind of scary surgery."

Concern crossed Louis's face. "Something with the formation of his foot. Congenital. I believe he's only four. Delicate surgery. And scary. Like any surgery, especially with a little child. Bin says it's expensive, too. She and her husband, Walt, been trying to help out with some of the bills."

Libby's mind began cranking right along with the copier, grinding out new thought after new thought, *ka-swish, ka-swish*. She started hesitantly. "Louis, before … you, we were talking about who on the staff *could* take that library money. I'm wondering, just wondering, who *would* take that money? I know everyone figures Jonah took it to buy lavish train trip tickets." She quickly jumped on her own barely gelled theory. "I'm not suggesting Bin would take it for her grandchild. But is there anyone else, just hypothetically, who really needed it?"

Louis reared up and back, but still spoke softly, "Woo-ee. Now that's asking something."

"Just hypothetically."

"Police got at this a little, but that was them asking me at my home. Feels a bit different standing right here and thinking those things."

He ran a hand back and forth across his forehead. "You asking who, in this place, really needed money?"

After a moment, he swept the room with a gentle wave of his hand. "Everybody," he said. "That's who."

At another time, Libby would have had a snappy rejoinder. But the copier quit spitting out its product, and in the naked absence of sound, she was left smarting at the simplicity and obviousness of the answer.

The security guard supported his point. "J'az surviving on a soldier-husband's pay. Wants to get her girls into good schools. Taking care of an ailing grandmother on lots of medication who lives with her. Paul. A single parent. Got a boy with a silver spoon in his mouth. Wants a rifle. Wants a bike. Wants a new phone. Me. I got bills. Fixed income and a wife with bad arthritis facing my future, and I, too, would sometimes like to take a lavish train trip. Bin with a little grandbaby she'd do just about anything to see it be healthy." He stopped for emphasis. "Just about."

He looked at Libby and smiled. "You want to know who needs money?" he repeated. "Everybody does. As for the moral character of who *would* take a pile of it sitting right there all the time? That I cannot tell you."

Of course, Louis was right, thought Libby. She walked out into the still-hot asphalt parking lot, the sun just beginning to let up on the heat it had been inflicting on the black surface all day. It was hardly satisfying to conclude that even though everybody in the world might have needed or wanted the library fine money, nobody, it seemed, could have taken it.

Except Jonah.

CHAPTER
THIRTEEN

Instead of returning home down the shadeless late afternoon alley, Libby took the front way down Apple Street. She was parched from instructing dancers and shouting over their excited chatter. She was hot and worn out, and nothing sounded better than joining Mae O'Malley for iced tea on her cool back porch.

Libby crossed between two parked cars in that direction. One of the Laguna boys riding his bike in the street stopped short for her, leaving Geoff Paterson, who was being pulled behind by a coiled bike chain, to have to make an unexpected jump off his skateboard.

"Sorry," said Libby. "You didn't need to stop."

But the boys were laughing, busy blaming each other. They were both breathless and seemed happy for the interruption.

"Hey, Geoff," said Libby, "you should be in our block party show."

"That's what I told him," said Javier. "He can sing. Anybody can sing."

Libby would have contradicted him, but for this project, she agreed. "Are you musical like your dad?"

Libby didn't know Geoff very well. Although he and his father had been in the neighborhood two summers, Geoff spent alternate weeks with his mother. He was a sophomore in high school and had only recently connected with the Lagunas, which was proving to be a great way to get him more involved socially. He was a good-sized kid, built for football, but apparently more interested in watching than playing. An only child with parents who both worked, he seemed used to being alone, used to amusing himself, used to talking to adults.

"I played the cello, too. For a while," Geoff told her, "but I really want a rifle. My mom's dating a guy who's taking me hunting."

Libby preferred cellos to rifles, but only said she thought he would enjoy the show practices and that it was not a problem to work around his schedule.

"I'll think about it." he said. The two boys got back on their separate modes of transportation, tethered by the coiled chain between them and cruised down the street.

Libby had to admit it looked fun.

Mae's caregiver was finishing laying out meds. A woman in her 60s, the caregiver called every morning to make sure Mae was up and had eaten. During the week, she came by to fix lunch, prepare something for dinner, and lay out the next set of pills.

At this point, Mae could be on her own for weekends. The caregiver filled appropriate pill boxes, stocked the refrigerator, and still called daily. Libby ran into the woman often and occasionally helped out if the weather or traffic held her up.

"I'm running a little late tonight," she said, letting Libby in the back door.

"Me, too," said Libby. "I had a hot rehearsal at the library. Was hoping to have some iced tea with Mae." Once summer arrived, Mae's custom was to set a large pitcher with several tea bags out on the south corner of her porch in the morning to brew in the sun.

"Hope there's some left. She's been drinking it all afternoon."

"Who's talking about me out there?" Mae called from the other room.

"Just me," Libby called back.

"Who's me?" asked Mae as Libby and the caregiver came into the living room where Mae was watching TV in her yellow Thursday sweater. "Oh. It's you. Well, come in."

"She's coming and I'm going," said the caregiver, who picked up her purse and a bag of knitting lying near the front door. And a letter. "This is yours," she said, handing it to Libby. "Came to Mae's by mistake."

"Is there any left?" Mae abruptly asked the woman.

"Yes. Unless you've been guzzling it."

"Then you may go."

The caregiver took the dismissal in stride. She winked at Libby. "She's all yours."

As soon as the caregiver left, Mae turned to Libby, "Got any news?"

"I always have news," said Libby.

Mae pushed up the sleeves of her yellow sweater. "Good. Let's get the tea, sit on the porch, and carry on till dark."

Mae stood, barely coming up to Libby's chest. She pointed the remote at two newsmen on TV and said, "Goodnight, boys," then flicked them into oblivion.

Libby didn't intend to carry on till dark. She hadn't had her own supper yet and neither had Dash nor BabyCakes, but there was time to relax with Mae and drink a cool drink.

The conversation flitted from the kids at the library practice to Mae's seeing police cars patrolling her alley, an observation given as a matter of fact, not of fear, for which Libby was grateful. With Jonah's murder happening right next door, Libby was reminded of Mae's vulnerability, and she was glad the caregiver made contact as often as she did, especially since

Mae's nephew and guardian lived over an hour away.

Libby took a long, refreshing swig of tea from the glass already sweating in her hand. Settling into a cushioned wicker chair, she watched Mae—whose small feet hardly reached the floor—tip her rocker into gentle, rhythmic motion.

Mae's front porch was only a modest stoop, but the back one was more than generous. Surrounded by a wood railing, it ran the full width of the house, and like most in the area, looked out over a decent-sized yard, which reached to the alley on the other side of the garage.

Libby relaxed into her visit. She admired the golden color of her tea and relished the quiet after the wild time at the library. "How long have you lived here, Mae? In this house?"

"I moved in the summer of that storm. When all the power went out. Right after."

Libby remembered it well. Remembered no electricity for a week in hideous heat. "About eight years ago."

"I was already good friends with Doc Whelan. She said, 'move in near me where people are around and can help if you need it.' She's a nut."

Libby did not think Dr. Whelan was a nut. Besides feeling as Libby did about living around people, Doc Whalen was, in fact, a prestigious former surgeon who lived catty-corner from Libby in the next block.

"She's older than I am," Mae said. "She's gone for the summer."

"Yes," said Libby. "With her kids at their lake cottage."

Northern Indiana was peppered with lakes left from the glacier melts. Some were large and resort-like with all kinds of boating and fishing; others just small fishing holes. Many of them were no more than an hour away. Hoosiers thought nothing of taking off for a day trip, renting a cottage for a week, or if they were fortunate enough to own a place, move up for the entire season.

"You were out on County Line Road before that?"

Mae nodded in time with her rocking. "My family home. Out in the country."

"Do you miss the country?"

"I like things and I don't like things. Always some of each. I was there till my mother died. There till my father died. Thought I'd be there till I died." She smiled impishly. "But I'm here."

"Are you glad?"

Mae rocked and sipped her tea. "I'm glad when you come."

Libby was not easily caught off guard in a conversation, but every once in a while Mae said something so disarming that Libby could not quickly respond with one of her flip comebacks. It endeared her even more to a woman Libby did think was, in the best sense of its meaning, "a nut."

Mae, however, was not an overly sentimental nut. "After Doc's husband died," she went on, "we took a lot of trips together. Ireland. Machu Picchu."

"Machu Picchu?" Libby had always been fascinated by this place. She couldn't watch enough National Geographic and PBS specials on it. "What's it like? Is it as stunning as it looks on TV?"

"Top of the world. Green, so green. Neat as a pin; feels like the Incas are still living there. We walked. Doc likes to walk. Up to Machu Picchu. Down the Grand Canyon."

Libby pictured the South American mountain and was amazed at the thought of tiny Mae and Doc Whalen scaling the heights. "How long did it take? To climb Machu Picchu?"

"I don't remember."

Libby looked out at Mae's back yard, visually a bit lop-sided, the result of a low picket fence on Paul's side, a high row of arborvitae on Jonah's. The imbalance was easily forgotten in light of two mock orange bushes by the garage, currently snowed over with fragrant white blossoms.

Libby breathed in their scent. She ran her thumb down the condensation on her glass. "They think maybe Jonah stole money from the library because he wanted to take his granddaughter on a trip," she said thoughtfully. "To Machu Picchu."

Before she could ask Mae if that seemed like something Jonah would do, Mae joined the chorus of the library security guard: "Everybody needs money."

A short time later, the Happy Trio sat with books on their laps, but not reading; Mr. Randall stood with his hose, but not watering. In the street near her house Mrs. Thorne swept a parking space, but looked elsewhere, all of which drew Libby's attention in the direction they all stared—her own end of the block.

Where a police car was parked.

Libby's heart jumped; her steps quickened. The only noise on the street was the *swish, swish* of Mrs. Thorne's broom and the Sparks' beagles across the way pawing at their curtains and yelping relentlessly. As Libby made out two uniformed officers on the Montgomery's porch, dangers shot to mind. Camille. The baby. Nikki and Honey.

Reaching the house, Libby saw Nick talking to the police and finally, Camille

behind them. Sitting—safely—with the two girls.

Nick and the police were slowly walking to the squad car by the time Libby reached them. "Everything all right?" she asked, breathless.

"Someone stole the girls' bikes," Nick said, his voice low, his tone disgruntled. "I could understand if they were out front where the girls usually leave them, just dropped on the grass, but they were on the back deck when we left for the Harlan Street Fair this morning." He leveled his eyes across the street. "Damn dogs. At least I shut mine up."

The older officer looked to Libby. "You from the neighborhood, ma'am? We're asking if anyone saw anything suspicious this afternoon."

"I was working in the house next door this morning. Then at the library later. Wait—" Libby interrupted herself. "I let Major—the

116

Montgomery's dog—out around three. I'm sure the bikes were still on the back deck then."

The officer consulted his report and started writing. "You're sure about the time?"

"Yes. My practice started at four. It was definitely around three."

"Gees," Nick grumbled. "stuff stolen in broad daylight. I thought you guys were patrolling the neighborhood. How else can I protect my family? We've had all this vandalism. And a murder."

The officer remained polite. "We do have extra cars in the area. We've been—"

Nick broke in as he regarded the house with the barking dogs across the street. "Not helping to have a rock band full of strange kids playing all night like thugs in some inner-city slum."

Libby tried to cut Nick some slack. It couldn't be pleasant to come home and see that your kids' bikes were gone. But it wasn't grand theft.

Besides, Libby had grown up in the "inner-city." They didn't think of it in those terms at that time. And it wasn't a slum. Just the city. They lived in town. Some people were friendly and nice; some were not. If something got stolen, it meant it hadn't been put away properly. That's what locks are for, her father would say.

Nick's comments irritated Libby, but she kept her voice even and addressed the police officer. "The kids in that band are not thugs," she said. "Mostly teens and pre-teens who go to school together. Half are from this neighborhood." She forced a small chuckle. "Believe me, they're more interested in getting their teeth straightened or their hair dyed than stealing little girls' bikes.

"*Expensive* little girls' bikes," muttered Nick.

Sush, sush went Mrs. Thorne's broom. Nick gave her a fake wave and an even bigger, faker smile. The expression on the one officer did not change. The other commented under his breath, stifling a smile. "According to all her calls, she feels that parking space is part of her property."

Libby was certain that, regardless of Mrs. Thorne's concentration on the few flecks of dirt at the curb, the woman was paying close attention to the police visit. Libby tried not to look in her direction. "Dumb thing is, she always parks her car in the garage."

"Nosey old bag," said Nick.

Libby agreed, but did not feel a need to encourage Nick's mood. She asked the officers if there was anything else she could help with. They thought not, except to keep an eye out for anyone unusual lurking around the neighborhood.

"They stole my bike," Nikki told Libby, as glum as her father, as Libby came up the porch steps.

Honey raced across the porch to entangle herself in Libby's knees, her eyes wide with excitement. "Me, too!"

"Maybe the police will find them," offered Libby. She unhooked Honey's pipe-cleaner limbs, found a chair, and sat.

"Maybe we can get new ones!" For Honey, this seemed almost better than having the police come to her house, which she regarded as a very grownup, very exciting occurrence.

She and Nikki assailed their mother with the new bike suggestion. "Please, oh, please?"

Camille, already exhausted from a day at the street fair, had little energy left to combat her girls' enthusiasm, which was compounded by all the cotton candy they'd eaten. She could only muster, "We'll see. All that matters is that everyone is safe."

"Even Major?" asked Libby, half-seriously, half as a distraction.

"Yes, Major is just fine," said Camille. "We can't keep him from barking when he's out here on the porch and we're trying to talk, but when someone goes in the back yard to steal the girls' bikes, he says nothing."

"True. He didn't say anything to me when I let him out," said Libby, earnestly furrowing her eyebrows.

Nikki pursed her lips. "Dogs can't talk."

"Maybe he can," said Honey. "Libby says Dash and BabyCakes talk to her. And she talks to the bees and lightning bugs all the time. Don't you, Libby?"

"I do. And sometimes they talk back."

At nine, Nikki appeared skeptical. She was prosaic by nature. Not Honey. Honey believed it all.

Libby and Camille yawned at the same time.

"Looks like we've both had exhausting days," said Camille. "How did your practice go? Sorry the girls missed the first one."

"It's all right. I can catch them up. Things went pretty well. Seems like hours ago." Libby checked the time. It had been. No wonder she was so hungry. It was after eight. "I'll tell you about it later." She tapped Honey on the head with the letter from Mae's. "I do have enough kids nine and under nine for a musical number of their own."

"I'm five," asserted Honey. She looked at her mom for confirmation. "Is that under nine?"

A nod from Camille sent Honey into cotton-candy fueled joy. "I'm nine and under nine!" she squealed.

Nikki spoke as if the entire world was aware of this. "We're both nine and under nine." But setting her sister straight swiftly took a back seat to being included in the block party show. "Can we wear costumes? And dance? Oh, let's dance," she cried.

On the spot, the girls launched into an impromptu performance, flouncing with unbridled rapture up and down the porch, showing absolutely no exhaustion or concern about the time.

CHAPTER
FOURTEEN

It seemed ironic that putting out energy for a walk could counteract the fatigue and lethargy, but tonight, after a long day, it was so.

Libby's tired spirits lifted as she started out with Dash for his final trip of the evening, finding the light breeze and warmth of the quiet summer night soothing. Winter was not so far away that she couldn't remind herself of how utterly freeing it was in June not to have to put on boots and scarf and coat and hat and gloves every time she went outdoors. She could simply snap on Dash's leash and drop into the night, free of all those coverings, a swimmer skinny-dipping under the moon.

"You *are* home," said Namita, pulling at her dog to catch up with Libby and Dash halfway down the block. "I texted you earlier about taking Paji out, but I don't think you were home."

"I am now," said Libby. "Sorry. Didn't see your text. Busy day."

Anything exciting?"

"My first block party practice. Oh, and Honey and Nikki's bikes were stolen."

"Stolen?"

"Off the back deck while Montgomerys were gone today."

"Gee. I'm getting a little nervous. One of the things I liked about this area was how safe you feel out walking, day or night."

Libby realized that that sense of vulnerability was close to the surface for her as well. Darkness tonight was relieved by a large bright moon, but she was suddenly grateful for Namita and Paji's presence in a way she normally took for granted.

"I am sorry I didn't get your message about taking Paji out," she said.

"It's okay. To be honest, I didn't really want to ask you so soon after you bailed me out with him last week." Namita untied a small bag from the leash and picked up after Paji, who was quick to do his business. "Besides, it got too late tonight for a movie. Just going out for a bite to eat instead."

"Now?"

This was another age marker for Libby. The thought of making herself presentable, physically and socially, after ten o'clock at night, was unappealing to her in every way. Not to mention being tired from it all the next day. She had found things like New Year's Eve the dumbest enterprise ever, even in college, even in her days of romance and youthful carousing. More power to her, Namita had different wiring.

The dogs fell in line, accustomed to walking together, and Libby and Namita let them set the pace as they all strolled toward the park.

"Is this a date? A new potential?" asked Libby, a spark of expectation in her voice.

"No. Just people from work." There was definitely no spark in Namita's tone. "No," she repeated, "I think I've reached the barren desert of dating."

Libby recognized the unhappy edge in her renter's voice. She had watched Namita be fixed up, do all manner of volunteer work, join on-line dating services searching for a true oasis in her desert. That most dates turned out to be mirages was not a totally inappropriate metaphor. Libby waited for Namita to complain, joke, or delve seriously into the topic.

Uncharacteristically, Namita chose avoidance. "How was your first practice at the library?"

Libby noted, but did not remark on the evasion. "Good. Good bunch of kids. And lots of them."

"Good."

"There've been some new developments in Jonah's murder case."

Namita had seen her landlady tie herself in knots figuring out everything from weekend crossword puzzles to strategies for grants to murders that somehow crossed her path. It did not surprise Namita that, having such unresolved events in their own neighborhood, Libby would be cranked to track down an explanation.

"Okay. What's the latest, Miss Detective?" Namita asked. "Why does it sound like you're somehow … involved?"

Libby smiled at how well her renter knew her. Besides companionship on so any dog-walking journeys, Libby found Namita to be a good sounding board. Tonight, Libby didn't hesitate to pass on what she'd learned. Which only served to renew her own curiosity about so many unanswered questions.

"The stolen money piece just doesn't make sense," she said. "Even if everybody in the world needs or wants money, it still doesn't fit Jonah. Plus, I keep thinking about his daughter asking me to help make sure her father gets a fair shake. I don't blame her. She's crushed that this would be his reputation and legacy. Not to mention that she thinks he'd go to hell."

"Wow," said Namita, as both women stopped to let the dogs sniff the grass. "That's a lot to have hanging over her head. And his. In my mother's religion, obviously being cast into Gehenna would be bad, but for some Hindus, a blemish on the family name—that would be even worse."

"See?" Libby said. "How could I not get involved?"

"Just so unlike you." The dogs started up again. Namita quit poking fun and gave serious consideration to Libby's concerns. "Other than wishing it not so and it not feeling right, why does it seem unreasonable for Jonah to take the money?"

"He was too … moral," said Libby. "His views—church and religion, the environment, education. Black and white. Good and bad. A blemish on the family would not sit well, but going to hell …."

"He sounds judgmental."

Libby had to agree that that fit Jonah. "But in this case, I just don't see him being anything but letter-of-the-law. Yes, he took delight in holding the money back and counting it like that, but stealing it? So contrary to his beliefs."

They crossed the street. Namita waited for Paji, who waited for Dash to mark a small bush once on the other side. "He wouldn't be the first moral hypocrite," said Namita.

Reluctantly, Libby agreed to this, too.

She paused for some calculating.

"Either Jonah took the money, or he did not," she said. "If he did not, someone else did. It seems plausible—even likely then—that one of the other staff people did. If Jonah is the one who took the money *and* it was lying out in his garage *and* a Random Vandal happened to be in the neighborhood…."

"Not as far-fetched as you're suggesting," said Namita. "My car window attests to that."

It was late. Instead of going through the park, they walked along the sidewalk edging the gardens. Here and there, a hint of roses in bloom found them.

The dogs went easily now, without pulling or stopping; the women strolled in peace. The flat vacant street beside them showed sharp-edged shadows of leafy trees, the full moon backing black silhouettes on the pavement.

"*White in the moon the long road lies,*" Libby quoted. "Something, something *above. / White in the moon the long road lies/That leads me to my love.*"

She paused. "A.E. Housman, I think."

They turned onto Old Orchard.

Namita looked straight ahead.

She said, "I want to have a baby."

Libby was too shocked to do more than flip out an unfiltered response. "So much for your barren desert."

"I'm not pregnant now," Namita said with a tsk. "But I want to be. I want to have a baby."

She sounded serious, although with Namita's penchant for unconventional ventures, it was sometimes difficult to tell what a realistic consideration might be and what a fantastical musing. "I thought there was no one on the horizon," said Libby. "Much less someone right here, right now."

"There isn't," said Namita. "I'm just tired of waiting. People make fun of the biological clock ticking, but slamming through my thirties, I'm starting to hear it loud and clear."

Libby's logical brain butted up against compassion for Namita, reeling off ten different thoughts and images at once: her friend's real longings, her friend's dreamy hopes. Her friend pregnant. A baby upstairs. Cute baby. Crying baby. Expenses.

A big step.

A no-going-back step ....

"I know you're happy living on your own," Namita was saying. "Didn't you ever want the whole family thing? Not just wouldn't it be nice, but really, really want it?"

"Sure. Handsome prince husband, kids, white picket fence, dog. There was always a dog in the picture." Libby reached down and scratched Dash behind the ears. "I do remember panicking when an older *and* younger sister got married—in the same year. Felt I was being left behind. When Bachelor #1 came along, he definitely made that family unit look pretty appealing. Until ... well, you know how some of those things end."

"Ummm." Namita let one syllable express her empathy for such endings.

For a moment, the feelings of sadness and loss, not just the literal events of the past, crossed Libby's heart.

Not for long. The anger and betrayal and disappointment also showed up in memory to balance any leftover heartache if there was any.

"When neither that guy nor Bachelor #2 some years later panned out, the whole scenario got revised," she said with conviction. "I quit thinking I hadn't done enough, become enough, dated enough, been fixed up enough. By then, I was loving my job, my life, and the people in it.

"There was no feeling of settling or giving up. Just going on my own path. I would never say never, because one must, I believe, stay open to life, but at this point, I do feel pleased with how things are."

Namita had heard bits and pieces of Libby's life story before, been happy for her things were as they are, but tonight it did not make her happy. Tonight, Libby was just another person who seemed to have everything they wanted. And were at peace.

"But kids," Namita pressed. "You love kids. I'll agree a lot of guys who've clomped through my doors haven't always fit the life-long partner image. But babies...."

Immediately for Namita, infants came to mind. The thought of their warm and tiny beings in her arms spread a soft ache through her, body and soul. "Didn't you ever want your own children?"

A ping on Namita's phone temporarily left the question hanging. She was being reminded she had dinner plans. She texted a recalculated time, then she and Libby and the dogs picked up their pace, taking the last stretch down Old Orchard towards home.

"I do like cuddly little bundles," admitted Libby. "I know some women yearn for the physical experience of being pregnant. Not me. *Making* babies, now that's another thing altogether." They both laughed. "I've often thought I would make a good parent. Decent at least. Maybe raise a kind human being. The world never seems to have enough of those."

"Ever think of adoption?"

"I did."

"And?"

"I know single parents are good parents and kids can do just fine, but I wasn't sure *I* could do it. Not without the support of another adult. Not just a neighbor or mom helping, but a true, in-the-house, up-in-the-middle-of-the-night, partner. And honestly, I was becoming quite content with being alone."

The women walked on thoughtfully without further comment.

The dogs turned on their own down the side street that led to Apple.

"No Blue Donuts tonight," remarked Namita. "Nice to have it quiet down this way."

It was Libby's turn for a question. "So. What's the plan?"

Namita paused.

"I'm working on it."

Camille sat on her porch in the dark, grateful for the respite after getting everyone to bed once the stolen bike chaos had subsided. She took a sip of cool water and thought about her baby, letting that crazy mix of love and concern, protectiveness and hormonal upheaval sweep over her.

Three. She would soon be a mother of three. A family of five. And a dog. How fast the time had gone by. Married already for ten years. Her Jamaican homeland seemed so far away. She still felt like a teenager sometimes. She and Nick dating. He had not been romantic. She knew that. Didn't care. He was so … solid. Dependable. Strong and handsome in his own way. Already successful in business.

But children had changed him.

No, that wasn't quite it. Children had brought out a different part of him. He worried about keeping everyone safe, about having a picture-perfect home. He was still a good provider. Of finances. But now that the girls were no longer babies, he treated them like employees. He had goals for them, was impatient when they didn't meet an expectation that sometimes only he knew about. He had been so loving when the girls were small. Babies. He could lie with them sleeping on his chest for hours.

Camille finished her water and thought she heard people coming home next door.

At the top of the first set of steps at 1901, Libby and Namita craned their necks to see around the blue spruce. "Hear you had some excitement over there tonight," Namita called out softly to the figure on the porch next door.

Camille's response was low and slow and musical like a lullaby. "Um-hmmm."

Libby lowered her voice to a whisper. "Everything okay?"

"Um-hmmm. Just a little restless."

CHAPTER
FIFTEEN

Sunday night. Dinner at Jane's.

Crazy big buckets of fried chicken, bowls of homemade potato salad and baked beans, platters of deviled eggs, fruit and veggies all crowded at one end of the buffet table; at the other end, plates and silverware for twenty-five.

Libby's oldest sister, Jane, hosted a weekly family dinner, which included her immediate family of married children and their children, an occasional drop-in friend or relative, abandoned neighbors, and almost always, Aunt Lib.

In the summer, everyone proceeded with platefuls of food to the back yard. Adults gravitated to two picnic tables on the deck; grandchildren landed on the grass, temporarily halting tree climbing, trampoline bouncing, hose spraying, and the bashing of cousins in toy disputes.

At the shaded end of one of the tables, Libby sat next to her niece Caroline. Until a toddler wedged himself between them. Libby scooted over for the child, kissing him on the forehead. In return, he gave her a grin with two new teeth. Awfully cute, she thought. Namita would have kidnapped him.

Libby put down the crispy chicken breast she was eating and wiped salty, greasy fingers on her third napkin. As a rule, she tried to eat good and healthy food, organic when possible, but she had also come to subscribe to the belief that surroundings—whether dining alone with a quiet vegetable stir fry or lively eating with greasy fried chicken, wedged in with toddlers and good cheer—had as much to do with eating well as anything on a nutrition chart.

"Things settling down in the neighborhood?" asked Caroline.

Before Libby could answer, one of Jane's sons-in-law took a seat between Jane and her husband, Joe, on the opposite side of the picnic table, juggling a plate of food and an icy bottle of beer. "No more dead bodies?" he asked.

Libby laughed. "No. Not that I know of."

The in-law took a lusty swallow of his drink. "It's been over two weeks. They still haven't caught the murderer?"

"Nope. One theory is that it was just a random vandal."

"Wow," said Caroline. "Scary. Somebody just coming down the street and strangling a person out in the garage."

"Did you really find a dead body, Aunt Lib?" A pudgy eight-year-old appeared at Libby's elbow.

Libby turned to her and spoke solemnly. "Yes. I did."

"Gross!" said the pudge, screwing up her face.

The in-law nodded at the child. "That's why I keep telling you to stop strangling your little brother."

There was a mixture of laughter and reprimanding clucks.

"What?" the in-law appealed. "I thought it was a teachable moment."

"She's only eight," said Jane, hugging the girl and sending her off for dessert.

"Oh, mother," Caroline said, "he was just kidding."

Joe motioned for a napkin. "Police really think that's what

happened? A vandal?"

Libby sent several napkins down the line. "I guess."

"You don't sound very convinced."

"It's possible," Libby said. "We've had some other vandalism in the neighborhood. Mostly property damage. The other discovery is that there could have been cash sitting out in the garage. Cash they think the victim stole. Five thousand dollars' worth of library fines."

The shock was unanimous.

"Dang," hooted the in-law. "Are you serious?"

Libby still found this as incredulous as everyone else. "Apparently he liked watching the amount grow. He'd collect it for months, then turn it in."

Caroline set out bites of chicken for the toddler. "So why steal it now?"

"The thinking is that he wanted to use it to take his granddaughter on a trip to Machu Picchu or—"

"South America?" asked Jane.

"Dang, Joe!" exclaimed the in-law. "You need to step up your grandfather game."

"Out of my league," said Joe, going back to his chicken. "I think big trips belong completely in the parent domain."

"Well," said Caroline, "that explains why he was killed."

"Except...," Libby began. The toddler fidgeted restlessly, and Libby moved him to her lap. "Except, they did find a brochure for the trip nearby in the garage, and it was for the right amount. Personally, I don't believe anyone would have five thousand dollars in cash just sitting out in a pile. Then have someone show up, randomly walking down the alley, see it, and attack him for it."

"Druggies would," said the in-law. "Shoot, they don't even need a thousand-dollar reason to attack somebody. They just need the opportunity."

"If I stole five thousand dollars," Joe reflected, "I don't think I'd go to Machu Picchu."

The eight-year-old returned with four cartons of ice cream, anchored under her chin like big, cold building blocks. "You wouldn't steal anything, would you, Grandpa Joe?" she asked, the ice cream cartons tumbling onto the table when she spoke.

Joe wiped his fingers. "I'd do almost anything for you, Pumpkin," he replied. "But probably not steal five thousand dollars."

Caroline pushed one of the tumbled cartons away from the toddler. "Not sure I'd put it past you. First of all, grandparents are one of the most protective—and indulgent—breeds known to man. There's no battle they wouldn't fight, no gift they wouldn't give if they could."

"Not steal," Jane said firmly. She stood and began to clear the table.

Caroline scoffed. "Close," she said. "I've seen *some* grandparents purchase, oh, let's say, an electric-powered toy car? Or a train set that takes up the whole basement?"

"That's different," Jane said innocently as she stacked plates and collected silverware. "Those were both from garage sales." She thanked her granddaughter for bringing the ice cream and reassured her that neither she nor Grandpa Joe would ever steal.

Suddenly, as if a piece of bread had been thrown into a pond of minnows, the other grandchildren swooped in from all directions and descended on the adult table, clamoring for dessert.

A big blue ceramic bowl, full of red ripe Indiana strawberries, now sliced and glistening with sugary juice, was set next to a basket of homemade shortcakes, warm from the oven. An assembly line formed until everyone got the combination they desired.

Libby gave the toddler up to his mother, then took the full offering. For the moment, everyone went silent, absorbed with dessert, watching their vanilla ice cream gradually swirl pink with strawberries before being sopped up by the last crumbs of shortcake.

When all the bowls were empty, the table was cleared. In the background the kids ran in and out of sprinklers for the first soak of the season, allowing the adults to sit and talk in peace.

"I have been thinking," said Libby. "Speaking of murder. Maybe ... maybe the stolen library money ... wasn't even part of it. Maybe—"

"Uh-oh," said the in-law. "I can see Aunt Lib's detective brain revving up here."

But dissecting the crime was far more interesting than any discussions of summer allergies or barbecue recipes. Soon the table was fully engaged in uncovering the murderer.

Libby described the library's logistics, how the money could possibly have been taken and by whom. She gave them the possible financial motivations of the library staff: retirement and a diabetic wife for Louis; a teen with bottomless wants and expenses for single father Paul; corrective foot surgery for Bin's grandson; and future schooling for the little girls of struggling mother J'az. Soon the group at the picnic table was weighing in as if Hercule Poirot had gathered all the suspects in one room for them.

Most agreed that Paul and J'az might have been extremely tempted seeing five thousand dollars under their noses. Every day. The overriding opinion, however, was that their normal parental costs were on-going, probably for life, as every parent in the conversation attested, and so there didn't seem to be any reason or pressure for them to take the money now. Louis, too, unless his wife was in immediate health crisis, seemed to be maintaining his lifestyle reasonably well.

That left Bin. A grandparent with a sick child gave a really strong and pressing incentive to steal. It beat out Jonah's trip to Machu Picchu, hands down.

"I must say," Libby said, "Bin doesn't seem the type. She's like Jane. Nice."

Jane bowed. "Thank you."

Libby looked at her notes, taken on a sheet of paper Jane had given her after the paper napkin she'd started with had been filled. "Maybe that's all there is," Libby said. "Bin took the money at the library, separately; Jonah was killed by a drug-crazed vandal."

She pushed a few leftover shortcake crumbs into a small pile on the table.

"Except," she started again slowly. "They happened on the same weekend."

"Coincidence?" offered Jane.

In-law was dismissive. "Naw. But what if the boss found out Gunga Din took it?"

"Bin," corrected Libby.

"No boss would let Gunga Bin get away with that. Not five thousand bucks."

"Maybe she thought she wouldn't get caught," Jane and the in-law said at the same time.

Libby pictured Jane as a frantic grandmother who needed the money. But who was also kind and helpful. And moral. "Maybe she thought she'd pay it back."

Suddenly the minnows began to pool around the table again. Libby grabbed her notes before a child's arms, wet from being hosed, leaned on them. She and the other adults rose up from their seats.

The end was at hand.

The late afternoon sun, the good food, last-minute fights over toys—with tears—replaced theories about the murder. The minnows darted about looking for kicked-off shoes as older siblings were still hiding from seek. In-law took a towel from Jane and wiped down the wet arms and legs of the leaning child.

"Here's what." He stood, folding the towel, and made his proclamation. "Gunga Bin steals the money for her grandchild's surgery. Boss finds out. Says he'll report her. Gunga Bin kills boss. Case closed. Thanks for dinner, Jane." He turned and shouted out into the yard, "Family! To the van!"

Aunts and uncles and cousins ran around, hugging and whining, eventually piling into four different vehicles. Not long after, the vans pulled out of the driveway and were last seen, like centipedes with a hundred arms, waving goodbye.

Libby stayed on to help Jane with dishes in a much calmer kitchen while Joe hosed down the deck. It was a sticky deck. It was a lot of dishes. Most fit in the dishwasher, and with the two women going at it, the work went quickly.

Jane finished with a few pans in soapy water. Libby leaned against a countertop and dried the big blue ceramic bowl, not one strawberry left. She looked around the room—a calendar marking birthdays and ball game times on the wall, a refrigerator littered with drawings and love notes to Grandma Jane and Grandpa Joe.

"Is this what you pictured when you got married?" asked Libby. "Sunday night dinners like we had when we were growing up?"

Jane put the leftover shortcakes in a tin. "Yeah. I guess."

"All these kids?"

"Does seem like a lot when they're all together, doesn't it? It's not like we sat down and came up with a number. We didn't want an only child. After two, we needed a tie breaker." She laughed. "I'm kidding. We thought about each one—did we have enough room? Enough money? Enough love?"

"What about Joe?" Libby asked. "He has only one sister. What do you think he pictured?"

Jane took the blue bowl from Libby and put it away. "We're both pretty traditional. I guess he pictured the usual husband, wife, kids. We were young. Didn't think that hard. Kind of left some of it to God, I suppose."

She looked past Libby toward the deck in back. "Joe did turn out to be a great father. Yes, he can drive me crazy, but when the babies came, I think it surprised him how much he enjoyed them. He got very protective, very concerned about them. Twice as frantic as I was when they were sick."

"I know this is purely sexist and times have changes," said Libby, "but it still surprises me to hear men be that baby oriented."

Jane stopped with a quizzical look at Libby. "With your godson? Counting the days till they get pregnant?"

"Point taken." Libby acknowledged that no one was more tender and besotted with an infant than her godson.

Jane took a sponge to wipe down the stove and counters. "Now my middle one—no children in that picture. Not with a husband who grew up in a house during a bad divorce. Not sure he has the same rosy picture of family. But then I don't believe everyone should have children anyway."

She put leftovers in various containers and found room for them in the refrigerator. "Why all the questions? You feeling left out?"

Libby was quick to answer. And firm. "No," she said. "I am not. Just a discussion I had recently about what constitutes a family... unit, I guess."

Jane took final stock of the kitchen, looking for errant dishes or food, and finding neither, let the dishwater circle down the drain. "You know what family is, Libby. Being connected. Having someone you love and who loves you back. Who takes you out of your own self-interest. Someone in your life—not necessarily in your house. You and my brood. You and Mae."

She wiped her hands on a towel and hung it on the oven door handle to dry. "I'm not sure the picture we start out with is always the family unit we end up in. Love's a little more unpredictable than that."

It was getting dark by the time Libby left. At the car, Jane handed her a small container. A piece of chicken and some potato salad that had survived.

Libby accepted them gladly. "Thanks. Thanks for dinner. Always so good."

"Do you think you should call when you get home?"

Libby stared at her sister, surprised by the request. "Why?"

"All this in your neighborhood. The vandalism. The murderer still out there. Do you have that whistle-on-a-wrist Mom gave you? I know you can't stop walking the dog, but wear that whistle. And take your cell phone." Jane gave her sister a hug. "Be careful."

Libby did call when she got home. She did rummage around for the whistle from her mom, and she did pocket her cell phone to take Dash out. None of this, however, kept her from jumping at imagined footsteps behind her.

The discussion earlier about stolen library money had been fun and productive, had given Libby new angles to consider. But her niece's simple, graphic description of somebody just coming down the street and strangling a person had Libby spinning around to check every little noise.

She did not like being made to feel afraid, and she told herself it was just prudent to take some precaution.

For the time being.

Given the situation.

Al Sparks was the only other human she saw, passing her on his way to third shift. Otherwise her walk down Apple Street was uneventful, a quiet Sunday with family units of all shapes and sizes retiring for the night.

Libby's solarium was cool when she returned, and she sank into the big comfy loveseat. She was pleasantly full—of good food and conversation, of the craziness from Sunday dinner at Jane's.

Family. All good.

But it was undeniably pleasant to be home alone. Without all the people.

Dash burrowed restlessly beside her until perfectly lined up alongside her thigh. He snorted once to declare that all was right and that he was duly settled in.

BabyCakes waited patiently on the footstool for the dog to come to a stop.

To keep the temperature down, Libby had left the lamp off. The big black cat was mostly a shadow moving against the light from the moon, full and white again, out the window.

She saw the cat's outline make a languid stretch forward. Then she felt him, paw by padded paw, climb up and over her leg onto the side opposite Dash, to curl, fitting perfectly, into her lap.

The ceiling fan rotated with a slow and measured cadence overhead, over and over, until Libby began singing simply, softly in time with it. *Are you slee-ping? Are you slee-ping? Ba-by-Cakes? Ba-by-Cakes?* until she felt quite safe, filled with pleasure and gratitude for her own small family unit.

"That's what *karma* means," said Simon Webster in the moonlit privacy of their back yard.

Late Sunday night, the Happy Trio family unit was debating the term.

Ann held a flashlight while Sarah read from the dictionary: *"Karma. The comic operation,* no, *cosmic operation of re-tribu-tive justice."*

She was skeptical but tracked down each unfamiliar word until Simon summarized their findings. "Payback. Getting even. The world getting even for doing something wrong. See," he said, "that's not the same thing."

Sarah ran her tongue over the pinching braces, new in her mouth. "Maybe Mr. Pemberton did something bad, and it happened all by itself. Maybe karma got him. Even without anybody else doing something."

Sarah closed the dictionary.

All three sat, together, in uneasy silence, for a very long time.

CHAPTER
SIXTEEN

Monday morning Libby pulled out a grant proposal and started to proofread.

It was not her own grant, but one put together by a nurse group Francie belonged to. It was written well, and Libby soon found herself reading as much out of curiosity as for the mechanical errors she'd promised to flag.

Part of the preliminary discussion focused on the infant mortality rate for a certain geographic area of the city. Studies outlined such influences as low birth weight, age of the mother, and environmental factors. While the proposal highlighted the need for prenatal care, which Francie's group hoped to address, Libby could not help thinking of a different neighbor with a different concern: Jonah and his campaign against pesticides and fertilizers, which the report implicated as well.

One chemical cited was the glyphosate. Jonah, too, had complained of it specifically because it was in so many commercial lawn-care products and in some cases, blamed for specific cancers. It had also been found in high levels in the area of the nurses' study, since the herbicide had been used for killing grass along the banks of a small arm of one of the city's rivers that wound through those neighborhoods.

Libby looked up possible side effects connected to births. According to the internet, children conceived in the spring during spraying season were often more likely to be underweight and have more of certain birth defects than those conceived at other times of the year.

Libby silently vowed, again, never to use any weed killers lining the shelves of practically every home-and-garden store. She did not even want to think about the tanks of it that rolled onto Apple Street several times a year to shower on local lawns.

It has to be like second-hand smoke, she thought. Even if I don't use the stuff, it is, like Jonah claimed, on common sidewalks, in the rain run-off washing across shared neighborhood streets—places I go daily.

Her brain went into overdrive. Had Jonah irritated someone so much? Complained one too many times? Had they tracked him down one night, argued, strangled him in a fit of fury?

Over pesticides?

Libby tried to imagine who, within earshot of his harassing, might react that way. Have this motive.

In the end, she could only conclude that, annoying as he was, Jonah never did anything much more confrontational than send fliers out once a year to the locals and talk your ear off about it.

She went back to correcting dangling participles for the rest of the morning, then worked on her own grants much of the afternoon.

For a break, she went outside to refill her birdfeeders and clean the birdbath. In the summer the water got warm in the sun and dirty quickly, and she imagined that her back-yard visitors enjoyed fresh water to drink or splash around in.

Among the leaves and feathers and debris in the birdbath, she found a bee floating. After her morning reading, she was quick to think glyphosate had killed it. The Montgomerys sprayed their lawn. Some may have drifted over to her place.

She scooped the lifeless insect out, hoping it might only be stunned or tired. She'd rescued others, maybe this one would revive once it dried off.

She waited.

Dead.

Others would think she was crazy, but holding something that used to have life and now did not always made Libby sad. She wondered how this one had drowned. Did the reflection of the water look solid, so it tried to land, like birds flying into the reflection of a window? Was it drinking on the side of the bath and fell in? She remembered Jonah's daughter saying her kids were out watering the bees. With no Jonah, were the bees down at Jonah's hives dying of thirst? Or drowning from lack of their own safe source of water?

The crime scene tape no longer cordoned off Jonah's yard, but Libby still felt as if she was somewhere she shouldn't be. The sun beat down hot on her as she stood and hummed, filling the clean bucket with water. Jonah had obviously read the same information Libby had found online about floating something in the water so the bees had something to land on to keep from drowning when they stopped for a drink. The entry had suggested Styrofoam packing peanuts. Jonah, the environmentalist, had chosen wine corks.

Libby watched the corks already in the bucket bob to the top as she turned on the spigot and let water gush in. She'd read that water for bees only needed to be in a reasonable vicinity of their hive, but she thought maybe in the heat they didn't want to work so hard and set the bucket of fresh water in the yard, close to the hives.

She did not have any of the official beekeeper clothing her online instructions suggested. According to the article, bees don't normally attack people anyway. Just as she had told Honey, they usually sting only if threatened.

But they could be curious. Want to investigate an exposed arm or slip up a pantleg. In light of this, she had put on a long-sleeved cotton shirt, long summer khakis, and baseball cap.

She wasn't really worried. After all, she'd visited the hives the night Jonah died. She'd been unprotected in any special way. She believed the bees knew then, and now, that she meant no harm.

As she watched them today, fascinated by their industry, she found the pitch of their buzz and hummed in their key. She hoped it was soothing to them; it was certainly soothing to her. Occasionally, she asked them softly out loud, "How are you doing?" and "Is everything all right here?"

She, however, was beginning to roast. She took off her cap and sopped the sweat from her forehead with her long sleeves and stood in a little shade by the garage door.

A noise in the alley made the hair on her neck stand up.

She felt again like a trespasser.

She swung around.

Saw no one.

Gosh, awfully jumpy, awfully fast.

Time to get out of here, she thought.

Slowly. Cautiously, she looked left and right.

Down a few houses to the north, past Mae's, past Paul's—

A man.

From the back it was no neighbor she recognized. Dressed nicely. Too nicely for a utility worker, too. Looking for something?

Nosiness and broad daylight made her brave, but she continued to tread lightly. Alert.

She crept toward the figure, ducking in at Paul's garage. Observing.

Suddenly she walked out and boldly went up behind the man, who was staring at wires overhead. "Are you lost?" she said.

She expected him to jump, was going to be perversely delighted when he did. Instead, Detective Grass turned to Libby and smirked perversely himself. "I am a policeman. I did see you coming."

Libby couldn't decide which was more disappointing—that she hadn't scared him or that she'd been so clumsy in her attempt to sneak up on him.

Grass wasn't disappointed at all. "There's been a report of cable wires being cut. First time, the owner thought maybe a storm pulled them down, or some animal chewed through them. Second time, the cable company guy asked if he had enemies. Said he recognized deliberately cut cables when he saw them."

Libby looked to see whose residence they were behind.

"Not here," said Grass. "A few doors down." His nod directed Libby to the house second from the corner.

"Mr. Motorcycle?"

"Don't know. Only talked to him on the phone. Supposed to meet him here after work. You know him?"

Libby squinted in concentration. "He kind of comes and goes. Cranks his cycle up every morning, U-turns in the street, then blasts off down past my house on his way to work. Blasts back on his way home. He's just a kid. Twenty-five. Maybe thirty. Don't see him much otherwise. Mostly just hear his bike."

Libby followed Grass toward Mr. Motorcycle's house. "He usually makes an appearance at the block party. Nice enough guy," she added.

"Nice enough he didn't want to cause any trouble about these wires," said Grass. "One of the neighbors encouraged him to report it, given all the recent vandalism."

"Not to mention a murder," said Libby.

Late afternoon sun pounded down around them, the asphalt in the alley hot beneath their feet. Any other time, Libby would have excused herself and returned home. But she was more than a little curious about another vandalism. Not to mention dying to find out if there was any progress in Jonah's case and worked to keep the conversation going.

"He parks in front" she said. "Mr. Motorcycle. I'll bet his back yard is cooler than standing out here."

"I was just double-checking the area for a possible—"

Libby finished Grass's sentence. "—Murder weapon."

Smart and annoying came to Grass's mind again.

"Unfortunately, just one more generic possibility," he said as he opened the gate to Mr. Motorcycle's place.

Libby had never been in this yard.

Most of it was shaded by an oak that rose up three hundred feet and fanned out over two properties. Underneath the tree was a large circle of paving bricks; in the center, a simple fountain, bubbling pleasantly.

Grass sat on a cool bench while Libby looked about the unfamiliar space.

"The marks I saw on Jonah's neck were odd," she said. "Jagged. No, not jagged. Hit and miss. They didn't seem smooth, like a cable wire."

Grass had to admit she'd observed this correctly.

She asked about lab reports. He gave rather listless confirmation that Jonah had been caught off guard, no sign of physical confrontation or struggle before he was strangled from behind somewhere after eight thirty. Likely before midnight.

Although Libby had roughly figured most of this, it was nice to have it verified. She focused for a moment on the bricks at her feet. Then asked, "Are you still thinking Jonah stole the library money, had it out in the garage, and that's what caught the killer's eye?"

"Something like that."

Grass's complacency was beginning to grate on Libby. "Definitely ruled out the rest of the staff?"

"Still doing some checking. But mainly, yes."

"You know," Libby said, a bit tartly, "they're all human. Could all undoubtedly use some cash. Some maybe more than others."

Grass nodded and tried not to react to the rise in Libby's voice. "So, it seems. Debt knows no stranger. Not surprising that most at-hand theft like this is prompted by hounds at the door."

"Like a family crisis."

"Or an uncontrollable temptation to splurge on something extravagant, something totally out of reach otherwise."

Libby failed to stifle a sigh. She did not want to hear about a lavish train trip again. "They all had means, motive, and opportunity. They're basically all the same as far as thieves go."

"Except Pemberton was murdered."

Libby flinched.

She looked away. Looked at the sky.

She amended her approach and spoke more evenly. "I suppose the police are on the lookout for money like this showing up somewhere."

"Nothing on the street with this price tag on it. Five thousand is enough to catch if it shows up in one spot, but not such a huge amount that it couldn't be divided or slipped out under the radar. Or even sat on. Although the kind of person who stumbles on it—either lured in seeing it on a garage bench or finding it after the fact by happenstance—"

"Five thousand dollars happenstance. Lucky guy."

The comment and delivery tipped Grass into feeling even hotter than he already was. He considered going back to his air-conditioned car to wait for this motorcycle guy. And stew in peace.

Stew about the cut cable wire not looking so hopeful as the murder weapon. Stew about Libby Kinder, who could sometimes be counted on for bits of evidence but had served only to remind him that he had uncovered nothing new. Her obvious skepticism about the notion of someone merely happening in on Jonah's cash cow bugged him.

"The money was discovered missing Monday morning. No one got in or out of the library over the weekend," he rattled off. "Jonah Pemberton was the last to check that money Friday night, after which he went home, watered his yard, yelled at kids in a neighborhood band, came back, and was murdered."

Libby listened to the rant, hearing nothing new. She found herself distracted, trying to make out the design in the patio bricks.

Grass stopped and stared at the leafy umbrella over them.

He debated about saying anything more. Then reconsidered ….

"What do you know about Al Sparks and the Blue Donuts?"

Libby let a snort escape at the image Grass's phrasing conjured: muscle-shirt Al as lead singer, backup by the Blue Donuts. "I know this. Al is *not* in the band."

Dumb move. She knew Grass was not in a humorous mood. She cleared her throat and started again. "The kids in that band are all decent. They either go to the same school or live here in the neighborhood. They're unusually good about sticking to their noise curfew."

"Feel like you know them, these kids, personally?"

"For the last four or five years, I've put on a modest, informal talent show, swing choir kind of thing, for our block party in August. Many of the band kids are in that. Why so many questions about them?"

"I assume you know Pemberton went down to their practice that night to … comment on the volume of their playing?"

Libby did know. Had dismissed it as something he'd done several times. None of which had ever come to anything.

"But wait," said Libby. "Didn't you interview all of them?"

"I did. Didn't tell me much."

"Maybe there wasn't much to tell."

"Maybe."

Libby couldn't decide if Grass's resigned tone was real or just the heat talking.

"Always disappointing," he went on, "when the last ones to see a victim alive have nothing to offer."

The comment hit Libby like a rock. Of course. Why hadn't she realized this before? She'd spent so much time thinking about the library staff, this had not registered.

The kids.

Of course, the kids.

"These kids are full of energy," she said thoughtfully, "but nothing malicious. Never seen anything to make me think they'd be involved in anything of this … caliber."

"Funny," said Grass. "I always find kids kind of a different breed in murder investigations."

He splayed his arms out across the top of the bench.

Libby began to walk along the spiral path laid out beneath her feet as if following the yellow brick road.

"What about the Sparks parents?" Grass asked.

Libby paused and pulled her thoughts back to Grass. "The parents?"

"Just trying to get a feel for what kind of adult supervision they might be providing."

Libby had known these neighbors at least fifteen years. Suddenly they were people she knew well and didn't know well at all.

"Al is kind of a rough, croaky guy," she said. "Not always sure if that's more bark than bite. He seems willing to help if he's around. Since he works the night shift. One time I was struggling with some ancient gnarled bushes in my front. He tied a rope around their base, attached that to his truck, and yanked those puppies out in about two minutes. Wouldn't take money for it."

Libby considered Cindy Sparks. "She seems like a good mom. Waitress. Runs the block party. Al is aloof and surly sometimes. Okay, a lot of the time. A bit of a blowhard. Let's just say I don't have the same philosophy he does on some issues. But I think he works hard, takes care of his family. Stays to himself. Maybe it's those weird hours he keeps."

"How about any of the other parents?

Libby stopped. Suddenly worried she might say something that would make someone sound suspicious. "You're not seriously considering these people? Or the kids? We're all pretty friendly. Neighbors. We all—"

Grass looked askance at Libby. A person who seemed to find mystery and intrigue in every corner. "It's surely no surprise to you that we're considering everyone. Lots of these ... neighbors ... could have killed Pemberton."

Before Libby could mount a defensive attack, Grass added, "But. Everyone seems to have an alibi. Parents and their band children got home. Even Sparks made it to work on time for those weird work hours, as you put it. Although it doesn't take long to choke someone."

He took a breath and let it out with an exasperated humph. "Meanwhile, your little Apple Street is rife with vandalism. Bikes, bushes, car windows, garden beds, cut cables ...."

Libby stared at the detective. "Do you think they're related? The murder and these other things? That there's a truly dangerous Random Vandal?"

Libby's defensive streak was abandoned for the very prying and probing Grass had found missing moments ago. A new line of questions rose up for her. "Would a vandal keep coming back to a place they'd already hit?"

"Depends. If it's an easy target. Things left out. Easy to get at."

"Like lots of items—tools, equipment—just sitting in a jumbled garage? Not necessarily money, but temptations for a later hit?"

Grass heard the implication. "First of all, coming back after a murder would be stupid and risky. Had there been anything worth it, they probably would have come during the night—before the body was discovered—and cleaned the place out.

"Criminals, returning or otherwise, are not that usual for your type of neighborhood at any hour. Too much going on, people out with dogs and kids, being in their yards, knowing and watching out for each other. All deterrents."

"Don't they normally take bigger items if they're stealing stuff? Like computers and TVs? Cell phones in cars."

"Bikes," he submitted.

"Bikes, yes," agreed Libby, "but everything else vandalized around here is more like damage, not theft."

No comment.

"Then all of a sudden it jumps to murder? Is that normal?"

"In the world of druggies and crime and poverty and need, there is no normal. There is only opportunity."

Echoing exactly what Jane's son-in-law had said at the Sunday dinner. "Dang," she muttered in resignation.

"What *are* you doing?" Grass asked as Libby turned one way, then circled back.

Libby glanced up and around her. "This isn't a patio," she said. "It's a labyrinth. Interesting. There's a church downtown that has a little one like this by its parking lot. See, bricks are laid out to eventually lead to the fountain."

"It's so small. What's the point?"

"It's for meditation. Prayer."

"I thought labyrinths were those high manicured bushes. Like Henry VIII's garden. Where people get lost."

"That's a maze. Lots of dead ends. And getting lost. A labyrinth winds around irregularly to keep your attention focused on the walk itself, not to thwart you."

Grass came over and stared at the unremarkable bricks and their seemingly haphazard layout. "Seems pretty lame to me. Can't take more than ten seconds to flip around and get to the middle. Or just walk directly to the fountain."

A distant revving grew louder and closer until it stopped very close, presumably out front.

"Mr. Motorcycle," said Libby.

She turned toward the back gate. "I'll just go the way I came."

"Straight down the alley. No twists or turns. You can't get lost."

Libby checked to see how big the grin was on Grass's face. Modest. She gave it right back. "Can't be sure in this alley.

And then the event that had them standing there talking in the first place came to mind. Grass spoke more soberly. "I don't have to remind you that this was a brutal and ugly crime. Random or not."

"Yes," she said with equal seriousness. "I know."

"And you are a highly … inquisitive person."

Libby smiled slightly, uncertain that he might be about to curtail that inquisitiveness.

Mr. Motorcycle came around from the front and waved at the detective. Grass waved back, then turned to Libby. "Be careful."

CHAPTER
SEVENTEEN

Late the next morning, Libby deadheaded the row of marigolds along her boxwood hedge out front as she pondered several remarks Grass had made the day before, certain now that she had missed a potentially important line of questioning.

She arched her back and followed Honey counting blossoms dotting the tomato plants, followed Al trimming bushes down the side of his house.

Any other time, she would have viewed all this poetically, a scene full of picturesque life and charm. But recent events had skewed the way Libby saw everything.

The budding tomatoes reminded her of Jonah's campaign against fertilizers. The strip of bushes Al worked on led back to the alley.

By the garage. Where the Blue Donuts practice.

Honey skipped away home, and Libby ventured forth.

"Hey, Al."

She marveled how easily he held the ch-ch-chittering hedge trimmer out over chest-high bushes. Her own arms gave out after only a few minutes doing the same thing.

"Hey, Al," she repeated twice more before he stopped.

"Got a second?" she asked but knew from the scowl forming on his face that he did not.

"What do you want?"

"That's okay. It can wait. Umm … is Heather around?"

He kicked the orange electrical cord out of his way to move to the next section. "The Shack."

Four blocks down and one block over, a crescent-curved street met up with the intersection of two others, forming a neighborhood corner the shape of a small wedge of pie. The tiny structure camped in the wide end might have been mistaken for a tool shed had it not been painted stark white with periwinkle blue trim. And courting customers busy choosing their favorite flavor of shaved Hawaiian ice.

The Shack.

Libby spotted Heather sitting with Harry on top of a weathered picnic table, obviously teasing and flirting.

"Blueberry?" Libby asked of Harry's snow-cone the color of a swimming pool.

"Blue Moon," he said with a slurp.

Heather leaned over. "Let me taste." But her tongue was left hanging as Harry pulled his cone away, and she almost lost her balance. She giggled with abandon, then playfully pushed Harry as she righted herself.

Libby smiled at their goofiness. It was part of the unguarded nature of kids she enjoyed. "Mind if I sit here till my turn at the window?"

With exaggerated fanfare, Heather and Harry cleared a spot.

Libby thanked them in kind. Made some casual small talk. Then said casually, "I hear Jonah Pemberton came down the night he died."

In a flash, the goofiness evaporated.

Harry picked at the paper cone of his Hawaiian ice. "Yeah," he said finally.

"Yeah," said Heather.

Two brief utterances reminded Libby again about the chameleon-like nature of kids—frivolous and goofy one minute; sullen and reticent the next.

"What'd he have to say?"

Heather and Harry exchanged looks. Licked their cones.

"Be quiet," said Heather.

"I'd heard this wasn't that unusual. I mean, did he come down that often?"

Toss of red hair. "Enough. It was like harassment."

"How so?"

He'd just show up sometimes," said Harry. "The big garage door in the alley stays half closed—for the noise—so Mr. Pemberton would stand in the other doorway. Behind us. Wait till we stopped playing. Then he'd say something. Freaked out whoever was standing right there." Harry started to laugh, then quit. "Sometimes he'd say the band was getting better. Then he'd say could we keep it down. Keep it under ninety decibels."

Libby could hear it as if Jonah were standing next to her. "Ninety decibels. Sounds like Mr. Pemberton."

Heather sighed dramatically. "Whatever. It wasn't nice. He tried to make it sound nice, but it was mean."

"Did he yell or raise his voice?"

"He never yells," said Harry, returning to his Blue Moon ice. "He's not so bad. He lives down by me, and that's just kinda the way he talks." He lowered his eyes. "Used to. Talk."

Libby heard Grass's words in her head about the kind of ugly event this murder had been. It had been upsetting for the adults. It had to have been upsetting for these kids. Part of her wanted to get to the end of her questions quickly so she could leave them to their innocent afternoon. Part of her kept thinking they were possibly the last to see Jonah alive.

"What time did Mr. Pemberton come down?"

As succinct as Heather's first responses had been, this one came out a fast and full-blown paragraph. "He came around nine because my dad went to work at nine thirty because he has to be at work by ten. No, I didn't tell my dad Mr. Pemberton came down. He just said goodnight and left. My dad."

She didn't sound peevish, perhaps more tired of being asked.

Libby didn't press Heather but looked to Harry. "Is that how you remember it?"

Harry stuck to his original syllable. "Yeah."

"Did you see or talk to anyone else?"

He shook his head. "Just her dad. Mr. Sparks. He came around nine thirty because he has to be at work by ten. The band quit when Tiffany's mom came. To take her home."

"Was Tiffany's mom there when Mr. Pemberton came down?"

Two head shakes.

"When Mr. Sparks left for work?"

Two more shakes.

"I suppose," Libby conjectured out loud, "your dad just got in his truck, drove down the alley, south to the side street, and toward the park to work."

"My mom's car," Heather corrected her. "My dad's truck is broken."

"Transmission." Harry added his bit of expertise. "Very expensive."

"Which means no dance camp for me this summer," grumbled Heather.

Pure peevish.

The Raspberry Razzle Hawaiian ice was completely gone by the time Libby crossed to her block of Apple Street. It had helped assuage her disappointment at what felt like an unproductive conversation with Heather and Harry. As she neared the Happy Trio's house, she heard lively jabbering from the porch and steered in that direction.

She paused.

The closer she got, the more it sounded like an argument. Rare to witness any strife among these siblings.

"I didn't do it!" said Ann, red faced as she darted off the porch and flopped onto the step ledge near Libby.

"I didn't say you did," Simon blurted as he and Sarah shot out next to Ann. Only then did they realize Libby was standing there.

"Sorry." Libby apologized. "Didn't mean to butt in."

Before Libby could move, Ann turned a face of desperation toward her. "Tell her. Tell Libby. She'll understand. I didn't do it!"

All four looked at each other for one, long, uncomfortable moment.

Libby finally spoke up. "Can I help?"

Simon surveyed the street. A cyclist rode by. Only Carrier Dobbs and Mr. Randall were talking several houses down. Even so, Simon motioned everyone up onto one end of the porch to a grouping of chairs and a table.

The explanation was slow and stumbling to start.

Their secret club.

Simon's kick on mysteries.

On murder.

A chill went up Libby's spine.

"We all got interested," said Ann defensively. "We all thought about murder. A lot."

Grass's comment about kids being a different breed in a murder investigation screamed at Libby. Worse—stories of sociopathic children flooded her brain.

"We weren't planning on *committing* a murder," Sarah said plainly.

Ann could not contain herself. "And we didn't! *I* didn't!"

"Maybe we did," said Sarah, urgently correcting her sister. "He died, didn't he? Right down the street."

Contentious squabbling broke out as Libby tried to listen, tried to sort out if she was really hearing what she thought she was hearing. The kids were talking over each other, at each other, clarifying, pleading.

"Please. Stop!" she said.

Silence.

The Trio sank into their chairs, grave, gloomy.

And frightened.

The fear infected Libby. She tried to swallow, but her mouth was dry.

"One of you," she said firmly, "just one of you, is going to explain, very slowly, what you're talking about. First. Is this in any way about Mr. Pemberton?"

Almost imperceptibly, all three nodded.

Libby felt the blood drain from her head.

"We wanted a murder," said Sarah, barely finding her voice. "We really did. We kept wishing for one because ... because then our Secret Clue Club could have something to solve."

"Like Sherlock Holmes," interjected Simon.

"That's all," said Sarah. "Really."

"Really," they repeated.

A long pause.

"Then Mr. Pemberton died."

At the mention of Pemberton's name, Sarah's bravado failed. Her words gushed out as if to be rid of them. "It's not karma! I thought it was karma, but Simon says that's not what karma is—"

Simon jumped in. "No. It's not karma! I told you. Maybe pre ... pre ... destination. We looked that up, but that didn't seem right either. I just know we made it happen. I've heard about it. We made Mr. Pemberton die!"

"We wanted a murder," Sarah said passionately. "Not Mr. Pemberton's. It could have been anybody. But it was Mr. Pemberton!"

Ann began to sniffle. "I didn't want a murder."

Simon spoke more adamantly. "We all did. We didn't *do* anything.

But we wanted a murder so bad we made it happen. Three of us. Wishing it made it happen."

Tears ran down Ann's flushed cheek, trickling out from beneath her pink glasses. "I didn't want it to happen. I didn't wish it. I liked Mr. Pemberton. He was nice at the library."

No one said another word.

The wind was completely out of the children's sails. They sat, trance-like, as if they had no power or energy left to move or speak.

Sympathy, empathy, and mainly relief washed over Libby.

Part of her saw the kids' claim as absurd, almost comical, but she recognized that their staunch belief was anything but. She tried to think of something meaningful to say that wouldn't make fun of their situation.

What came to mind was the time Libby and her sister Jane had saved up allowance money and spent it all, per Libby's choice and insistence, on a debauched afternoon of hot fudge sundaes at a nearby Dairy Queen. That night Jane had had an attack of appendicitis. Eight-year-old Libby had been certain that it was the indulgent fudge and ice cream. Certain Jane was going to die. Certain her sister's death was all her fault.

Libby made eye contact with each child in front of her. "You," she said as emphatically, yet as kindly, as she knew how, "did not murder Mr. Pemberton. No karma, no predestination. You did nothing wrong, caused nothing bad to happen."

"Are you ... sure?" asked Sarah.

"Positive," said Libby.

The Trio exchanged looks.

They sighed separately and together.

It was as if the tenth request for a reprieve from the Governor had gone through, unexpected, unhoped for, but granted nonetheless.

Libby let the sense of absolution wash over them.

When relief, even a smile, began to light up their faces, Libby tried to reassure them, easing into normal conversation.

"You kids don't even go down Mr. Pemberton's alley, do you?"

"Sometimes," said Sarah. "They throw good stuff out in the trash on that side of the block."

"Well," Libby said lightly, "at least you weren't over there the day of the murder, so—"

"Yes, we were," said Ann.

Libby was stunned. "What time?"

Simon didn't hesitate. "Between six and seven."

"What makes you so sure?"

"The Blue Donuts were playing," he said like a well-trained detective. "They start at six. Dinner was ready when we got home. That's usually around seven."

"Did you see anybody?"

Sarah poked at her braces. "Only Max Sparks. Geoff Paterson. And Punk."

"Punk got loose," said Ann. "We all helped catch him."

Kids.

A different breed.

What an understatement, thought Libby as she took up the last item on the day's agenda.

Louis spied Libby. He held up his ring of keys and came toward her. "Ready for rehearsal, Miss Libby?"

Libby had a lot of recent news she could have gone into with Louis, but there was no time now. She merely smiled. "As ready as I can be."

A little crossword puzzle banter got them down the hallway.

Near the practice room, Louis lowered his voice. "I've been asking the staff more specifically about their monetary needs." He tipped his head in close. "But subtle. Discreet. Circumspect."

Libby lowered her voice in kind. "And?"

"Nothing I didn't already tell you about. I did, however, think more assiduously about somebody having time to steal that money."

Libby could hear the sound of kids gathering in the library vestibule.

"On second thought," he continued, "I do believe someone *could* have ducked into that office, if even for the briefest moment, and pilfered the cash."

Louis let the meeting room door swing open to allow the throng of boisterous kids shove between them.

He saluted Libby. "I shall continue to cogitate on these matters. I'm off at six. In the meantime, they're all yours." He swam upstream through the steady flow of performers jostling, singing, dancing around, and poking each other.

Libby's mouth had fallen open, prepared to ask for details. But Louis was gone, and the kids were swimming in around her.

Ready to roll.

Practice had been moved to accommodate an afternoon swim meet, so it was already six when Louis opened the doors.

Unfortunately, the meet had not depleted everyone's energy. While some did take to sitting earlier than usual, there was horseplay from the regulars, Heather and Harry were back to their flirtatious selves, and the Happy Trio was literally buoyant in light of their reprieve from execution for murder.

Libby cajoled and encouraged and praised the group through two plus hours of practice. When words to their songs went out the window along with all the dance steps, she gave in to her own fatigue.

"Okay! Time to go!" she shouted.

By eight forty-five, Libby was alone.

She stared at the list of finale suggestions from the kids, too worn out to move or decide anything.

Behind her, the sound of the door to the hallway opening broke in on the stillness. "Is that you, Louis?" she called to the back. "I'm finished here."

The reply was terse. "No. Not Louis."

Libby turned.

Bin closed the door. It locked automatically.

Bin was not a large woman, and sixty-seven years had left their mark, but as she bore down on Libby, she appeared formidable in a way she never had standing at the library check-out desk.

"It's not Louis," Bin repeated. "Louis and his big mouth are gone. Done asking questions. He says *you* got him thinking. Thinking who of us in the library might have taken that money. He was asking me alone, like I might tell on someone else, but I know he did the same to the rest of the staff. Getting us to rat, to tell about people's movements the night Jonah was murdered! Who was here, what time we left—"

Libby pulled herself together and stood but still felt cowed. "I'm sorry. I never meant—"

"I don't care what you meant. The insinuation was clear."

A knock at the locked door interrupted them. Libby haphazardly collected her things tried to take steps in that direction.

Bin stayed in Libby's face. "You need to quit nosing around and talking about things you don't know about." "You come in here asking about my grandchild, asking how we all got along with Jonah. It's none of your business."

More knocking. "Time to go home, ladies." Paul. "Do you need help putting things away?" he said through the door.

Libby inched toward Paul's voice. "That would be great," she said over Bin's head, close and still blocking the way.

"From now on, my family and me are off limits."

Libby's niece's description of protective grandparents flashed before her. Pretend it's Jane, Libby told herself. Just pretend it's Jane. "I'm really sorry," she said, aware it had more than one meaning.

Either Libby's deferential tone, Bin's burst of fury wearing out, or the jangling of Paul's keys as he unlocked the closed door momentarily stalled Bin. She made one last, defiant statement. "The police are satisfied that Jonah took the money. Let it go at that."

Paul popped his head in. "Your husband's here, Bin."

CHAPTER EIGHTEEN

T hick clouds decided dark would come early, and the small library parking lot sensor lights were already on for closing at nine o'clock.

"That's her husband?"

Libby stood next to J'az under the overhang, lingering to let Bin leave before passing her to walk home.

"Yep," said J'az. "Dwarfs Bin, doesn't he? Good 'ol Walt. Always out here waiting for her."

Even Walt's leaning against the car did not diminish his height, well over six feet and well over Bin's five. Libby couldn't hear the specifics, but it didn't take great detective work to figure out the conversation. Bin's scowling glance in her direction and the similar one that soon showed on Walt's face made it clear. Libby wondered if Louis had interrogated the others as discreetly as he'd been with Bin. Wondered if they'd had the same adverse reaction.

Paul gave the library doors one final tug behind Libby and J'az.

"You walking?" Libby asked him.

"No," Paul said, crossing to one of only two cars left. "Taking things to Geoff at his mother's. She couldn't be bothered to pick them up. 'Night, ladies."

"I'm right behind you, Paul," J'az said. "Goodnight, Libby."

It was as if the music for an amusement park ride had started, jerking all the cars into motion at the same time. Bin and her husband, Paul, and J'az pulled their vehicles back, circled around, lined up, and one by one became part of the traffic on Oak Avenue.

Libby stood alone.

Feeling alone.

Bin's attack had unnerved her, not just the physical affront, but that nagging pit in her be-nice stomach from feeling she'd done something wrong.

Just a long day, she told herself.

She decided to skip going home down the alley. It was faster, but isolated. More people would be out front. A witty remark by Mr. Randall would help. A friendly hello from Camille. Just seeing another human being.

But it was late June. And hot. Everybody was inside where it was cool.

No one was on the street.

It was hard for Libby not to think about it being the same time of night Jonah had been murdered. Hard not to recall her niece saying how creepy to have someone just strolling by stop and strangle him. Even worse to have heard Grass jump from considering a vandal to suggesting the murderer might be a neighbor.

A neighbor.

In one of these houses.

She wished she had brought her safety whistle. Or Dash.

A car drove slowly down the street.

There. Company.

It drove on through the intersection.

No little girls out playing. No lights on at Namita's upstairs.

Almost home.

Another car. This time speeding, coming up behind Libby.

She was already past her front yard.

At the corner, she turned. Get to the back entrance.

The car careened around the corner, up onto the park strip. It swerved in front of Libby and slammed on the brakes!

By the time Libby twisted to go in the opposite direction, a man had rushed out of the running car to cut her off.

"Get in!" he commanded.

Even in shadow he was big, blocking her way.

Libby spun to avoid his grasp, her foot catching where the grass met the sidewalk, dropping her to one knee.

The front car window went down. "Just kill her!"

Kill her? Tell her? What had she heard?

Libby got up. Steadied herself enough to try to run.

And stared.

Bin.

The streetlight from the corner showed a face that no longer looked huffy and angry as it had at the library. Instead, Bin looked rattled. Anxious. "We can explain," she said.

Walt's husky voice remained insistent. "Get in or we won't explain anything. I'm not doing this out on the street." He stood back, his height still intimidating. Was he really going to hold the door for her?

All of Libby's instincts screamed, "Don't get in!" like the audience's warning at a horror movie.

But it was Bin. Who Libby had known for years as a friendly, helpful librarian. A person like Jane. Who didn't sound threatening now. Walt had backed away. Curiosity had stepped forward. It was enough to consider hearing the explanation

Not enough to get into the car.

Libby nodded ahead. "Come to my back yard." She did not worry out loud that no one was at the schoolyard to call for help or that it was not a traveled side street. She kept that to herself. But also, the fact that Camille and Nick could hear a good scream from their bedroom in back.

Walt pulled the car forward on the side street. Then he and Bin joined Libby inside the low wrought-iron gate.

Dash immediately started barking at the back door. Libby pulled a third chair out to the patio, far enough away from the door that Dash might calm down. In all other circumstances, his watchdog tendencies would be welcomed. Now she thought it might kill the deal.

"What kind of dog?" Walt asked, gruff, as if he had military background.

It was an unexpected question and made Libby hesitant. She wanted to put eighty pounds on Dash and lower his bark, claim he was a Rottweiler-Shepherd mix. "He's a Dachshund-terrier mix. A little rabid and antisocial. I wouldn't —"

"Let him out. The barking will drive me nuts." Another unexpected comment.

Libby was happy to get Dash out for the same reason, but also for the protection the dog would be if Walt tried to harm her. Dash could shred a pantleg and the skin beneath it in a heartbeat.

Inside the back door, Libby rushed to instruct the dog, who was panting with excitement, awaiting orders. "You pee, you sniff these people out, then you sit by me. They make one wrong move, you take them down."

It seemed ridiculous, but giving instructions helped Libby focus.

BabyCakes stood on the kitchen chair below one of the windows that overlooked the back yard. Even with the room air conditioner going in the stuffiest heat of summer, Libby indulged the cat by leaving that window open far enough for him to sit, butt on the chair, head and front paws on the sill, one with Nature.

BabyCakes arched his back in a lazy stretch. "You," said Libby, "dial 911 if anything looks out of line."

BabyCakes had not really been trained to do this, although Libby had seen a video of a cat who could, and she fully expected animals to do miraculous things if the occasion called for it. Firmly instructed, BabyCakes yawned. Others might have read this as a blasé response, but the cat sat back down, crisscrossed his front paws on the sill, and took up his post.

Outside, Walt spoke first. "We're only doing this so you quit asking my wife all these questions."

"And Louis," added Bin. "He's nice enough, but if you get his curiosity going, he doesn't give up. Sometimes he doesn't have enough to keep him busy." She hesitated, then added, "I think he thinks I stole that money."

Libby waited for a denial.

"And I did not. Yes, I have a grandchild who could use it. Five thousand dollars could pay a lot of hospital bills. But I didn't take it. Why would I take it now? The surgery isn't for several months. Besides, the way Jonah left it sitting around, I could have taken it anytime I wanted."

Dash had finished the first part of his directives and came to stand near the leg of Libby's chair. She picked him up, adjusted and quieted him on her lap.

Libby considered Bin's angle, not denying that what she laid out might very well be the case. "Since Jonah often called out the tally, you must have known it was nearing the five-thousand-dollar mark. Maybe that sounded like he was getting ready to turn it in. Maybe it just clicked with you—that it was now or never."

Bin folded her arms. "Well, it didn't click."

Walt's beefy paws curled around the front of the chair arms. "And it could have clicked with anyone else in that library. Or in off the street."

The idea that persons other than staff were in a position to steal had always been on the table for Libby. At this point, it wasn't Bin's accessibility that set her apart.

"Let's say you're telling the truth," began Libby. "That you didn't take the money. You told me to butt out. Wasn't that enough? Why practically run me down, threaten me like this, to make your point?"

Bin looked over at her husband before answering. "Louis really gets into playing detective. Really. Always throwing out these possible scenarios. Says what if Jonah found out who took the money, and they killed Jonah to keep his mouth shut."

Son-in-law calls it again. Dang.

Walt's fingers twitched. Dash lifted his head.

Libby held her breath.

Bin let hers out and spoke haltingly. "I could tell Louis was starting to get … something else into his head. That maybe that was why Walt … was late. That night."

Libby was beginning to get it into her head as well. Monster Man. Already in the neighborhood to pick up his wife. At the exact time of the murder. With a credible motive.

Libby sat very still.

There were lightning bugs and crickets. There was the loamy smell of earth punctuated by the perfume of lilies. She found herself again listening to someone on the verge of a confession. Again, she struggled picturing the crime that she had imagined—the angry, brutal strangulation—and picturing what the ones confessing were describing.

It had been easy to dismiss the Trio. Walt presented a whole different image. Had it been an accident with Walt? A confrontation, just like this, that had gotten out of hand?

Or a premeditated plan?

"You have to tell her," Bin said to her husband. "She and Louis will keep asking, keep prying, trying to make something out of what they don't know. It'll get to the police."

Walt's fingers curled and uncurled on the chair arm. He spoke to his wife as if Libby had disappeared. "What if she doesn't believe me?"

Libby had not disappeared. She could not deny how badly she wanted to hear what Walt had to say. But now she worried that Walt might tell her something she wouldn't know how to respond to. Not as easy as reassuring three neighborhood children.

Libby tried to sound practical, hoping to encourage Walt. "If you tell me something I can believe," she said, "maybe I can let it go. If you tell me nothing, I will probably feel like I have to say something to the police."

At that, danger shot back on the table. Walt was adamant. "I don't want the police in this! At all!"

Libby tensed at his reaction but tried to keep her tone reasonable. "But if what you have to say makes sense—"

"No police. They don't need to know."

Feebly, Bin came to her husband's defense. "Privacy is very important to Walt."

It was pitch dark now. Libby sat back as if they were sitting around a campfire. She rubbed Dash's ears and waited for Walt to tell his story.

"Jonah was a bully," he began. "A self-righteous bully. He cheated my wife out of vacation pay, made her practically beg for a day off. If anybody did take time off, even for something serious, he wouldn't get a sub, he'd make you find your own sub or just make everybody on staff cover for you. He made rules about how many pencils had to be at each station; no chairs to sit on behind the desk, because it made you lazy. He wouldn't offer services like free lunch in the summer for poor kids. Didn't want to bother. Didn't think they deserved a handout.

"So, first of all, Bin, as you call her, did not steal that money. She did ask for some days off for our grandchild's surgery. And Jonah was pissy. No other word for it. Pissy. I usually come down Apple Street anyway. I like to be early, like to be waiting out front when the library closes.

"That night I saw Jonah out front by his house watering stuff, then go around back. I drove down the alley to find him. I was just going to have a word with him. Over and over I had heard the complaints, and I wanted him to know it wasn't appreciated. My wife has been there a long time, and even without that, everybody deserves some respect and consideration."

There was no crescendo, no buildup of anger as Walt spoke.

And then he didn't.

The crickets filled in the void until they and the human silence drove Libby to press for more. "So, you went down the alley and … what happened next?"

It was as if Walt thought she would have guessed it, that anyone in their right mind would have, because they would have done the same thing.

"I chickened out."

He said it plainly. "Oh, I drove down the alley. Went around the block, thinking what I would say, then came up the other way. Passed that rock band that was banging around."

"Was Jonah there?" asked Libby. "In his garage?"

"Yeah. Garage door wide open. Looked like he was tinkering with something at a workbench. And, I don't know. He just seemed … it just didn't seem worth it by then to stop and say anything."

Her eyes now accustomed to the dark, Libby could see Bin's foot jiggling against the grass. Gently, Bin said, "Walt's not really an aggressive person."

Libby pictured Walt, demanding that she get in the car like some mafia thug. She hesitated to give him a complete pass. "What did you do after you saw Jonah there?"

"Just drove down the alley up to Oak Avenue."

"And Jonah was alive?"

"Yes."

"What time would you say this was?"

"Probably nine or a little before. By the time I drove around the block, it was getting dark. I wasn't sure which place was his, so I drove kind of slow. Then I was afraid I might run into somebody."

"And did you? Run into anybody?"

Walt shook his head. "Legs. The garage door where the kids were playing music was closed partway. You could see their legs. Drove down the rest of the way, saw Jonah; just kept driving. Stopped at Oak for traffic—Wait," he said. "Maybe. Some guy. In my rearview mirror. I hardly even remember. Just that split second, you know, when you check what's behind you before you pull out?"

Libby rose up enough in her chair to make Dash go on the alert. She patted away his sleepy low growl, but her excitement was difficult to contain. The Random Vandal? Could this be the person the police were looking for?

Walt was less enthusiastic. "It was such a brief blur. Getting dark. Probably just somebody taking out the garbage."

But this was possibly a big clue. "You really should tell the police."

Walt, however, was finished.

He stood, looming high above Libby. Dash did not like the posture and growled.

The husky thug returned. "I wasn't there. That's what I'll tell the police. If they ever find out. And they better not." He turned to Bin. "Come on. We're leaving."

He turned and added gruffly to Libby, "We never had this conversation. Understand?"

Libby latched the low wrought-iron gate. It kept a small dog like Dash contained, but it was mostly decorative. It certainly kept no one out. She had never been tempted to replace it with a high privacy because she liked the historic look and the open view it allowed.

She'd always considered herself lucky. She lived on a quiet side street overlooking a mostly uninhabited schoolyard. Big oak trees, two spindly pines, and a lilac bush at the rear gave some sense of separation.

She hugged Dash close, brushing her face along his jawline. Softly she called to BabyCakes in the window, "We're okay," and crossed back to sit in her chair next to those vacated by Bin and Walt. Dash put on his adoration gaze, and Libby rewarded him with robust scratching all over his head, both to please him and to release the pent-up tension—the fear—that had gripped her since a car had threatened to run her down.

"You would have protected me, wouldn't you, Dashy?"

Dash pushed his nose up against Libby's palm, a bid for more scratching. Libby switched to gentle stroking. She looked out over the yard and took several deep sighs. The lightning bugs had gone to bed, but not the crickets. "We're safe here, aren't we, Dash?"

Safe? Libby wondered. Anybody can come into this yard. Anybody can steal money from a public library. Go down an alley. Murder a neighbor.

Anybody.

CHAPTER
NINETEEN

"Do you believe him?" was Namita's first question after hearing of the night visitors.

The sun was up and preparing to put out a lovely day. The air was warm and clear; the sky blue in every direction. Libby had tossed on comfortable shorts and an old t-shirt, but Namita had already showered and was in the sundress she planned to wear to work. With the dogs at their feet, the two women sat on the shady back deck, drinking freshly brewed coffee.

"I actually tried it out," said Libby.

"When?"

"This morning. Drove down Jonah's alley, gave a quick glance at the rear view before turning onto Oak."

"Test results?"

"He described it pretty accurately. Would have been a brief blur. Of course, this in daylight. And no one standing there." Libby gave that a second thought. "Guess he could have made that part up."

"You think? I ask again. Do you believe him?"

"It is a rather simplistic excuse," admitted Libby. "He was mad at Jonah's treatment of Bin, went to tell him off, got cold feet. Just conveniently skipped the murder part."

"Sounds like Walter covered all the bases."

"Yes. Maybe a little too pat."

Namita cradled her favorite yellow mug. "You mean if he made it up, it should have more flair?"

"No," said Libby, "I guess if it's true, it's true. But in some murder mysteries, the killer throws you off *exactly* by telling the truth."

"Is that the manual you're consulting? Murder mysteries?"

"All I've got at this point."

"Are you going to tell the police?"

Libby had thought late into the night about this. "To what end?" she said. "If Walt didn't do it, as he claims, his story adds nothing to the investigation."

"Except he may have seen the vandal. The killer."

"True. Big point. But it only confirms what Grass already believes. If, however, Walt did murder Jonah, I guess I'd like a little more proof before I told the police."

Namita slowly turned her head and eyed Libby suspiciously. "And Walt made you promise not to tell."

Libby hesitated. "Not in so many words."

Namita stopped, mid-sip. "He threatened you, didn't he?"

Libby did not want to think of the unnerving conversation from the night before in those terms. "Not in so many words," she repeated. "Mostly he was adamant about his not telling them. And denying it if someone else did."

She complimented Namita on the coffee, asked its country of origin, and in all ways tried to move to a different topic. "Hey, still going down to Kentucky next week?"

Namita looked out over the back yard and smiled. "I am happy for the conversation to be diverted here. Just saying, be careful."

A much-anticipated vacation made it easy for Namita to switch gears. "Got Monday off, too, so I'll leave in the afternoon."

"Paji invited?"

"I love this dog dearly, but she's such a p-a-i-n to take. All the stuff you have to pack. Get her out when she needs to go."

"But you're hiking. She'd love it."

"She'll love being boarded, too. Won't you, Paj?" The dog's tail wagged at being mentioned. "It's expensive, but it's so nice not to have to deal with a d-o-g."

"Sorry she's not more cat-friendly. Dash would love the company, but BabyCakes isn't thrilled being chased under the bed in his own home."

The dogs tagged along as Libby and Namita walked into the yard along the garden.

"Everything smells so good out here," said Namita. "I do love flowers. And I will," she vowed, "get those annuals on the front porch in. Soon."

Libby laughed. "At least you don't have a huge investment in impatiens. Hey, the daisies in the alley are in bloom. Want to take some to work?"

"No more lilacs?"

"Sorry," said Libby.

"They always smell so sweet. I can smell them all the way upstairs when they're in full bloom."

"The really old varieties like mine have much more fragrance than the new ones."

"Did you plant them?"

"Lucked out. Came with the house."

Libby traded her mug for clippers. When she and Namita reached the other side of the garage, Libby nodded at a big car creeping toward them from further down the alley.

"Criminy," said Namita. "Can she go any slower?"

"Or come any closer to— really, Namita. Get out of her way!"

Libby and Namita each reached for their dog's collars, pulling them to safety. Then both stood, backs flat against the garage, letting Mrs. Thorne brush past them and crawl out into the street.

"Always complaining she can't see around my stuff," said Libby. "She's halfway into the intersection before she even looks this way."

As Libby set about cutting from a row of white daisies, a white and green lawn-care truck pulled up at the schoolyard directly across the street.

"Oh, no," said Namita. "What a way to ruin a nice morning."

"Not to mention our lungs." Libby started to turn back to the yard, then paused. "Wait. He can't be spraying here. The playground is asphalt. Neither the folks across the alley nor I use that stuff."

"The guy's just sitting there. Maybe he's checking where to dump his next load."

"I'm proofreading a grant about local infant mortality for Francie," said Libby. She snipped long stems on the daisies for a bouquet while Namita tugged at a weed. "Studies about why certain birth defects are higher in some areas of the city. Made me check the background on one of the chemicals used around the river there. Did you know statistics show that women who conceive during the spring spraying season are more likely to have children with some of these defects?"

"Around here?"

"It's one of the things the group is examining."

"Wow," said Namita. "Just like Jonah Pemberton's fliers."

"Here, hold these," said Libby, handing over the bunch of flowers. "I'm going to cut some for myself."

Once the subject had come up, Libby couldn't let it pass. She pretended to be engaged with the daisies. "Speaking of conception …."

Namita smiled, not surprised to have pricked Libby's interest.

"So, what are you thinking?" asked Libby.

Namita considered before she answered. "Not sure yet. Doing some research."

The lawn-care truck ground into gear and pulled away. Namita waved at it. "Good riddance," she said. "By the way, you haven't run across a green manila envelope, have you? Or is that a misnomer? Is manila the color? Okay, a large green envelope. I've been expecting one in the mail. Should have a blue-and-white star logo on it."

Libby thought back through the last few days of the post since she was usually the one to separate hers from Namita's. "Nope, didn't see it, but we have had some mix-ups lately."

"I know. That's why I'm asking. It would be funny if Mae or Mrs. Thorne got this one!"

"Wonder if summer subs are botching things up."

"Let's go in," said Libby. "Sounds like the truck stopped at the end of the block. I don't need to be out here if someone's getting sprayed."

Namita walked over and dropped her weed in the garbage can. Glancing down the street, she said, "Relax. The lawn-care truck is gone, but, hey, is that Carrier Dobbs?"

Libby visored her eyes with a hand to better make out the man in uniform shorts and shirt loading up his bag at the rear of a small red, white, and blue postal truck that had pulled into view and parked. "It is."

"Can you believe some people get their mail this early?" said Namita. "He must zig-zag a lot through the west side of the neighborhood not to get to us before four o'clock."

"Not a bad job to have on a day like this." Libby looked up the sun-speckled, tree-lined street. "Unless they're spraying chemicals."

Namita called the dogs and picked up their leashes. She tugged Paji toward Carrier Dobbs. "Let's go ask if he's seen my envelope."

"Hello, dogs." Carrier Dobbs first acknowledged Dash and Paji, who sat obediently as commanded by their owners.

The postal worker had been on this mail route for many years. Over time, his hair had grayed, but he was still slender and as friendly as ten years ago. Because of his long tenure, he knew almost every name on his route.

"Kinder and Green," he said. "1901 Apple Street."

"We sound like a personal injury law firm," said Libby.

They laughed, then remarked about the beautiful weather. As Carrier Dobbs hoisted the large leather bag of mail up onto his shoulder, Namita said, "I know you might not remember every piece of mail you handle, but I'm looking for a large green envelope with a logo of—"

"Delivered it yesterday. Possibly Monday. Unusual. Blue-and-white star in the corner."

"Yeah," said Namita. "That's it."

"We've been wondering," Libby ventured cautiously, not wanting to offend Dobbs, "if you've had subs in the last few weeks. Seems like there have been some mis-deliveries. You know, mail ending up at the wrong houses?"

"I do know," he said. "Driving me crazy. No subs to accuse. Makes me feel like I'm losing it. People aren't happy, and I don't blame them. I've been extra careful, double-checking, especially over on Apple Street. Your block in particular."

"I gather we're near the end of your route," observed Namita. "Maybe you're starting to wear out by then."

"I sort everything in the morning—before the brain cells shrivel." He waved at his truckload. "This is all ready to go when I leave the station. I don't know. I don't get it, but I am aware, and I'm sorry if you've had trouble. I'll ask about where your green envelope might have ended up, but I'm pretty sure I folded it and stuck it in your mail slot on the front porch. It did come with all the ads, which makes a thick pack, so I might not have shoved it in all the way."

Dobbs slammed the door on the back of his truck, wished the dogs and women a good day, and set out.

Libby and Namita watched him cross the street, go up a flight of cement steps; then down the sidewalk beneath shady maple trees, and up the porch steps to the next house.

"Sure is a lot of walking," commented Namita.

"Every day," said Libby.

"Rain or shine."

"Sleet or snow.

"Or spraying."

"Whoa!"

In looking one direction to avoid Bin, Libby had practically run into Paul. "Sorry," she blurted.

"Want me to unlock the meeting room for you?"

Libby followed him. "That would be great. Thanks."

"Sounds like you and Louis are treating Jonah's death like one of your puzzles. Louis is a smart guy. Sometimes not very smooth asking all his questions."

Paul parted the clump of kids and unlocked the door. "Me," he said with a smile, "I don't care. But some of the … other staff find it a little … invasive."

Libby nodded. "Believe me, I hear you."

Honey's Fireflies did not meet every practice, so today there were only the Middies—ten- to twelve-year-olds and Top Dogs, as they named themselves—thirteen and older. Age cutoffs were flexible, so brothers Javier and Manny shifted to the upper group, while the whole Happy Trio stayed together with the Middies.

Libby gathered the Middies towards the back with a recording of the Shaker hymn *'Tis The Gift to Be Simple*. They had the best voices and could pull off the harmony of this particular version.

In another area, she set to work with Heather and the older kids on choreography for some popular hip-hop song. Libby had barely heard of it, but this group knew every word of it. By heart.

It was a productive practice, even with everything still in the early stages. Pulling the room back in order went smoothly. Several kids clustered around Libby, yammering about some private joke. Simon handed her a large green envelope. With a blue-and-white star in the corner.

Libby stared in amazement. "Where'd you get this?"

The cluster quit talking on the spot, all eyes on Simon.

"Came to our house by mistake. It's for Namita Green in your upstairs apartment."

"It is," said Libby. "She'll be very glad you found it."

"We didn't find it," said Simon. "The mailman just put it in the wrong mailbox."

One of the Top Dogs threw up her hands. "Why does he keep doing that?"

"He's old," said another. "That's what my dad says."

Libby defended Carrier Dobbs. "He's not old. He knows there's a problem. He's not the one doing it."

"Who is?" asked Harry.

Behind her pink glasses, Ann's eyes got wide with her theory. "Maybe it's the Grinch. He switches mail."

"That's in the movie," came the retort. Although improbability did not keep them from offering zombies or the devil as other options.

"Monster Man?"

"My mom says it's Mrs. Thorne, who really works for the CIA. She's only twenty-five but dresses up like an old lady."

"Okay, Okay," said Libby. "Let's not worry about the mail. Somebody will figure this out."

Wild imaginations and neighborhood lore could be a lethal combination for kids at this age, and Libby knew enough to call a halt to it before their conjecturing descended into the silly and ridiculous.

There was no silliness on the bench outside the library's entrance.

Simon, Sarah, and Ann sat, each with a nose in a book. Upon Libby's approach, each nose lifted as if prompted by three successive notes struck on a xylophone.

"Waiting for someone?" she asked.

"Yes," they replied in unison.

"You," said Simon.

On the walk home, the Happy Trio buzzed with excitement. Their Secret Clue Club had a new goal: they would solve the Mystery of the Mail Mix-up! They were obviously pleased with the alliteration and punched the m's as they pronounced the title of their proposed undertaking.

Libby thought that after their foray into karma and murder and predestination they'd have sought another line of summer diversion.

Not so.

"We just have to watch," Simon said. "Carefully. If it's not Carrier Dobbs doing it like a prank or something, it's somebody else. They must go up on people's porches, steal the mail, then take it to another house."

Libby couldn't help being impressed with their logic. Nor could she deny her own temptation to be sucked into the mystery and intrigue. Besides, neighbors would be grateful to find out who was doing this.

"Do you think the switcher will stick out?" Libby asked. "Be easy to spot?"

Simon gave this serious consideration. "No. I think they'll blend in. Unless it's somebody like—" The Trio looked furtively at each other, then turned big eyes to Libby and whispered, "*the killer!*"

Libby didn't think it was the killer, but she couldn't tell if the kids were relishing the thought and hoping for some danger on their mission or praying that that case was permanently closed.

"Don't tell anyone we're doing this," implored Sarah. "Especially no adults. It's our secret club."

In exchange for Libby's promise on this, she made them promise not to do anything but watch. If they did uncover the culprit, they were to tell her. Not confront this person or persons, not say anything, not do anything.

Agreed.

Libby sat on the Happy Trio's front porch and helped them scheme.

With twenty-six houses on the block, the first logistical problem was of watching so many at one time. Reluctantly, the Club decided to enlist a few trustworthy friends.

"No adults," reiterated Sarah, the freckles across her nose bending to the seriousness of her plea.

Soon, the plan was hatched. Code name: *Grinch*.

The Happy Trio would hang a flag from the pole on the porch pillar when Carrier Dobbs started at that end of the block around three o'clock. Lookouts would join them outside—play, ride bikes, throw a ball—normal activities, not to arouse suspicion.

And watch.

Surveil.

Libby would be on her porch every afternoon, if possible, as Command Post. The calculation was that the switch probably took place soon after the drop, since by four thirty or five, most people were home and already collecting their mail.

If a lookout saw something, they would either 1) text Libby if they had a phone or 2) come down and let her know.

Libby extracted more promises not to confront any person or persons directly.

Agreed.

Libby stood to go. "When do we start?"

"Tomorrow!"

CHAPTER
TWENTY

Libby did not know what to expect. She had been a kid and worked with kids enough to know they could go either way—tenaciously committed to a project or interested with a flash of inspiration that was over just as quickly.

The next day, at the appointed time, Libby picked up her grant notes. She slipped on a baseball cap to be observable to those who needed to know she was at her Command Post. She moved out front, thankfully in shade by the afternoon, and prepared to oversee the enterprise.

If anyone did, indeed, show up.

To surveil.

2:41 p.m. Libby roams over to her small garden at the top of the steps and gives a cursory glance up and down a very tranquil, very unpopulated Apple Street.

2:44 p.m. At the other end of the block, noiselessly, as if in some silent movie, a flag unfurls. Moments later, an invisible, phantom director calls, "Action!"

Not suddenly, but steadily, smoothly, without the least fanfare—one here, two or three there—kids from the neighborhood appear.

By the sides of houses. On porch steps. With a book. Pretending to check a bike tire. Some were wearing Superman shirts and sunglasses, some with caps pulled down low. It looked as if the block party was in full swing already, so many kids at one time on the street.

And yet eerily low key. No one spoke but moved and performed like unpaid extras with no lines to speak.

By the time Libby could see the star player, Carrier Dobbs, come into view, she could also see every pair of eyes on the street following him. Every head turned as he went up on a porch, dropped off mail, came down off the porch, and walked over the lawn to the next house. He covered the west side of Apple Street, greeted Libby at her corner, crossed, and did the same up the east side until his route on the block concluded.

And he was gone.

For almost a half hour, the cast stayed in character—watching, glaring, keeping an eye on the likes of Mrs. Thorne, Mr. Randall; Francie Ellison, one of the Two Sues, and Mae as they came out for their mail.

Nothing.

No sightings. No captures.

The director must have called, "Cut!" for without fuss or ado, the kid cast made an orderly retreat off the set, back into the wings of their homes.

The flag came down.

That was Friday. On Saturday, Libby had to sing at afternoon Mass and only saw that the flag reappeared, while the number of lookouts had greatly diminished.

Sunday, no mail; no surveillance.

Monday, heavy rain. Even the flag did not brave the elements. Only Carrier Dobbs, true to his motto, showed up for his part.

At Tuesday's rehearsal, hyper was the operative word. No one could focus on singing or dancing, much less on the switching of a few pieces of mail. Activity in the library was hyper, too, as more patrons than usual were picking out movies and books and games for the next day.

The Fourth of July.

No mail.

I'll tell you how the sun rose,—

    A ribbon at a time.

    The steeple swam in amethyst,

    The news like squirrels ran.

Just after 6 a.m. Libby found herself catching the ribbons of Emily Dickinson's sunrise as she stole down Jonah's alley to water his bees.

It was so still and quiet that she turned the spigot on to only a thin stream so as not to disturb anyone.

People were either gone for the holiday or not yet awake. No rushing to work, no school buses, no motorcycles. The city's busyness fell away, and Nature made a shy appearance: the cooing of a solitary mourning dove above on a telephone wire, the sweet-smelling tiny white blossoms of privet hedges; chimneys swimming in amethyst skies.

At home, Libby fed her own birds and put fresh water in their bath.

She sat on her back steps, taking the day off, taking in the fresh air, taking the extra time to watch a fat robin plop his chubby self in up to his neck in the bath, fluttering and splashing with joy like a naked two-year-old.

Which was possibly the age of the child fussing a few back yards down. Another child added sobbing briefly to the commotion. A shout quieted them and peace returned.

The robin hopped to the edge of the birdbath, fluffed and preened for a few moments, and flew away.

Now all Libby could think of was what a mess things were.

Being at Jonah's had only reminded her how little she had accomplished in clearing Jonah's name, in proving for Charlotte and herself he had not stolen the library funds.

Then again, maybe he had. People do funny things.

Maybe she needed to renew her efforts. Regroup. Double down on her determination.

Or maybe she should let Grass have his way with the investigation. Since he seemed certain.

Detective Grass arched his back as he sat on metal bleachers, shielding his eyes against the bright morning sun so he could see his son leading off at second base.

A double! There. That should get this dumbass coach to take notice.

Sitting next to Grass, his wife handed her husband a bottle of ice water, hoping it would cool him off. He was a good father, and she loved his protective streak. But she also knew, holiday or not, he was bugged not only by his son's coach, but by an unsolved murder case. Some guy killed just out working in his garage.

Before piling into the van for the Independence Day Parade in North Manchester, the Happy Trio convened a meeting of the Secret Clue Club. Simon dictated, and Sarah took notes; Ann found and spelled *surveillance* for them. They listed all the clues they'd gathered in their brief stakeout and outlined future plans.

High-fives and congratulations.

They were making real progress.

First there was screaming back and forth. Then sobbing that made the complaints unintelligible.

Mrs. Thorne lifted her kitchen window and shouted at the wailing children. "Stop that racket or I'll call the police!"

She returned to her coffee and computer, read the news headlines, then the obituaries. Hospice, Alzheimer's; heart, diabetes, had taken folks by the looks of the donation suggestions.

She didn't much care or dwell on how she might go in the end. She distrusted doctors and took her chances, took her own remedies to deal with the arthritis. She hated the growing stiffness, cursed the slowing of physical functions.

The Fourth of July.

Holidays had stopped having any effect on Mrs. Thorne years ago. Her family was distant in every sense of the word. Besides, she liked things to be predictable, under control.

After she finished her coffee, she washed her mug, emptied the grounds from the coffee maker, rinsed the pot, dried it, and put it away. She scoured the sink and sprayed down the counter until it looked as if no one had been there.

Midmorning and so hot already, thought Camille.

She sat in a webbed lawn chair and let her feet swirl the water in the girls' wading pool. She didn't care how it looked in the front yard. Nick's mother, whom she would have to endure later, would not have approved. Her son had similar feelings about how things looked. But it was hot. And easier and cooler from poolside to watch the girls happily setting up a lemonade stand.

Out front.

Libby had finally declared it a true holiday for herself and refused to do any work. Mental or physical. On grants or murders. Instead, she joined Camille to share a bowl of wild black raspberries.

The two women sat, nibbling the fruit, feet dangling as if they were fishing at the end of a dock, and listened in as the two youngsters set up their business down on the sidewalk.

Nikki made assignments. "You sit here and take the money. I'll pour the lemonade."

Honey took on the finances. "I can count. Five cents, eight cents, fifteenth cents." She fidgeted in her chair behind the card table, where pitcher, cups, and money box were laid out. "I'm thirsty."

"Not yet," said Nikki. "No drinking till the end of the day. We get all that's left."

The end of the day sounded very far away to Honey.

"How much does a new bike cost?" she asked.

Nikki was confident. "About six hundred million dollars."

Libby leaned over to Camille. "Must be the deluxe model they're working for."

Camille laughed. "I keep telling Nick that girls are expensive. Probably another reason he's hoping for a boy."

"Hoping to pass on the family name?"

"He's mentioned that," said Camille. "Kind of an old-fashioned thought that must go through men's minds. My father in Jamaica didn't care, but then he had several boys. Nick's the only Montgomery male; maybe it occurs to him more."

Camille shifted to find a comfortable position. "Is that what Namita's thinking? That she wants a baby to leave some part of herself to the world?"

"She hasn't put it in those terms. I think it's more basic."

"Procreation? Continuing the human race?"

"If anything," said Libby, "avoiding population explosions would be more her philosophy. No, I think she mostly wants to have someone to share her life with."

"This may be crazy," said Camille, "but raising a child makes me feel like I've accomplished something, that I've contributed." Her face went flush, and she laughed a deprecating laugh. "Sounds kind of corny, doesn't it?"

She scooped water from the wading pool and patted it against her neck, damp with sweat. She pictured Nick on his ten-mile bike ride. It made her sweat even more.

"How's the big mail stakeout?"

Libby wiggled her toes in the pool. "Interest has waned considerably."

"Too bad."

"Why?"

Camille dipped her hand into the pool again. "Don't want to burst your bubble, but you already missed one."

Libby lurched forward. "What? In the last four days? When?"

"One of the Two Sues brought a bill of ours left at their house on Saturday."

"Seriously?"

"Nick thinks it's Mrs. Thorne. That's she's really CIA."

"So, he's the one pushing that theory."

Libby slouched back in defeat. All intentions for a pause in thinking about murder, vandalism, and mail switching down the drain. "So disappointing," she muttered.

Camille patted her friend's hand on the way to more berries. "Oh, Libby. Don't take it so personally."

"All this crime happening right under our noses," Libby said with a spit of irritation. "I should be able to fill in some of the blanks. At least for what's going on in the neighborhood."

"You make it sound like you've been given an assignment."

In a way, Libby did feel that way. An assignment, along with the Happy Trio, on the mail switch; an assignment by Charlotte—even Grass— on Jonah's murder.

"Let it go," said Camille. "Let the police handle it." She leaned her head back against the chair and closed her eyes. "Just let it go."

The city fireworks display took place at the vocational college. Hundreds from far and near spread blankets on the campus grass, unfolded folding chairs, or sat on the hoods of cars parked in local lots.

Libby loved fireworks. She had succumbed to Camille's advice—for the day—and let things go, renewing her vow not to work on the holiday. Dash and BabyCakes were delighted to have their mistress home by their sides for a full, sedentary afternoon, lost in a good book.

At dusk, Libby had walked the two miles to the school, met up with her sister Jane and family, settled in with popcorn and gummi bears, and waited in the still hot evening for it to get dark.

At ten thirty, cheers went up along with the first ground-thumping explosions. For the next forty minutes, spectacular cascades of color lit up the July night sky to the oohs and aahs and applause of the crowd.

By the end of the wait and the show and the thundering finale, overtired children, cranked up on sweets and freedom and fresh air, began crying and falling asleep on laps and shoulders.

Libby said goodnight to all and left for the walk home. Technically, she was by herself at the start, but she was hardly alone. Streets were jammed with happy traffic; sidewalks, too, full of people walking, riding bicycles, pulling wagons of drowsy babies. Everyone moved slowly at the late hour, languid with a fatigue that rose up on them like the wavy heat from the pavement.

On other Fourths, Libby had made the trek with friends. This year that had not worked out, and tonight she walked without them. Halfway home, she peeled away from the main drag and started down the far end of Apple Street.

The contrast was sharp, and Libby felt the isolation immediately. No cars. No other walkers. The silence. The dark.

No wonder Walt and Bin came to mind.

And Namita's question: "Do you believe him?"

Up to this point, Libby had spent most of her energy wondering if Walt's story was plausible. Now she gave more serious thought to his being the actual killer. Had it been a spur-of-the-moment decision to strangle Jonah? Walt had come only a few minutes early to pick Bin. He couldn't have counted on Jonah being vulnerable out in the garage. Or even having gone home. Unless Bin had informed him.

According to Walt, he'd been in Jonah's alley a very short time. Supposedly seen Jonah. Seen someone else as he left the one end. Who else had been or was actually in the alley?

The Blue Donuts? Al going to work at the other end?

Earlier, the Happy Trio. The kids rescuing Punk.

The phantom Random Vandal.

"Hey, Libs!"

Libby jumped. So did her heart.

She turned to make out Francie in the shadowy light, a child in tow. "I thought that was you," she said, breathing hard. She checked the youngster at her side. "You okay, baby? Whew," she declared. "Too hot to run like that!"

Libby agreed and calmed her own breathing. And pounding heart. She greeted Francie's granddaughter, asked how she liked the fireworks, getting an unintelligible mumble in return. The three took up the lazy late-night stroll, a few crickets still on duty.

"Kind of dark down these side streets," Francie said, glancing about warily. "Lamar would not be happy to see us walking out here alone. We thought there'd be more people down this way."

"Where is he?"

"Home with a bloody stubbed toe. Not his." Francie lifted the small hand of her granddaughter. "This little lady's brother."

"Nurse not needed?"

"Not this nurse. Shoot. Lamar was happy for the excuse. No

walking for little brother so no walking for him. Right?" Francie asked the child.

The little girl shook her head and yawned.

Bang!

A firecracker went off.

Knowing what it was didn't keep any of the three walkers from jumping.

"They can stop that now," said Francie. "I love 'em with the aerial display, but oh my, I hate it when they pop off out of nowhere like that. Scares the … scares me. Scares me good." She swatted a night bug. "You sure seemed all lost in your thoughts. I had to call you more than once."

Libby fell back into her crime quandaries. "Do you think anybody on our block could ki—." She looked at Francie's granddaughter, who was not paying much attention to the conversation, but still …. "Anybody could … do Jonah in?"

"Girl, you need to give this business a rest."

Shades of Camille.

"I keep thinking how sad Charlotte is, knowing they think her father stole the library money. It's just not like him."

"You don't think it's like Jonah to take the money, but you have no problem thinking some neighbor ki— … did him in?"

Libby felt thwarted. And tired.

She let it go.

A few more blocks, a few more firecrackers, light chit-chat about the day, and the group arrived on their block of Apple Street, even more dead, since midnight was not far away.

Libby hesitated at first, but seeing yawns from the little girl, declined Francie's offer to walk her to the corner.

Francie and her granddaughter said goodnight and left Libby to take the last part of the block on her own. No Dash. No whistle-on-a-wrist.

A smoky haze from grilled hamburgers and firecrackers and the day's heat hung in the air. Houses were dark.

None darker than Jonah Pemberton's.

Libby thought about people moving out of a neighborhood, how odd it seemed that even though they were still alive somewhere else, they were definitely no longer part of the community.

Then here was Jonah, dead and literally gone, but lingering in everyone's mind like the wind chimes on his porch. The unresolved nature of his going left his pots waiting for him to be watered, bees expecting him at the hive, bills expecting to be paid.

It suddenly made Libby sad.

As she passed Jonah's house, she had a flashback: jagged marks on the neck, wild eyes …

Bang!

Libby jumped and shivered at the same time. She looked over her shoulder for Monster Man or Walt or the Random Vandal. Or possibly all of them standing behind her.

C.S. Lewis was certainly right that grief could feel like fear, but tonight that fear was being surpassed by Libby's sense of pure frustration; her ability to figure things out, stifled.

Strangled.

Was she failing her assignment others had counted on her to help with? That she had given herself? Failed by not being more thorough?

She thought about Francie's remark. Was she being selective about who she let off the hook and who she pursued?

She began to think maybe she'd been too easy.

On everyone.

CHAPTER
TWENTY-ONE

"No, I think it's great to have a set time for family meals. In the summer, seven seems perfect for dinner. Bet you're glad your kids are so punctual."

Libby hated making this call to the Trio's mom, but she had made more lists and, with renewed vigor, was ready to verify even seemingly little things.

Like the whereabouts of the Happy Trio. Who on the night of the murder it turned out were, as they said, home and at the meal table. By seven.

Confirmed by mom.

But had they been in Jonah's alley?

Libby lucked out finding Max Sparks in his yard.

He was hard to miss.

A howling competition between Max and one of his dogs was in full swing. They were not the majestic bays of a wolf, but the elongated, pained siren of a beagle. Perfectly duplicated by eleven-year-old Max.

"Hey, Max. What's up?" Libby asked.

Max sat cross-legged on the grass, his baseball cap on backwards with hair the color of his sister Heather's sticking out from all sides.

"Not much." He flipped the dog's ears several times, which elicited another howl.

"Is that Rocky or Punk?"

"Punk." Max's responses were succinct, but not unfriendly.

"He seems pretty good right here," Libby went on. "Does he ever run away or get out sometimes?"

"Once in a while."

"I heard he got out a few weeks ago."

Max shrugged his shoulders, more interested in the rhythm of flipping one dog ear then the other. "Yeah. Maybe a few weeks ago."

"Is he hard to catch? Dash can be pretty fast."

Max lit up with a chance to brag about his dog. "Oh, yeah. Punk is fast!"

"Did you catch him all by yourself? That last time?"

"Geoff Paterson helped. He helps me if Punk runs that way to Oak Avenue. Those kids from across the street helped, too."

"Simon and his sisters?"

"Yep."

"Anybody else out there? In the alley that day?

"Nope."

"What'd you do after you caught Punk?"

"Everybody went home. I gave Punk a treat. Kept him with me in my room with Rocky. My dad gets mad if they get loose." The boy went nose to nose with Punk, who was rested and ready for more howling. Max obliged.

Trio in the alley. Geoff in the alley. Max and Punk in the alley— before seven.

Then no one from this group.

Confirmed.

Libby was not the only one in the neighborhood re-committed to getting to the bottom of things.

2:52 p.m. on Thursday, the 5th of July, the flag at 2013 Apple Street went up the pole. It was a fluke for Libby to be out front in the first place. She was snipping a handful of parsley when she spied the stakeout signal.

She had to smile. Of all the kids who were so excited those first few days, only the Happy Trio had stuck with it and shown up.

Sarah remained on her porch and appeared to be coloring or drawing, periodically looking around. Ann, the rover, pedaled her bike up and down, stopping for an occasional swig from her water bottle. Simon made a seat leaning against the trunk of Sparks' catalpa tree directly across from her. Libby did not wave but continued snipping parsley as Simon began reading a magazine, binoculars and notebook at his side.

Libby thought of the summer after fifth grade when she was allowed to ride her bike to the Edith Hamilton branch library. It was a hot, four-mile ride down city side streets to an even hotter—pre-AC—small branch library.

She would sit on a stubby wooden stool in one, large, airless room full of nothing but books. Books about everything—the Civil War and African lions and drawing and Nancy Drew. It was the summer Libby flirted with science, devouring the biographies of Madame Curie and Thomas Edison, absorbing their sense of the patient, methodical hunt for answers to help humankind.

Libby understood this about Simon and Sarah and Ann: catching the mail switcher was a golden opportunity. On otherwise ordinary days in stifling July, it was a chance to be intellectually engaged and challenged, to do meaningful work with one's brain and mind.

Every day the Trio showed up—on porches or under umbrellas in the rain; under trees and beach hats in the unrelenting afternoon sun. They became part of the norm, no different than Mrs. Thorne on her swing, Mr. Randall or Paul or Francie out with their hoses; other kids on skateboards and bikes. Libby held practices and worked on her grants. She walked the dog and tried to remain available during the Happy Trio's stakeout hours.

During the second week, there was another undetected mail switch by the Grinch.

The Trio was not deterred and continued to show up, even though some days Libby did not. In fact, she began to think the whole endeavor seemed interminable.

And fruitless.

Then.

"Libby, Libby! We know who it is!"

Sarah stood at Libby's back door, breathless. "The Grinch is doing it again! Simon says come watch because we're not sure which house is going to get switched on, but we've seen it happen before. We've *seen* it! Come on!"

Libby followed Sarah out the back, around the side of the house to the front. "Be quiet," Sarah cautioned in a low voice. "Act natural. Like you and I are just talking. Like no big deal."

They crossed the street. Simon had moved up onto the porch steps of the corner house. Through a fake smile, Simon instructed Libby and Sarah to sit, to keep pretending. But watch.

Libby tried to remain calm, tried to carry her end of the meaningless babble with Sarah and still keep an eye on Carrier Dobbs going from house to house on the opposite side of the street.

He finished the west row. Crossed the street and came toward Libby, greeted her and Sarah while Simon seemingly read, and moved on.

Next door at the Sparks' house, Rocky and Punk inside went nuts as usual, barking and pawing at their window during the postal invasion.

And on Carrier Dobbs went.

Suddenly, it seemed to Libby there were a lot of moving parts to track: Camille came out for her mail and slipped back into the house. Mrs. Thorne picked dead leaves off a hanging basket of petunias. A car drove by.

A skateboarder click-clacked across the sidewalk cracks; mid-block a child squealed. Sparks' dogs kept barking.

It all seemed like normal activity, but now on the alert, Libby was having a hard time knowing where to focus.

Simon cleared his throat.

Sarah nudged Libby and nodded across the street. "The Grinch," she said through a phony smile.

The Grinch was passing out blue fliers.

Sarah whispered, "Watch."

A flier was put in Camille's mailbox, but with a closer look, it was seen to be immediately taken back out and returned to the original pile in the Grinch's arm. The Grinch quit the west side, crossed Apple Street, and calmly greeted Libby and Sarah at the corner house, then stepped over Simon and made the same pretend drop in the mailbox behind them.

But as the dogs barked insanely at the Sparks' next door, the Grinch did something slightly different. It was obvious if a person was paying attention. The fliers were blue; the envelope plucked from the Sparks' mailbox was white.

Simon didn't need binoculars to catch this switch. Neither did Libby.

Libby let her chatter with Sarah slow to nothing. She held her breath. What should she do? Was this really how it happened or—

Sarah stood. She waved at Ann on the opposite side of the street, now leaning on her bike several houses north of Mrs. Thorne's.

The Grinch strolled down the block, not hitting every house, but enough to look busy.

Simon cleared his throat again. Sarah tugged Libby's shirt, getting her to follow along as they crossed over to the third member of their team.

Ann's eyes could not have gotten any larger. "That's the Grinch!"

"Really?" asked Libby, skeptical, not wanting to believe them. "Are you sure?"

Sarah gave an exaggerated nod. "Oh, yeah," she said.

"We've observed, taken notes, and confirmed," explained Simon. "We didn't want to tell you until we were positive."

Simon then positioned himself so they could all look like they were talking to him but could really be looking across the street. "Keep watching."

Ann gushed with excitement almost too difficult to contain. "One time he acted like he was putting somebody's ball back on their porch."

"It's harder to tell when he's dropping the envelopes out of the fliers," said Sarah. "But if you keep watching, he takes longer at that house, especially if it's a mail slot."

Libby knew there were only a few houses left for the Grinch to hit. She was starting to formulate her plan of action. If this truly was the mail switcher, she needed to confront him during an actual switch. "Wait," she said, "he's going up on Mr. Pemberton's porch."

"That's camouflage," Sarah said confidently. "No one's home there. Mr. Pemberton's dead."

Libby told the girls to wait there. She crossed back over and down the street.

After the Grinch.

Casual. Like no big deal.

A short distance away, she called, "Hey. What have you got there?"

Geoff Paterson looked at Libby. "Nothing. Just some fliers." He was friendly. Very calm.

"You know Mr. Pemberton isn't here anymore?"

"Oh. Yeah. Forgot." He kept walking as if on a pleasant afternoon excursion.

As if he were passing out fliers.

Libby walked closer to him. "What's up? I don't think I got one of those. Can I see what I'm missing?"

Geoff tipped the pile of blue sheets enough for Libby to see that they were printed fliers, but not enough so she could read anything.

"Oh, come on," she coaxed.

She read the one he finally handed her. It didn't take long. Yes, it was a flier. "This is for your school food drive. Last Thanksgiving."

Geoff took the flier from her, looking mildly concerned. "Must have picked up the wrong pile. They were both blue. I meant to grab some for a vacation bible study camp at my church."

"What else have you got there?" Libby asked. "It's kind of a thick pile."

"Yeah," came a defiant voice from behind them.

A few feet away, Simon stood with his sisters. "It's the Sparks' mail. We saw you take it."

Sarah stepped forward. "We saw you take Mr. Motorcycle's last week and put it in our neighbor's mailbox."

"We saw you," chimed in Ann.

"You did?" There was genuine awe, even admiration. "Wow, you guys are good."

It was not the reaction Libby expected, did not fit the plan of action she had formulated. Geoff was neither defensive nor belligerent. He shrugged. "It was just a little prank."

Simon was not so nonchalant. He waved his notebook. "A prank? You're not allowed to mess with the mail. We've seen you do it before. And there were all those other times before we started watching."

Ann backed up her brother's claim. "We know. We have a list of all the times you switched. You're the Grinch!"

Sarah added her part. "We went door to door and asked everybody. We made a list."

Libby knew this was so. They had asked her and Namita early on. Geoff's non-aggressive posture might have persuaded Libby to let his excuse work, but the long list Simon was pointing to in his notebook made *prank* seem too mild a term. Her adult responsibility bones kicked in.

"Tampering with the mail is not a prank," Libby said.

"It was just a practical joke," countered Geoff, still affable, not arrogant in the least. "Nobody got hurt."

Libby was no longer being swayed by the casual attitude. "I think I'd better talk to your father."

Geoff told her he was at work. Wouldn't be home until six. Libby said she'd be by then to speak with him.

"Okay," Geoff said easily. He took his fliers and his time and returned home two doors down.

Libby walked with the Happy Trio toward their house. The Secret Clue Club could hardly stop buzzing about solving the case, offering to help further in any way.

Libby had no doubt they wanted to be in on the trial, the conviction, and the sentencing of the apprehended Grinch.

"We're witnesses," said Simon. "We kept records. We've got names and dates."

"I'll let you know if I need them," said Libby.

At the Trio's front porch, Libby thanked them and commended them on a successful stakeout.

Wow, thought Libby on the walk home. It worked. There was a crime puzzle, we put our brains to work on solving it. And we did.

They did. The Trio.

With patience, perseverance, and thoroughness.

Libby plucked a leaf from a bush. She twirled it happily and felt inspired.

CHAPTER
TWENTY-TWO

"What possessed you to do this?" Paul asked, an obviously pained look on his face.

Geoff shrugged with a child-like grin.

Paul looked away. "This isn't like you."

Libby felt like an intruder witnessing the conversation between father and son. She distracted herself by focusing on the Paterson living room, beautifully decorated with antiques and oriental rugs from Paul's grandmother. It was one thing to own such lovely pieces, another to know how to arrange and display them for effect. Libby, who tried to have some aesthetic plan, but usually succumbed to comfort over everything else, admired this. It made her feel better to see a skateboard sticking out from a clump of clothes undoubtedly dropped by a teenager who probably cared little about visual impact.

She also appreciated Paul's reasonable tone as he tried to understand his son's actions rather than fly off the handle in anger. Or the other extreme, merely dismiss them.

"Is this something kids at school are doing now?" asked Paul. "Like the toilet paper hanging all over trees?"

"No."

"Something in the movies you've been watching?"

"No."

Paul explained to Libby that Geoff had always been fond of CIA and espionage films. "I like them, too," he admitted. He turned again to the boy. "You keep this up and you will not get that gun."

"Geez, dad, that's for hunting."

"It's a real thing. Not like pretending you're in the FBI. This mail business makes me think you're not old enough for the responsibility."

Geoff started to object, but Paul raised an eyebrow and gave what must have been the parental cut-off look.

Geoff did not argue.

Paul shifted his attention to Libby. "I'm sorry about all this. Geoff will be apologizing to every person on the block whose mail was affected."

There was a heavy sigh from Geoff. Paul softened and looked at Libby. "I don't think any real harm was done, do you?"

"Not that I know of," Libby said. "Not like we need a major police investigation of it."

She was half joking, but Paul took it seriously.

"I was hoping the apologies would be enough. There are things I can do here at home, like … grounding." He derailed Geoff's objection with a second raised eyebrow.

Libby hadn't thought about punishment. Paul was right. It didn't seem as if there was any real harm done. The prank needed to be addressed, but making a personal apology to half the neighborhood, especially for a fifteen-year-old with a scowl on his face, sounded unpleasant enough to qualify.

"I assume people will be okay with that," she said. "Probably better ask to be sure. Most of them have kids. I think they'll understand."

"Do you remember who all you switched the mail on?" Paul asked Geoff.

"We have a list I can get for you," said Libby. "And maybe he should apologize to Carrier Dobbs. He's the one who's been getting the blame for everything."

"Certainly." Paul put his arm around his son and gave it a small, but sturdy squeeze. "No more mail pranks. Okay?" He thanked Libby. "I'll take it from here."

Libby left Paterson's house mulling things over: Geoff's low-key heist operation; the Happy Trio's secret club and stakeout; even performers in the block party show acting like it was Broadway.

The sum total of all these kid things reminded her of *Bugsy Malone*, a serious old gangster movie, but with the gangsters and victims and police played by child actors. The girls wore Roaring Twenties flapper dresses; the boys sported striped suits, mustaches, and fedoras. Their cars were vintage replicas powered by bike pedals, and their tommy guns shot whipped cream.

Who needed to have their own kids to make life interesting?

The next afternoon, Libby stood at the copying machine in the library, running off the list of mail switch victims happily provided by the Secret Clue Club. She smiled at the thought of informing Louis about their amateur sleuthing. And their success.

J'az, with today's flamingo pink wig, came towards her with an armload of books.

"Where's Louis?" asked Libby.

J'az looked around for the normally ubiquitous security guard. "He must still be talking to that police detective."

Libby did not drink a lot of caffeine. Nor eat a lot of sugar. She had not had anything that morning that would have cranked her up. But at the mention of Detective Grass's presence and interrogation, it was as if a pinball had been sent bing-banging around her brain, lighting up images, and bumping into obstacles.

Bin standing at the front desk—Libby had promised her not to rat on Walt. Let him come clean on his own about his being in the alley the night of Jonah's murder.

Paul by the computers—Libby had promised him not to go to the police about Geoff and the mail switching.

Coming towards her, gray slacks, plaid shirt and tie, and friendly confidence was Grass—the man she'd promised to tell exactly such things.

If, she rationalized, if they were important.

If telling would help.

Libby took a deep breath and let her ricocheting pinball slow down, let it hit on another option—she could do the asking first.

"Something new on the case?" she began. Friendly, too. Plus, honestly curious.

Grass's first thought was that here was Libby Kinder coming at him, friendly and curious. His second thought was that she does seem to show up a lot during a murder investigation.

"Hello," he replied. "Nothing new. Just going over some things. Crossing t's, dotting i's. Re-checking some timing. Have a quiet Fourth here? No stolen bikes? No smashed car windows?"

"Nope. Quiet. Vandals on vacation."

"Hope that's true."

Libby braced herself for Grass to ask her directly if she'd found out anything.

She pushed the button for two copies and mentally scrambled to find a way to steer him in a different direction.

"Yes. Timing," she said, piecing together a plausible theory as she bumped along. "Not so much people's comings and goings, but ….

"I've been thinking. Let's assume seriously that everybody *can* use more cash. And if we consider—just consider—that Jonah didn't take the money at all. And if it looks like no one could have taken the money *before* Jonah was killed, could someone have taken it … *after* the murder?"

Grass had considered this option but had found little support for it. "How would you figure things in that case?"

"Well. Maybe someone was upset about something … totally different. Once Jonah was dead, maybe they said to themselves, 'I might as well take that money.'"

For Grass, getting a new angle on his facts was like getting a new tire on the car. It might replace the bad one that had gone flat, but a new one also threw the alignment out of whack for the whole car, and eventually everything had to be adjusted.

In a murder case, this was not something he undertook lightly or without sufficient reason. Then again, he was talking to Libby Kinder, who might just have uncovered one. He studied the look on her face to see how serious she was.

Before he could ask more, Bin came up beside them. Polite. Not particularly friendly. "I'm on break, Detective. I can talk to you now."

Grass stepped aside, allowing her to lead the way to a small study room. "Don't worry," he said to her, "I don't think this will take long."

"I don't think so either," said Bin. As Grass turned, Bin smirked toward Libby. "I have nothing new to tell you."

So much for Walt coming clean.

Paul appeared from the stacks and pulled Libby's attention away from Bin. "Is that the list?" he asked, gesturing toward the sheets of paper dangling from Libby's hand.

"Yes," she said, giving one of the copies to Paul. "Everyone whose mail got switched is listed here."

"Good. Geoff will be with me this weekend. He can start apologizing right away."

Libby pulled the original from the copier. She smiled at Simon's neat handwriting and meticulous documenting skills on the lined notebook paper he'd given her. She folded it carefully to fit into her shorts pocket. She looked around but did not see Louis and decided to leave before Grass—or Bin—returned.

Even on the most oppressive summer days, there could be some peace for the soul being outside at twilight.

If Libby placed her deck chair just right, her view could pass between the hard lines of the garage and the loose, carefree shape of the heirloom lilac bush guarding the alley. She could watch the fiery ball of the sun sink into black trees at the horizon, taking with it the heat, the work, the conflicts of the day.

Not tonight. Tonight, she was too anxious. An impromptu game of baseball across the street had kids shrieking and cheering. Just feet away, gnats had gathered like a tiny storm cloud. Outwardly and inwardly, Libby felt agitated.

And guilty.

She had purposely avoided being honest with Grass. Thank goodness she hadn't had time to ramble on into her impromptu theory implicating Bin or J'az as Monday morning thieves.

Bin and J'az. How lame.

Although the money certainly would have been tempting.

They could have landed on the same idea at the same time. Justified it. Talked each other into it.

A mosquito buzzed closer. Libby swatted at it.

But what if she was on to something? What if Walt killed Jonah because he was honked off? Then Bin took the money because why not?

Dang.

In her childhood, Libby's father had planted a small plot in their inner-city back yard with a half dozen beefy tomato plants. Every night, after a day in a noisy factory and dinner with his six noisy kids, he noiselessly inspected his tiny crop. Foot by foot, plant by plant. From leaf to bud, then finally saw the fruits of his labor. At twilight.

Libby quit the deck and began to walk slowly around her own back garden. Tried to stop thinking of what she knew and didn't know. What she could figure out and what was going to have to remain a mystery.

Maybe it's time for me to bow out of all this, she thought. Certainly, she wanted to clear Jonah's name, but if Jonah was involved, that's just the way it is. The police would figure things out. Eventually.

The sun disappeared.

Mosquitoes began attacking in earnest.

Not like any of this really affected her personally.

Or hadn't.

Until the next morning.

CHAPTER
TWENTY-THREE

At 7 a.m., Libby swiped away tears between curses at the sight of her hacked and disseminated heirloom lilac bush.

There was a pause only when Namita showed up next to her, yawning. "You know, 'Shit, shit, shit,' carries pretty far on a quiet Saturday morning?"

"I don't care if the whole block heard me!"

Namita surveyed the pile of eight-foot branches, hacked to the base and strewn every which way. "Gosh, you think this is more of the same vandalism spree?"

"This is not a normal vandal."

Namita looked around, half expecting some unusual creature to be lurking about. "Is it time to start being a little more … scared here?"

Libby stared at the destruction, a certain suspicion beginning to grow.

She narrowed her eyes. "I know who did this. That rotten Mrs. Thorne! She's always complained she can't see around my bushes when she drives down the alley. But she can't see, period. And she shouldn't be driving!"

Namita was awake now. "Maybe she took advantage of the other vandal attacks for camouflage. Snuck this one in. Still," she said, "she doesn't strike me as this good with an axe."

Libby kicked at a large dismembered limb. "Shit!"

A cell phone rang. Libby picked hers up and took the call. Her furor came to an unexpected and abrupt end. She confirmed that she was awake and had what the caller needed.

"Is she all right?" Libby asked. She then said she would get the number and be right down.

"Mae cut her hand," Libby explained as she started for the house. "Mr. Randall wants to get hold of the caregiver in case Mae needs stitches."

"I should have figured she was on blood thinner." Paul stood to the side while Mr. Randall gently tugged at Mae's blue Saturday sweater and held Mae's arm steady, so Libby could spray the cut, blood appearing as quickly as either one of them tried to blot it out. The caregiver was on the way, and Libby thought the liquid bandage would hold until a doctor could look at things.

Paul offered to get Mae something to drink, but she declined.

"I was watering her flowers," he said, recounting the night before. "This time of year, she practically lives on her back porch. We were looking for something more than her famous iced tea. Mae offered me an apple. I got her a knife to cut it with from on top of the refrigerator. Should have figured they were up high for a reason. The knife must have slipped. I don't know. I just looked over and she was bleeding."

"Mae, Mae," Libby mildly reprimanded the old lady. "You know you're only supposed to use the butter knives in the drawer."

Mae's eyes stayed glued to the cut where Libby had sprayed it. "I don't use knives. They're too sharp."

Libby carefully daubed at the wound with a damp paper towel to see if it was new blood or just some from before the spray. The cut was quite small, but the skin was a sheer layer, barely covering the bone, and Libby knew even the tiniest nick for someone on blood thinner could be dangerous.

Paul looked over Libby's shoulder. "We cleaned the cut, didn't we, Mae? And two Band-Aids. It looked like it had stopped when I left. I'm so sorry."

Mae finally looked away from her cut and tilted her head toward Mr. Randall. "Thank you."

"You're very welcome." Mr. Randall leaned back and looked at Libby. "I was out in the alley this morning spraying Pemberton's weed patch. Heard this little shriek. When I saw the blood dripping out of the Band-Aid, I knew we needed reinforcements. Francie wasn't around, so you got the call."

Although the liquid bandage seemed to hold, when the caregiver arrived, she decided that a trip to a ready-care facility was probably a good idea.

Out front afterwards, everyone thanked everyone else for being there for Mae. Especially so early on the morning.

"Not unusual for me," said Paul. "My son may be a night owl and will sleep till noon. Me? I'm early to bed, early to rise."

"I don't need much sleep," said Mr. Randall. "Up late, up early. Good you were on deck, Libby. I know you're sometimes out with your dog."

"I was up," said Libby. "But my dog wasn't the half of it. Somebody chopped down my heirloom lilac bush in the back yard."

"What?"

"Are you kidding?"

Both men shook their heads. Like Libby, they were at once incredulous and unsurprised, having had so many similar events occur in the last few weeks.

"Will it grow back?" asked Paul.

"I don't know," said Libby. "It was really hacked."

Mr. Randall shoved his hands in his pockets and rocked back and forth on his heels. "Sometimes the old ones are pretty resilient. Seems like you got the worst hit."

"I was going to say Sparks's truck." Then Paul reconsidered. "I keep forgetting the slashed tire was the vandalism. It has other problems, I think."

"Transmission," said Mr. Randall. Besides it's being a general piece of crap."

"Transmission. Expensive," remarked Paul. "No wonder it hasn't gotten fixed. Glad it's not my problem."

Paul excused himself, leaving Mr. Randall and Libby to amble toward their respective houses

"Do you know what Charlotte's doing with Pemberton's house?"

Libby shook her head. "Haven't heard."

Mr. Randall stopped in front of Jonah's. "It's a great little property. Historic. It's quite old. That rolled roof. Not many of those around." He scanned it further. "Would have to restore the landscaping. Couple coats of paint. Vintage colors, of course. Yes, a great little property."

Libby had always appreciated the special elements Mr. Randall pointed out, but it had been a while since she'd viewed Jonah's house as anything other than Jonah's house.

She stood for a moment and admired it as well.

Libby felt as if she'd put in a full day, although it was only a little after nine.

A summer Saturday was just waking up—a pack of joggers making a weekend run, lawn mowers humming, other yard work getting done early before the predicted ninety degrees sapped the joy out of being outdoors. Visitors often pointed out that temperatures got much higher in the south and west, and that was more uncomfortable, but anyone melting in the sky-high humidity of Indiana's version of ninety got nowhere with that argument.

Libby was too fair skinned for the sun and heat to have no effect. Sweat appeared on her upper lip; she pulled her shirt away from where it clung to her back.

Helping Mae had granted her a reprieve from the anger about her lilac bush.

It ended the minute she reached the edge of Mrs. Thorne's property.

Libby clenched her teeth, more heat flaring up inside and outside. Even Major stood on the edge of his porch and let the old lady have a piece of his mind with a throaty bark.

"You look really, really hot."

Honey called it as she saw it, crouched on the small hill in front of her house, waiting for her sister to arrange chairs for their dolls.

Libby was not in the mood. She started to blow by the girls when Honey offered a dead bee for her to examine, then pulled it back, seeing Libby's rushed state.

Libby sighed with guilt.

At first, she feigned a quick interest. Then chided herself. Honey's a child. This is what meditation is all about. Calm down. Smell the roses.

Sitting on the damp, cool grass, Libby relaxed for the first time that day, and earnestly joined Honey's mourning.

She apologized. "Sorry I was so sharp with you, Honey."

Honey held the bee up to her cheek. "That's okay," she said gently and lay the bee to rest at her side. "My dad gets hot, too."

Maybe children should run the world, thought Libby. They can be so forgiving. So able to live in the present.

She looked across the street to see where Harry and Heather leaned against the disabled truck, the bane of Mr. Randall's property values. About which they didn't care. The Happy Trio came flying, calling "Goin' to the park!"

For children, it seemed, every day was an adventure only a bike ride away.

211

Certainly, these kids were fortunate. She was fortunate. But here she was, all fuzzed and hissy, blaming an old lady for something she could not possibly have done. Namita was right. It made Libby laugh, picturing Mrs. Thorne in those blue puckered sweatpants and that cement-coiffed hair, wielding an axe, clearing the land like a pioneer.

When Libby started to get up, Honey held her hands out—stop! — to block the move. "Wanna hear?" she begged. "I can sing that song."

She rose to her full three feet. "*Fair-y jack-et. Fair-y jack-et.*"

The melody was clear, and adults at the block party would find Honey's version of *Frere Jacques* even more charming than the original French.

Libby clapped her hands with delight. "Perfect, Honey! Just perfect."

She stood and dusted the grass from her shorts, dislodging a forgotten folded paper in her shorts pocket. Honey couldn't be helpful fast enough. She dove to retrieve the paper, then let her busy fingers work to shove the note properly back into Libby's pocket.

"Thank you so much," said Libby, patting the clunky bulge as she turned to go.

Suddenly, unexpectedly, one of several pinballs broke loose—bing, bang, bing—and dropped into a home slot.

As usual, BabyCakes took the more measured approach, waiting, tucked along the back of the couch for observation. Dash knew right away something was afoot and followed Libby from one end of the house to the other as she rifled through disparate piles of papers.

BabyCakes yawned at the sight of Libby making one of her umpteen lists, while Dash stayed with the program. All were rewarded when Libby collapsed onto the couch, BabyCakes peering from over the shoulder; Dash nosing in from the lap side.

Libby smoothed the now unfolded note on her knee. She held it up along with another—two lists on two sheets of paper, side by side.

"Can it really be true?"

Unbelievable.

By 3:15 that Saturday afternoon, Libby sat in the cool quiet, the lights not on yet, in the dim congregational seating area of St. Hedwig's Catholic Church. As cantor, she and the organist had already practiced the music for the Mass that would begin at four. Easy things today. It was the end of July, Ordinary Times in church terms. The priest was setting things out on the altar for the service and would shortly open the doors for the parishioners who came early, which, on a summer afternoon like today, would be very few.

And so, Libby could sit, alone with her thoughts. She felt small in the cathedral-like structure surrounded by flickering vigil lights; the wooden pew under her slightly sticky even with the air conditioner blowing.

She stared at the stained-glass windows behind the altar, but because her attention was elsewhere, the scenes depicted there mostly registered as blurs of blues and reds and golds. What she was visualizing in her mind's eye were the images from that morning: the two lists she'd compared—one of everyone on Apple Street who had had their mail switched; the other, of everyone vandalized.

It had seemed like a match column quiz from school days. For every name in Column A there was the same name somewhere in Column B. No more, no less. Exact correlation. Not random at all.

What Libby was left to deduce was that Geoff Paterson, who had admitted to all the mail switches, was the likely candidate to have done all the vandalism on Apple Street.

It still caused her to shake her head.

Go over it again.

Means. Motive. Opportunity.

Geoff was a kid. A fifteen-year-old, part boy, part man. He was certainly strong enough to break a car window and bust up some garden beds; to cut bushes and cable wires. How hard was it to steal children's bikes or slash a tire?

Bare hands mostly for means, probably supplemented by a hatchet or clippers or baseball bat.

Opportunity. Between times she actually knew of and ones she'd found out from a few phone calls, Libby had penciled in dates for almost every event. Was Geoff even in the neighborhood, at his father's, when these occurred? It shouldn't be that hard to find out, but would Paul be willing to have the conversation once he understood the implication?

Motive. What could possibly be Geoff's motive?

Libby knew kids loved playing tricks. A prank, Geoff had called the mail switch. In his mind, were these other doings just more of the same?

Libby sat in the unlit church. Off to the side, the priest entered the confessional, a small cubicle behind ornately carved doors, to hear penitents tell their sins and ask for forgiveness. Was it Libby's job to confront Geoff for justice's sake or to be more understanding, forgiving, like Honey had been?

Maybe none of it was her job at all.

Once again, she considered that it was time to contact the police. Call Detective Grass and turn Geoff in.

Wait. Maybe she was way ahead of herself, her sleuthing tendencies in overdrive. Just as she'd jumped to blaming Mrs. Thorne for axing her lilac bush, was she jumping, albeit with good cause, to accusing Geoff?

She had been wrong before.

Relax.

Don't get ahead of things. There was enough evidence about the vandalism that she needed to approach Geoff and his father. It had been easy before; no need to think it would not be relatively so a second time.

One by one the lights came on in the church. Pews were filling up. Libby took her place at the cantor's podium in the sanctuary, and refocused. Singing was always cathartic and a joy.

She opened the hymnal and announced the number for the gathering song. She almost choked laughing, going up the scale on *For the Healing*—contemporary words set to the old Latin *Tantum Ergo* tune.

The first four notes were exactly the same as *Fairy Jacket, Fairy Jacket.*

CHAPTER
TWENTY-FOUR

There was no humor in Libby at 6 p.m.

Standing at the Paterson's front door, all the doubts and hesitations she'd repressed during St. Hedwig's Mass came flooding back.

But for good or bad, it was not in Libby's nature to let things slide. She knew if she didn't speak up about her suspicions, she would not sleep well and would eventually have to deal with it.

Deep, soothing notes from his cello confirmed that Paul was home. Libby hoped it confirmed a soothed disposition in the man himself. Her best-case scenario placed Geoff in the house to talk to. If he wasn't, at least she could find out if he had been staying at Paul's when so many vandalisms had occurred.

Or not. That would be great. Totally let off the hook.

Paul was surprised but cordial. He was having a Saturday evening drink and offered one to Libby, who declined as she took a seat on the couch. Geoff, she was told, was in his room playing a video game, waiting to be called to go out to eat.

Libby tried to appear neutral. She presented Paul with the two lists. One he already had; the second had to be explained.

"They're the same," said Libby. "The people who had their mail switched are the same who got vandalized."

Paul looked from one list to the other. "Because they're the same, are you saying the same person did them? You think Geoff did all this?"

Libby's inner detective faltered. "Just … trying to figure it out. My lilac bush got destroyed last night. Namita's car window smashed. I'd like it to stop. I thought Geoff … might have some ideas. Help clear it up."

Libby could see that Paul was struggling.

He said first what seemed natural for any parent. "I don't think Geoff would do anything like this. He's not a mean kid. Even the mail prank was not normal for him. Must be some odd coincidence."

After studying the lists, a little longer, Paul went halfway up the center staircase and called to his son, who came bounding down, ready for supper. "Let's go to AJ's Steakhouse. Mom says their New York strips are huge—"

Geoff stopped on the spot when he came into the living room and saw Libby. "Oh. Hi." He was as friendly and at ease as the day Libby had caught him fake-dropping blue fliers into mailboxes.

Everyone sat. Paul said nothing but passed the two lists to Geoff.

As Libby watched Geoff reach for the papers. "What happened to your hands?" blurted from her without thinking.

Geoff tried to turn his hands away as he awkwardly took the sheets. "Nothing. Being pulled on my skateboard."

"Let me see. Both of them," said Paul.

Geoff had to set the papers aside to comply. His palms were red; white blisters lined the pads at the base of each finger.

So much for children running the world, thought Libby.

She also thought Paul was better at this than she ever would have been. She'd have gone ballistic. Her voice, even if trying to ask for a reasonable explanation, would have been loud and accusatory, and she'd have had a hard time waiting for an answer. Liking kids was one thing; addressing things they did wrong was a different story.

Paul remained calm, more curious than outraged. "How'd you get those?"

Libby kept expecting Geoff to lie, to pout, to become a snotty or hostile teenager. But as he had been when being asked about the mail, he was merely straightforward. "I did some work for Mrs. Thorne."

Libby now wished she'd accepted that drink. It was 7 a.m. all over again and ballistic was on its way. "Like cutting down my lilac bush?!"

Paul wasn't happy, but he saw another hand in the events. "I don't understand. Were you doing Mrs. Thorne some kind of favor? Did she know you were doing this?"

"Know?" said Geoff. "She hired me."

The words hung in the air as if a foreign phrase had been uttered, and everyone needed a moment to translate it. Paul got it first.

"She hired you? For money?"

As Paul's only child, Geoff was obviously used to standing alone, presenting his own defense to adults.

"Of course, for money. But I like her, too. Mrs. Thorne." Geoff looked to his father. "You're the one who sent me over with one of those dumb nut breads. And she was nice to me. Other people say she's mean, but she's nice to me. I asked if she needed any help. So, I took out her recycling. Carried some things up from the basement. Her kids don't even come see her. Mrs. Thorne is all alone."

"But she asked you to do damaging things," said Libby. "You stole bikes and broken car windows and—"

Geoff shrugged. "She said she was going to give the bikes back. They were kind of in her way. She couldn't see past your lilac bush in the alley. Said it'll grow back. And," he shrugged again, "she paid really well."

Paul reached for his glass, swirled the ice cubes in his drink. Then set it back down. "Dear God."

Apparently, Geoff was not affected by his father's lament. "What?

218

All mom ever talks about is how expensive everything is. My shoes. My school. And you, Dad, stuff for the house. How are we going to pay for the roof? The water bill?"

Paul shut his eyes, pinched the bridge of his nose, and said nothing.

Libby had calmed down. Geoff's simple, almost plaintive explanation, along with Paul's moderate response, tempered her tone.

It did not temper how she viewed what had happened.

"Geoff, this is vandalism. Not just putting a few letters in somebody else's mailbox." She leaned into the back of the couch. It was very comfortable, and for a minute, she wished she hadn't brought up the whole situation. She should have talked it through with Namita or her sister or Francie. Anyone.

The only plan she'd had was to inform Paul by way of confirming or denying Geoff's involvement, leaving the fallout primarily to his father. She hadn't thought there might be others. That there might be a Mrs. Thorne in the mix. She'd bumbled into it now, and now she wasn't sure what to do.

"Maybe we should just tell the police."

Paul rubbed his forehead as if a migraine was on its way and there was only one word that would stop it. "No. No. No, no, no. Not the police. It'll go on Geoff's record. Mrs. Thorne put him up to it. He's just a kid. She lured him with money."

Libby had no soft spot for Mrs. Thorne. "Maybe she's the one we should be reporting."

"No! Please," Geoff said with more emotion than Libby had ever seen in him—not when caught red-handed switching the mail, not when confronted with being the vandal. He pleaded, "She's ... my friend. Please don't call the police."

"Oh, God," said Paul. He shook his head. "Your mother. This will be another opportunity for her to claim I'm an unfit father."

Libby looked from father to son.

Geoff sat waiting. Paul took a large swallow of his drink.

Libby did not move. Did not speak. No pat or thoughtful response came to mind.

Instead came images of neighbors. People Libby saw every day, mowing lawns, walking dogs, going to work, pushing babies in strollers, exchanging recipes and gossip. They may give a wave, a shout of irritation, a sympathetic comment—all unrelated, surface interactions really—until something, like a jigsaw puzzle piece fitting perfectly, snapped all kinds of people together more tightly, more intimately. What had started as the uncovering of a small crime had come to expose deeply personal connections: Paul and his ex, Geoff and Mrs. Thorne, and all the victims on those lists.

"Maybe," Libby started tentatively, "maybe you could offer to pay for some of the damage."

She had meant the suggestion for Geoff, but Paul took it first. "I don't have the money for this kind of thing." He looked at Geoff. "If Mrs. Thorne paid you so handsomely, you can use that money to make amends."

Geoff gave a sheepish, uncomfortable grin. "I already spent it."

Libby wondered if the charm of this only child worked on Paul.

"Shoot, Geoff," said Paul, his tone exasperated but already softening. "You haven't even apologized to the neighbors for the last dumb thing you did."

Libby pictured her lilac bush. Lying on the ground in shreds. "I don't know if an apology is going to be enough," she said. "A person might let you off the hook once, but not twice. It's not like Mrs. Thorne has racked up a lot of good will."

Paul was on Libby's side. "Mrs. Thorne should be footing her part of the bill. If not all of it."

Geoff objected again. Libby considered it a fruitless effort. "Good luck getting her to admit anything, let alone coughing up any money. Or apologizing." Libby didn't say it out loud, but her thought was that if Mrs. Thorne was so devious to plan such things, she probably was not above lying to the police. Geoff was decidedly not going to rat on her.

Libby had no idea what the police would do. Not a clue except what she'd gleaned from movies about what got put on a kid's record, at what age. Or the kind of punishment he might receive.

She felt boxed in. Paul was begging her to promise not to call the police on Geoff; Geoff was begging her not to call them on Mrs. Thorne. But Libby could not, nor would not—for her sake or the others—just let it go.

"What about some kind of community service hours?" she proposed. "Yard work. Pet-sit or something?"

Father and son seemed separately to roll the idea around. After a silent visual exchange, both shrugged a kind of acceptance.

"Just a suggestion," said Libby, reminding them that it was not completely up to her. "You need to ask those on the list how they feel about it."

The early morning lilac bush massacre, Mae's cut hand, lists disclosing weird alliances in a vandal operation, church, and lastly, punishment negotiations for crimes committed.

After the Paterson's door clicked shut behind her, Libby stood on the porch to get her bearings. It was close to seven. The sun was still radiating heat on a summer Saturday night. She felt completely drained as she started home.

She caught the delicious aroma of a barbeque and finally had time to feel hungry.

A piece of fresh salmon awaited her and a salad with almonds and fresh blueberries. It was refreshing to think of something else for a moment.

However, her appetite took a dive at the sight of Mrs. Thorne on her porch swing.

Let her go, said one voice.

Tell her off, said the other.

Libby went up the first set of steps and paused.

Mrs. Thorne's head of tight white hair, moving not left, moving not right; the swing going forward, going backward.

Libby was plain and forthright. "I know you had Geoff Paterson chop down my lilac bush."

Mrs. Thorne did not alter her swinging, but her head swiveled mechanically to keep her eyes riveted on Libby. "He's a nice boy."

"You had him do awful, not nice, things."

Mrs. Thorne's eyes bore into Libby.

Libby turned to go. It was enough for her to know that Mrs. Thorne knew she knew. Halfway down the steps, Libby heard it, not loud, but sharp and direct like a dart thrown at her. "Wait until you're old."

On Sunday afternoon, Paul hosted the meeting of all who had been vandalized. Geoff made a sincere apology, and although he tried to keep Mrs. Thorne out of it, he eventually admitted only that she had known about his activities and had had a "few suggestions" on who and what to hit.

Because she had been a fixture in the neighborhood for so long, and because of her age, people did not see much point in trying to get satisfaction—financial or personal—from the old woman. Beyond locking her up, which was not likely, she was viewed as a pesty wasp no one wanted to antagonize, worried she might have even more stinging "suggestions."

Geoff offered to make amends. This, too, was sincerely given. At first, people were hesitant to extract payback. Mr. Motorcycle was content that this was a kid thing and that the cable company had already replaced his cut wire. No big deal.

Others were reasonable. Cleaning the inside of her car and a couple of washes would be a luxury for Namita. Libby and the Two Sues were happy for help weeding their gardens.

At the other extreme was Nick Montgomery. He had to be talked out of calling the police or the CIA, honked off about his girls' bikes. Especially when he found out Mrs. Thorne had set them out for the trash even though Geoff swore he had left them in her garage. Nick settled for dog-sitting and poop-scooping his back yard.

Al Sparks did not want the police involved in any way, but he, too, unloaded vociferously. Although Libby thought he had every right to be angry, she was uncomfortable hearing him yell at Geoff, even briefly. When Al finally calmed down enough to consider what reparations Geoff could make, it was as if he had acquired an indentured servant. One who could move a pile of bricks, mow the lawn, and if he was so good with a hatchet, take out some old bushes. Truck tires were, after all, expensive.

Halfway down the block, as the vandal victims dispersed, Francie caught up with Libby. "What'd I miss? Another murder?"

For a frantic second, Libby was afraid there was yet another crisis. "What makes you say that?!"

"I don't know. Guess it doesn't leave my mind very often. And it looked like you were all coming out of Jonah's."

Libby told Francie of the meeting at Paul's, the story of Geoff, the mail switches, the vandalisms. And Mrs. Thorne. "The consensus was not to call the police. They didn't want to give Geoff a record, and what difference would it really make to report Mrs. Thorne?"

"How terrible," said Francie. "Using a kid that way."

"He's going to do service hours to compensate, but nobody knew what to do with Mrs. Thorne."

As the two neared that woman's house, they lowered their voices until they saw that she wasn't out, and Libby continued. "The Two Sues volunteered to go with Paul to let Mrs. Thorne know she was caught and had to stop. For some unfathomable reason, Geoff has a protective streak about her and wanted to make sure she didn't get yelled at. Al and Nick were politely, but firmly, discouraged from being the ones to confront her."

Francie considered all this. "Maybe she doesn't know what she's doing. I've worked in geriatrics, and I've seen some awful behavior. Maybe she doesn't even remember."

"Oh, she remembers all right."

Francie's phone went off. "Well," she said, checking the message. "You're not going to change the spots on that old cat." She nodded at her phone. "Lamar. I'm meeting him and the grandkids at the park. He sounds ready for reinforcements."

Libby pulled back a strand of hair lifted by a slight breeze. The air was warm, but it was moving. "How do you think you get that way? Mean, like Mrs. Thorne? Can't just be old age. Mae's old, and she's nice. My mom and dad both lived long, but neither one of them got nasty. Dad got quieter; mom actually got sweeter."

"Could be meds. Could be she's this way naturally. Sometimes a person has a choice; other things happen in life that make you go in a certain direction."

"Who would choose to be an old crab?"

"It's probably more subtle. Every time she chooses to call the police instead of letting things go reinforces that choice. After a while, everything looks like an offense to her. That makes her not friendly to others, so others don't want to be friendly to her. Could be she just got into the habit."

At the corner they stopped before parting. "The Two Sues suggested we contact her kids," said Libby. "What do you think?"

The clinical nurse took over. "If this were your mother, wouldn't you like to be apprised of the situation? I'd want to know so I could check with her physician, evaluate her condition, determine an appropriate course of action so her needs are met."

"You sound like my sister Jane. I'm busy looking for justice—you and she are asking what the old bag needs."

Francie laughed. "Oh, Libs, it's not a setback to justice to be considerate."

"Easy for you to say. You and Jane are nice naturally. I have to work at it."

Francie's phone buzzed again. She didn't even check it. "Gotta run. I'm sure Lamar is desperate."

As Francie crossed the street, she laughed again. "Wait till you're old."

CHAPTER
TWENTY-FIVE

Namita, home from work late Monday afternoon, took the hose from Libby. "It is so creepy," she said, as she watered each individual impatiens still languishing in one of her flats on the front porch. "What do you think?"

"About the plants or Mrs. Thorne?" Libby was skeptical on both accounts. "I've seen impatiens revive in pretty dire conditions, but I keep telling you they need to get in the ground or in a pot soon. Indiana clay is not very forgiving this far into July. As for Mrs. Thorne, she's like Fagin out of Charles Dickens, training Geoff to do her bidding like some Oliver Twist."

Namita lined up the flats as if tidiness might ensure their resurrection. "I did notice at last night's meeting, no one brought up the one—really creepy—possibility."

The notion Namita hinted at had not escaped Libby. "You mean how far did that bidding go?"

Namita watered her toes. "I suppose it's kind of a big jump to murder."

"It's that everything else seems so … banal. So ordinary," said

Libby.

"I don't know." Namita nodded at the gray house two doors down. "At this point, I'm not sure I'd put anything past that woman."

Libby uprooted a defiant weed in her coleus planter. "You have to admit the vandalisms could be seen as revenge for some ordinary things. She hated you parking out front in *her* space—go smash Namita's car window. Roots from their trees bumping across her lawn—go smash the Two Sues' garden beds. Although she's not the only one Punk and Rocky's barking drives crazy. All in all, petty retaliations for petty grudges."

Namita handed Libby the hose. "So. You don't think things just escalated? To killing Jonah?"

Libby rinsed her muddy hands and turned off the hose. "I was thinking that Jonah's murder came more in the middle of all these other rather minor events, not in a neat progression. Things were just as petty after the murder."

"That would be Mrs. Thorne. Neat. And petty," said Namita. "Somehow murder does seem a departure as payback. For what? Jonah asking Mrs. Thorne not to fertilize her lawn?"

Libby turned off the hose and rolled it up out of the way. Namita checked the time. "It's after six. Hungry for whatever the city has to offer?"

Every week in the summer, a different ethnic group took over the downtown park to show off their cultural roots. A huge, open-sided tent the size of a football field gave cover from the elements. It sheltered tables to eat at and a stage area for bands playing native music. Best of all, was the serving of that country's gastronomical specialties: Greek and German; Arabian and Latino and on through the season with other international cuisines.

A bike ride took Libby and Namita through weathered old neighborhoods to an undisturbed street that ran along the double-track railroad by the river. White Queen Anne's lace and wild blue chicory waved them on, and in twenty minutes, they landed at the gates of Germanfest.

227

Bratwurst, sauerkraut, warm potato salad, and apple kuchen for dessert. Thirsts quenched by cups of frothy beer.

They two sought out a table on the outer edge for the breeze and to be farther away from the polkas so they could talk and be heard.

"You know," said Namita, evenly distributing the sauerkraut smothering her brat, "that Geoff child. He's another creepy thing altogether."

"I suppose," said Libby, "if Mrs. Thorne was to be considered the brains, Geoff might then have to be considered the brawn."

But recalling the frightful sight of the murdered Jonah brought a gravity to those considerations. In the end, though, neither she nor Namita could mount much evidence against Geoff, citing his youth, his solid but average size, his alibi of being at home with his father waiting for pizza. And what Libby kept seeing as his apparent lack of meanness.

"Did you ever see the movie *The Bad Seed*?" asked Libby.

"About impatiens that die?"

Libby laughed, but then recalled the story of the cute little six-year-old girl who was all sweetness and light and who turned out to be anything but. Not a possessed alien or mutant being. Just pure human malevolence. "Scary kid. Scary movie."

"Speaking of seeds," Namita said, wiping beer foam from her upper lip, "I'm looking into artificial insemination."

A mouthful of potato salad kept Libby's jaw from dropping.

Namita went on as serenely as the breeze passing through the tent. "I've done some research. Weighed different options. I thought about asking a friend to impregnate me. That way I would know some things—medical history, possible personality traits, health of the donor."

Libby could not be nearly so blasé. She swallowed and collected her wits. "Do you have someone in mind?"

"Well, I did. Kind of. For a while. But then I started thinking that for as many positive reasons there are to pick someone local, it might also be a negative. I mean, there he'd be. All the time. What if they looked alike? What if we stopped being friends? What if after the fact he wanted more to do with 'his baby'?"

While Libby knew her renter did not always follow through with every proposed venture, she did not know her to be anything but thorough when it came to gathering data, so she was not surprised by Namita's examination of her various options.

Libby did not care how old-fashioned she seemed. Yes, Namita was an adult. Yes, a friend would stick by her and her decisions. Libby's genuine concern spilled out in a flip remark. "No. You don't want any bad seeds."

Namita avoided snorting her beer. "Okay. Will make sure no sociopaths or murderers in the background. In light of recent events," she added quickly, "I guess that's not so funny. Relax. I'm checking out, and probably going with, a local doctor or clinic." She patted Libby's hand. "Better?"

"I guess," Libby said, still a bit rattled.

Friends of Namita's from church joined them. For the rest of the evening, the worries of Apple Street were overridden by loud oompahs and hoists of more cups of beer.

The quiet on the bike ride home was palpable after the noisy tent crowd.

Both women were tired but at ease. Namita was glad to have updated Libby about baby plans; Libby was glad to have put mail switching and vandalism out of her mind. Maybe now people could start recovering their sense that the neighborhood was safe, and she could turn her problem-solving brain off for a while.

"Look," said Namita as they climbed up the steps at 1901, "my impatiens are revived."

Libby yawned. "Not me. I'm ready for bed."

Namita held open the front door. "That's good. Because now that those other situations are resolved, you'll need your rest to put everything into tackling this murder."

It was still light at eight thirty the next evening. After a visit to Jonah's bees, Libby was checking Mae's window boxes when she noticed a vaguely familiar car parked in front of Jonah's. Squinting, she recognized the more-than-vaguely familiar face of the man sitting in one of the green Adirondack chairs on Jonah's porch.

"Detective Grass?"

"Kinder?"

Libby accepted his offer to sit in the matching chair. She leaned back into the generous seat. "Kind of late, isn't it? What's up?"

Grass was slow to answer, partially from having other things on his mind, partially from the lethargy of the day's lingering heat.

"Not much."

"Just happen to be in the neighborhood?"

He smiled and came out of his reverie. "Pemberton's daughter thought of another place her father might have stashed the illusive library money. Which she still adamantly does not believe he took."

"And?"

"And I was in the neighborhood."

"I mean, and did you find anything?"

Grass's forearms lay along the chair's wide arms. He lifted a lazy hand just at the wrist. Then let it drop. "A few mint-condition U.S. coins. Downtown guesses worth a few hundred dollars. Some old stock certificates from a family company that went out of business years ago." He lifted his hand again, curled the fingers and let them down to tap noiselessly on the wood. Several times. "Actually, I've been busy. Couple other tough cases. Thought if I sat here a little while, at this crime site, I'd get ... inspired."

Libby smiled. Not from delight at the detective appearing stymied, but because it seemed so unlike him to be without firm conviction and direction. While she rarely passed up a chance to poke fun at him, she asked now out of genuine interest, "How's that going?"

Grass's eyes followed a squirrel crossing the lawn. "Nothing so far." The squirrel darted from place to place in a quick survey of the property. "Anything happening around here?"

Lounging on the shady porch, out of the heat, lulled Libby physically, but it did not dull the joy of scooping the detective. "We discovered the neighborhood vandal. Not the murdering Random Vandal," she quickly added, "but the vandal of lesser crimes. Wire cutting, bike stealing, etc."

Grass perked up. "Caught or confessed?"

"Confessed?" Libby guffawed. "Not likely. A kid in the neighborhood did them."

"Really? Nothing crossed my desk. Just happen?"

Libby did not mention Geoff and only told Grass how the neighborhood association had taken care of it.

Great, he thought. Just great. I'm working my tail off on this case, and the neighborhood bookworm solves half of it.

He was unsuccessful at hiding his annoyance. "You know, lesser crimes are still crimes? Given the circumstances, didn't you think this might be something the police should have been brought in on?"

Libby shifted uncomfortably in her seat. She would have thought Grass would be pleased to have the culprit caught and taken care of with no sweat on his part. She could see now that that was not the case. Still, there had been an explicit agreement with Paul and an unspoken one with the neighbors not to involve the police. She said nothing.

Libby watched the squirrel bury its treasures. All things being considered, she felt she had been helpful and tried to encourage Grass to see it this way. "I must say, it's nice to have that piece of the puzzle in place."

"Yes. Good for you," he said a little too sharply. He leaned forward, hoping that cooler air might circulate around his back. "I know how things sometimes just fall into a bystander's lap." He spoke quickly so she wouldn't have time to get her fur up. "You were never keen on the vandal murderer theory anyway, were you?"

He didn't wait for an answer, but went on, sounding like he was putting out a challenge more than a question. "So, what are you thinking now?"

Libby wasn't thinking anything. In fact, even after Namita had remarked that she would need her rest for solving the more complicated crime of murder, she had relished falling into bed much more than consulting her list of clues and hypotheses.

She kept her gaze on the busy squirrel. "Guess I've been happy just thinking the two-bit criminal, as they say in the books, has been accounted for."

Grass tried to overlook the pseudo-detective babble and Libby's tight-lipped responses. She was obviously still coming up with things that might help. "Sounds like you've taken a vandal totally off your list. I haven't dropped the idea entirely, but I have moved it to the bottom of mine."

"In my experience," Libby said, "if anyone moves down on that kind of list, someone else moves up. Who's the lucky guy or girl?"

"If," Grass said, stressing the word, "if we eliminate the Random Vandal, we might have to consider a more personal motive." He leaned back in his chair. "Like who gains by Pemberton's death."

Libby had only thought about gaining financially in terms of someone stealing the library money, not benefitting some other way from Jonah's death. She allowed that Grass had a new point for her to consider. "Like?" she asked.

Grass patted his chair arm once, then swung his head around to glance behind him.

Libby followed his glance.

"The house?"

"Inheritance. Always a good motive."

The shade of the porch became irrelevant. Libby attempted to hold down the heated rise in her voice. "You can't mean Jonah's daughter? She wasn't even here!"

Grass remained cool. "Could have hired someone."

Recent experience gave Libby pause. Getting someone to do the dirty work was more plausible than she wanted to admit.

But that was different. This was Charlotte, Jonah's only daughter, his little girl. Whom Libby had known since birth.

Libby's protective side flared up.

Grass could see the flush showing up on Libby's face. That she was so easy to provoke was hard for Grass to pass up. He surmised that the only thing taking time for her to respond was her mounting of a logical defense.

"Relax," he said, lazily lifting his hand to stifle the onslaught. "Daughter gets the house. And the hassle of emptying it and selling it. All the rest—pension, savings, life insurance—modest as they all are—go directly to the grandchildren. And no, I don't think Daughter is the kind to kill off her father to get the money into her kids' hands sooner. She and her husband are doing just fine financially."

It was not the first time Libby wondered if Grass had purposely baited her. She adjusted her tone. "Jonah's daughter probably didn't hire a hit man, either."

"Probably not."

"Family the only beneficiaries?"

"Yes. Of money."

Libby carefully eyed Grass to see if this was more bait or if he really had something. "Like what?"

Grass now wished he had a payoff to cap the interest he'd aroused. He shrugged. Improvised. "Something intangible. Something Pemberton could give. Or take away. I've seen other cases where someone might be trying to get a company, a divorce, a child. Or get out from under one."

They both watched the squirrel run up a leafy maple tree and out of sight. Both speculating how the animal moved so rapidly in such heat. Both speculating what intangibles Jonah Pemberton might have.

"Anyone else, specifically, on your list?" pursued Libby.

Grass wanted to get up and go home, but inertia had set in. He was getting punch drunk on the heat. "Well, you did find the body."

Libby's own inertia allowed her to let this bait go by. "I figured I was ruled out from the beginning."

"Okay. You were cleared. Movie-watching neighbor and renter corroborated for you."

Grass contemplated the tan line at his wrist. "Do you remember anything else from that morning?" He was not baiting Libby; in fact, he only wished he had some bait to toss out. He was hot, and not a little frustrated. "Sometimes after the shock of finding a dead body wears off, images or sounds or something you felt bubbles up in the memory."

Libby looked out across the yard again, trying to free her mind for just such a bubble. She closed her eyes slightly…

Cool. Cool that morning. Cool in the garage. The body. Cold. Bending down to the floor, cold. Hard, cold metal under her knee. Ouch. Swat! "What was that?"

"Hard, cold metal on the floor that you swatted away?" Grass pulled out his small black notebook. "There's nothing in here about anything like that near the body. If I remember correctly, the original thought was that you knelt on travel brochures."

"This seems like it was a lot harder," said Libby. "But it was gone in an instant. Maybe the cement floor just felt that hard and cold."

"There was a small combination padlock under one of the benches. Not too far away. Generic. Jonah's prints, but otherwise clean. I'll look the report over, but that might be what you hit."

Libby sighed. "Not much of a weapon."

"Definitely not good for strangulation. Anything else?"

Libby remembered the birds, the shadow of the fence slash across the sun in the alley, the musty smell of the garage, but …

No more bubbling insights.

"Sorry," she said. "That's all that seems to be in there. Anyone else on your list? Besides me?"

"How about Mae?"

"Mae! That's not even a good joke."

"I didn't mean as the murderer." Grass felt his shirt sticking to the back of the chair. "Wondered if she'd seen any more monster guys."

"Monster Man? No, she hasn't said so. You have to understand, he's been a neighborhood figure for a while, even a person who takes out the garbage or puts a shovel away might qualify."

"Is she the only one who sees him?"

"Some of the kids think he's out there. Don't get me wrong, Mae has some well-worn brain cells and a quirky sense of humor, but she's not senile. Like the kids, she's sometimes prone to a vivid imagination and likes telling a good story. I assume you take that into consideration."

"We do," said Grass slowly. "But the killer might not."

"What do you mean?"

"Directly or indirectly, the killer might get wind of Mae's claim of seeing someone. Take her seriously. Especially if they think she could identify them."

A small, sudden gasp came out of Libby's mouth. The thought scared her more than threats to her own safety. She stared at Jonah's lifeless wind chimes just beyond Grass's shoulder. Mae was alone a lot. Out of sight mostly, but not to someone who was looking for her. An old lady sitting on her back porch. A sweet, funny, vulnerable old lady, sitting on her back porch.

"Same goes for you."

"Me?"

Grass was direct. "Asking questions and trying to figure things out—on your own—comes naturally to you. Any killer paying attention is going to know this or find this out. Which is why I always tell you to be careful."

Libby slumped in her chair. Such scenarios would have seemed plausible in a book. "Does this stuff really happen?" she asked. "In a place like Apple Street?"

As a veteran detective in a good-sized city, Grass had worked on more than a few of what the general public would consider peculiar, even unbelievable, and bizarre setups for crimes. Ordinary folks hatching and carrying out gruesome plans. Murders.

"People who are threatened tend to see things a certain way," he said. "If they've already solved what they see as a problem in a violent way, they have nothing to lose by employing the same methods again. And yes, in a place like Apple Street."

As soon as Libby saw Mae's good friend, Doc Whelan, talking to Carrier Dobbs, she cut catty-corner across the Apple Street intersection to the big brick house.

Chances were that Doc Whelan would be returning to her summer days at the lake shortly, and Libby didn't want to pass up the opportunity to catch her before that happened.

The sense of urgency appeared to be mutual.

"Come in and sit down right now if you can," Doc said, swinging the door open wide. "Fill me in on all the crime business going on in this formerly bucolic little neighborhood."

A walker was the only concession Doc Whelan had made to age. Libby had never seen her not smartly dressed or without hands beautifully manicured. "Doc" was almost too informal for such an accomplished medical doctor, but "Doc" is what she preferred, a term bestowed on her by her late husband.

Libby talked through two glasses of ice water, bringing Doc up to date.

"A more personal motive, eh?" Doc said, repeating the last angle Libby indicated Grass was pushing. "The human psyche covers a lot of territory. Old grudges. Jealousy. Petty differences. Fear. Shame." She shook her head. "And this possibly inspired by Jonah Pemberton?"

"Hard to believe, isn't it?" asked Libby. "Even harder when you try to connect such dark impulses to someone right here in the neighborhood. But I'm past believing everything is merely random."

"Knowing you, there are people you already have in mind."

Libby pulled out a piece of paper with its doodled-on list. "I've been trying to think beyond the names that seem most logical. So remember, these are purely speculative."

"Understood."

"Okay. First. Harassment," said Libby. "Jonah was a regular, coming down to complain about the band noise, the hours, kids today in general. One or more of the parents of the Blue Donuts could have gotten fed up. Taken matters into their own hands. Literally."

Doc Whelan nodded, listening thoughtfully. "Parents can be extremely sensitive."

"Although," Libby added, "if this were the case, it makes you wonder why they haven't done in Mrs. Thorne, who yells at kids—and adults—all the time."

A smile played on Doc's lips. "Mrs. Thorne has always been, shall we say, aggressively miserable."

It was a great phrase, and Libby admitted it captured both the sourness and ramrod defensive posture Mrs. Thorne had presented to the world as long as she'd known her.

"My second new thought is about conflict of interest, I guess you could call it. Jonah and Mr. Randall butting heads."

"Randall still trying to get the Old Orchard area on the historic register?"

"Perpetually. Why?"

"Just thinking how important that is to him."

"They were really cranked up about fertilizer use this spring."

"I'm on Jonah's side for that," said Doc.

"Drove Mr. Randall crazy living next door to Jonah's more free style landscaping. Especially when he knows how effective a good dose of weed and feed would be. Don't know who got angrier. Jonah was a hot head because Mr. Randall used so many chemicals; Mr. Randall more of a slow burner, mad at Jonah for just the opposite." "I've always appreciated Randall's efforts to protect this area. Preserve its history. He can, however, be a proud and stubborn man."

Doc's solarium was also lined with windows that framed Apple Street. Libby took a moment to gaze out at the afternoon view.

She sat back.

She folded the paper with her list once. Then unfolded it.

"Pretty slim roster, isn't it? And flimsy."

Doc's smile turned into a grin. "Given that you're looking for a murderer in my neighborhood, I'd like to think that's a good thing.

CHAPTER
TWENTY-SIX

D own the hot alley to Thursday's block party show practice. Any route to the library was hot; the alley was just the shortest. Libby wanted to move quickly, but that only made her more flushed. Her steps were sluggish; sweat dampened every inch of her skin.

Nothing else was moving today. Every leaf, every swing set, every shirt on a laundry line, inert in the sweltering sun.

Passing familiar yards and houses, Libby began to feel as if she'd spent a ridiculous amount of time thinking about the people in these houses.

Thinking bad things. Picking the scab off spiteful retaliations and simmering feuds that could have, perhaps should have, remained undisturbed, leaving the quaint English village aura intact.

Or was the block party in August—so like an English fête—more like Christmas for dysfunctional families? Was it the one day out of the year the residents of Apple Street seemed pleasant and tolerant and generous, but in reality were mean, grumbling, vengeful people?

Libby stood in the shade of the small barbershop, waiting to cross the sticky asphalt of Oak Avenue. She was hot, but she was genuinely happy to have shown practice. It wasn't mental diversion like her daily grant work, but a safe, playful distraction from thinking about suspects and murder.

Outside the library, she found kids waiting for rehearsal lounging on the grass, listlessly pushing a soccer ball around their circle. She caught sight of Geoff Paterson in the group with the Happy Trio. She smiled when eye contact was made but said nothing.

Kids sure were funny. Some loved being singled out, others wanted to blend in. Libby did not know Geoff well enough in this situation to do more than acknowledge his presence. Given his recent behavior, she was glad he'd come. Giving kids a chance to work creatively together was why, even on uninspiring hot August days, she trudged up to the Riley branch library for practice.

In the vestibule, Harry and Heather leaned against the bulletin board. Before Libby got her greeting out, she realized they were having a serious conversation, their voices low and intense.

"No one cares anymore," said Heather.

Harry looked at the floor. "It's your stupid secret."

Heather was more petulant. "You swore."

A glare from Harry. "I'm tired of being bossed around."

Libby hurried past, curious, but not wanting to intrude.

The air inside the main room was almost shockingly cold. Louis spoke as he came toward her. His voice was low, but hardly intense. "Trouble in paradise?" he said, nodding at the two teens on the other side of the glass doors.

"Not sure," said Libby. "Something's up."

"Important to air important things right away. Not let them fester."

"Certainly not my problem," admitted Libby. "I get mad and bang! I'm off like a string of firecrackers."

Louis narrowed his eyes. "I like to save my perturbations for true disagreements. Not just shootin' off for trivial things."

Libby had always shot off her feelings and her mouth with speed. She held back blowing up in most professional and public situations, but to stifle an annoyance with family or friends took conscious restraint. Even then, sooner or later her dissatisfaction snuck out in a snide comment. Not good. Not always nice.

"Insignificant or important—that's what I try to discern," said Louis. "Show of power. Somebody needing the last word. In my opinion, those can be downright deleterious. But," Louis took in and let out a deep breath, "happens all the time."

He raised his wiry gray eyebrows. "'Course me and my wife are the exception."

Like anteing up, Libby raised her eyebrows in return. "Can't be much arguing there. From what you tell me, you two have worked things out pretty well. Of course, you're awfully sweet on her."

He offered a slow, shy smile. "You got that right."

Louis held up his keys, and he and Libby discreetly slipped into the entranceway, past the on-going spat.

"I don't care if I get yelled at," Harry said through gritted teeth. "My dad yells at me enough already. I'm used to it."

Heather's red hair made her face look twice as florid. She folded her arms and hissed, "You swore."

"Looks like everybody's a little hot today," commented Libby as she and Louis headed down the short hall to the practice room.

"*Sudorific*," he said. "'*causing to sweat*.'"

Inside the room, he volunteered to help set things up.

"Thanks," said Libby. "But I'll get the kids to do it. Might be a good distraction for the wrathful lovers. Keep their spat from getting too … sudorific."

Louis took in the ceiling and smiled again. "They do take me back. My Sugar and me, we argued all the time. In the beginning. Too much pride going on when you're young."

Chuckling, Louis went back to the main room. "Hardly ever now. But in the beginning … woo-ee," he whistled. "She was peppery!"

The exchange left Libby wondering if that would be how Harry would describe Heather in years ahead. If they made it that far.

For the present, Heather chose not to come to practice, leaving Harry grumpy the rest of the afternoon.

By 6 p.m., Libby rued her decision to let the kids do a noisy, pounding hip-hop number. Moreso that she had waited till the end to practice it.

She'd taken the *Fairy Jacket* children first and let them go, then worked on the Shaker song, a gentle piece meant to be a break in the program. She braced herself for the stomping, clapping, and frenetic movements of the older gang.

The number actually went well the first time through, and Libby judged it good enough for the time being. These kids had been squirrely before they'd begun, testosterone boasting and chasing; estrogen squealing and being chased. Geoff had clearly felt more comfortable and was beginning to show off; Harry had stayed mopey.

Because it was summertime, because rain, possibly severe, was on the way, but mostly because this show was supposed to be fun, Libby decided to stop early.

Naturally, the excitement over early dismissal only added to the rowdiness. Javier wheeled in the chair rack. One of the girls loaded a chair, then hopped on for a ride. Tables were shoved like battering rams. More chasing and squealing.

"Stop it!" Libby bellowed. "Someone's going to get hurt!"

The universe always hears adults make this prediction and complies accordingly. As soon as Libby uttered the words, it happened.

It wasn't "someone" who got hurt. It was Libby.

Not badly.

Javier had pushed the girl riding the chair stacker at the same time Geoff shoved a table, and Libby got caught trying to stop the collision. Most of her hand escaped, but two fingers were pinched hard. Not broken. Painful, but not terrible.

And not enough to derail her fury.

Into the sudden silence of kid guilt, Libby unleashed a diatribe about juvenile antics and danger and not listening. Some of the teens slinked out while she was yelling. Most hung their heads and winced at her pain when they realized what had happened.

Once spent, Libby took a breath. "Sarah. Simon. Go out to the desk and see if they have an ice pack. Please." Like soldiers dispatched to the front, the two responded without question.

While Libby did not take pleasure in making anyone feel bad, she did not regret getting angry. As long as there was remorse in the air, she could calmly direct the remaining troops to finish straightening things up.

Lights out.

Libby made her way back down the alley, a borrowed ice pack wrapped around her two pinched fingers. She looked to the west where a bank of clouds brought cover from the sun but hardly from the heat.

It was peaceful watching Libby check her tomato plants. Camille had determined that if she sat very still and concentrated on something else moving, purposefully, fluidly, like Libby's nightly inspection of her very small front garden, the heat, the ache in the small of her back, the throb in her swollen ankles could be manageable. It wasn't like watching the girls. Their animation was so skittish; joyful, yes, but frighteningly unplanned. At any moment a bony elbow might stab an unsuspecting thigh, or a jubilant yelp pierce an eardrum.

"Supposed to rain," Camille called out past the blue spruce. "Hard."

"So I heard," said Libby. "We can use it. Just so muggy before it comes." She located five cherry tomatoes ripe enough to eat.

"How you feeling?" Libby called back.

"'Bout the same."

"Want any basil?"

"No, thanks."

In her cool kitchen, Libby realized how hungry she was. She'd cut a slice of good chewy bread and toasted it.

Holding a knife in her uninjured hand, she halved the cherry tomatoes, smeared a thin layer of mayonnaise on her toast, flattened leaves of deep green basil against the white spread, and meticulously laid down a tidy grid of ten little red tomato domes.

'Tis the gift to be simple, she thought, and sat at her small kitchen table, the cat and dog settled nearby, obviously glad to have her home.

Only one finger had had enough of a cut to bandage, and she was grateful for the care J'az, Louis, even Bin had provided at the library. She'd also gotten an earful as they'd griped about Jonah's miserly use of first aid funds, his miserly ways as a whole except for his always special allowances made for Paul. The saintly single father.

Libby's thoughts had receded into the background as they'd discussed the scary broken wrist of one of J'az's little girls last winter, then an update on Bin's grandchild's surgery. So much to worry about with your children, reflected Libby as she lifted her open-faced sandwich, careful to bite between rows of tomatoes to keep the grid in place.

Honey's words came back to her: "my dad gets hot, too." And Harry's from his intense conversation with Heather: "I don't care if I get yelled at. My dad yells at me enough already."

What also came back were the faces of some kids, ones shocked at her outburst in the library tonight, which made her think they were not, like Harry, used to such a thing at all.

I'd be a terrible parent, Libby concluded. Always getting hot.

She wiped a dab of mayonnaise from the corner of her mouth and thought Louis's wife was lucky she had found someone who liked her "peppery."

CHAPTER
TWENTY-SEVEN

It was after nine, eerily dark, not as much from the hour as from the blue-black clouds of the predicted storm lumbering in.

"What happened to your fingers?" asked Namita, meeting Libby for a last outing of the night with the dogs.

Libby's injured fingers were already streaking purple, more garish in the given light, and noticeably stiff when she went to push away a strand of hair stuck to her sweaty forehead.

She held her hand out for further observation. "Occupational hazard."

"Didn't realize grant writing was so dangerous."

Libby laughed. "Block party show practice. Kind of a rough time all around today. Started with a Heather and Harry spat. Something about secrets. She was miffed. He was mopey."

"Trouble in paradise?"

"You and Louis have the same read on that," said Libby. "Rehearsal was fine, but then everybody got a little rambunctious putting things away. My hand ended up pinched between some chairs and a table."

Namita cringed. "Ouch."

Libby shrugged. "Show biz."

The air had become lifeless. Even Dash and Paji barely inched their way along the sidewalk down a deserted Apple Street.

Namita stopped when Paji stopped. "Are you sure it was an accident?"

Libby stopped and Dash stopped. "How do you mean?"

"Like Bin from the library and her husband. Who tried to run you down. Maybe this was meant to … intimidate you."

It was too hot for Libby to roll her eyes as they resumed their stroll. "This was a bunch of kids rushing and being careless because they got let out early."

"Need I remind you," said Namita, "that there are some funny kids in this neighborhood?"

Namita rambled on, her delivery as unhurried as her steps. "Word on the street is … you're setting up another sting operation."

"Are you serious?"

"Instead of snagging the mail switcher, you're out for Jonah's killer."

If Libby hadn't been talking to Namita, she'd have thought she was in some B-movie. All they needed were cigarettes dangling from their lips and a black sedan trailing them.

"What on earth are you reading these days?" Libby asked.

"Your fault. All those mystery novels you leave out for me."

"I guarantee you that Miss Marple, while she may have availed herself of the information, never referred to anything she picked up as 'the word on the street.'"

Namita persisted, half-amused, half-serious. "The scuttlebutt is that you're working with the boys in blue."

"I see," Libby observed. "Me and the Feds."

"At least you and Detective Grass."

Namita pulled out her phone, scrolled and flicked, then read from the small lit screen: "*Scuttlebutt. Nautical term. A hole in a cask of drinking water where a dipper can be introduced. To scuttle. To cut holes in a ship for the purpose of sinking it. Scuttlebutt—slang. Gossip. Rumor.*"

"There you have it, Miss Marple." said Libby. "Gossip and rumor."

"Not gossip and rumor if it's true. You are, indeed, out asking people about the night of the murder, are you not? You're either run off the road or you come home from friendly neighborhood show practice all banged up."

"Two pinched fingers."

Namita let her interrogation-style manner drop and asked sincerely if the fingers hurt much.

Libby flexed them gingerly. "Got ice on them right away. That helped. They do ache a bit. The kids were sorry."

"Just reminding you to watch out for those little bad seeds. Especially a whole room full of them."

The air pressed down around them, the smell of the coming storm concentrated, thick and earthy, as if everyone had simultaneously mowed their yards and mulched the neighborhood.

Libby thought of her last conversation with Grass. "He's convinced himself that clues fall out of the sky and land in my lap."

"Like word on the street."

"Yes."

"Scuttlebutt."

"Rumor and gossip."

They turned at the park, waved at one lone dog owner waiting to pick up after her charge. Funny, thought Libby. Seeing only one person instead of dozens out walking made the night seem more desolate than if no one were out at all.

"I had my suspect list narrowed down to only those around during the hour Jonah was killed," she said. "Just when the list was starting to look manageable, Grass tells me time of death isn't set in stone—it might only take five minutes to choke somebody to death. Whammo. Half the gang is back on the list. Plus a few more."

Namita took in the sky. "Isn't that amazing?"

"Frustrating."

Libby followed Namita's gaze. "Oh. You mean the storm clouds."

Namita looked back at Libby. "No. I mean that it only takes five minutes to choke somebody. I guess that makes sense. Kind of scary, though, how quickly life can be snuffed out."

"Shoot. A bullet takes two seconds. A bash on the head," Libby snapped her uninjured fingers, "like that."

Lights in houses on Old Orchard glowed a soft gold in the downstairs, occasionally blinking on upstairs, as the end of the day darkened. The stillness outside was broken only by the slap of flipflops, the friends' subdued conversation, the jangle of Dash's and Paji's dog tags.

Namita looked at the threatening sky. Then at Libby. "You need to be careful."

Out front at 1901, Libby said goodnight to Namita and Paji and started around to her back entrance. A small breeze had arrived, making the air slightly more tolerable, and she decided to go once more around the block by herself with Dash.

Walking with Namita was always welcomed, even helpful, especially when there were things on her mind that benefitted from talking them out.

But it was not the same as walking alone.

Solitude could help thoughts emerge more freely; solution present themselves.

A low rumble of thunder and a quiver of lightning prompted Libby reassure Dash the walk would be a short one.

At first there was just the echo of flipflops lightly slapping against the sidewalk. Rhythmical. Lulling.

Libby was city born and bred, but something about being outside before a storm, one coming on slowly like this, tapped her rustic bones. She noticed the slight uptick in the wind, leaves being roused, gray on gray in the clouds, and that smell of impending rain—the air not yet clean, not fresh. Musty.

Then a different kind of movement. Libby had given solitude its chance, and it had obliged. Nothing specific. A snippet of a conversation with Doc Whelan. A reminder by Namita.

Enough impetus that as she neared home, Libby got the idea to copy Grass's visit to the murder site for inspiration. She had to tug Dash off his set path to coax him into the deserted alley.

She stood and imagined the Blue Donuts playing at roughly the same time of night.

Walt driving toward Jonah's garage.

Monster Man on the prowl.

Mae on her back porch.

Jonah coming down in the dark to—

"What the—?!"

Libby froze.

Out of the blue, out of the black, Al Sparks appeared. Hoisting a club above his head! Libby recoiled with fear, Dash snarled. Then began barking. And barking. And barking.

"Christ Almighty!" Al barked in return. He lowered the club but still towered over her.

"I'm sorry," Libby said, picking the dog up to quiet him.

Al moved in closer. "What the hell you doing out here?"

"Just … just walking the dog."

"Well, stay out on the sidewalk," he said gruffly. 'Specially at night. People drive up and down this alley like maniacs."

Libby stuttered, trying to sound unfazed. "That's what… what Mae says."

"Not surprised. Sitting out back like she does all the time."

He turned toward his car. Of course, thought Libby. He's on his way to work. She wanted to get out of there, but she wanted to ask more. "Did you see anybody like that, driving down the alley, the night Jonah died?"

"Nope."

"I know it was a while ago."

He tossed the club into the front seat. "I'd remember."

Libby bit her lip and rushed another question. "Were you out here when Jonah came down that night?"

"No." He slid into the car. "I'd remember."

Libby had to speak up over the gusting wind. "I know Jonah could piss a person off."

Al slammed the car door, responding through the open window, "Jonah needed to mind his own damn business. These are good kids. Better being in their own neighborhood doing something harmless like playing music than out doing drugs or drinking. Or doing damage like that kid down the block. But he's not my concern. I take care of my own. And you—you need to mind your own business."

The window started up.

Libby leaned into the disappearing space, cradling Dash against her chest. "Were all the kids from the band in the garage when you left for work? What did Heather tell you about Jonah coming down? Were the kids upset?"

The window stopped. "I told you before. The kids handled it. Wasn't the first time Pemberton bugged them. Heather didn't tell me he came down. I just said good night to her and left." His tone sharpened again. "I'd be careful asking all these questions.

A crack of thunder. More wind.

Libby jumped. "The police still think there's a murderer out there!" she shouted.

"They can butt the hell out, too!" he spit back.

A flare of lightning and another clap of thunder.

And Al Sparks was gone.

Libby started to set Dash on the ground when huge raindrops splashed on her cheek and hand. Her weather bones knew enough to judge by their sudden and rapid increase that she needed to move—now!

It was faster to run with Dash in her arms. Spurred on by more claps of thunder, Libby hunched over her little dog and rushed into the wild wet wind, which in seconds was sweeping rain sideways in sheets across Apple Street.

She could barely see as the downpour blew at her from all directions. Her hip snagged the railing up to the back porch. Her pinched fingers fumbled to hold Dash and open the door.

She was drenched.

But inside.

Libby's chest heaved. To catch her breath from running. From having faced Al Sparks in a dark alley.

She set Dash down and went for towels.

BabyCakes was already in the basement. Libby started down the steps to check on him. Dash was not about to be left behind.

Libby's basement was more storage area than entertainment center. Pantry shelves of canned goods, plastic containers of seasonal clothes and decorations. A tool room with the boiler at one end; laundry room at another.

Libby had no idea which cranny the cat was tucked in. She spread towels on the floor, leaned against an old couch, and began to dry Dash, her hands still shaking. As the wind howled and rattled things overhead, she called out gently, "We're home, BabyCakes."

A smack of thunder!

Power off.

Lights out.

In the pitch-black basement, Libby's shoulders slumped. She could not now put two thoughts together. She didn't want to make one more list of suspects. Didn't want to figure out the murderer. Didn't care who stole the library money. Her head hurt, fingers hurt, hip throbbed, and water dripped from sopping hair onto her cheeks.

Dash crawled up into her lap. In the dark, she wrapped him in a towel and held him close. In the dark, a warm purring body at her neck said nothing but reassured her just the same.

CHAPTER
TWENTY-EIGHT

Things always seem better the morning after a storm clears out. With power back on, the air clearer and lighter, it was not a terrible chore for Libby to be outside for the first forty minutes picking up debris that had come down during the blustery night before.

Renewed, she had breakfast and went on to plow through to the end of a sticky section of a grant summary, finishing earlier than expected.

It was Friday. For a reward, she decided to walk up to the library, sit in a quiet corner and do something she didn't do often enough—pleasure reading.

She sauntered down Apple Street. Tina Laguna stood by the back of her van midblock, and Libby stopped. "How did you guys do last night?"

"A few big branches snapped in the alley. Nothing too bad. How about you?"

"Same. Nothing terrible. Some planters knocked around."

"Feels like it's going to heat up again."

"It is August," said Libby.

Tina handed bags of groceries to her boys who'd come from the house. "If you see Geoff Paterson," Javier said to Libby, "tell him we're home if he wants to come down to shower and have dinner with us. His phone must be dead or turned off."

Farther down, Libby spied Mae in her red sweater setting out her sun tea.

"Need any help with that?" Libby called out.

Mae shielded her eyes to see better. "Just to drink it," she said.

Libby waved and promised to come by later.

Near the end of the block she ran into the Happy Trio.

"Our lights went off last night!" said Sarah, the thrill of it still in her voice.

"Mine, too."

"Scary. But fun."

"How are your fingers?" asked Ann.

"Not too bad," said Libby.

Simon still looked worried. "It was kind of scary when that happened."

Sarah made a pained face. "I thought your whole hand was broken."

Libby wiggled her fingers as convincingly she could. They were sore, but flexible enough. "Thanks for getting the ice."

"Some kids tried to make jokes about it," said Sarah with a disapproving air.

Libby had noticed. "Everybody reacts differently when something like that happens."

Simon added his observation. "Harry was so … reserved. But he was like that all night."

Libby weighed the term. "I don't know if *reserved* is the right word."

"Grouchy," said Sarah. "Plain grouchy. He's usually so nice." Her expression changed to a sappy sweet grin. "I think he was missing his girlfriend."

"No," said Simon, lifting his eyebrows and glancing knowingly from sister to sister. "You know why."

Sarah and Ann hit on it at the same time. "Secrets!" they whispered dramatically.

So much for the resolve to quit being concerned about such mysteries. It was as if Libby had, on the spot, become a member of the Secret Clue Club. She leaned in and asked, "Do you guys know what Harry's secret is?"

Delicious conspiracy all around.

"Something about 'that night' and how mad Heather's dad would be," said Simon.

Libby hesitated. Maybe this was more than she wanted to know. She was curious, but she had no desire to pry into private lives, especially of teenagers.

Until Sarah added in hushed tones, "'That night of the murder.' Then Heather said, 'We can never tell.'"

Before Libby could gulp in horror, Sarah added off-handedly, "Or something like that."

"So, you don't really know what the secret is?"

"No," admitted Simon, "but we are … observing."

Libby wasn't sure what she'd hoped for. Whether the Happy Trio had picked up on something or was merely inflating an overheard remark for a club activity, she didn't know. She was, in fact, on the same level of their investigation: observing.

Libby saw Geoff and his skateboard come from his house on the other side of the street. "Hey, Geoff!" she shouted.

While Geoff crossed in the direction of Libby's call, she found herself repeating a recent refrain aimed at her, one she now aimed at Simon, Sarah, and Ann. "You kids be careful."

Libby delivered the Laguna invitation for a shower and dinner to Geoff.

"Great," he said. "Thanks." He turned to Simon and hitched his thumb down the block. "You going that way?"

"Sure."

Geoff was affable and Simon equally agreeable as Geoff attached himself to Simon's bike and skied, clackity-clack, down the sidewalk, as if riding the waves behind a speed boat.

Libby marveled how these two factions, the Happy Trio and Geoff—one recently having spied on the other—were laughing and playing nice together. She had read that warring nations should act more like children in a sandbox, who often solve problems or get over things quickly, because the ultimate mutual goal in the sandbox is to have fun.

The happy thought encouraged her to make a detour.

A quarter pound of licorice All-Sorts from Betty's Sweet Shoppe found its way into Libby's pocket, which she patted in happy anticipation as she passed through the double glass doors of the library.

It was freeing for a change to come with no rehearsal on the agenda. The place was busy. All the computers engaged, an afternoon story time for little ones, and Louis directing patrons to areas like a traffic cop.

"I've got something I want to run by you," he said, catching Libby's eye. His eyebrows twitched. "About the pilfered loot. I'll find you later," he said and went back to assisting a gentleman.

Libby wandered over to periodicals. She was worried about what was going to happen to Jonah's bees if the house was sold. She was looking at some nature magazines that might have a clue when Bin came up next to her to shelve an armload of stray issues.

It had been weeks since the night of Walt's confrontation. Bin hadn't spoken to Libby for much more than minimal library interactions since. Yesterday's episode with pinched fingers had been more of a community effort involving several of the staff, so nothing between just the two of them had occurred.

Libby was not one for uncomfortable silences.

She saw no reason for them not to play nice. Like children in a sandbox.

"Hi," she volunteered.

Bin kept shelving.

Libby shifted her eyes back to the magazines but said, "I'm sorry you think I've butted in so much about this Jonah thing. He was a neighbor to me, a friend, not a boss. Plus, I found the body. And, for better or worse, I'm a naturally inquisitive person."

"Nosey."

Libby shrugged. "You're not the first to point that out."

Bin didn't laugh at Libby's self-deprecation, but she did stop slapping magazines on the rack.

"Walt told you everything he could remember. Which isn't much." Bin glared. "So there's still no reason to say anything to anybody. Like the police."

"And I haven't. I do wish I would have asked Walt more questions about whoever he saw in his rearview mirror. Was it a man? Were they wearing a hat? Carrying anything like garbage? Walking? Slinking?"

Bin's frustration lashed out. "It could have been a midget or a giant for all he saw!" She whapped a magazine down and took a deep breath. "It was a brief flash of a figure moving halfway down a dark alley in the rearview mirror."

Libby decided the sandbox analogy was overrated.

She stepped away from periodicals to let the librarian finish her job and pretended to search for a book.

But at the end of a long aisle of history and politics, on the floor, legs out as he leaned against a corner wall, sat Harry. He had earbuds in. Even though his eyes were closed, he seemed awake. Libby squatted down, lightly tapped the bottom of his shoe. He opened his eyes slowly and gave a wan smile of recognition at Libby's wave.

"Hi," she said when the earbuds were pulled.

"Hi."

"How you doing?"

The music leaking from the earbuds was more soulful than wild. Harry looked like he didn't have the energy to shrug.

"May I join you?" she asked.

When given permission, Libby sat on the floor next to Harry, offered him some of her stash of licorice, and said, "I have a few questions I'd like to ask."

Louis never did come back to Libby.

Didn't matter. On the way home from the library, she already had enough new pieces of information to suck her back into the fray.

Dropped into her lap, so to speak.

Was it time to talk to Detective Grass?

Or not?

What if she was wrong? Should she keep tracking down things herself until she was more certain? Even if signs were pointing in one direction, was that enough? Did she really want to be the one to make a formal accusation?

Everyone had said to be careful.

Maybe that finally sounded like good advice.

She would call Grass tomorrow. No. Today was Friday. She would wait until Monday. Sleep on it. Sort through things. Flesh out her theory.

She would have iced tea with Mae. Just sit with the old gray head and let things simmer.

CHAPTER
TWENTY-NINE

They sat on the back porch as usual. The yard they overlooked faced east, so by this time of day the sun had moved around to the front, taking its radiant heat with it. The shady space was cooler, and beyond, past the alley, soothing greens were on display like a giant color chart at a paint store. Forest green. Sap green. Chartreuse.

The view, the iced tea, a bit of a breeze, and just plain sitting refreshed Libby.

It wasn't long, however, before the view also revved her. Although tall bushes obscured most of Jonah's yard next door, the back part of the house was visible. The charming—and historic—rolled roof. The object of Mr. Randall's architectural affection.

"Bunny's having a snack," Mae said.

Rabbits, squirrels, and chipmunks frequented Mae's place, but at the moment, it was a small rabbit that munched on grass by bushes that lined the other side of the yard. "Bunny's a baby," she said. Then added, "Flannery O'Connor kept peacocks."

Libby had not heard. "Really?"

A car drove down the alley, kicking out gravel as it went faster than necessary, making Libby think of Al's comment the night before about them flying by.

"Did the police ever ask you about cars going down the alley the night Jonah died?" she asked.

"They did."

"Did you remember any?"

"I did. Some went fast. Some went slow."

Libby's eyes widened with anticipation. Could Mae confirm Walt's being in the alley—so Walt could confirm others?

"Do you remember what time you saw any of them?"

"After dinner. Before bed."

As loose—and unhelpful—as this description was, it was, no doubt, accurate. It outlined Mae's typical summer schedule on the back porch.

Libby drank her tea and resigned herself to her original goal. Sit with Mae and let things simmer.

Another car came by. Slower, but still too fast for a neighborhood alley.

"I guess you just get lots of cars," said Libby.

"Cars. Bikes. Kids. Cats. Dogs. Bunnies," listed Mae. "No peacocks." The small woman rocked, her toes barely touching the ground on the *to,* lifting off completely on the *fro.* "Died at the age of thirty-nine. Never married."

Mae grinned at Libby. "O'Connor. Not the peacocks."

Libby grinned as well. She rattled the ice cubes in her near-empty glass of tea till she was told to pour another round for everyone. "You never married, did you, Mae?"

More rocking.

"Spinster," she said. Statement of fact.

"If I may be so bold," started Libby, "was that by choice or circumstance?"

"You are bold," Mae said, but didn't miss a beat. "I couldn't get married."

"Couldn't?"

"Didn't have what it takes."

Mae never disappointed Libby.

"Didn't have what it takes? What does that mean?"

"I couldn't cook and I didn't want children."

Libby choked on a laugh and on tea that had gone down the wrong way. She cleared her throat. "I thought you lived at home and cooked for your father all those years."

"Fixed him something to eat. Mostly cold meat sandwiches. Yes, until he was ninety-six." She rocked easily. "I wouldn't call that cooking."

After a night of storms and a full day of work, Libby didn't last long on the porch. She told Mae to stay put in her rocker and watch Bunny, took her own glass into the kitchen, and headed home.

It was late. Out front, facing the western sun, it seemed unbearably hot.

Humidity wrapped Libby in sweat. The Blue Donuts were in full swing and their thumping music only added to the oppressive feeling.

Libby made her way down the block, overwhelmed by a longing to get home and flop on her bed in front of a fan. She was nearly thrown off balance when Francie rushed up to her from behind.

"Hey, girl!" Francie's enthusiasm vanished when she faced Libby. "Oh, Libs, are you okay?"

No. And now she was nauseous and unsteady. Damn heat.

Francie steered her friend up the first set of front steps at 1901.

Just before the second set, Libby leaned over the grass and threw up. It was vile and black as tar.

Libby's first thought was of the time one of her sisters had helped clean out a high school chemistry lab. Exposed to a toxic mix of old chemicals, she had brought up a similar colored gunk.

Francie's voice didn't sound alarmed, but it hardly matched her words. "That's scary. What have you …? Where have you …?"

Libby retched black stuff a second time. The sight scared her a second time.

It was not easy to focus, and she leaned against Francie.

Finally, after the initial shock, Libby was able to figure out the black stuff coming up was the licorice from the candy store.

"How much did you eat?!"

"Quarter of a pound." Libby swallowed hard at the thought of it. She gripped the railing, and during a break, made it into the house.

Dash and BabyCakes came to Libby immediately, but sensing the situation, trailed her unsteady steps from a distance.

Francie kept up with the questions. "When was that?"

"About four."

"What else did you eat today?"

Libby forced herself to concentrate. "Brunch."

"What time?"

"Eleven maybe."

"Anything unusual?"

"Soft-boiled eggs. Toast. Same as yesterday. Not sick then."

"Anyone else eat the candy?"

"No. Harry doesn't like licorice."

After another heave in the bathroom, Libby stumbled a few steps, and collapsed on her bed, begging Francie to quit asking about food.

"I keep asking because this looks like food poisoning. Quick-onset vomiting. Although it's already been a couple hours since the licorice binge. If you're lucky, your system will eliminate it on its own."

Which it continued to do. Back to the bathroom.

Libby sat on the linoleum floor, exhausted, dozing for a few minutes between bouts of upchucking.

Francie offered her a damp washcloth for her face and a glass of water. "You don't need to drink it, just rinse out your mouth."

Libby mumbled, "Tea."

"No," Francie cautioned her, "just water."

"Ice." Libby marshalled all her energy to speak. "Iced tea."

Francie was adamant. "No, nothing iced. I know it sounds good right now—"

Libby was weak, but just as adamant. "Iced *tea*."

And then she got frantic. "Mae's. Both ... we both had iced *tea*! Check Mae!"

Tiny puffs of warm air on her eyelids and the hum of a very small motor gradually roused Libby. Eyes closed and still in bed, she lifted a listless hand to pet BabyCakes, discouraging the cat from making a more detailed examination of her face.

BabyCakes was noted for sticking to a routine, and when Libby deviated from it, such as staying in bed so late in the morning, his curiosity spiked.

Suddenly, Libby emerged from her stupor.

"Poison! Mae!"

She only realized she had spoken out loud when, her eyes shooting open, she saw BabyCakes jump from the bed, and Dash come to attention at her feet. And her sister appear at her bedroom doorway. "Jane?"

"Good. You're awake," Jane said. "Mae is fine. Before I ask how you are, how much food does that chubby cat get? The only time he left your side was to circle his dish."

"Third of a cup," said Libby. She took in and let out a long breath. "Mae's okay. That's good. Come here, Dash."

The dog needed little coaxing to come up close, bury his face in the covers, and get his head and ears tousled. Libby sat up, adjusted her pillow, and called after Jane, who had left to feed the neglected BabyCakes. "I am tired, but oh, dear God, I feel so much better than last night, most of which is a blur. When did you come?"

From the kitchen, Jane spoke over the clatter of cat kibble tumbling into BabyCake's bowl. "About nine thirty or ten. That band down the block was still playing. Francie said they'd quit soon. We thought you were probably all right, but it never hurts to be careful. I think that black licorice coming up was a little disconcerting, even to a nurse. Like you might have gotten into something truly harmful."

The mention of licorice sent a lurch of memory to Libby's stomach. "So, you think that was it? The … candy?"

"The iced tea." Jane returned. "Good thing you had Mae's key on your ring. She was on the floor. Had thrown up. Francie called her husband to go over while Francie stayed with you. He and a daughter-in-law took Mae to the hospital. They kept her to make sure she got her fluids back under control. As long as you keep drinking these tasty juice-and-electrolyte concoctions, I think you'll be okay."

Libby accepted the glass Jane offered and gingerly took a sip. She rubbed a thumb along her dog's eyebrows. "Did you take Dash out?"

"Francie walked him earlier when she came by to check on you. Said she fed him according to package directions." Jane pushed aside a blanket and sat on the chair she had pulled next to the bed. "From what Francie and I could make of it, you were the only one who had licorice. Mae had half a peanut butter sandwich earlier, but you didn't. So far, the tea is the only thing you both had."

"It was just sun tea," said Libby. "The caregiver is scrupulous. I can't imagine it would be a dirty jar. We didn't even do lemon juice or sugar. I don't know, can bacteria or mold get in there?"

"Only if it sat there for days, I would think. But you said she'd just put it out there in the afternoon."

Libby scratched Dash under his chin. "Yes," she said thoughtfully, "I'm sure it was sitting on her front porch all afternoon. In the sun. As usual."

She furrowed her brows as the idea jumped at her. "Someone could have put something in it. Poison!"

Jane was not given to the same fascination with murder as her sister. "Way too many Nancy Drew mysteries as a child." Jane touched Libby's forehead. "Maybe it's your feverish brain. Nah. You're okay."

"You read them, too," said Libby defensively, as if she and Jane were twelve years old.

"But I alternated them with Cherry Ames nurse stories. At least what I got from them comes in handy." She fluffed Libby's pillow. "I'm sure this was just a fluky accident. Although I can see knocking you off. You're such a Nosy Parker with stuff like this murder. Honestly. You need to be more careful."

Libby's instinct as a sibling was to come back with another juvenile comment at yet another warning to be careful, but current the situation compelled her to be more serious. "No one could be sure I was even stopping at Mae's. I do go often, but it's not any regular day or time."

"What are you thinking?"

Libby stroked Dash's front paws. "I'm thinking about Mae being in danger."

Jane stood and folded the blanket she'd pushed aside. "For heaven's sake, Libby. Who would ever want to hurt Mae?"

CHAPTER
THIRTY

Two ten-gallon clear glass water coolers welcomed customers at the Muffin House, a local bakery and tea shop in a converted old firehouse on Oak Avenue, just beyond the Riley library.

Clean white walls, white wooden tables and chairs. Vases of yellow, pink, and coral snapdragons from the garden out back. All of it a pleasant change of scenery for Libby, who'd spent most of the weekend inside. Resting. Thinking. Simmering. Working things out. Working up the courage to be sitting now at the Muffin House.

All summer, the Muffin House coolers would be filled with ice water spiked with herbs and colorful slices of fruits. When Libby came in mid-morning Monday, thin wedges of pale cantaloupe and sprigs of green mint pressed their faces against the frosty glass. Because tea still did not sound appealing, she was glad to have the clear drink to accompany a Bluebell Blueberry muffin. Her stomach still wanted to take it easy after Friday night, and she was glad that some of the muffins were not outrageously rich or sweet.

This morning, even the mild Bluebell sat untouched.

However, the muffin was neglected more because Libby's mind

was occupied with other things than with her stomach's wishes.

She already knew how Jonah had been killed. Now she was pretty sure she knew why. And who did it.

Through the wall of low mullioned windows that used to be the firehouse doors, Libby stared at the traffic and argued with herself.

It wasn't the divulging of her conclusion that gave her pause. She was confident she was doing the right thing.

Someone had to report it now that it was so clearly obvious. That it could be firmly substantiated.

Such information had, in fact, dropped in her lap. Not so much things completely out of the blue, but things that had been out of focus.

Paralyzed by thinking she might be wrong, she'd examined, over and over, the conversations, the timing. Considered whether other conclusions could be drawn from what she'd picked up. Actually, considered telling the would-be killer first, giving them a chance to turn themselves in.

She figured there would be grief.

But there could also be danger.

She'd taken notes, made lists, and doodled two pens dry.

Instead, she'd made this call.

She still had time to change her mind.

Not much.

Grass sat down, blocking Libby's view of the street.

He ordered coffee, black—no muffin, thank you.

The detective scanned the quaint shop. Monday morning. People not at work. Just casually meeting, chatting away. These scenes always made him think of retirement and the luxury of such free time.

Then he looked across the table.

Libby Kinder was hardly one to call him for a casual cup of coffee. When his arrived, he aligned his tie with his shirt front and said, "Okay. What's up?"

Libby began with the iced tea episode from two days before.

Grass looked both concerned and perturbed. "It was bad enough she needed to be taken to the hospital but not bad enough to call the police? I thought I made it clear I was to be notified if anything unusual went on around here."

Libby wasn't surprised by his reaction. Knowing it was one more time she hadn't let him in on something didn't help. She tried to skim over that part.

"I'm not sure an elderly lady with what looked like a touch of food poisoning would qualify as unusual."

Grass cocked his head and eyed Libby. "What makes you think it only looked like food poisoning?"

"You, to start with."

Grass added perplex to perturbed.

"That day on Jonah Pemberton's porch," explained Libby. "When you said Mae might be in danger if someone thought she saw something incriminating."

Grass pulled out his pen and black notebook. "Go on."

"First of all," said Libby, "everyone knows Mae sits on her porch every night. Including the night Jonah was murdered. You yourself said common knowledge like that makes it easy for anyone who wants to know to find out.

"Second, this sun tea jar is also totally predictable. Sits in the same spot on the side of the porch in plain sight. All day; all summer. So why, after all this time, all those jars of tea, prepared the same way, same tea, in the same container—why does everybody suddenly get sick?"

Grass glanced up from his writing. "Did you save any of the tea? Or the jar?"

Libby was embarrassed. She knew it was the proper thing to do. Would have been. She stammered. "The caregiver … threw it out. The tea."

"And the jar? Even if it's in the garbage—"

Libby stopped him. "Caregiver scrubbed it and ran it through the dishwasher. High heat. Twice."

Before Grass could criticize the action, Libby vouched for the caregiver. "She's very careful about keeping things clean for Mae. She was horrified that a dirty jar might have been the source of food poisoning. On and on about washing it every morning before Mae puts the whole business out fresh."

Grass sighed. "Your Apple Street is getting a little too efficient for its own good, Is she all right? And you? You don't seem to be too worse for wear, although I know food poisoning is no picnic."

"Not food poisoning," said Libby pointedly. "Poison."

His voice rose. "Which is why I keep saying be careful. To tell me when you find out something!"

Libby's voice met his pitch. "I *am* telling you!"

Grass sat back. He looked at Libby. Looked at her untouched muffin, which he had attributed to her recent stomach troubles. He now realized she was nervous.

Unusual for Libby Kinder.

If something had dropped in her lap, Grass knew he needed to let her tell it in her own way, not scare her off with badgering.

He took a sip of coffee and settled in. "I'm listening."

Libby watched Grass settle in. She poked at her muffin and took a deep breath. Here goes.

From her shorts pocket, Libby pulled a folded sheet of paper. She unfolded and smoothed it on the table before her, a list embellished with elaborate doodling. She began with the offenses of Mrs. Thorne, not only her instigating the mail switch, but masterminding and overseeing all the vandalism.

Grass had heard a lot of whacky schemes in his time. This broke new ground.

"She used the same kid for all of it?" asked Grass.

"Same."

"Not like any summer job I ever had. Want to give me his name this time?"

"Not really."

Grass traced the line of the handle of his delicate china coffee cup to channel his frustration. "Neighborhood take care of it as well?"

"Yes."

He regarded the ceiling, painted pale blue. Apple Street was taking on a new image in his mind. One guy murdered. A hefty chunk of money missing from the local library. One old lady poisoned; another old lady hiring a kid for a crime spree. So much for a nice family neighborhood.

"I can guarantee," he said, "that old lady would be the first to throw a fit if the police came after *her*."

He didn't especially like or condone how things had been handled with Mrs. Thorne. He might appreciate neighbors taking care things, but he didn't need a vigilante mentality getting out of hand. After all, there was still a murderer to be dealt with.

He would look into the poisoning. That was possibly a serious new development. But for now, it was almost a relief to set the vandalism piece aside.

Grass accepted fresh coffee.

He glanced at Libby's list and braced himself. "What else you got?"

It was harder for Libby to tell him about Bin and Walt. About Walt's being in the alley the night of the murder. At almost the exact time of the murder.

Grass had quit looking so settled in for this. Perturbed return.

Libby raced through her justification for waiting so long to pass on this information. "Walt said he didn't even stop at Jonah's. Only saw a blur of a moving figure, maybe, in the alley in his rearview mirror. Said he'd deny it if I told you anyway. He didn't threaten me. Really. I mean, he could have snuffed me out right there. Run me down. Besides," she slowed to take a breath, "I … I believed him."

She hung her head with embarrassment, chagrined at the pitiful reasoning she'd used to hold back telling Grass in the first place. What she had left to offer sounded lamest of all. "And I promised."

Grass was more than a little irked. He tried to keep his voice restrained. "You realize this is withholding evidence? Snuffed you out! Hell, you have the lingo down from those damn mystery books, you must know about withholding evidence!"

Libby wished she had a pen. There was a line of circles doodled across the top of her list she wanted to add to. She stared at them.

Grass stared at her. Stared at her list buried somewhere under what looked like designs for a gang tattoo.

But he knew—for absolute certain—if he wanted more information from Libby Kinder, from that scrawled-on list, that he had to stay calm. It infuriated him.

Penning a few strokes in his own notebook allowed him to focus and settle down.

He pushed his coffee cup to the side. Folded his napkin in half. Then in half again. Finally, he sat back and spoke with more patience.

"Look, Libby," he said. When she lifted her head and made eye contact, he tried to sound as sincere as he was. "You've got to start trusting me. Things may not seem important to you. I understand that. But you can't necessarily see the whole picture."

Libby met Grass's eyes squarely. His manner could infuriate her. Why did his sincerity come across to her like he was talking to a ten-year-old?

She let it go. She knew she had something important to say. Something that would add to that whole picture.

She straightened up in her chair.

And told him Harry's secret.

It was overcast later when a squad car pulled up and parked

271

noiselessly behind the disabled truck.

From her solarium window Libby watched two blue uniforms go up to the door of the house across the street. She heard the barking beagles they roused; saw the officers let in.

As she raked her fingers down BabyCakes' spine, making light furrows in his soft, black fur, she thought about her part in what was happening.

Harry had told her that Mr. Sparks had gotten furious when Heather said Mr. Pemberton had come down complaining about the band's racket. Madder than usual; "freaking out," as Harry put it. Sparks had declared he'd "shut that jerk up" and stormed out of the garage toward the alley.

The police—and Heather's mother—eventually convinced the girl she had to tell what she knew, given what Harry had described.

In the end, Heather had backed Harry up. Together they admitted that although they both had seen Sparks leave the garage, they had not witnessed his return. They had heard a car door slam and the car peel away sometime after that. Even with all the wiggle room, timing had put Al within the damning window of opportunity.

Acting on Libby's tip, the police had also confronted Bin's husband, Walt, who had reluctantly cooperated. His recall improved greatly in the presence of law enforcement. He realized the figure he'd seen in his car's rearview mirror was likely male, that the person had his back to Walt, facing Sparks' end of the alley, and was moving quickly. Rushing? Libby had wondered. To get to work? To get away from a murder?

At the Muffin House, Libby had wondered out loud about Al's hands, aware of their prevalent use in his everyday life. From the first days of the investigation, Al had claimed the callouses were a result of his job, of his normal summer yard work. While this was verifiably so, the marks were also the same type the murderer could have gotten strangling someone with the suspected cord weapon.

On top of all this was the fact that Al had lied about his actions that night. Even worse was covering up those actions by asking his daughter to lie as well.

It had helped no one that she had then asked Harry to do the same.

The sum total of all these disclosures seemed critical and incriminating in Libby's eyes.

Grass had been grateful for Libby's input, even though he kept reminding her that much of it was circumstantial.

The one concern Libby had had was that Al and Al's family would find out that she had clued-in the authorities. Ratted on, in genre parlance.

Grass had told her the police would only say that they'd received multiple tips. He assured her that Al would not know about Bin's husband, or Libby's own part in the matter. That he would not know about Harry unless Heather or his wife told him.

However, Libby knew that if neighborhoods were like family, sooner rather than later, everyone would know where everything came from.

Libby looked up from a purring BabyCakes at the house across the street. What was taking so long? Being asked to come in for questioning, no matter where that might lead, seemed a quick and simple procedure.

Libby glanced up and down the block. Apple Street seemed unusually unresponsive. The police had shown up. Were people off about their business, inured to any official presence as the murder investigation dragged on?

Or were they inside, like Libby, glued to their windows?

The quiet was broken by the Sparks' front door banging open. Heather and her brother, Max, stood in the front window holding Rocky and Punk, who were barking their heads off. Cindy Sparks stood next to them.

Al shot onto the porch, an officer on each side gripping Al's arms, pinned behind him as he twisted against their hold.

Libby now saw the handcuffs, saw Al—disheveled and red-faced; contempt firmly fixed in his eyes—led down the steps.

Al Sparks could be helpful around the neighborhood, pleasant when it suited him, but he was snarly with his children, sharp with his wife, and gruff with his pets.

Any hesitation Libby had felt about turning him in dissipated as she watched Al Sparks, not compliant or submissive, but physical and defiant, as his head was bowed down by the police to deposit him into the back seat of the squad car like a full-fledged criminal.

CHAPTER
THIRTY-ONE

So. Al Sparks sat in jail.

A few simple questions by the police in the Sparks back yard had turned into a confrontation, had brought out the club, had resulted in battery. Battery had gotten Al handcuffed, taken in, and booked. A prior assault, while not recent, was enough to set bail higher than his family could afford.

So. Al Sparks sat in jail.

It was mid-August.

Apple Street was unquestionably not the same place it had been two months before.

The murder of Jonah Pemberton—one of their own—had turned the seemingly placid neighborhood upside down.

The arrest of Al Sparks—also one of their own—had been equally shocking. But his arrest had returned some equilibrium to the place, some freedom to feel safe, comfortable returning to routines without constantly glancing backward.

For many, there was residual fear, traces of extra caution as parents continued to watch their children more closely, residents to keep more lights on in the house and on porches through the night. Some still refused to walk alone or late, no matter what time of the day.

Responses to Al's arrest were as varied as the block's inhabitants. The Two Sues saw justice served. The Lagunas and Paul Paterson understood a parent sticking up for his kids, while Francie searched for a clinical explanation. Stress? Medications?

Mr. Randall felt free to call Al a loud-mouthed bully, an opinion which united usual enemies Nick Montgomery and Mrs. Thorne, vindicated now in their mutual assessment of the man.

The Happy Trio regarded the event as thrilling, further adventures in a mystery right under their noses, a summer distraction they could not have imagined in June.

One response was more complicated, affected Libby more than the others.

Preoccupied with her thoughts one afternoon, she walked Dash in the park, skirting a fishing tournament underway at the pond.

A few yards ahead in the playground area, an older kid listlessly let the chains of a swing twist and untwist above him.

Staring at the rut he had dug in the pea gravel at his feet, was Harry.

Dash recognized the boy and pulled toward him, panting with excitement.

In the library during Libby's last conversation with him, Harry, too, had been excited.

And relieved.

Not today. Today he looked miserable.

It had not been hard to get Harry to talk. He was so full of guilt from not talking that it took very little to open the floodgates and get him to tell about the night of Jonah's murder.

When it was discovered that Jonah Pemberton was dead, Al had made Heather promise not to tell anyone how mad he'd gotten when he heard Jonah had come down to complain. In turn, Heather had made Harry promise not to tell anyone about her father's outburst, his storming off,

276

which only the two of them had witnessed as they'd stood at the back of the garage behind the band.

And Harry had promised. Promised a friend. A girlfriend.

In the beginning, it had been kind of romantic, he had told Libby. Just the two of them knowing something. "Keeping the secret made me feel important," he said. "Like Heather really trusted me. Really liked me."

But then everything came to be about the secret. Whenever Heather didn't get her way, she held the secret over Harry's head. When she wanted him to do something or not do something, the secret always put Heather in charge.

"She was in a tough spot," said Libby. "Would be hard to turn in your own dad."

"But what Mr. Sparks did was wrong," said Harry.

He stared at the gravel. "I just couldn't lie anymore. Feeling that bad all the time was worse than telling." He looked up and wrinkled his nose. "I still feel crappy."

A light breeze drifted over from the pond.

People fishing fished. Dash found grass at the edge of the gravel to lie in. Libby sat on the swing next to Harry.

"There's a famous character in a novel called *Crime and Punishment*," she said. "This guy kills somebody and escapes the police. But he's so riddled with guilt that he starts to wonder if it's more punishment than prison could ever be."

Harry stared at Libby, confused. "But I didn't kill anybody. Mr. Sparks did. I just told the secret."

He had a point.

"You told the truth," Libby said. "That's what we all had to do."

Libby felt a twinge of guilt for holding out on Grass for so long.

Harry hung his head. "Now he's in prison. I'll bet it's awful. It's awful in the movies."

Harry twisted the swing chains again. "Do you think what I told the detective will make Mr. Sparks be put in solitary confinement?"

Libby cringed with misery that Harry had to think about this. She reassured him that solitary confinement was not likely.

It did not keep her twinge of guilt from growing. Did not keep her from picturing more graphically, and thinking more soberly, that what she'd told the detective had helped put Al Sparks where he was.

She waited for the breeze off the pond to come again.

"We have to remember what you said before, Harry. That what Mr. Sparks did was wrong."

Harry covered over and re-dug the rut in the pea gravel. "They said he took all this money. He should've paid for Heather's dance camp. He should've fixed his truck. Why didn't he just go down there and yell at Mr. Pemberton? He could've just yelled. He yells all the time. And if he killed Mr. Pemberton, why didn't he just say it was an accident? That's what I think happened. It was just an accident. Or ...." He glared wide-eyed at Libby, "hat if he didn't really do it?"

w

Walking home, Libby ambled down Old Orchard, too lost in thought to see the lush canopy of trees over her or notice the approaching car until it was right next to her.

"Kinder! Libby Kinder!"

Being hollered at by the driver startled her. Dash, who had become very attuned to danger of recent times, barked at the rolled down window.

"It's okay, Dash," said Libby. "Detective Grass enjoys sneaking around. He means no harm."

"I don't consider driving down the street in broad daylight all that sneaky."

He pulled to the curb. "How are things over on Apple Street?"

Libby shrugged. "Getting back to normal, I guess."

"Anything else come up I need to know?"

Libby raised her hands in surrender. "Given you all I've got," she said. "The ball's in your court. I just talked to the boyfriend. He still feels pretty bad."

"I keep trying to impress on you how important it is for people to come forward with information," said Grass. "We needed Harry to tell the truth. For you to tell us everything you'd picked up." He pointed a finger at Libby. "Everything."

Libby chewed her lip. Going over stuff with Harry had dented her confidence. Made her see things from a different angle. "What if Al Sparks isn't guilty?"

Grass blinked. More than once.

He ran a hand through his hair. He wished Libby Kinder would land on one square. First, she withholds facts, then she spills her guts—positive she knows the killer—now she regrets that. "We have a suspect," he said. "Remember, it's our job to collect as much evidence as possible. From any source we can get it. Then it's our job is to put it together."

He smiled, hoping it would make him sound agreeable. "Things on Apple Street will get back to normal. People just have to be patient."

Patience, however, was not Libby's strong suit.

She crossed her arms and leaned up against the car by its window. Dash laid down in the grass.

Libby couldn't help but recall leaning in at Al Sparks' car window the night of the storm. When he wouldn't answer her questions. "Did Al explain about the poison in the iced tea?"

"No," said Grass. "Clammed up completely on that."

Libby didn't want to hear clammed up. She wanted to hear that he had confessed to everything. Fit all the pieces together. "Did he see Bin's husband driving at the other end of the alley? What about the money? Was it just lying there in plain sight? What did he do with it?"

Grass was sitting in an air-conditioned car, but Libby's bombardment of questions made him reach to lower the temperature. He did not feel like going over everything with her. Again. He'd already been pulling out his hair at Sparks' lackluster and unproductive interrogations. Libby's queries only made them more obvious.

"This is a pretty stubborn guy," he said. "Not very police friendly to start with and dead set on making us do all the work. It's true. No one saw him do it or even positively saw him in the alley. I told you from the beginning, some of the evidence is circumstantial, but there's an awful lot of it."

Grass wiggled his fingers in front of the blower of cool air.

"Look," he said, unloading his best defense. "This was a parent who got mad, fed up with a jerk of a neighbor. According to half the people on your block, Jonah Pemberton could be an annoying pain in the ass. He complains about the kids—Sparks' kid—one time too many. I understand this. I've got kids. I don't like people ragging on them, getting in their faces. Sparks goes down, flips a little too far, takes this guy out, steals a nice chunk of change just sitting there. Why not? He can use the money.

"Now all that's bad enough. Then he lies about it. Okay, normal reaction. The choice he makes. But worse, from my personal point of view, is he asks his kid to lie for him. That's not right."

Grass sat back and looked ahead, tapping his steering wheel. "That little girl is a good kid. She knows her father's not perfect. Said she knows he yells a lot, but he still loves them. She idolizes him like kids do. And this guy takes advantage of that. Maybe it was aggravated, not premeditated, but it's not a bad bet that Sparks did this."

He turned to Libby, leaning in at the passenger's window, with her furrowed brow. He sighed. "I'm sure you and Harry feel worse than Sparks does. For what it's worth, I can tell you not all murderers feel guilty."

Libby nodded. It had been reassuring to hear Grass lay out so firmly and convincingly the same line of reasoning she herself had followed when deciding to go to him in the first place.

He was right. They all—she and Harry and Walt—had had to tell what they knew.

The rest was up to the police.

Libby felt her brows relax. She stepped away from the car.

"Thanks," she said.

Grass rolled up his window. As he pulled away, he saw Libby tug at her dog and walk in the opposite direction, her head up, seemingly more at ease.

He shook his head. "Wonder how long that will last."

CHAPTER
THIRTY-TWO

Libby took the hose to the plant containers in her back yard. She had slept much better since talking to Grass two days before. With Al Sparks securely in custody, she could finally quit spending every waking—and sometimes sleeping—moment trying to track clues and formulate theories about the murder.

Not that she didn't still have questions. But she had begun to let them fade as immediate concerns.

Next door, Honey, swinging wildly on her playset, belted out *fair-y jack-et, fair-y jack-et* for her block party debut only ten days away.

Nikki belted out with equal gusto, "Mom says pipe down! It's too early!"

7 a.m.

Early but not cool, as the hottest and muggiest dog days of Indiana moved in permanently.

Although Libby usually let her lawn go brown and dormant in the heat, the tomatoes out front were worth keeping watered. They were one of the few things that flourished in this weather. Well, and zucchini.

Down the way Paul watered Mae's window boxes; Mr. Randall

hosed the sidewalk. The Two Sues moved sprinklers to their raised beds, spilling over with cucumbers—and zucchini—that had jumped the wooden confines and were wandering out into the grass. Everyone was watering before the sun could suck the earth dry again.

The high temperatures and humidity did not deter early morning joggers or dog walkers. Or Mrs. Thorne from sweeping her street.

All normal.

Maybe Grass was right, thought Libby. Apple Street would settle back into its routine.

"I've made the appointment!" Namita announced as she appeared in baggy mint green pajama bottoms and a tank top at the front door with Paji. She bypassed the dried-up orphaned plants on the porch, and lazily dropped down each step.

"Wow," said Libby. "An appointment. To get information or to actually … do the deed?"

"It's called artificial insemination, Libby. I'm starting my child out using the correct terminology. Good idea, don't you think? Studies show even in utero babies pick up this stuff."

"Your child will have the best vocabulary in the nursery."

"Not mine. No nursery. Home birth."

"Hmmm," said Libby and sprayed her toes, perpetually exposed in August. She turned off the hose. "Is that why you've gone back to your book club? In Utero Lit 101?"

"Can't hurt." Namita and Paji started down to the sidewalk. "By the way, a few friends suggested a conception party. What do you think?"

Libby shielded her eyes from the sun to see if she could read how serious Namita was. She struck a neutral tone. "Always open to new experiences."

"Good. You might be hosting it." Namita tossed out a laugh. "Just kidding. My only request is no iced tea. And maybe your detective friend can patrol the alleys that night." She laughed again. "Just kidding."

Libby laughed but thought to herself that normal hadn't quite fully returned if these were the first things a person planning a party in the neighborhood considered. She continued to push aside the fading concerns, replacing them with Namita's infectious joy.

"Hey!" she called out. "What do you think those party favors look like?"

"I'll just say this—if you have *hammer* at 27-Across for *to pound*, you need to re-think that."

Louis stood at the library copier, his uniform so crisply ironed that Libby wondered how many he had in his closet; he certainly never wore the same one two days in a row.

"I do have *hammer*," she said. "Almost every other word fit. Are you sure?"

It was foolish to question Louis. He had undoubtedly solved the whole Sunday *Times* crossword. It was Tuesday, and Libby was still struggling with hers

"Haven't seen Romeo and Juliet for a while," said Louis. "They drop out of your show?"

"That relationship may have taken a hit when Heather's father was arrested. Kids are funny. They can be pretty resilient. Harry said he'd be back. Don't know about Heather."

Louis nodded towards Bin checking in a pile of books at the desk. "Heard you did some conversing with that detective. About a certain husband."

"Bin tell you?" asked Libby.

"Oh, yeah."

"Probably never talk to me again."

"I think she realizes you had to divulge it. Personally, I think her husband should have divulged all of it. Himself. Of course, one can surmise why he might not, if you get my drift."

It was a drift Libby had encountered before. But. It was out on the table now for the police to deal with.

Louis greeted a patron, then rocked back and onto the balls of his feet. "I assume the authorities disclosed what fate befell the library fine money."

"Only that the arrested guy keeps denying he took it. Apparently at this point he's denying everything. I suppose he'll eventually come clean. Or they'll go back to believing it's not connected."

Louis crossed his arms and rocked more. "In my experience—with mystery novels—everything is connected."

Libby admitted to having the same experience. "In books," she said. "However, my real-life experience seems to be leading me to a different conclusion."

The rocking stopped. "Libby. I have had some postulations about that money."

"Oh?" Libby's brain consulted its file of unanswered questions. "I must say, some things about it still don't fit. I'm thinking about when Harry brought up the truck."

"The what?"

"Al Sparks' truck has been dead for months. Needs a new transmission."

"Expensive."

"Exactly. Why," Libby wondered out loud, "if Al went down to yell at Jonah, strangled him in a rage, and only took the money as an afterthought, why didn't he use it to fix his truck? I heard he was anticipating a bonus at work. Could have just said he got it. Nobody would have given it much thought. Been happy he got the thing off the street."

"Hmmm," said Louis, mulling this over. "I started to say something to you a while ago, but when this guy was apprehended, I let it go. I see now, it might be more pertinent than—"

The double glass doors opened behind them, stopping their conversation. Libby turned and greeted Geoff Paterson. "Here's one of my star dancers."

"Oh, right," Geoff said with a friendly scoff.

"Okay, okay," said Libby. "But you do have a nice singing voice."

"That's a real joy," said the security guard.

Paul and J'az came from the children's section, carrying boxes of jigsaw puzzles. J'az went to the back room while Paul detoured toward Geoff.

"Hi, Paul," said Libby. "I was just saying what a good voice your son has."

"Happy he's using it for a change. I hope you're not interrupting these people, Geoff."

"Just neighborhood gossip," said Libby. "Louis was asking about Al Sparks' arrest and the library money."

Paul set his box of jigsaw puzzles on a table near the copier. "I assume, like everybody, that Jonah took the money. That Al found it lying around in the garage that night and then he took it."

"Big surprise," said Geoff. "If Mr. Pemberton was dumb enough to leave it sitting behind the desk over there, he was dumb enough to leave it sitting out in the garage. He should've known anybody could take it."

Notwithstanding Geoff's penchant for speaking with adults like an adult, it was a kid who marched over, slipped surreptitiously behind the main desk, and held up an imaginary money pouch to demonstrate.

"Geoff!" Paul's raised voice raised looks by computer users nearby. Instead of saying more, Paul turned to Libby and Louis and sighed heavily.

When Geoff returned, Paul did what parents do to a mischievous four-year-old in public—divert.

"Why don't you ask Libby about having a skateboard surfing race at the block party?"

"Oh, yeah," said Geoff.

286

Libby was not above going along with the diversion tactic. She told Geoff what she told every child who came up with a block party suggestion. "Sounds good. All you need is a parent or adult who's willing to organize it, run it, and give out a few prizes. And no, I'm already putting on the show."

Geoff looked to his father. "Dad?"

Divert and delay. "We'll talk about it. I have to get back to work. That far study room is free, Geoff. Why don't you go play some of your games till practice? Come on, I'll unlock it."

As Paul and Geoff walked away, Libby cocked her head toward the hallway to the practice room. "Come on, Louis. Unlock the door for me. And bring your postulations."

She shut the door behind them and spoke quickly. "I've only got a little time until my cast busts in. What's up about the library money?"

Louis didn't hesitate. "Jonah was killed late Friday. The fines were discovered to have vanished Monday morning. It was determined that no one could abscond with the money over the weekend as per the alarm system's setup. The police and you asked repeatedly about Friday night. Who was here? Who was at the desk? Who was the last to deal with the money pouch? What time did people leave, etc., etc."

Libby nodded with every point Louis presented. "Yes. Yes. Which is why the final ... postulation was that since no one could have taken it after Jonah left, Jonah must have stolen it."

Libby paused, calling up an old idea. "I did once propose that someone could have taken it *after* the whole episode."

"You mean Monday morning?" Louis pursed his lips in consideration. "That would mean either Bin or J'az who opened. Or Bin and J'az colluding." He closed his eyes briefly. "I'll have to give that some thought. It doesn't ring very true to me for those two ladies."

Immediate frustration for Libby. "Then we're back to Jonah stealing it. From there, the killer—either the Random Vandal or, in this case, Al Sparks—must have found it in the garage."

"Exactly as we have previously conjectured," said Louis. "But. Then you asked what changed? What was going on? Bin's grandchild getting ready for surgery; J'az going for an atypical dinner out. Summer programs beginning; you starting rehearsals."

Louis halted his list. "You know," he said, "how sometimes you're eating your cereal or buttering your toast when 6-Across just pops into your head? On the spot, you know it's not *hammer*; it's something else?"

"Yes. Yes."

"Sorry to mix so many metaphors."

Libby could hear kids gathering in the hallway. "So, what popped into your head?"

Louis rocked forward with a big grin. "Nothing."

Libby gave an elongated blink. "Nothing?"

She frowned. A big frown. "Nothing?"

"Just like Sherlock Holmes. Not what did happen, but what didn't. For the last twelve years, I've watched and listened to Jonah Pemberton amass small fortunes in library fines, talking them up at the end of every day, bragging like it was his personal Wall Street portfolio. A ballyhoo for every penny. When he reached his self-imposed goal, he'd turn the money in, and start all over again. It was just a game."

"That's what his daughter keeps saying. That her father only piled up the money for sport. Said he never did before, and never did this time, intend to steal it. There was nothing to it. Is that what you mean?"

"No," Louis said coyly. "I literally mean *nothing*. For at least a week, Jonah said nothing. He stopped counting. Stopped commenting. Before this, even if he'd hit some mark and started over, he always—and I mean always—made a big deal of it. To summarize," Louis said with momentous gravity, "Jonah. Said. Nothing."

Libby waited. No light bulbs went on. No pinball machine lit up. A complete blank.

"What do you think it means, Louis?"

The glee disappeared from the security guard's face. "Now that did not rise to my mind. Remember, I solve crossword puzzles; you solve murders."

Polite knocking, then impatient pounding at the door.

Libby would have to ponder Louis's new angle later.

Before opening the door to let kids in and Louis out, she suddenly paused and smiled. "*Pummel*, not *hammer*," she said. "27-Across. *To pound* is *to pummel*."

Louis smiled back. "See. Sometimes you're only just a little off."

CHAPTER
THIRTY-THREE

N othing.

Beyond the initial promise that Jonah saying nothing held, nothing else fell into place for Libby after Louis's postulations about the library money.

She had been busy with work during the days and a summer star-gazing camp in the evening for most of the week.

On Sunday, she sought the shade of the front porch with Dash to read the newspaper. The humidity had temporarily cleared out, so even at noon, the breeze teasing her pages predicted a lazy, comfortable time of it.

And yet Libby could not relax. Could not look at the crossword puzzle without stewing over Louis's comments.

Al Sparks' truck across the street taunted her. Harry's plaintive questions about Al languishing in prison popped up every time she looked in that direction.

Finally, she abandoned the unruly newspaper. She watched the leaves lift and flutter until they were not the focus, until she was looking but not looking.

She imagined the library humming along smoothly. Then at some random moment, Jonah taking center stage and broadcasting the library money numbers like he was caller at a church bingo party. The hoopla. The applause at the tally.

Every day.

Then. Nothing.

Nothing new in Libby's thinking either.

She decided she needed to do something physical. Like Louis buttering his toast, it might distract one part of her brain while another came up with some useful insights.

She settled on brushing Dash. Sliding the brush along the dog's back, over and over, she began to wonder …

What reason would Jonah have to quit making his normal big deal of the library fines?

Was the money really gone already? Possibly a whole week *before* the murder?

Stolen? Surely Jonah would have reported it.

If Jonah himself had taken it that far ahead … wouldn't he have pretended it was turned in and start over? No one would have been the wiser.

But the police didn't find it anywhere. He hadn't bought costly trip tickets or hidden it or given it away.

And if it wasn't Jonah who had taken the money, then who?

Libby went back to imagining the library. Not the desk and computers, but the people. The staff. Patrons. She pictured Geoff Paterson easily reaching in for the money pouch.

Libby scowled. For heaven's sake, she thought, almost everyone who came into that library had access to it!

Everyone who came into that library.

She stopped. Held up the brush. It wasn't a new thought, but an old one with a new spin.

Dash twisted his head around to see what was causing the disruption in his grooming.

"I'll have to verify it of course," she told him.

She squinted, concentrating. Wasn't it Cindy Sparks at the first block party meeting ... didn't she say she didn't think her husband had ever set foot in that library?

Libby patted Dash's head.

Several times.

Until this dropped into her lap: he may very well have killed Jonah Pemberton, but Al Sparks did not take the library money.

What else did he not do?

"Hey, Miss Libby!"

Libby turned to see Honey standing by the blue spruce in a red polka dot bathing suit. "Hey, Miss Honey."

Honey squatted next to Libby and pointed at Dash's brush. "Can I do that?"

"Sure," said Libby, even though her mind was gaining speed, rumbling down a different track.

Honey proceeded to apply the brush with precise and gentle strokes as if preparing the dog for Westminster. "Will you buy some of our lemonade?"

"Maybe. Who made it?"

"My mom. Two times. We drank the first one."

"Then I will. I might take two cups."

"One for Dashy?" Honey backcombed the wiry tuft on top of the dog's head and giggled at the electrified look it produced.

Libby pulled her attention back fully to Honey. "Lemonade's not good for dogs," she said. "I may take one to Miss Mae."

Honey flattened Dash's ruffled head of hair and chatted on as if she and Libby were college roommates planning their futures.

"Nikki and I are going to make a million dollars."

"You are?"

"Yep."

"That's a lot of lemonade."

"Yep."

"What are you going to do with all that money?"

"Buy a present for the new baby. And maybe a swimming pool. A big one."

There was a clunking noise next door.

Libby looked to see Camille tugging at an extension cord attached to a vacuum sitting by the parked family van. "What's your mom doing on this pretty Sunday afternoon?"

"Cleaning up after us," Honey reported matter-of-factly. She bent down, doubled over at the waist, to examine Dash's eyebrows before carefully, carefully tidying them. Dash kept his head still, his eyes looking upward following Honey's movements.

"Does your mom want help?" asked Libby.

"I don't think so. She told me, No, go help Nikki."

Libby could see Nikki struggling to drag a chair from their porch down to the sidewalk. "What's Nikki doing?"

"Building a better lemonade stand. She told me to go bother you."

The vacuum roared.

Camille had resigned herself to the heat. It was summer, she was very pregnant, and some things just had to be done.

Not everyone would have put vacuuming out a van on their must-do list, but here she was, the nozzle noisily sucking up cracker crumbs, bits of a paper birthday hat, the plastic leg off the miniature pony her oldest had begged for, and the green gummi bears her youngest hated. A scrapbook of her girls. Before Baby #3.

Camille arched her back in a stretch and regarded her children. Nikki, so grown up at nine; Honey, her baby, but not for much longer.

She let out a nostalgic sigh.

Now don't get all weepy, she admonished herself. You still have the back seat to do.

"Need any help over there?" Libby called out.

"Almost finished," Camille called back. "You're doing me a favor keeping certain little hands busy."

Libby gave a thumbs up.

"Hi there, ladies." Namita came out and into Honey's grooming salon. "Oh, Honey, I love your polka dot bathing suit. So cute. What's going on?"

"We're selling lemonade and I'm brushing Dashy."

"What a lucky dog. How about you, Libby? Going to your sister's for dinner?"

"Not tonight. They were invited up to the lake. Lazy day for me. Didn't see Mae after church. Promised her I'd visit."

"No sleuthing? No arresting any—" She caught Honey's ears perk up and curtailed her comment. "You know what I mean."

Libby not only knew but was itching to tell Namita her new speculations about Al, but ….

Camille fired up the vacuum again.

Namita stared at the pregnant woman wielding the defiant vacuum nozzle. "What is that Camille doing?"

"Nesting," replied Libby.

"Nesting?"

"Making a nest. Getting ready for the baby."

Given her current preoccupation with all things related to birth and babies, Namita leveled a keen eye on her neighbor. "Is that a real thing?"

Libby nodded. "My mom always said so. My sisters, too. Say they get this burst of energy near the end, this crazy desire to clean, sort cupboards, go through closets."

Honey stared at her mother. "Will my mom's nest be in the van?"

Namita and Libby stifled chuckles.

Libby reassured Honey. "It's just something people say. Birds make nests, but people just get things ready for babies. Make room."

Namita gave a cockeyed grin. "Most of my apartment could use some nesting work."

"Getting excited?" Libby asked.

"Tuesday's the day."

"Conception party still on for Monday?"

Ever the entrepreneur, Honey said, "You could have lemonade at your party."

"There's a good idea," said Namita.

Honey jumped up. "I can get it for you now!"

"Oh, no thank you, Honey," said Namita, starting down the steps, "I'm meeting friends for an art show. I'll get some later if you're not sold out."

The vacuum roar ceased.

Camille abandoned the machine and waddled over to a chair next to the lemonade stand.

Honey tore across the yard. "Hey, mom! Are you all done making the baby's nest?"

Before the story could get out of hand, Libby started after Honey.

"Don't forget the brush," Honey shouted.

"Nest?" said Camille.

"Nest-ing," corrected Libby as she joined Camille to watch Nikki make a sign for their business.

"Ah. Afraid so."

Camille turned and winked at Honey. "Did you tell Miss Libby about your surprise?"

Honey shot off into the house. "I just remembered it!"

Libby sat on the cement steps near the sidewalk and the stand.

Camille stretched her legs out. "How about a drink?"

"I'll take two cups, please."

Nikki jumped up and filled the order, carefully managing the pitcher.

"Thanks," said Libby. "I'll get them in a minute. Can I pay for them later?"

"Okay," said Nikki and returned to drawing her sign.

"Two?" asked Camille. "Thirsty?"

"Helping with their college fund. How about you? My treat."

"Thanks. I'm lemonaded out."

"Sure? You look a little flushed."

"Hormones. And wrestling that old vacuum."

"Should you be doing all that?"

Camille smirked. "It's that or make another pitcher of lemonade."

Libby looked more closely at her perspiring neighbor. "I was only going up to Mae's. Want me to stay out here with the girls? You go in and rest."

"I'm fine. I'll sit up on the porch." Camille's hands slid over the globe in her lap, then she winced trying to adjust her position.

Even though Libby knew this was the norm for really pregnant women, she was concerned. "Nick around?"

"Sales meeting in Arizona. He'll be back Tuesday. He fixed dinner before he left this morning. There's a park program tomorrow to entertain the girls, and we'll order pizza. I'm okay. Really. Go to Mae's. I've had the lemonade, so you're both safe."

Libby ignored the comment. "I have my cell. Call if you need me. Don't do anything crazy."

"You're the one going to Mae's. I should be telling *you* to be careful."

Libby took the jab good-naturedly, but secretly thought the phrase was starting to be grossly overused.

Out danced Honey. She held up a shiny black coil. "We got new bikes, and this is for a lock with a come vacation, so they never get stoled again."

"A lock? With a come… combination," Libby construed the meaning as the child flounced over and sat next to her.

"I've heard this part," said Camille, "I'm going in for short break."

Honey laid her new security gizmo at her side and picked up the dog's brush.

"Are you ready for the block party?" asked Libby. "Only five more days."

"That's why we got new bikes for the parade." Honey leaned in, lifted one of Dash's ears and confided, "Ours got stoled."

Honey continued to perfect her grooming method: brush fur, smooth fur. Brush fur, smooth fur. "Good thing we save money in Piggy. Daddy says, 'Bikes don't grow on trees. Don't like tomorrow money you don't have.'"

"Tomorrow mon—? To *borrow* money?" Libby checked to confirm this translation.

Honey nodded confidently. "Tomorrow money is tomorrow trouble. That's what my daddy says. Mine's pink. My bike. With a mermaid."

"How pretty."

"I might get to ride it to the library."

Conversations with Honey were always a delight, but mention of the library threw Libby back to thinking about the stolen money and Al.

Honey gave Dash's topknot a little flourish with the brush. "Isn't Dashy beautiful?"

"Yes, very," said Libby. "I think I'll take him down and show him off to Miss Mae." She snapped on the dog's leash.

"Can I use your brush to brush Major? He's in the house sleeping."

Honey jumped up. "I can make him beautiful, too!"

"Oh, Honey!" said Libby. "Are you okay?"

The black bike coil had left bright red marks on Honey's bare thigh where she'd been sitting on it to groom Dash.

Libby stared.

She remembered seeing those marks with the wavy, intermittent pattern.

Only one other time.

Generic.

One more generic possibility Grass had said of Mr. Motorcycle's cable.

As Libby walked toward Mae's, she kept telling herself that there were probably hundreds of black bike coils in the city just like Honey's. Generic. Non-specific.

Non-helpful.

Half of Libby's attention was focused on her steps, each made cautious by lemonade sloshing in the two cups and Dash's leash pulling where it was looped over her wrist.

The other half went to her mind, leaping to conclusions, then leaping to refute them.

A bike went by.

Libby watched it fly down the street. Just a rider. No one hanging on.

Her eyes widened. Her mouth went dry.

And then a score of pinballs was set loose.

A puzzle piece thrown on the table—all the metaphors colliding at one point: she *had* seen another black coil on Apple Street.

Libby's foot tagged a hump of sidewalk jutting up over a tree root.

She caught and righted herself, barely holding on to the dog and drinks.

She was antsy now.

She needed to do more than deliver this lemonade.

Because once a certain thought, a certain person, had dropped into Libby's consciousness, she could not let them go.

She knew they had *a* generic cord. Potentially *the* specific murder weapon.

Had they been around at the crucial hour?

And why? Why would they murder Jonah? Money? Prank?

Libby tripped a second time, bumping up the curb as she crossed over toward Mae's. She turned to make sure Dash was still in stride and spilled lemonade.

"What the heck are you drinking, Kinder?"

The comment startled Libby as it shot out from Mr. Randall, set back and tucked away on his porch.

Unnerved, she tried to cover by toasting her neighbor. "Lemonade," she said and made light of the spill by walking a straight line of sobriety up the sidewalk to where he was perched.

Mr. Randall dialed down the baseball game on his radio. "You know, we have open carry laws in Indiana. Although if it's good stuff, I won't turn you in. If you share."

"It really is lemonade. Sorry, one for me; one for Mae."

The striking white hair stepped out of the shadows and leaned over his perfectly painted railing. "Don't you think it's time for Mae to be somewhere … safer? Her mind has gotten all fuzzy." He fluttered his fingers to demonstrate. "Can't really trust anything she says."

"Now, Mr. Randall, you've lived next door to Mae for years. Most of that is Mae's quirky sense of humor."

He straightened up. "I love the old gal. Even so," he said, "I'm going to suggest it to her nephew next time I see him. She has plenty of money. No offspring to speak of. Mine?" he added with a sarcastic chuckle. "They've been draining the coffers since the day they were born." He fluffed the matching striped pillows, sat on his wicker love seat, and turned his game back up. "Now, you be real careful."

Libby nearly lost the rest of the lemonade. "Excuse me?"

Gesturing to her beverage, Mr. Randall pantomimed drinking. "I'm a good designated driver."

Be careful.

The warning was beginning not only to irritate Libby but to haunt her.

It only added to her agitation that she had to cross Jonah's front yard.

A house where someone is murdered has scars, and even a breezy Sunday afternoon could not undo the ominous feeling Libby had as she passed the empty rooms and lightless windows.

Jonah's tiny wind chimes sent up a ghostly jingle, and she hurried on, her mind shifting pieces of the puzzle, moving them around, turning them to fit together.

CHAPTER
THIRTY-FOUR

M ae carefully eyed Libby, who held out one of the cups of lemonade. "Better not be anything funny in there," said Mae.

"It's been checked out," Libby assured her. She took a seat across from the Sunday yellow sweater as Dash spun around twice and settled at her feet. She tried to sound casual. "Where did the sun go?" she asked, puffs of fluffy clouds mixing with the blue sky. Still, there's a nice breeze."

In the distance, the faint sound of fans cheering from Mr. Randall's radio rose and fell. "No baseball game for you today?" Libby asked.

"Double header. I'll watch them tonight."

Libby swirled the lemonade in her cup, the pinballs too active for small talk.

"Mae," she said, "what or who—exactly—did you see in the alley the night Jonah was murdered?"

"Oh, I don't remember."

"They've arrested Al Sparks. Was that who you saw?"

"I don't know that guy."

It was an answer Mr. Randall would have used as evidence against Mae's mental faculties. "Sure you do," pressed Libby. "What did you tell the police you saw?"

"Monster Man."

"Are you sure it was a man?"

"Yes, big."

"What about hair?"

"Of course, hair. On the top. Where it belongs."

"What color?"

"Too dark."

"The hair?"

"No. The night."

Was Mae being silly—or sharply and evasive? Libby wondered. Did she know more than anyone had been able to pull out of her? Yet. More than she was possibly aware she knew?

"How was he moving?"

"Walking."

"Slow or fast?"

"A little fast. Over there. In the alley."

Libby sat up and followed Mae's finger, pointing in the direction of Oak Avenue.

Dash lifted his head at Libby's abrupt movement. "Over there?" she asked.

Libby looked left and right. She wanted to be certain. "Not down the other way?"

"I need a taller fence," said Mae. "That one isn't high enough to keep things from flying over here. What do you think?"

Libby was still zeroed in on the alley, her answer absent-minded. "Maybe plant some bushes like you have on the other side. By Jonah's."

"No, they're too high. Bad as Goldilocks. That side's too low; this side's too high. Nice if they were just right, so that kid doesn't keep coming over to get his boomerang."

Suddenly Libby froze.

Mae wasn't describing some once-in-a-while event.

Out of the blue, the wind lifted Geoff Paterson's frisbee unpredictably as he tossed and chased it into view, apparently by himself, in his back yard just beyond the too-low picket fence.

Libby's pinballs slammed into each other and came to a halt.

She hadn't planned on confronting anyone until more evidence fell into place.

But here was Geoff.

Should she talk to him now? Get answers before jumping to any conclusions?

Or wait?

"Geoff said he'd trim those tall arborvitaes for me," said Mae. "For a tidy sum. He's a nice boy. Likes to make money. I think he's big enough. Maybe I'll let him."

The yellow sweater popped up. "I'm going to ask him right now."

Before Libby could intervene, Mae was at the edge of her porch calling, "Geoff! Geoff! Come over here, please."

"Hey, Mae! Just a second."

Mae went back to her rocker.

Libby, who'd never had time to move from her chair, scrambled to organize her thoughts.

But within minutes, the summoned teen was standing on Mae's back porch. Cradling his skateboard.

And holding a black bike coil.

"You just caught me," Geoff said. "Going down to see if Lagunas are home." He sat on the railing, leaning his skateboard against one of the posts. "Hi, Libby. Hi, little dog."

Libby watched him chat effortlessly. Watched him spring and unspring the coiled cord like a slinky toy.

"I asked you to stop playing with that."

Libby jumped at Paul's voice coming up the porch steps next to her.

Paul and Geoff.

Right here. Right now.

The opportunity.

"I was just going to ask Geoff where he got that," she heard herself say.

"I don't know," said Geoff with a shrug. "It was just sitting out on the kitchen counter one time. I figured Dad bought it for me. It's perfect for bike surfing. The spring is great."

"Sorry to interrupt here," said Paul. He waved his leather garden gloves toward the rocker and smiled. "Good afternoon, Mae."

He turned to Libby. "You can get bike cords anywhere. I don't even remember where I picked that one up." He gave a mock serious glare at Geoff. "It was originally meant to lock your bike with. Why, Libby? Need one?"

Mae returned Paul's wave. "I was going to ask your son if he wanted to earn some money trimming those old bushes. For work, I'll pay."

"Geoff'll be happy to trim them. Whenever you like. For free."

"Free?" Geoff stood, lodging his objection.

Paul countered with parental calm. "You don't need any money, Geoff."

"That's a change. Just because *you* don't think I need it."

The sun was blotted behind some large clouds, dropping shade over the whole yard and alleyway.

Libby waded in further.

"Mae and I were just talking about the night Jonah Pemberton was murdered."

Paul tucked his gloves into the side of his belt. He leaned against the tall post by the steps and folded his arms. "You're as bad as Louis. Always wanting to know what's going on with everybody. Maybe you should both let it drop since it's moot now that Al Sparks is arrested."

"Not completely moot," said Libby.

"Anything specific or is this just more playing detective?" He uncrossed his arms and stood forward. "Come on, son. Let's let these ladies have their Sunday afternoon back."

Hurry, thought Libby. They're going to leave.

She turned to Geoff. "Mae said she saw the Monster Man that night. I know you were out much earlier catching Punk. But what about later? We know somebody drove down this way about the time of the murder. He saw a person in the alley. Any chance you were out there?"

"Boy, people did say you were nosy," said Paul. "Look, the police have the killer locked up. Everyone knows Al was upset with Jonah's complaining about the noise those band kids—his kid—were making. Just went off the deep end. If Geoff saw anyone, it was Al Sparks."

Libby stayed seated; stayed calm. She nervously scratched the top of Dash's head and tried to keep her voice even. "It couldn't have been Al Sparks."

Paul looked perplexed. "What do you mean?"

"Was Geoff home when you got there after work?"

"No. Yes. What difference does it make?"

Geoff began, "I was—"

"Be quiet, Geoff."

Libby kept going. "Mae saw a male figure in the alley."

Paul frowned and glanced at Mae. "I'm sorry, old dear, but I can't always take what you say seriously. You do say some silly things."

"Hey," Geoff jumped in. "Don't hurt Mae's feelings."

Paul didn't seem to care, his words more deliberate. "Remember, if she saw anyone, she saw Al, whether you believe it or not."

"Al lives in the opposite direction," said Libby. "At the south end of the alley. If he killed Jonah, he would only have to come as far as Jonah's garage. Not past the garage. Not past Mae's bushes. Not this far down so she could see him."

Libby rose. She pointed north toward the Paterson house. "The Monster Man Mae saw was coming from there."

Paul looked but swung back around quickly. "Or further down. Could have been that kid with the motorcycle. Or anyone in any other house—beyond ours."

"They all have alibis. Weren't even around."

"I was around," said Paul. "Home from work."

Libby didn't let go. "Surprising someone from behind makes strangling a short affair. And he had time before you got home to do it."

Geoff looked from his father to Libby and back again. "Do what?"

"Nothing!" Paul said sharply.

"You think I killed Mr. Pemberton?!"

CHAPTER
THIRTY-FIVE

Suddenly there was questioning, defending, everyone talking over each other. Dash began barking.

Mae marched over to Geoff. "You killed Jonah Pemberton?"

"You're both crazy," said Paul.

Libby knew immediately this would be another blow to Paul. For the third time she was accusing his beloved son. But so much, so much finally made sense.

Sun and shadow fidgeted, disturbing the light in the yard.

Paul got louder. "You've been on this kid's case all summer. You're as bad as his mother. First the mail. Then the vandalism."

Libby turned to Paul and got louder, too. "He did criminal things!"

"They were pranks. They weren't murder! Come on, Geoff. Let's go."

Geoff stepped into the fray, facing Libby. "Why?" he asked.

Libby couldn't place the tone. Not nonchalance, the easy-going confidence she'd always witnessed from Geoff. At the moment, he seemed genuinely confused.

"Why do you think I'd kill Mr. Pemberton? He wasn't so bad. Most of the time." Geoff reared up defensively. "He wasn't nice to everybody, you know. But it wasn't enough for me to kill him."

In truth, this piece had not fallen into place yet for Libby. "Maybe for the money? Mrs. Thorne paid for all that vandalizing. Maybe this was just an opportunity to make more. A whole lot more."

Dash panted. Mae shook her head. "You said you'd do anything for money."

Geoff was now defiant. "Mrs. Thorne would never ask me to do that! She's a nice lady. Lonely. People do mean things to her. Mr. Pemberton even wrote letters to her family to get rid of her. To put her in a place for old people!"

The implication of the statement hit home hard.

Motive.

Libby knew it.

So did Paul.

He latched on to saving his child from saying anything more incriminating. "Stop talking, Geoff. Just stop!"

Geoff's defiance faded. "I didn't do anything, Dad. I swear."

"It's all right," Paul said, speaking to soothe his son even as the most threatening pinballs fell into their slots for Libby. "Nothing's going to happen to you," he said. "She doesn't have any evidence."

Child or no child, Libby bristled at Paul's attitude. This was not a prank. Not some juvenile mistake.

"What about this?" Libby reached over and flipped at the bike cord in Geoff's hand. "This morning Honey Montgomery sat on a cord just like this. It left a red welt on her leg. Red, irregular because of the way it coils. A mark I remember. On Jonah Pemberton's neck."

It was frightening for Libby to hear it said out loud, to imagine the murder, with the real weapon in front of her. And the real murderer. "We can all see Geoff's hands are calloused from when he used it."

Geoff unconsciously flipped them over as everyone stared, even

Geoff, who seemed to regard the rough palms as if they belonged to someone else.

Libby had never heard this father get angry.

Paul sneered. "Thanks to your payback plan, he got most of those callouses honestly. Besides, there a million cords like this."

"We'll see," she said. "Let the police decide if this is the cord used to choke Jonah Pemberton."

She reached for the weapon.

"Give me that!" Paul shouted.

He lunged for the cord, knocking Mae to the ground, sending her tiny body in one direction, her glasses in another.

Dash barked uncontrollably.

Geoff dropped the coil and bent to help the older woman. "Mae, Mae! Are you all right?"

When he looked over at his father, his face registered something Libby had never seen there: fear.

"I didn't do it, Dad. Tell them I didn't do it!!" He tenderly guided Mae back into the rocker. "I didn't kill him, Mae. Really."

Libby held on to her frantically barking dog. "Everything's okay, Dash. Sh-sh-sh. You're fine." She glanced toward the rocker; the yellow sweater being clasped at the neck by shaky, arthritic hands. "Are you okay, Mae?"

Geoff handed Mae her glasses. "Thank you," she managed.

For a moment, the barking stopped; Dash panted. No one spoke.

Libby found the reprieve confusing.

She petted Dash, as if he were a frightened child. Geoff was being no less gentle with Mae, and Libby caught herself second-guessing her suspicions. He was so sincerely earnest in his denial. Was he such a skilled liar? Truly a bad seed?

Or was she wrong again? Close, but not exactly on the mark? Her mind raced: gentle with Mae, so caring about Mrs. Thorne. Could Geoff really kill Jonah Pemberton? If Jonah had threatened Mrs. Thorne by telling her family she should be in a nursing home, how much was Geoff, like his father, terrified to lose someone he loved? How angry at the person who might cause such a thing?

Libby looked at Paul. He'd picked up the shiny black cord and was stretching it between his two hands. She saw the expensive garden gloves folded neatly, hanging over the belt at his waist.

Before the pinballs in Libby's brain had a chance to do more than begin careening again from side to side, Paul spoke.

His voice, low and steely.

"Leave him alone, God damn you."

Wind chimes jangled; a baseball game played on the radio.

"Geoff didn't do it. I did."

Silence.

Too much to take in.

To register.

The serene voice of Paul Paterson then went on as calmly and reasonably as if he had a family anecdote to relate.

"I only borrowed the money from the library. I had bills. The car. The gun Geoff wanted. Jonah kept it in that pouch, collecting it month after month. It was just library fines. Not like it was somebody's money for food or stolen from the payroll. What difference did it make if I … used it for a while?"

Libby found herself blinking, as if that would make sense of what she was hearing.

She felt cold and tense, like she needed to tiptoe, but Paul's eerily rational tone compelled her to ask, "Why didn't you just give it back? A week here or there couldn't have made any difference to Jonah."

"Almost five thousand dollars," Paul said. "Just sitting there. Day after day. I did. I told him I'd give it back. A week he gave me. Set a deadline. He was expecting it."

"On Friday," Libby said under her breath.

"Yes. Friday."

"Did you argue about it?"

"No. I had already argued. Pleaded. He didn't have a clue how demanding creditors can be. Calling all the time, showing up at the house. I thought he'd understand. That's when he got all righteous about it. All about God and justice. Set that stupid, unrealistic deadline. Said he'd turn me in to the police."

A weariness crept into Paul's voice. "I called everybody I knew. My own mother said, 'Enough is enough.' Nobody. Nobody would loan me any more money."

Paul swallowed several times. He began flexing the coil in and out between his hands, as if the rhythm calmed him.

It was difficult for Libby to watch, thinking of Jonah, thinking of the marks on his strangled neck. "Maybe the police would have understood," she offered quietly. "Couldn't you have worked something out?"

"It wasn't the money. Not even the debt. I've been in debt before. I've been in debt my whole life."

He looked at Geoff. "It wasn't the money. It was him. They would take him. The only child I have left"

Anger returned. The look in Paul's eyes got as steely as his voice. "Where's God's justice in that? To take one twin at birth and let the mother take this one now? She would have given me nothing—no rights, no visitation, no access! I couldn't. I just couldn't. God, damn you all!"

At each word, Paul pulled tight the bike cord.

Suddenly he was behind Libby. The cord at her neck.

Dash fell to the ground.

Mae shrieked.

Geoff rushed at Libby.

Choking, Libby's eyes bulged with horror. Geoff pushed against her, and she realized he was as strong as when she thought he could have strangled Jonah.

Libby grabbed at her throat, tried to gouge up under the cord, tried to kick at the bodies and limbs engulfing her, trapped between the two men. It didn't matter if they were caught. It didn't matter that the pinballs would drop into all the right slots. It would be too late. For her. For Mae.

Dash wriggled and flipped himself over, recovering enough for his terrier genes to kick in. He barked ferociously, snapped and bit at Paul's legs, then Geoff's.

At Libby's ear, Paul grunted, "Why didn't you stay out of this?"

In between Mae's whimpers, Libby heard Geoff shouting. "Dad! No! Don't. Please don't!"

The porch was too small. As Libby struggled, she stumbled over the chair. Pain slammed through her ribs as she dragged Paul and Geoff with her to the floor. The chaotic tumble was enough to make Paul lose his grip on the bike cord, allowing air to return fitfully to Libby's lungs.

Dash, snarling and biting, kept up his assault. When Libby realized Geoff was trying to subdue his father, she pulled the dog away, stifling his attack, but not his furious barking.

"Dad!" Geoff shrieked. "You can't do this. You can't hurt them!"

Panting. Everyone was panting.

Libby sucked in air, in and out as fast as she could.

Paul and Geoff wheezed from exertion.

Mae, visibly shook, each breath countering the adrenalin pulsing through her.

On the ground, pinned against the house by Geoff's body, Paul finally took in his son's voice. It was the adult, in-control voice Geoff had used with grownups all his life. "Please, Dad. Let them go."

And it was over.

Libby could not say how long the struggle had lasted. It was her sense that Paul was overcome as much by his son's appeals as he was by his son's youthful strength. She freed herself from the legs of the chair she'd fallen into. A small gash on her leg was bloody but not bleeding hard. She sat, leaned against the porch railing behind her, and looked to Mae, who had curled so far into her rocker that she looked like a small yellow pillow.

Paul and Geoff, not far away, untangled their limbs like two snakes.

All Libby could think of were so many warnings from so many people: be careful.

Dash was still on the alert, darting toward the men, then backing away to Libby's side, uttering his most guttural disapproval.

Libby fumbled for her cell phone. She needed, wanted help.

Not in her pocket. Must have fallen out in the scuffle.

Paul sat up against the house, brushed his arm, brushed his slacks.

Geoff leaned back on his heels. "Are you all right?" he asked his father.

Paul said nothing, but continued to straighten his clothes, smooth his hair.

"Dad?" Geoff asked again. "Are you all right?"

When Paul spoke, he, too, was in control.

"We'll just drive," he said. "I have a little library money left."

He smiled at Geoff. "We can tie them up." So pleased, as if he'd remembered to cancel the mail. "No. Wait. Take them with us."

Libby struggled to stand up. Her side ached. She was dizzy and slightly nauseous Her throat and lungs stung. Try as she might, no scream for help would come out.

Paul stood.

Dash went nuts, his barking more frenzied than ever as the man towered over the dog. Over Libby.

Libby was frantic. The chair was in her way. Paul was in her way.

She tried to get her bearings, considered a leap over the porch railing to run for help, find something she could use as a weapon ... get some—

"What's all this ruck—"

Libby didn't think she'd ever witnessed anything that truly happened in a flash.

Until she saw Detective Grass come around the side of Mae's house.

It was like one of those flip books, still photos clipped together so that when fanned through there's a sense of continuous movement, like a movie.

Action:

… the look on Grass's face, changing instantaneously from curiosity to on-guard alarm … the pulling of his gun, scanning the scene, locating each person … noting the overturned chair, the dog, the bloody leg, the cowering yellow sweater … registering the look of panic on Libby's face, a different kind of panic on Paul's.

In a flash.

For a moment, everyone froze. Stunned.

Then the interruption dissolved into the sequel:

… the son, numb and silent; the father with facile explanation and justification … the backups, the handcuffs, the rights read … the takeaway … the relief … the gratitude.

In a flash.

CHAPTER
THIRTY-SIX

"**D**oes that need stitches?"

Grass rested against the railing of Mae's porch. He watched Libby, sitting on the chair that had been righted, daub the gash on her leg with hydrogen peroxide, which Mae had brought out along with ointment and Band-Aids.

On the grass below, a uniformed officer waited for further instructions.

"It's not deep," Libby told Grass. "Fortunately, I'm up-to-date with tetanus. Thanks, Mae," she said, smiling at the yellow sweater, now back to rocking.

She turned again to Grass. "What about Geoff?"

"His mother was going to meet them at the police station. He wanted to ride with his dad. I saw no harm in it once Paterson was handcuffed and in custody."

Libby stared at Grass, still astonished by his materializing when he did. "How in heaven's name did you end up here?"

Grass folded his arms. "Didn't I tell you to trust me?"

"I know this is how police show up in murder mysteries, but I always thought it seemed a little contrived."

"It is," he said. He nodded at Dash. "You'll be happy to know that Mrs. Thorne called in to complain about that dog's incessant barking."

"Oh, Dash!" gushed Libby.

She involuntarily grimaced as she bent to pick up the dog, only then realizing how much she'd been banged around in the scuffle. It didn't keep her from burying her nose in Dash's neck. "You did call 911! Sort of. All those drills paid off!"

She hugged him again, kissed him several times, and let him gently slip back down. Within minutes his head hit his front paws and he seemed finally able to relax from being on duty.

Libby pulled off the thin paper covering on the Band-Aid adjusting its position. "But you, Detective, surely you've got more rank, more clout than to be taking calls from the Mrs. Thornes of the world."

"Thankfully, yes. Officers were already on a call nearby. When I saw that it was in this infamous block of Apple Street, I needed to see what else was going on. Since I'm not always informed directly," he added emphatically. "First, a pregnant lady down the block having trouble. Then Mrs. Thorne—"

"Oh, dear!" Libby broke in. "Camille! The pregnant lady. Is everything all right?"

"Don't know. I left them to come check out the reported ruckus down here. Afraid to imagine what was going on at Mae O'Malley's. Seemed a little too close to the poisoned iced tea incident not to find out."

"The pregnant lady's husband's out of town," Libby said, collecting her first aid supplies. "Maybe I should go down." She took quick stock of Mae. "Although I ... I kind of hate to leave things alone here. Just yet."

Grass glanced over his shoulder at the officer below him. "Jones. What was up with the pregnant lady?"

"Everything good when I left. Someone from next door said she knew the kids. Officer O'Brien located the husband, who's on his way home from Arizona. He gave the okay for this neighbor to stay with the kids. Somebody named *Bonita*?"

"Namita," said Libby. "Yes, she'll take care of things."

"They needed to get that lady to the hospital," said Jones.

Libby felt terrible not being able to help. "Poor Camille. Did she go to the hospital alone?"

"Are you kidding?" Jones scoffed. "Ten different neighbors showed up and offered. A nurse, tall African American woman, went with her."

"Francie," said Libby. "She'll be good. Yes. It's a good neighborhood."

Grass coughed. "With a few notable exceptions."

At the edge of the porch, escorted by another officer, Mr. Randall appeared. "I only wanted to give the lady her cell phone," he was telling the officer. "It keeps ringing, and I thought it might be important." He handed the phone to Libby. "Must have dropped it when you were juggling your … beverage."

Libby reached for the phone. She winced at the stretch. "Must have banged my ribs when I fell."

"Maybe you should get checked out," suggested Grass.

Libby pushed up and down her side. "I'm fine. Probably just be a little stiff for a while." She took the phone from Mr. Randall. "Thank you so much. No wonder I couldn't find it when things got crazy back here."

Mr. Randall put his hands in his pockets and jingled the coins there. "I wanted to come sooner. During the seventh inning stretch I turned the radio down, and I heard shouts and dogs, but by the time I got over here, the police wouldn't let me come any closer. What was going on?"

Grass explained the situation to Mr. Randall while Libby checked her phone texts.

Namita: *I think Camille is in labor.*
Namita: *Not good. Calling 911.*

Namita: *Francie with Camille to hospital. I'm with kids. Where are you?!*

Libby wasted no time texting back.

Libby: *Paul Paterson murderer. Arrested. Big tussle, but everybody OK.*

Namita: *!!!!!*

Libby: *Would like to stay with Mae till caregiver comes. Do you need help?*

Namita: *Stay put. Reading Honey and Nikki's complete library. Grandparent here in a few hours. Nick flying home when flights worked out.*

Libby: *How is Camille?*

Namita: *Don't know.*

Libby: *How when she left?*

Namita: *Scared.*

"Wow," said Mr. Randall. "Paul Paterson killed Jonah Pemberton. Took all that money from the library." He ran a hand through his wavy white hair. "You think you know your neighbors. Wonder if it would have made any difference if I'd loaned him money when he asked for it."

"He asked you for money?" Grass and Libby had the same question and issued it with the same surprise.

"Last year. Car problems, I think he said." Mr. Randall put his hands in his pockets again as if to make sure the money there had not gotten away. "But I was stiffed one time by a brother-in-law, and I decided never to get into that situation again. You know, the old thing about neither a borrower nor lender be?"

Or, thought Libby, Honey's version: *Tomorrow money is tomorrow trouble.*

After Mr. Randall was assured no other help was needed, he left.

Officer Jones was dismissed, and Mae began to nod off.

Grass dotted an i in his black notebook and directed his attention to Libby. "So. How did you know it was Paul Paterson?"

Mae's breathing had become regular enough to produce a soft snore, and Libby finally felt herself relax. She could tell she would be sore the next day, but for now, nothing was more comfortable than where she sat on Mae's back porch.

"How did I know?" She repeated, more to herself than anyone else, "How did I know?" Her smile was thin. "I didn't."

There was no other way to put it. "I believed it was Geoff—the son—again. He was our mail switcher and local vandal."

"Ah," said Grass, pieces of his own puzzle falling into place.

"I had also seen him bike surf up and down Apple Street, pulled by that black coil on his skateboard. I realized it must have been what the murderer used."

"What made the connection?"

"I'd seen Jonah's neck when I found him in the garage. This morning, similar marks showed up on the leg of the little girl next door after she'd been sitting on the same kind of coiled cord she'd gotten for her new bike. Really, I just happened to see them on Honey."

Grass couldn't help it. Yes, he was grateful Libby had uncovered the real murderer, especially saving him, as lead detective, the embarrassment and headache of going after the wrong guy.

But he was also slightly miffed. "The old 'dropped in your lap,' eh? And why didn't you call and tell me what you'd figured out?"

Libby was more than grateful that Grass had shown up when he did, but that did not mitigate how irritating he could be. "Why didn't you tell me the marks on Jonah's neck were from a coiled bike cord? Assuming your lab got that right," she blurted out. "All this might have occurred to me sooner. So much for trust."

"It did occur to us, and the lab did get it right. Eventually," adding the last word under his breath. "Sometimes it's necessary to withhold information from the public. We checked every house and garage in the area. Even more after you said you knelt on the combination lock that presumably went with it on the floor of Pemberton's garage. You must have really swatted it aside. Took my crew a lot of rummaging around to locate it. But the actual cord? Never showed up." He returned to under-his-breath delivery. "Until now."

Libby skipped taking delight in Grass's admission. She was more interested at the moment in loose ends. "Geoff said he found the bike cord on the kitchen counter. Paul must have strangled Jonah, still had the cord with him when he returned home, and just thoughtlessly set it down. Like Macbeth returning with the bloody daggers, wishing he'd left them at the scene."

"No wonder they gave such convincing alibis for each other," said Grass. "Paul lied outright, and Geoff legitimately covered for his father because he came home after the murder."

"But before Paul disposed of the cord."

"By the time Paul went to deal with it, Geoff had claimed it."

Libby had seen enough dynamics between this father and son to guess how that might have played out. "Believe me, if Geoff wanted that cord for his surfing, Paul would never have denied it to him."

"He may also have thought it was good camouflage," said Grass. "Hidden in plain sight."

"Hmmm," Libby agreed. "Classic."

"By the time we were looking specifically for that kind of coiled cord, I can probably figure that Paul's kid had gone to the mother's. He and the cord were out of the range we'd established. And of course, we did not see him in the neighborhood—the times he was around—to observe him using it. Like you were … privy to. In the right spot at a fortuitous moment."

Libby regarded Grass. And another poorly veiled suggestion about her being merely lucky. Not about the hours she'd spent following up leads with neighbors or questioning library staff; working on theories to clear Jonah's name, to find his killer.

She started to be miffed.

But she was also physically spent, relieved, and starting to get punchy with the strain of the day.

More importantly, she realized she was safe—in no small part because of Grass's arrival.

"Thank you," she said.

Although Grass's more sarcastic side usually prevailed, like Libby, he was relieved. In the end, he, too, had been in the right spot at a fortuitous moment. A murderer had been caught and people were safe.

"Thank you," he said.

CHAPTER
THIRTY-SEVEN

She'd been there all afternoon and now into the late evening. Long enough to play tea party, watch movies, learn songs by heart, read a million books, and settle several squabbles.

During one extended lull, while Nikki and Honey amused themselves unattended, Namita had stood at the living room doorway and thought about something she had only given lip service to prior to that moment: these two girls were full-fledged persons. They had desires and goals, points of view and philosophies—all these adult elements in miniature.

Fascinating.

A little after 9 p.m., Libby stood with Dash on the Montgomery's porch and looked in the front window.

Namita sat on the couch reading aloud from a large picture book. Honey, sleeping like one of Mae's bunnies, was curled under Namita's arm on the right; Nikki, awake, twirling a strand of hair and following the story, on Namita's left.

When Libby softly tapped at the glass, Major rose up from lying on the floor and barked. Namita hushed the dog and sent Nikki to the door.

"My mom's having the baby! They took her in an ambulance! We're waiting up for Grandma Dee Dee."

Even with Nikki's enthusiastic news flashes, Dash and Major's barks of greeting, Honey did not stir.

"She's been out like a light for over an hour. At least through four of these," said Namita, adding the book she held to one of the piles stacked up on the coffee table in front of her. "On the other hand, Big Sister here might outlast me tonight."

The room looked as if Nikki and Honey had provided plenty of entertainment for Namita's babysitting marathon. On the table by the books, DVDs mingled with CDs. A doll house on the floor, emptied of all its furnishings, appeared to have a tiny garage sale in progress. Dress-up clothes and shoes were jumbled in with stuffed animals attending the tea party.

Libby bent to scoop together several magazines and coloring books from a chair to make room for herself. She did her best to ignore the ache in her side and sat while Nikki, standing inches away, rattled on. "Mommy got a bad pain, and I had to call the police emergency. I had to tell them my address. Very. Very. Slowly. Honey was afraid. I was brave."

"You were brave," said Libby. "Did you call Namita, too?"

"Mom said go get Miss Francie first. Major was barking and people were coming to help and then Namita came and then the police came. They called my Dad and Mom went in the ambulance and Namita fixed dinner and read books and we watched two movies."

Libby registered appropriate awe. She cleared her throat and smiled at Namita. "Sounds like good practice for motherhood. Kind of like never forgetting how to ride a bike."

"Not a bike I ever rode much. Remember, I'm an only child. Never did do a lot of babysitting." Namita curved her arm around Honey and gave her a gentle squeeze. "Adorable when they're sleeping, aren't they?"

Nikki danced back to Namita. "I got a new bike."

"That's what I heard. You know, Nikki, your Grandmother Dee Dee will be here in a little while. I think you should have your pajamas on. Maybe even be in bed."

Nikki knelt and started sorting and re-piling the books into a tower on the coffee table. "I wanna wait."

Namita gave a reluctant sigh and looked at Libby. "Nick's mother is on her way. Thinks she'll be here around ten. But wait—" Namita's eyes widened with concern. "What happened at Mae's?! How did Paul get caught? Who figured it out? And what's with the Band-Aid on your leg? Ooh, is it the light or is your neck all red?"

Libby gave a self-conscious touch to her neck. Nikki's interest was piqued, and she unleashed her own barrage of questions. "Who caught Mr. Paterson? How did they do that? How did you hurt your leg? Want me to call the ambulance for you?"

Libby threw up her hands in surrender. "I'm fine. Mr. Paterson is fine. Even Mae is fine. The caregiver is with her. And it's just a little cut on my leg."

Nikki seemed satisfied, and Libby shifted to let loose another flood of questions. "First, what's happening with Camille? The baby? What's the latest? Have you heard from Francie?"

Namita's look of concern took on a shade of anxiety. "We haven't heard anything."

"We haven't heard anything," echoed Nikki, then became engrossed in a new organizing principle for her coffee table library.

Namita softened her voice, trying to sound more casual. "Francie said she'd text, but last I heard they were hoping that bedrest and drugs would hold the baby off."

Libby nodded. "Maybe something just got jostled cleaning out the van."

"Remind me not to do any nesting. Or cleaning," said Namita.

Nikki kept filing her books. "Why won't they let the baby come out?"

Libby and Namita exchanged looks. Nikki appeared occupied, but it was obvious she was paying close attention.

Libby adjusted her explanation. "It might be too early. The baby might need more time to grow."

"Can't it grow outside my mom?"

"It can," said Libby.

It was too late for Libby to determine what facts of life Camille and Nick had imparted to their kids. She opted for a simple, plausible alternative.

"Maybe your mom just pulled a muscle or got a bruise somewhere."

Nikki popped up and stood tall, all attention. "I'm growing taller." She hopped across Namita's legs and tussled Honey's hair. "Honey's growing, too."

It surprised no one that this woke Honey up. The child stretched out of her bunny ball, half whimpering as she tried to verify her surroundings. Her hair looked backcombed like the way she brushed Dash's; her cheek red where it had been plastered against Namita's side. While Namita had been sufficient comfort in the interim, it was now definitely, "Where's my mommy?"

Nikki jumped in with her version of things. "She's still in the hospital growing the baby some more. Daddy is finding a plane. And Dee Dee is coming."

Honey rubbed her eyes. "How do you grow a baby?" She yawned. "I'm thirsty."

Libby stood, happy for the change of topic. "So am I!"

"Me, too! Me, too!" Namita and Nikki joined the chorus.

When Libby added, "So is Dash," Honey bolted from her warren, sending Nikki's tower of books flying across the living room floor, into the garage sale and tea party. Honey wasn't deterred and once on Dash's level,

325

showered the dog with affectionate pats and kisses. "Oh, Dashy," she crooned, then gave no less affection to Major. She put on an instructive voice. "But just water. No lemonade."

Lights on in the kitchen and a late-night buffet ensued, its offerings dictated by the Montgomery girls. Libby and Dash had not had supper; the little girls had but were hungry again. Namita couldn't remember what or when she'd eaten, and Major was eager to chow down any food any time it was put in his bowl.

Daddy's hamburger and noodle casserole was reheated a second time; carrots and celery and cucumbers set out with a yogurt dip. Honey dragged a chair to the sink and helped Namita wash purple and green grapes. Nikki located her favorite crackers to go with the cheese Libby cut.

Conversation revolved around favorite books, favorite songs, and new bikes. No further mention of mommy or baby or the capture of a murderer down the block. Instead, the girls were engaged dreaming up suggestions for some party Libby and Namita were organizing for Tuesday night. It seemed at their age a party could be thrown together at any moment. A reason for it was not necessary; half the fun was in the planning.

Fortunately, the eating and planning and frivolity were winding down when Grandma Dee Dee arrived. Nikki and Honey ran to the door when the bell rang but had hardly gotten their effusive hellos out when they were admonished by the new adult. "Why are you girls still up? Not even ready for bed?"

"Let's go, kids," said Namita, scooting the girls upstairs to remedy the situation, with Major and Dash trailing behind.

It was always a little jarring for Libby to remember that she and Grandmother Dee Dee were almost the same age. For the most part, Libby found Dee Dee Montgomery polite, if not a little aloof. Tonight, a little insensitive to her grandchildren as well.

On the other hand, watching the woman set down a small paisley travel bag in the dim hallway, even in her pressed capris, print blouse, and neat blond hair, Libby thought Dee Dee looked weary.

Libby, after confronting a murderer who had tried to choke her to death and being worried about a friend and her baby, could identify with weary. She tried to empathize with Dee Dee and pushed herself to be pleasant. As simple as they were, hospitable words took effort.

"How was your drive?" she asked.

"Long."

"Are you hungry?"

Libby led Dee Dee to the kitchen and continued to offer what was on the menu. "There's still some noodle casserole. Fixings for a sandwich? A salad?"

Libby stopped to catch Dee Dee staring at the island in the center of the room cluttered with half-eaten cucumber sticks; a line of grapes, artistically alternating purple and green; several small stacks of cheese and crackers. Lots of plates and napkins and crumbs.

"My. What a big mess you have."

Right out of a grim fairytale.

Libby promptly forgot the fun she'd been having with the little girls.

Forgot pleasant.

Went past peppery, heading toward pissed.

She directed all her energies to swiping food into the trash, bagging fruit, loading the dishwasher. And stifling all spoken interaction lest some snide version of "you're welcome" or "no, no problem for Namita to spend hours watching the kids"—all ready to spill out.

The other woman got herself a glass of water.

Namita came down to report sleeping children. Libby hugged Dash and Major effusively, their wagging tails and friendly faces a welcomed contrast to Dee Dee's sour demeanor.

Libby gave a final, determined swipe of the island and hanging up the dish cloth, calmed down enough to speak to the only important thing she wanted to get from Dee Dee. "Have you heard from Camille?"

A sterile report.

"They put her on bed rest to see if they could slow things down. Nick booked a flight and will take a cab directly to the hospital. I'll stay the night with the children and see where things are in the morning."

Dee Dee finished her water. She addressed Namita. "I certainly hope those girls sleep through the night after eating so late and then going to bed late as well."

Libby didn't trust herself to keep being civil. She was tired and wanted to get out of there. "It is late," she agreed. "We should go. Besides, I need to walk Dash."

Namita reassured Dee Dee. "I'm sure they'll sleep fine."

As they passed the living room, Dee Dee gave it a silent glare.

Libby was finished. "The girls can pick things up tomorrow."

Namita didn't even stop to look. "I wouldn't bother. They'll get it all out again, I can assure you. Come on, Libby. I have to take Paji out, too."

"I tried. But I wasn't very nice," said Libby, waiting for Dash to take his turn watering the corner bush after Paji had marked it as his. "She didn't seem to try to be nice at all."

Namita yawned. "She was a little contrary. I'm sure she's just worried about Camille and the baby. Plus, she had to rush around to get down here tonight."

True, thought Libby. It did not, however, put a dent in her irritation.

"And she's not real young," Namita added.

Libby nearly shrieked. "We're almost the same age! That's not so old."

Namita put her arm around Libby. "You're not old. And I'm sure you were nice. Dee Dee's just … efficient."

"I guess."

Libby took in deep breaths of fresh air. "Maybe she's on medications."

"She's what?"

"That's Francie's go-to line of explaining a person's behavior."

"I see," said Namita.

Sunday night on Apple Street was quiet. It was late and dark.

Libby sighed. "Do you think Dee Dee knows how she's being, that she chooses to be … efficient instead of friendly and gracious? Nice. Or is it just how she is? Her nature?"

"Ah. The old Nature vs. Nurture."

"I know my nature is to flip out sometimes. But I work hard to counter that. At least I try."

"Maybe this is what Dee Dee trying looks like."

Libby stopped and looked at Namita. She had to think about that.

"Libby. You are a nice person," Namita said with conviction. "You're nice to me. Nice to Mae."

"You're easy. Mae's easy. Mrs. Thorne—not so easy. Grandma Dee Dee …."

"Maybe not everyone deserves nice. You cleaned up that whole mess in the kitchen. Looked like a miracle when I came down. All the dishes. Dishes from before we even got there. I would have left some of that."

"I wasn't being nice. I was mad the whole time."

Libby's gestures got more animated. She threw out one hand after the other. "Mad at myself for not being more pleasant and understanding. Mad at Dee Dee for being … ungrateful." Her voice began to climb. "You took care of those girls. For hours. Fed them. Entertained them. She should have seen that."

Namita laughed outright. "You're so funny. I usually pick one. I can be mad at myself for something. *Or* the other person. The way you work it, you can't ever relax. Somebody's always wrong."

Libby's shoulders sagged. "You think I'm being too judgmental?"

"Look," said Namita, today, I did what I wanted to do; what I thought was helpful. I was glad to sit with those kids. I didn't think about it being right or wrong, good or bad. Nice or not nice. I didn't, and still don't, really care about how Dee Dee sees things. She's a big girl. She doesn't like that living room mess, she can pick it up or help the kids do it. She wants them in bed earlier, more power to her. I think we all start somewhere—and not everyone at the same spot—and progress from there. Hopefully in a positive direction. How much is just nature and how much is choice, I don't know. I try to let that stuff go."

Libby tugged gently at Dash to keep moving.

Another yawn from Namita. "This is all a little too deep for me tonight. Besides, I only have enough energy to hear about you catching the killer."

Libby was happy to change the subject.

"The path only led to Paul because of Geoff. I was really convinced it was Geoff. Big, strong enough; had that bike cord; had the opportunity as a kid on his own, alone, waiting for his father the night of the murder. Had access to the money, either at the library or on Jonah's bench in the garage."

"Certainly spent a lot of the summer with Bad Seed written all over him. Would Paul really have let his kid take the blame for murder?"

"Geoff's being in danger was the one thing that made Paul own up. According to Paul, Jonah had no right to demand the money back, or at least not put what he considered an unreasonable time limit on returning it."

As they rambled by habit toward the park, Libby filled Namita in on Paul's financial woes. "He apparently owed money like crazy. Instead of cutting back, he just spent on what he—or Geoff—wanted and then tried to hit up everyone he knew for his debt. He'd drained his relatives, his ex; had asked Mr. Randall, Mae—"

"Mae?!"

"Very sneaky with Mae. Said he'd pick up groceries or drug store items for her. Wanted cash. The caregiver caught on early when not all the items showed up. Mostly thought it was Mae confusing things until Grass suggested otherwise tonight. Grass said that even when given the chance, Paul didn't pay this huge water bill. The water had actually been turned off.

"He told Geoff it was a plumbing problem he couldn't afford to get fixed; he tells the neighbors it's a city water main problem. Geoff showers at the neighbor's, he waters his yard and gets his drinking water by pretending to water Mae's things. God knows where he showered."

"Could have gone to a gym or splashed around enough in the library restroom," said Namita. "We have homeless folks at the university who do that. Or it's hot enough, he could have just hosed himself off in his back yard or garage."

Libby took a moment to imagine the lengths Paul had gone to.

"So much work to hide everything. I almost feel sorry for him," said Namita. "Debt is really demoralizing. And it can be like quicksand once you're in it. But come on, tell me about what happened to your leg. And your neck."

At the park, they found a bench facing the pond. In the summer, a fountain in the middle was lit with pastel lights. On warm nights, it sent out a refreshing mist and lulled watchers with the steady pshhhh of its spray.

It seemed an incongruent background as Libby explained Paul's admitting that he had murdered Jonah. "Then came the attack on me. It's scarier than I can tell you," she said, staring at the fountain. "Being choked. Terrifying. But it happens so fast there's no thinking about it. You just fight for your life and nothing else is on your mind. I didn't even know I fell or got that cut."

Libby's throat went dry reliving the moment. She cupped her hand over her mouth then wiped the sweat that had collected on her upper lip.

"Before that, before the choking," she said, searching for a description, "it was … creepy. Paul was creepy. On the spot, he cooks up this plan to run away. To tie Mae and me up and just run away. When you stand next to someone who is so calmly irrational …. It's frightening."

Until Dash jangled his tags as he re-circled the grass he had chosen,

Libby had been lost in the retelling. She reached down, and with effort picked up her dog, and snuggled him profusely in her arms. "Thank goodness for Dash! My hero. Barking and attacking and calling the police!"

Namita joined in the petting fest of Dash, then leaned over and included Paji. "Such good dogs."

"And Geoff," said Libby, stroking Dash down his back, out to the end of his tail. Geoff really did save us. So ironic. Paul hellbent on giving Geoff things, scared he was going to lose him to his ex, then doing the very dangerous and stupid thing that ends up causing exactly that."

"Is that what happens to Geoff? He goes to his mother full time?"

"Grass said that would likely be the outcome. He's fifteen. In few years he'll have adult status and can decide for himself."

"Ironic, too," said Namita, "that it was Geoff, the one Paul stole and killed for, who stopped him. Caught him really. Kind of sad."

They watched the fountain, feeling the wind that carried the smell of flowers and grass and pond over them.

Then they headed home.

"How soon do you think they'll let Al Sparks out?" asked Namita.

"I didn't even ask," said Libby. "I sure hope he never finds out I had any part in suggesting he might be Jonah's murderer. I just felt I had to tell all the things that were, at the time, pointing in his direction."

"You did have a lot of scuttlebutt to unload. Besides, it's not your fault Al waved a club at the police."

Libby sighed. "That probably did as much damage as anything I feel guilty about divulging."

"You *and* the boyfriend," said Namita. "Personally, I think you did the kid a favor. He would never have gone to the police on his own, and from what you described, he was totally conflicted over what he did know."

It was slow going on Old Orchard. The breeze had stayed behind in the park. Each step was like lifting lead feet. Libby's neck smarted, the cut on her leg stung, and the muscles in her side were beginning to stiffen. She no longer cared about being nice or getting old; about catching murderers or letting suspects off. She was tired.

"Nobody's ever tired in murder mysteries," she said. "They stakeout somebody all night on one puny cup of coffee. They literally run for their lives, wrestle guns from killers, and fight off guys choking them. Then, even at 3 a.m., they have wild sex or go out to dinner. Fix an omelet. I guess once in a while there's curling up with a brandy by the fire." She was mumbling now. "Me? I just want to be home in my own bed."

Soon after, right before that wish became a reality, Libby's phone lit up with a brief text.

Francie: *Nothing yet. Camille resting. Just waiting. Nick on his way. Will stay till he arrives but won't bother you any more tonight. Say some prayers.*

CHAPTER
THIRTY-EIGHT

Monday morning. BabyCakes and Dash put out their wake-up call early.

Too early.

Dash got a run in the back yard instead of a walk. BabyCakes was content with a minimal amount of attention. And food. There was light and birds and grant work to do, but Libby, who was sure she'd caught the flu, pulled the blinds, flipped to the cool side of her cotton pillow, and crawled back into bed.

Even in decadent youthful days, Libby was not one to sleep late. By nine thirty she was up, a little more refreshed and drinking strong coffee instead of tea.

Libby did not have the flu. More than her ribs ached, and her assaulted neck—courtesy of Paul Paterson—made every swallow of the usually smooth, home-brewed coffee remind her of the experience of the day before.

She sat out back with her coffee and for long, lazy minutes watched yellow and brown finches eat modestly from the tubular feeder, pecking at holes too small to allow them to be gluttonous. Not so the nuthatches and sparrows, scrapping for every morsel on the ledge of their suspended feeder, swinging and competing as they stuffed themselves.

Before Libby could hit the shower, the sound of the girls, chattering next door as much as the birds, drew Libby out front.

"Mommy had a baby! We got a baby!" Honey squealed and clasped onto Libby's legs just missing the bandaged gash.

Major barked at the edge of the Montgomery porch, and Nikki raced over brandishing a long pole. She circled Libby, pumping the stick in the air like the drum major of a marching band, joining Honey's cheer: "We got a baby! We got a baby!"

"How exciting," said Libby, adjusting to keep her balance. "Boy or girl?"

"A girl! A girl! A baby sister!"

Libby didn't need to ask any questions. Nikki and Honey were too full of answers to bother with such preliminaries.

"Mommy's very tired," said Honey, all seriousness and concern. "She and the baby are going to stay and sleep at the *house little.*"

Nikki butted in. "She needs to grow more. Just like you said."

"We didn't put a name on her yet," Honey offered. "I like Marigold. Or Morning Glory."

Nikki sniffed. "Those are dumb."

"I kind of like them," said Libby. "What about Tomato? Or Parsley? Parsley Montgomery?"

Honey thought these were wildly hilarious and giggled rapturously, while Nikki stood at attention to announce that "Mommy says wait till we see her to pick a name."

"Is that a fishing pole?" Libby asked, examining the rod at Nikki's side.

"Dee Dee said I could bring it. Papa's going to take me fishing."

"I'm fishing, too," declared Honey.

"You're too little."

"I am not."

"Be quiet!" Dee Dee was speaking to Major, still barking at the edge of the Montgomery porch next door, but her reprimand was loud enough and cautionary enough to stop Nikki and Honey in their tracks.

Not to mention Libby.

By the time Dee Dee reached the three of them, she wasn't as loud, but was still in command mode. "Nikki, I told you to put that pole over by the car. Honey, you can take Frog or Bear, but not both. And set out your bathing suits."

The two children rushed away with the buzz of preparation, leaving the two women standing in the front yard. Namita had told Libby that the girls only got excited about visiting this set of grandparents because their grandfather was fun and crazy about kids, certainly more than Dee Dee.

In the light of day, Libby granted that not all grandparents were doting like her own mother, like her sister Jane. Or Francie. Or even Bin.

She admitted that neither of her own grandmothers had been the cuddly type but showed more affection, albeit in their own way. One was civic-minded and socially busy, making sure they saw live theater productions; the other let them watch her crochet, do crossword puzzles, and taught them to cheat at euchre.

"Looks like a trip to Grandma's," said Libby.

"Just a few days."

"How's Camille? How did everything go?"

"C-section. After a long night. I knew she was in trouble the last time I saw her."

Libby was immediately apprehensive. The weight of that answer piled anxiety on top of the foreboding that had started with Camille's fall last June. It had visited often throughout the summer like the blue jay that landed periodically at the edge of her birdbath, frightening the other birds with his puffed chest, his long sharp beak, and menacing screeches.

"And the baby?"

"Some complications."

Screech. Screech.

Libby's heart sank. She thought again of her own mother not caring about anything but that her babies be healthy.

As Dee Dee turned to go, Libby rushed to get what information she could.

"Can Camille have, or does she even want visitors?"

"I'd wait."

"Are you taking Major?"

"No. Nick will be in and out."

"Will the girls be back for the block party on Saturday? They've been looking forward to it all summer."

"We'll see."

It was the dreaded adult "We'll see"—more full of *probably no* than *probably yes*.

Dee Dee left.

Libby's phone buzzed with a text.

Namita: *Forgot church meeting after work. OK to move concep. party to 7? Nothing fancy. Can you walk Paji @ 5? Text if not OK. Thx.*

As Libby trudged back and up the steps to her own house, murders and babies and children, parties and parks and walking dogs—continued to wear on her, and her feet went lead again. She stumbled and knocked over Namita's flats of dead and dying plants, sending dirt and black plastic containers across the porch.

Screech. Screech.

Out of the shower, Libby saw another message on her phone.

Francie: *Left before Camille's C-section. Too much to text. Heard it was a girl. Details when I see you. Busy day.*

Prompted by Francie's message, Libby set the proofread nurses' grant proposal on the buffet table near the back door to deliver later. She, too, had a busy day on the agenda. For the time being, she took a conference call, then prepared for and went to a long meeting with one of the university's grant underwriters.

Off to the store. Ice cream and pickles for fun; fancy petite sandwiches plus cheese and white wine spritzers for sustenance. Libby was content with generic napkins and balloons when none with conception party themes could be found; a bag of sperm-like gummi worms would have to carry the theme.

At 7 p.m., the partygoers arrived: a friend from work, one from church, a couple Namita had known forever, and Libby.

Namita had hurriedly pushed things aside to make room for people to sit, having already cleared one end of the table for the food Libby had brought. The unexpected babysitting the night before had quashed any time or inclination of Namita's to clean. In the end, the excitement of The Appointment on Tuesday, the comfort level of close friends, and the festive mood overall softened her concerns about having a scrubbed and tidy venue.

"Wow, Namita," teased the husband of the couple she'd known forever, "You sure have a lot going on. Guess we haven't been over lately." He stood at the edge of the living room area which ran across the front of the apartment, a tiny kitchen to the left. Canning jars were part of the pushed-aside items on the food table, joined by a pressure cooker, ladles, immersion blender, and dozens of tomatoes and green peppers on towels awaiting transformation.

"I'm doing salsa again," Namita proudly announced. "Might try spaghetti sauce this year. Branching out."

The church friend wandered into the room. "I didn't know you played the flute." She eyed an instrument standing next to its open case. Whether it was going in or coming out was uncertain.

"Haven't for about two years. I need to look for a new instructor," said Namita, then turned to show off a box of alpaca yarn she'd ordered to support Third World women starting businesses. To be knitted into Christmas presents. There were the labels she'd collected for the church fundraiser next to books for the block party read-a-thon she was hosting.

The wife of the couple cast a practical eye about. "Namita, dear, you know you're going to have to make some room for the baby?"

Namita let out a slow moan, deflated but not defeated. "I know," she said. Then brightened. "I'm hoping that nesting instinct kicks in when I'm pregnant."

The church friend admired triangles of material cut for a quilt already underway. She laughed. "You may need to start a little sooner."

The wife gave Namita a supportive hug. "We'll help. We know you're a free spirit and creative soul."

"In so many areas," added the husband with a wink.

Libby looked with new eyes at her renter's space. Where was that baby going to fit in?

Namita had lived upstairs long enough to become a friend, companion, and vital sounding board for Libby; walking the dogs together, literally and figuratively in all kinds of weather. She was intelligent, helpful, generous, and easy-going. But Libby also saw her friend at times untethered to schedules, unhampered by thinking things all the way through, which could yield spur-of-the-moment fun—or chaos.

Then again, thought Libby, in the words of the woman herself, Namita was a big girl. She wasn't the first free spirit to have a child. It wasn't the way Libby would have done it, but this was Namita's choice, Namita's life. And she did have so many wonderful qualities to pass on.

"Put me down for salsa!" exclaimed the husband of the couple as he started to pull a chair out from the table, bumping tomatoes into motion and onto the floor.

There was laughter and scrambling to catch the rolling salsa ingredients. "You know," said the husband, "it's so beautiful out, I vote we take our party down to the park. Conception picnic!"

Perfect.

They paraded merrily to the park and spread blankets on the grass overlooking the pond. They broke out wine, cheese, and sandwiches—saving pickles and ice cream for dessert when they returned.

Namita reveled in the buoyancy she felt surrounded by friends. They had been there for her in the past and would be there for whatever came next. She let all the apprehension regarding the huge shift about to take place in her life vaporize with the misty spray of the pond fountain, shimmering with sunset golds.

Libby raised her glass to toast with the others. She smiled at Namita, blushing with wine. And at all the verbal and visual jokes about gummi sperms.

That night before she retired, Libby picked a small bouquet of black-eyed Susans and yellow snapdragons and set them next to a good-luck note—plus one gummi worm—on the mail table in the hallway for Namita to see before she went to work.

And to other appointments.

Libby spent Tuesday morning on her grants. And checking her phone for any update from Namita, who was apparently keeping herself too busy to reply.

By late afternoon, Libby set off for practice at the library. After all that had happened, she was anxious to connect with Louis and fill him in on how things had turned out.

She went by way of Jonah's alley to put out fresh water for the bees.

It meant passing the Sparks' garage. And wondering about Al. She'd heard he'd been released, although no one had seen him.

It meant standing outside Jonah's garage, looking towards Mae's. Looking at those fateful bushes and knowing that behind them Mae was undoubtedly sitting in one of her many-colored sweaters, once again rocking serenely on her back porch.

It meant shaking her head to see how many dead bees lay along the property line that Mr. Randall had sprayed.

And it meant looking at Jonah's house as she filled the water bucket, knowing that the whole place would sooner or later go up for sale. Jonah and his daughter would become neighborhood ghosts, permanently departed, permanently removed from the block party directory.

She had eventually found Jonah's bee garb in the garage and now slipped the veiled hood over her head like an authentic beekeeper. It was hot work, but there was growing satisfaction and peace in the effort. She had become attached to the bees, as much as to the birds in her yard, to Dash and BabyCakes.

The Happy Trio was camped out in their traditional spots on porch ledges and steps, so engrossed in their books and notebooks that she had to speak before they realized she was there.

"Hi, kids. What's going on? Back in school yet?"

Sarah looked up and replied with breathless joy as if she'd been asked how soon they were landing on the moon. "Yes, but today we're writing our own murder mystery!"

Simon bookmarked his place and echoed his sister's enthusiasm. "Think of all the stuff we know about now—the mail stakeout, discovering a vandal!"

With obvious pleasure, Ann touted the highlight of their portfolio. "And murder! Right here on Apple Street!"

Simon had reporter questions for Libby. "Did you talk to the police? Were you there when they arrested Mr. Paterson? Did he confess, or did they figure it all out ahead of time? We heard you and Mae got hurt."

Sarah popped up and stood on the nearest ledge to examine Libby's neck. She pointed gingerly. "Is that where it happened?"

Ann joined her sister, on tiptoes to see.

Sarah's reaction was serious. "I don't want a lot of blood in our murder. Too messy. Choking is kind of yukky, too."

"Yeah. Gross," said Ann.

Libby had no opposition to that evaluation.

"Poison is always good," said Simon. "No blood. No gun shots to give it away. Lots of mysteries have people getting poisoned."

Sarah began fleshing out the particulars of using this method. "Remember, at camp they told us some plain old ordinary plants are poisonous? The ones with the little bells."

"Foxgloves," said Simon.

"Rhubarb leaves," said Ann.

Sarah put a finger to her cheek and furrowed her brow in consideration. "Hmm… *Death by Rhubarb*," she proposed. "Is that a good title?"

Libby had heard lamer ones. "I like it," she said.

Simon got on a roll. "*The Rhubarb Murders. The Secret Rhubarb* … no, no … *The Mysterious Rhubarb. Caper.* I like *caper*."

Libby liked them all but had other things to do. She excused herself, leaving the Trio to their imaginations.

Libby's imagination had also been pricked.

Poison. From ordinary plants. As a gardener, Paul would easily have known this. Could he have brewed up something at home, slipped it into Mae's ubiquitous pitcher of tea? Something mild in taste. And effect— except on Mae, who is fragile, who might be harmed more critically?

Libby stood still for a moment. A residual pin ball showed up.

What about Mae's cut hand? Had Paul given that sharp knife to Mae with a more sinister purpose the night they were cutting up an apple? Did he help guide it a little too forcefully into Mae's hand?

No one would probably ever know if Paul had been trying for some time to get his old, too-observant neighbor out of the picture.

Permanently.

CHAPTER
THIRTY-NINE

It was the end of August. Since June, the James Whitcomb Riley Library had lost two-fifths of its staff—its manager murdered; its assistant, arrested for that murder. As stunning and disruptive as this must have been, everything in the place, outwardly at least, appeared to be functioning as normal.

Pleasant weather outside meant a relatively quiet afternoon inside. Bin anchored the front desk; J'az roamed, assisting the few people at computers. A small number of patrons browsed. No babies or children; no older kids.

Except Harry.

When Libby tilted her head, she could see him not far away between stacks of non-fiction, picking through volumes at eye level and seemingly muttering to himself.

It was hardly the oddest thing Libby had seen a teen do, especially since half the time kids had earplugs in and were jamming along to some private concert. But there was Harry. Hmmm ... no ear—

Whoa! Suddenly Louis was standing at Libby's elbow whispering, "You're only getting one side of the story." He crooked his finger, bidding her to follow him a few steps to the right.

From this vantage point, Libby could see the other side of non-fiction. In a similar stance, quietly speaking, not to the books or herself but past them—to Harry—was Heather, her long red hair hiding her face, but not her identity.

"Romeo and Juliet," whispered Louis with a nudge.

"More like *Midsummer's Night Dream*," said Libby out of the corner of her mouth. "Talking through Pyramus and Thisbe's chink in the wall."

The two adults crept back toward the library's main area. With so little activity to absorb the teens' conversation, Louis kept his voice down. "Can't decide if they've been forbidden to see each other and this is the clandestine destination or if they're just ironing out their relationship. Got the impression it's been going through some upheaval."

"Have they been here a lot?" asked Libby.

"Almost every day. Since her father was arrested. We all kind of pretend not to see them."

Libby smiled—at the thought of the kids thinking they were sneaking around undetected and the thought of the adults watching but not letting them know.

"I'm actually glad," she said. "They probably need somebody to talk to who understands their situation." She did not let on how much of that situation she was privy to, but merely added, "I heard Heather's father is out of jail. No one's seen him yet. Could already be back to work on third trick and we'd never know."

"But Louis!" Libby swung around to face the security guard, straining to keep her voice low. "What did you think about Paul?! I couldn't get in here yesterday, but I'm dying to know! When did you find out? And how?"

The faster Libby asked the questions, the slower and more deliberate Louis became.

"Well now, my wife is a long-time police radio scanner aficionado.

Knows all the codes. Always keeps an ear out for anything going on near the library. I can say the assiduity of her monitoring has increased these last few weeks.

"Then Sunday night—woo-ee! All hell broke loose on Apple Street! Pregnant lady in trouble; dog barking nuisance; backup for crime in progress, possible deadly force. Drove us nearly apoplectic knowing *what* was going on and *where*, but not *who* it was going on with. By the late news on TV we had a clearer—but considerably more disturbing—idea."

"That wasn't the whole picture either." Libby gave some of the background with Camille, then told about own her part in the deadly force incident. And Mae's. And Geoff's.

Louis bent slowly and peered at Libby's neck. "Paul Paterson did that?" Louis shook his head. "I never would have reckoned him to be that violent. Much less a killer."

"Gosh," said Libby, "I didn't think you'd be surprised. You helped figure it out."

Wiry gray eyebrows flew up, then crashed. "How's that?"

"You guys talking about Paul?" Bin sidled up to Libby, joined shortly by J'az, both visibly enticed.

Libby stepped back to include the two women. "I was just telling Louis what an important piece of the puzzle he uncovered in the investigation."

The women looked quizzically at Louis; he just shrugged.

"Louis told me Jonah hadn't announce the book fine money totals for a week *before* he was murdered," said Libby.

"Guess I wasn't paying attention," said J'az. "After a while you just tune it out."

"Not Louis," said Bin. "He's always paying attention."

Whatever dig Bin meant, Libby let it go. "Once I remembered Al Sparks's wife's comment and realized he never comes into the library," she said, "I went back to thinking the money was more likely taken by someone on the premises. Even Geoff Paterson, who hung out here, made more sense than Al. But because we all assumed the money was taken Friday night, even the police thought Jonah had to be the thief."

"Faulty premises," said Louis, "lead to faulty conclusions."

Bin looked uncertain as she let this sink in. "But it was Paul? Paul who took the money at least a week before?"

J'az folded her arms, her powder blue Afro not softening the scowl on her face. "I can't say I am shocked. All that man talked about was wanting money, needing money, getting money. He said it in a sweet cultured voice, but it was the only song he played."

"But why?" asked Bin. "Why did he kill Jonah? If he got the money he wanted?"

"Jonah threatened to turn him in," said Libby.

"Couldn't he have just paid the money back?"

Libby was still dismayed by this herself. "Didn't have it. Spent it already. Yes, almost all five thousand dollars. Spread it around so it didn't even register on any police radar. A water bill, a car loan payment, plants for the yard. A $3,000 rifle for Geoff along with an antique oriental rug for himself. These last two were apparently bought privately from people I heard were not inclined to say anything after the fact. And not inclined to give the money back. Paul said he tried to borrow from everybody he knew."

Louis gave a knowing nod. "You got that right. Tried to borrow from me early on."

J'az poked Louis. "Me, too. About a year ago when he first came. I never even connected it till now. Said he needed it for Geoff's tuition. Said his wife was being a pain about it. Was all earnest about paying it back."

"Did he?" asked Libby.

J'az squealed loud enough for patrons to look her way. She clamped her mouth shut, then said more softly but no less emphatically, "I didn't have any money to give to that man. I've got two little girls who use up all mine."

Bin laughed. "He was in with the wrong crowd if he thought any of us were in the lending business. So, wait," she said, putting things together. "Paul steals the money. Jonah says pay it back. Paul can't."

"And trust me," said J'az, "Jonah would have been adamant. All moral and righteous."

They all clucked in agreement that that's exactly how Jonah would have acted.

"So, Paul just went down there and killed Jonah?" said Bin. She shuttered. "Choked him to death for that money?"

"He did like awfully nice, expensive clothes," said J'az.

"There was more to it than the money," said Libby. "He was convinced his wife would take Geoff away if she found out. He couldn't bear losing his son."

Bin let out a long moan. "Oh, my goodness," she said, "after losing that twin baby."

It was obvious all of them knew the story. All had children of their own and understood in the core of their parent souls what devastating depths it would have touched to lose one, then be threatened with losing a second.

There was a solemn pause.

Bin picked up her end of the explanation. "That must be who my—" She hesitated, then quickly amended her wording, "who was seen in the alley that night."

"Unless it was Al Sparks," said Libby. "Movement in the alley that night must have looked like a choreographed vaudeville show, with timed entrances and exits. Just picture it:

Jonah is home and in the garage by 9p.m.

Paul comes home from work.

A car goes down the alley. Before it disappears at one end, the driver sees Al Sparks at the other.

Before Al gets to Jonah's to yell at him about harassing his kids, he changes his mind, turns back to the other end, and drives off to work.

Paul leaves his house, hellbent on settling things, and heads to

Jonah's.

Mae, on her porch, sees Monster Man—Paul, not Al; the Blue Donuts, finishing their practice in Sparks' garage, see none of it.

Paul returns to his house; Geoff comes home.

By 10 p.m., the Blue Donuts have disbursed; Al is at work; Paul and Geoff are eating pizza."

Louis rocked forward and back on the balls of his feet. He shook his head very slowly. "I still can't reckon that Paul Paterson could kill someone, then go home and eat pizza."

Had Libby not seen the Paul Paterson who tried to choke her, she might not have believed it either.

It was a decent show practice. With only days until the performance, a giddiness spread through the cast. Almost everyone was there. Harry had stuck around after his rendezvous in the stacks. So had Heather. With so many kids in and out for vacations and camps and sports tournaments all summer, her absence was hardly noticed.

Obviously, not in attendance was Geoff; Honey and Nikki were at Grandma Dee Dee's.

Libby ran through every song and all the movements or dances that went with them. Finally, she started from the top and literally just walked through the complete program, ironing out the sequence of numbers, inserting the solo talent acts, all in an effort to cause the least amount of chaos for the actual performance day.

If that was possible.

Harry and the tech crew wrote down cues for the portable microphone, listing when each piece of accompanying music had to be switched on; the volumes, the fades. She tried to remain patient as they mixed things up and kept reminding herself this was just a summer diversion for all involved.

Before turning the gang loose, Libby talked about what to wear;

costumes was too strong a word. The suggestion was only that everyone wear shorts, t-shirts, plain with no printing if possible.

She had a few ideas of her own to surprise them with on the actual day. A surprise mostly because she wasn't sure she'd have time to get anything before Saturday.

She packed up her bookbag, and as she left the tidied practice room, checked her phone once again for messages.

Namita: *I'm OK. Everything OK.*

Pretty spare. Probably too much to text, figured Libby. I'll find out soon enough.

CHAPTER
FORTY

Because the library air-conditioning was set so low, the sun outside after practice felt good. Odd how skin can hold that chill.

For a moment.

Within ten feet, Libby had warmed up. By the time she crossed Oak Avenue, she was sweaty. She chose the front way down Apple Street, where she saw Francie unloading her van.

Libby quickened her steps, hurrying to catch her friend before she went in, busting with a million questions about Camille. Before she could do more than offer to help, Francie thrust a small pile of orange papers at her. "Fliers for the block party. Schedule of events. Willing to pass them out?"

"Sure," said Libby. "But I've been dying to find out how things went with Camille and the baby! It got so late Monday night, and last night we had an unusual kind of party for Namita. But I'll let her tell you about that."

"Believe me, I understand. Last few days have not been my—oh, Libs, I see your neck now." She tilted her head several ways to give a thorough look. "Hope you're keeping it moist."

Libby was impatient. "I am. But what about Camille? Rough time in the delivery room?"

"Always a concern when the infant's premature. We tried to stall things, but babies are in charge. Camille seemed prepared that something might go wrong. Some people are like that. Some are all positive and upbeat; some go with the flow. Others, like Camille, ready for whatever. She was worried but stayed calm."

"Good thing you were around," said Libby.

Francie feigned smug importance. "Someone had to step up—while you were dealing with the neighborhood murderer."

Libby waved off the teasing. Francie only laughed. "Better get used to it, girl. Everybody's heard. Guess Sunday was a wild night in general for our block."

"Things at Mae's were a little scary, but so was your night with Camille."

"Well, that is true," said Francie. "You try to let the baby do its own thing. But the longer we waited, the more concerned Camille got. The doctor, too. Under those circumstances, every minute seems like an hour. By the time Nick arrived, the baby was experiencing stress, and they were proceeding with a C-section."

"The grandmother was kind of tight-lipped," said Libby, slipping the orange fliers into her bookbag. "Would only say there were complications."

"I didn't stick around. It was already after three. Nick was there by then, and I wasn't really needed." Francie lifted out two bulging pharmacy bags. "I did hear that she, the baby, had some upper respiratory difficulties and was under weight. Breathing problems. Lungs possibly underdeveloped—all concerns for preemies. There may have been other issues that did not manifest themselves immediately, but by then I was home and in bed."

"No update since?"

Francie shook her head. "Privacy regs. I wasn't on any list to be informed."

Libby stood back as Francie slammed the rear door of the van. "Anything else to go in?" she asked.

"This is it." Francie raised two bags, one then the other. "First aid supplies for Saturday. Just in case. Candy on sale for winners of Lamar's egg toss competition. How's your show coming?"

"A little ragged. Could be good; could be a disaster. Hoping at least it'll be fun."

Libby followed Francie up the steps to her house. "When do you think they'll get to come home—Camille and the baby?"

"Unless there were more serious issues that I was unaware of, it will largely depend on the baby's weight. They won't release them much under five pounds. Camille will need a few days to recover."

"Grandma Dee Dee said Camille didn't want visitors. Does that sound right?"

"I would honor that request," said Francie. "Even if there was no other specific trauma, Camille will be exhausted."

"Anybody have any idea what brought all this on?"

Francie leaned against her front door. "As I said before, babies dictate a lot of this. You don't always know the reason for why things happen."

Francie yawned. "Excuse me. Crazy day at work. And I haven't caught up with my sleep yet. Getting too old to do that night shift."

Libby caught the yawn and mumbled through it, "Are you going to be home tonight?"

"Home, but in bed early."

"I have your grant proposal all proofread. It's a great project. Can't believe you were able to track down those infant mortalities to one area of the city."

"That's been a statistical fact for a long time," said Francie. "It's just that this group of African American nurses have been dedicated to eliminating some of the known factors. Education is primary. But thanks, I really hope we can get the monies to offer more programs to help."

"It's well written and thorough. Looks like you're applying to the right agencies, too, so I think you have a good chance. I'll bring it down now if you want."

"Hey, Mrs. Ellison? Hey, Libby!" The Happy Trio called as they blasted out next door and landed on their porch with plates of food.

"We're having macaroni and cheese!" Ann informed not only Libby and Francie but half the neighborhood.

"Sounds good!" Libby called back.

"That group," said Francie. "Up to something, I bet."

Halfway down the block, Libby found herself chuckling, wondering if what they were up to was plotting *The Macaroni Murders*.

The thought so lifted Libby's mood that it prompted her to wave at Mrs. Thorne, sitting, barely in motion on her swing. Was that a twitch of the hand gripping the chain? A semi-wave? Or was it a completely involuntary gesture?

Whatever the case, it brought to mind Geoff's defense of the older woman. Libby had to wonder if she was missing something. Had she misjudged Mrs. Thorne? Even when she was nice, the response was less than positive.

Before Libby could assign Mrs. Thorne big girl status, she heard the sound of objects hitting something with ka-clunks. By the time her view had cleared the big blue spruce, she could see not only a large plastic garbage bag being pitched into with ka-clunks, but that it was Namita, rather vigorously, doing the pitching.

Libby made it up the first set of stairs. She stood at the bottom of the ones leading to the porch before Namita was startled into discovering her standing there.

She looked at Namita, flushed and perspiring, her hands covered with dirt. The porch, for the first time all summer, was cleared of flats and pots, of all the plastic containers of annuals which never made it to the garden.

Libby started to ask if nesting was underway, but something in Namita's unflinching focus and demeanor stopped her.

She searched Namita's face for clues. Her friend wore a neutral expression, as if even her features were unsure of their emotion. Libby saw neither joy nor relief; but not sadness or anxiety either. It was as if getting the porch cleaned was the only thing on Namita's mind.

The instincts of friendship also stopped Libby from her usual glib opener.

"Hi," she said plainly.

Namita chucked the last flat into the garbage bag, a sooty cloud of old dried up dirt rising above it. She looked at Libby. "Sorry I let this stuff sit out here all this time. It really was a mess." She took a broom and started sweeping dirt off the side of the porch, throwing up more clouds of dust.

Libby watched for a minute, then ventured, "What happened?"

Sweep. Sweep.

"Nothing."

Sweep. Sweep.

"Didn't go."

Libby had anticipated many possible answers, but she had not considered this one at all.

Namita did smile briefly, but countered it with, "I don't really want to talk about it."

Nothing stops a conversation more starkly than that.

Libby skidded to a halt on curiosity but couldn't shut down concern. "Are you okay?"

Namita stopped sweeping and gave long consideration before answering. "I am," she finally said. "I'm okay."

Libby waited a second to see if there was more. When there was not, she left Namita and went around to her back entrance. She trusted that eventually, on some walk with the dogs around the pond, dotted with fishermen or frozen for skaters, she would get the full story.

If Namita wanted it told.

CHAPTER
FORTY-ONE

L ibby hardly noticed that everything was cleared and gone when she came back around front.

Down the street she went, her feet flying faster and faster, her mind agitated, new thoughts roiling.

Was there really a connection? How worried should she be?

Dinner was getting underway at Francie's kitchen counter. Libby sat at the nearby table, nervously fingering the pages lying in front of her.

"Atrazine. Glyphosates," she rattled off. "The most common weed killer in the U.S.—banned in Europe—but sitting in cans stacked on every garden center shelf in America. Hosed out by every lawncare company's application; beads of it all over the sidewalk for animals to pick up. I brush Dash's paws off every time we walk, while Mr. Randall straps on his personal tank, spraying the tiniest crack like Agent Orange. To kill a dandelion!"

Francie turned to her friend. "Are you sure you don't want a glass of wine?"

Libby sailed past the offer. "Not to mention killing honeybees. When apples and carrots and broccoli disappear, they'll realize how badly pesticides have affected the world."

Francie glanced over Libby's shoulder as she passed to the sink with salad greens. "Is that Jonah's flier you're reading from?"

"Some were sitting near your grant. After what you said earlier, I started to see a thread running through all of this. The flier about the danger of lawn chemicals, the grant proposal and health threats. Especially to fetuses."

Libby swung around to face Francie. She had been thinking of nothing else since the connection had occurred to her. "Do you think there might something here to do with Camille's baby's?"

"So that's where you're going."

"You have to admit, they're the exact same complications you said Camille's baby had—low birth weight, respiratory problems, possible hormonal damage later. And I know Montgomerys use stuff on their lawn."

Wrinkles spread across Francie's brow. "Gosh. I don't know."

A floor fan directed at the table whirred softly as Francie unwrapped a package of hamburger.

"Exposure to those chemicals needs to correlate with the time a woman conceives," she said. "Has to happen during spring spraying times. That doesn't line up with Camille's dates. Besides, our data shows other causes for low birth weight in our focus area—limited pre-natal education, poor health of the mother due to limited access to nutritious food." She gave Libby a resigned smile. "Sad and dangerous as it seems, the use of pesticides is low on our list of issues to address."

Francie tossed the meat tray and coverings in the trash container under the sink. "Don't be too bleak, Libs. First of all, it's hard to know causes for certain. Secondly, babies are very resilient creatures. And remember this, there may be absolutely nothing wrong with Camille's child."

She shaped and salted a platter of patties. "But here's my hamburger, wrapped in plastic. Depending on who you talk to, an artery clogger and a carcinogen. Lamar and I can't afford organic beef or fish all the time, and the world is currently coming to us mostly wrapped in plastic."

Francie rinsed her hands. "My nurse group will try to have some small effect on the lives of mothers and babies in this one zip code. You have to start somewhere."

Libby slumped in her chair. "How can people want a perfect lawn more than healthy children or good, clean water in the lakes?"

"I hear you," said Francie, "but frankly, I'm too old to tackle the whole world." She dried her hands, set mustard and ketchup on the table, and began slicing a large red onion into rings. "Now you, you just helped catch a murderer. Isn't that enough laurels to rest on for the week?"

"Oh. Yeah. Paul," said Libby. She sighed as she looked out Francie's back window onto the small cutting garden. The walkway was lined with a row of herbs that she and Francie traded throughout the season. "He grew such pretty flowers. Made such good nut bread."

Francie laughed out loud. "Nut bread?!"

"He brought nut bread to Mae all the time. It was very good. Although I'm beginning to wonder if he didn't also poison her iced tea."

"Are you kidding? How? Why?"

"Because Mae was on her back porch, as usual, the night of the murder. Paul could never be sure what she saw or what she'd say. Must have felt threatened from all sides."

"He's turning out to be one scary guy."

"A strange mix, for sure. Devoted to his son; seemingly gentle; played that beautiful cello. And underneath a streak so ... deadly."

"Just wonder what gets into a person."

"You probably didn't know, but Geoff was a twin. His brother died at birth."

Francie stopped chopping, a look of sadness crossing her face. "How tragic. Not surprised he doted on Geoff."

"I wouldn't doubt that Paul thought God or the universe had been unjust to him all along, starting with the loss of that infant. Everything he ran into after that—money troubles, a mean-spirited ex-wife—were seen in that light."

"It's the same as I was telling you about Mrs. Thorne," said Francie, returning to her onion. "All those big and little events. Times in our lives we make choices. Forks in the road. How we react can take us in one direction or a completely different one."

When Namita felt the red flesh of the tomato in her hand sink beneath her thumb, she knew their time was up.

She pulled the shades on her front apartment windows against the August sun bursting in early. She had to go to work. By the time she got home, it would be sweltering outside and cool in the apartment if she did this. The room air conditioner was effective, but the heat of August was not to be trifled with.

The hose downstairs, which had been running for a while, went off.

Namita hadn't talked to Libby since yesterday afternoon at the porch restoration. She reached for Paji's leash and called the lanky greyhound. Before heading out the door, she chose three decent tomatoes.

"No salsa this year," she explained, bowling the tomatoes into Libby's hands. "Compost them if they're bad."

Libby happily accepted the load. "Thanks."

"Have you already walked? It'll be short in this heat."

"Let me put these inside and get Dash. He's been ready to roll since seven."

The foursome sought as many spots of shade as they could possibly find, crossing the street to take advantage of the cover of a big sycamore tree and two oaks in a row. For a minute, Libby thought she needed to be more grateful, more often, for the gift of trees. The difference in temperature from being in pounding direct sun to being in the slightest bit of shade was incredible.

Libby tried to imagine the major shift of intention Namita must have made. Libby herself was just beginning to catch up with her own adapting to no longer thinking about a baby upstairs.

"How are you this morning?" Libby started out. She watched for a signal for how much Namita might want to talk or not, whether she was dealing with grief or disappointment or—

"I'm feeling good," said Namita.

Libby checked Namita's tone. Had the little group not been sluggish with the heat, it seemed genuinely upbeat.

"It's a little warm, and I wish I didn't have to go to work, but I'm good." Namita looked at Libby and saw the concern; had heard the wariness in her questions. She stopped to firmly punctuate the word. "Really."

Once convinced, Libby stopped treading lightly. "So, what the heck happened?"

Namita looked ahead. "Ooh," she said.

She inhaled, then exhaled slowly. "A combination of things. Mostly a … a gut instinct. Just didn't seem like the right thing at this time."

"Hmmm," said Libby, also inhaling and exhaling deliberately, as she let more adjustments, practical and emotional, take place.

Admittedly, the turnabout was jarring, as if someone had dealt out cards for hearts and then said they were playing gin rummy. Similar cards but certainly needing to be rearranged.

They walked. The dogs did their duties. The morning sun slanted hot between the houses.

"I'm thinking about being a Big Sister," Namita said as they took the short route down a side street.

The card game had changed again.

Libby stuck with "Hmmm."

"Yeah. One of the directors came into my resource center. We got to talking. Thinks I'm in a perfect situation. Did you know a city this size has over 3,00 kids, waiting, who need a mentor? 1,500 already being served."

The lawns along the way were a lush green if still being watered; brown and dormant if the homeowner had given up, leaving hot and rainless August to call the shots.

One oscillating sprinkler waved optimistically over grass eager to be revitalized.

CHAPTER
FORTY-TWO

Friday, the day before the block party, found Camille sitting inside by her living room window, her legs stretched out along the couch.

She knew she had to prepare an answer, a set of words that would steady her in the face of all the good wishes people would be extending. Words that would accept the joyful comments graciously. Then words for the sudden looks of pity. Most especially, words she could tell herself over and over until she herself believed them.

She had been home already for two days, although she had not seen or talked to anyone outside the house. She was tired and sore; taking it easy. Nikki and Honey were home but had been so only for the last hour. After hugs and questions and stories about their visit with Papa and Grandma Dee Dee, they had rushed to slip on bathing suits and fly into the hot afternoon to reclaim their neglected wading pool.

Just as Camille had predicted, the girls looked as if they were ready for middle school when she returned after the birth of her tiny new child. She had missed their giggling and bickering. She watched them now, moved as only a parent is by their unbridled silliness.

Beyond them, she could see Libby, halfway down the block, stopped to engage with the mailman.

"Don't forget the block party tomorrow," Libby said to Carrier Dobbs as their routes intersected. "I know you can't have any beer on company time, but you're welcome to hit the food line."

Carrier Dobbs thanked her for the invitation. He went one way with the mail, while Libby went the other with her fliers.

One was the finalized *Schedule of Events*. A second was about using lawn pesticides and fertilizers. Couldn't help it.

She'd updated Jonah's statistics about possible birth defects and the danger to pets and children, trying to make it sound more encouraging to change than damning of practice, a tact Jonah could never pull off.

She outlined easy household concoctions to replace the chemicals, described methods as innocuous as pouring boiling water on weeds to kill them in sidewalk cracks. She did not go into how helpful at cleaning the air those weeds and any green plant life actually was. She could be judicious. She didn't have to be overbearing.

As she made her way home, Libby saw Nikki and Honey running through their sprinkler, hopping in and out of their wading pool on the front lawn like sparrows returned to Capistrano.

"I'm so glad you're home!" Libby exclaimed, returning Honey's enveloping hug.

"Can we have some tomatoes?" asked Nikki.

"Dee Dee doesn't have tomatoes," lamented Honey. "Butterflies are okay, but she doesn't like bees. Papa likes bees. And grasshoppers."

By now Libby's cherry tomato plant branches were drooping with the weight of so many red and golden specimens. The crop was abundant, not only because they thrived in the August heat along with Indiana's corn-on-the-cob and the ubiquitous zucchini, but because Libby's usual little neighbor harvesters had been away.

Libby, Honey, and Nikki stood there, unrestrained, eating and laughing and telling of recent adventures; sweet juice and seeds squirting out and down everyone's chin.

When she looked up to see that Camille had appeared on her porch, Libby urged the girls to return to their sprinkler and followed a short distance behind. She could always turn around if their mother did not seem in the mood to talk.

Instead, Camille invited Libby to come have a seat.

"You're home," said Libby, patting the head of the ever-vigilant Major, who greeted her at the edge of the porch.

"I am," said Camille.

Libby thought Camille looked tired in a way that had little to do with rest or sleep. She had on a loose white cotton shift with blue cornflowers. Her black hair was pulled back, and there was a paleness to her usually dark skin.

"How do you feel? Physically?" Libby asked.

Camille smiled at the distinction made. "I had always heard C-sections can take a lot out of you."

Libby waited. Finally, she ventured, "And the baby?"

There was an awkward pause.

"She's home, too."

Camille then searched for some of the generic points she'd rehearsed. "We weren't sure how long it would take her to gain enough weight to be released, but fortunately she's a good eater. No surprise after these other two."

Camille seemed to latch on to the more neutral topic of her other girls, visibly more comfortable glancing down at Nikki and Honey, dancing in and out of their pool.

Libby followed suit and repeated Honey's description of fishing with Papa and Nikki's perfect, if irreverent, impersonation of Dee Dee instructing them on how good little children act at the dinner table.

Which got the two women laughing.

Which Camille realized she had not done for many days.

She relaxed and asked about Namita; became subdued and thoughtful at Libby's details about the change of plans.

Libby then filled her in on the dramatic arrest of Paul Paterson.

"Nick was shocked to hear it wasn't Al Sparks," said Camille. "No secret he's never been a fan, but still …."

Suddenly, Major set on a barking binge. Camille didn't wait long, but got up and put him in the house.

She sat again on the porch swing, started to say something, then stopped.

Libby's propensity would have been to help, to encourage, but she tried to take to heart Francie's caution to let Camille proceed in her own way and time.

Camille twisted the chain links that held the swing.

She didn't speak the words out of courage.

She spoke out of need.

The need for someone to know. Suddenly her plans to be measured and careful dropped away.

"Faith," she said simply.

Libby didn't follow. "Faith?"

"That's what we named her. Nick's not crazy about it. She looks like a Faith."

Before Libby could delight in the name, Camille added plainly, "She failed some tests. There may be … problems."

Libby struggled for a response, but Camille spared her by not waiting for one. She was ready to talk. "We don't know everything yet. Whether she'll need surgery to correct some respiratory issues. Preemies often fail the hearing test, so no one—except me—was freaked about that. Oh, my." She took a deep breath. "I really miss my mom."

She found a tissue and pushed tears aside.

"Nick is staying upbeat, telling me not to be melodramatic, but it feels more like he's not facing the realities. And you know Dee Dee. Hardly the most compassionate mother-in-law. Already embarrassed by a child who might have *issues*."

Her voice and eyes lowered. "Oh, Libby. I did so many things wrong during this pregnancy."

Libby had listened to Camille make the most painful of revelations, she would not now let her blame herself on top of everything else. "Camille," she said, "please don't take that on."

Camille folded in the edges of her tissue. "Remember, I fell."

"Even if that did any harm, it was an accident."

"It wasn't an accident when I drank mulled wine, even for a while after I knew I was pregnant. Or the pesticides I cleaned up in the garage."

Libby froze; Camille went on. "I've read Jonah's fliers," she said. "And I knew when I cleaned up the spilled weed killer in the garage last winter that I should have been more careful. But it smelled so strong, the place all closed up like that, and Nick was gone. I just wanted it out of there."

Winter, thought Libby. January? February? Not during spring spraying season, but a winter conception. When she was exposed to the chemicals in the garage.

Again, Libby relied on Francie's words. "I'm told it's really hard to trace the cause of …."

But Libby couldn't pretend to be upbeat or dismissive. Camille already had people in her life for that. It was rare for Libby not to know what to say. Her mother had been a role model of compassionate, appropriate comments for even the most difficult situations. Even so, Libby tried to imagine what she would have said in this circumstance.

"Whatever happens, Camille, you're strong. And you have friends."

It sounded lame.

Camille, however, did not think so. The nurses at the hospital had been gentle, but realistic. Dee Dee had been self-oriented and harsh. Nick was in denial, and the comments of other mothers in the nursery had been either laced with pity or full of overblown optimism about the baby's future.

Only Libby reminded her that she was strong. That no mother would fight harder or care more completely for this child. Faith.

Camille looked over at Libby and smiled. "I don't want to go into a lot of details with people," she said. "Especially because there are still so many unanswered questions."

She cleared her throat. "How does this sound: they're running some tests, watching Faith because she came early. But she's home. And she's beautiful."

CHAPTER
FORTY-THREE

At 9 a.m., orange barricade horses went up at either end of Apple Street. Two porches hosted coffee and donuts and egg casseroles for the early risers who helped set things out.

The night before, the entire block had emptied itself of vehicles. Mrs. Thorne might have been pleased except that by breakfast, the area had filled up with all manner of kid transportation in preparation for the parade: bikes and trikes and scooters; strollers and wagons, all with crepe paper trailing from every handle or handlebar, woven through every spoke.

The block party was underway.

It was as if a huge playpen had been dropped down from the sky, allowing pets and children to roam largely unattended, yet safely confined. It wasn't a fête in the English countryside, but there were enough activities coming to life up and down the twenty-six houses, 1901 through 2022, to qualify as a small fair.

There was a water balloon toss and chalk drawing contest. A badminton net was strung across the street for continuous games. Namita read books on the lawn; Mrs. Laguna painted insects and flowers on the faces of any child who could sit still long enough to have it done.

At noon, no one cared that it had gotten hot. Most of the kids were running around anyway in clothes drenched from exploding water balloons.

Adults rolled out grills to a central spot, while tables and chairs were pulled from porches and back yards and set up in the shade. The charry smell of meaty bratwurst and burgers cooking called everyone to eat.

Libby had brought finger sandwiches with a cream cheese-dill spread topped with cucumbers, courtesy of the Two Sues. She set them next to a taco dip and warm corn soufflé. There were bags of every conceivable kind of chip and a few casseroles, but the main fare was Indiana August fresh: watermelon and cantaloupe wedges, sliced tomatoes, marinated zucchini, onions, peppers—red, yellow, and green. Some tossed with vinegar and oil, dusted with cilantro or parsley; some simply sliced and circling a homemade dip.

Once the majority of people settled down with plates loaded with food, general announcements were made. They were the usual reminders about association dues; about picking up after pets; a plug for the fall community garage sale.

And the review of safety tips.

Frivolity withered at the very first note.

Watch for anyone destroying property.

Be on the alert, aware always of your surroundings.

Leave porchlights lit; don't walk alone.

Report any suspicious activity.

It didn't help the mood for Libby to call for updates in the block directory, everyone acutely aware of the names and numbers being taken off the list.

And the obvious, unspoken reasons for those removals.

As usual, it was the children who could not stay serious for long, and soon an impromptu contest to see who could spit water between their front teeth the farthest ensued.

Eating and visiting resumed, the lighthearted mood prevailed.

Not long after, Francie bumped her hip into Libby's canvas chair. "You falling asleep?"

Libby turned a lazy eye upward. "Digesting."

"Come help protect me from the desserts."

Libby could refrain from lots of the sweets laid out, especially gooey, sugary, kid-oriented concoctions of pulverized cookies and candies mooshed up in whipped cream or cupcakes laden with sprinkles. But there was no passing up a small piece of Francie's warm, homemade blueberry pie. She kept to a small piece, not because she was being judicious, but because she also wanted a piece of Mrs. Randall's peach pie, too. A scoop of ice cream accompanied both.

"Nice turnout," said Libby.

"Food or people?"

Libby laughed. "Both, I guess. Some at the lake or on vacation as usual. Mrs. Thorne boycotting as usual. Otherwise a decent showing. Any casualties yet?" she asked as she searched for her fork.

"One skinned knee. One splinter. One mosquito bite."

Francie helped herself to a piece of pink raspberry cake and a large spoonful of banana pudding with vanilla wafers. "How about you?" she asked. "Your show biz kids all here and ready to go?"

"Hope so. Never surprised when somebody doesn't turn up. Or gets embarrassed, too shy to go on. Or like Geoff Paterson. Missing obviously for a different reason."

"That's all just so sad." Francie opened a cooler and reached into the ice for a bottle of water. Libby tucked her own container of water from home under her arm, balanced her pie slices with fork and napkins, and followed Francie to two abandoned chairs in the shade.

"I know Geoff did some despicable things," said Libby. "He was an odd kid. Not unlikeable, even a good heart deep down. He really did save me and Mae. In a way, this neighborhood was good for him."

Francie licked pudding from her finger. "Except for Mrs. Thorne."

The highlight of the late afternoon was Mr. Motorcycle letting anyone who wanted to sit on his big roaring red beast. Parked, it was not roaring at the moment, but formidable just the same. Even Carrier Dobbs climbed on, pretending like a five-year-old to be revving his motor and zooming down the highway. Mae demurred about getting on, but with very little coaxing, delighted all by strutting around in the shiny black helmet bobbing on her tiny head.

Another big event was supposed to have been the moving of the bees.

From Jonah's to Libby's.

There was no way around it. Libby had spent the summer reading and studying about them, caring for and protecting them, gradually feeling responsible for them. She just could not let their hive be dismantled or destroyed or they merely be left to fend for themselves as Jonah's house sat empty. New owners quite probably would do away with the hive as well.

But the county extension office had informed Libby that this move couldn't take place until it was cooler. To relocate a hive the distance Libby wanted, the bees must be quarantined in the hive in that new location for one or two days so they can reorient their radar, literally getting their bearings. Otherwise, they keep returning to their former spot and, having no home there, eventually die. Closed up that way for a move in the August heat could be just as lethal.

A few weeks later, on an unseasonably chilly weekend, there would be another Apple Street parade, no less exuberant than the block party one that morning. This time, human streamers of children would trail behind Jonah's hive, strapped to a dolly. Honey, who was over the moon about the bees moving in next door, would direct the crowd, instructing them along the way about bees being a danger only if *frettened*.

The hive would then come to rest in Libby's back yard.

Like Honey, Libby would be pleased.

Jonah's daughter, Charlotte, too would be happy that a part of her father would still be buzzing around her childhood home, annoying some, pricking the conscience of others.

Dinnertime did boast one other anticipated event: pots of hot, fresh corn-on-the-cob. No one passed up the sweet and tender corn, picked that morning, and brought to the local farmer's market for purchase. Butter dripped from cobs and chins; fingers and faces smeared salty.

After indulging on two ears of corn, Libby ducked out to take Dash for a quick walk, fed him and BabyCakes.

She checked the clock.

An electric bolt of excitement shot through her.

Showtime!

At 7:30 p.m., Libby blew her safety wrist whistle, giving the half-hour heads-up signal. Within minutes, Mr. Randall's place became the focus of attention. Food tables were cleared away; chairs rearranged. Kids who would perform, already hyped from eating crazy and running wild all day, went into a frenzy of bathroom stops, going over lyrics, and primping as they began to alternate between feelings of exhilaration and sheer terror.

Ah, the thrill of a live production!

Into the midst of the audience assembling and children preparing, came Camille.

And the new baby.

Libby watched everyone ooh and ah and smile and part like the Red Sea to give them preferential seating. She also watched Camille, who looked more relaxed than she had the day before.

"Libby! Libby! The boombox's not working!" Sarah rushed to Libby's side.

This was not good news. Yes, all part of the charm of a live show, but not what Libby wanted to have to deal with fifteen minutes before a whole summer's worth of work was to be presented.

Harry had been the main tech guy, had trained Sarah to help, and was currently back at Sparks' garage getting other band equipment together. In checking the operation of the portable speaker box, which housed music for almost every single number, Sarah found she could not get it to work.

Libby knelt next to the box, frantically examining all the wires and extension cord connections.

"Want some help?"

Libby turned to see a tall person next to her, in shadow from the sun beginning to descend behind him.

"Geoff?" Libby stood. "Where did you come from?"

He hitched his thumb toward an unfamiliar woman off to one side of the chaos. "My mom brought me."

Before Libby could comment, he added, "You know, she's not so bad."

"Good. I'm glad."

"Is Mae okay?" he asked.

"A few bruises, but she's fine."

He did not seem any less confident—or sincere—than he always had.

"That's good," he said. "I … she had kind of a rough fall." He eyed the crowd. "I thought she might be at the block party." He grinned. "I didn't expect Mrs. Thorne."

You are disarming, thought Libby. She looked around. "Mae was sitting over there a little bit ago. I expect she'll be back for the show. Meanwhile, do you know anything about portable speakers like this one?"

He did. He poked about—front, sides, and back. He adjusted some of the preset buttons he said must have been knocked or changed in carting the box around.

He smiled. "Good to go."

Sarah smiled.

Libby smiled and thanked him. "You're welcome to stay and sing," she said.

Geoff shrugged noncommittally.

CHAPTER
FORTY-FOUR

"Faith."

Namita nudged Libby and stood with the new Montgomery baby tucked and sleeping in the crook of her arm.

"Her name is Faith," repeated Namita. "They're running a few tests on her, but she's home. Isn't she beautiful?"

She was.

Libby had heard Camille's practiced lines, but she had not seen the baby.

Honey squirmed between Namita and Honey. "That's my baby."

"She most definitely is," said Libby, noting Honey's same black hair and cocoa skin.

The baby coughed. Libby watched Namita run a tender finger lightly against Faith's chubby cheek. "How are you doing with all this?"

"Not too bad," said Namita. "Not too bad at all."

Then a sudden rush, the Blue Donuts flooded in from the back yard and alley. Heather herded them to one side of Mr. Randall's porch with a continuous stream of instructional encouragement.

Namita dodged a set of drums being carried out in pieces, going to the spot Heather pointed to. "I'd better get out of the way," Namita said. "Looks like the other director is taking charge."

"Really glad she's here," said Libby. "I don't doubt that she could run the whole show."

Namita escorted Honey to the youngest group of singers sitting on the grass and waiting with one of the parents. She returned Faith to Camille, thinking that this was, perhaps, the best outcome for her—a new baby next door to hold and spoil, at the same time being a big sister and mentor to an older child who needed what she had to offer. And had room for in her nest.

She looked around at the swelling crowd and snagged a seat near a refreshed-looking Mae.

It was a perfect setup: The audience of forty or fifty could sit in chairs and blankets all along the ample grass park strip or in the street. The performers had a cement runway, centered, that led to eight wide steps, then up to the deep porch, which stretched across the entire front of Mr. Randall's house. Plenty of room to accommodate a cast of twenty-eight or allow for a smaller group just on the steps for a more intimate number.

A little before 8 p.m., thin layers of clouds pulled across the sky like a curtain, dimming the sun and stirring enough air to make having so many sitting so close on a warm August night quite bearable.

The microphone and portable speaker worked.

As predicted, Honey, Nikki, and company silenced everyone with their pseudo-French version of *Fairy Jackets, fairy jackets; stormy, too; stormy, too*," complete with hand gestures. For the English lines "*morning bells are ringing*," each child vigorously shook ribboned bells which Libby had unearthed from her box of Christmas decorations.

Adorable.

Libby stood to the side, stage managing: lining the acts up, bringing them on with an introduction, scooting them off with a call for a round of applause.

It was a relatively short program:

Two baton twirlers. All tossed spins caught.

'Tis the Gift to Be Simple. Harmony not bad. Karaoke background music on the boombox made it sound professional.

Second year appearance for a saxophone solo. A little boring but improving.

Three card tricks performed down front on the grass, which kept the audience engaged while the Blue Donuts set up center stage on the porch.

The normal cacophony of twangy guitar tuning, and unrelated drumming almost lost the crowd as it got late, and they got restless. In the nick of time, Harry, poised to push the button for sound, gave the nod; Libby made the introductions and handed the mic to the lead singer.

Heather dropped her head forward dramatically. She held out her palm at full arm's length. All extraneous noise ceased.

On the count of four, the music was cranked up, Heather keeping everything together. They weren't perfect, but they were awfully good.

Libby looked out at the audience. They seemed both amazed and delighted that such a coherent and pleasing sound could emerge from the Blue Donuts, from what they had always considered mere noise and discord of practice going on all summer down at Sparks' garage.

Practice, Libby could not help thinking, that had annoyed Jonah Pemberton—and the reaction to that annoyance that had almost cost Al Sparks his freedom. Practice that had been the cover for a murder by Paul Paterson.

The first song ended, and Heather cued her drummer. She handed the mic to Libby and fell in line with the beat, clapping, waving the entire cast onto the steps, the porch, the runway.

Libby had bought them colored baseball caps, but now realized they were all wearing black or white tops and putting on sunglasses, even the nine-under-nine section, giving the group the look of one, huge, almost professional, ensemble.

Heather's hip hop choreography was sharp and athletic. Her mother was in the front row, clapping along to the beat with the rest of the audience right down to Mae.

Nothing like a live performance, thought Libby. So rousing, moving.

She'd been both singer and audience member and knew the thrill from both angles. It was with great satisfaction for herself and joy for the performers to see Mr. Randall's porch covered with Blue Donuts, the Happy Trio, Geoff added in the back row, Honey and Nikki, all the kids from up and down Apple Street at this one moment, rocking this block party audience.

Libby thought about how kids sang and jumped around all over the place in their homes, just goofy most of the time. It was the organized singing and jumping—the dancing—that parents rarely saw from their children that was so fun and gratifying for her to be a part of.

Heather finished by picking up the mic and bringing everyone in singing the last grand section.

Libby looked out front.

Past Mae, past Camille, leaning against a maple tree at the far edge of the crowd was Al Sparks.

Libby could not imagine what might be going through his mind. Maybe, she hoped, at this minute, he was only thinking of Heather, that he could melt back into the ordinary, be just a parent, like all the other ones, watching his child with pride.

The standing ovation was well-deserved.

No, it was not Broadway. Far, far from it. But it was so much better than anyone had expected.

If there is an adrenalin rush for the performers and the audience during the performance, there is no less a high in the congratulatory moments that follow.

Singers, dancers, technicians, parents, siblings; neighbors and friends in the show, neighbors and friends in the back row, all slightly astounded at what they had done and seen.

Even the bad and the boring were swept into the net of congratulations and patted on the back for a job well done. A wagon carrying a big cooler with ice cream bars was wheeled into the crowd, completing the sweetness of the event.

Almost everyone and everything was cleared out by 10 p.m.

A few adults sat around a small portable fire pit, drank beer or ate 'smores, but the rest were home collapsing after washing painted butterflies off their children's faces, sorting out grass-stained outfits for the laundry, or taking a cool shower after a long, sweaty, successful day.

Libby stood in her back yard. Above the night sounds, she heard Major bark occasionally and a few bursts of laughter erupt farther down the street. Dash nosed around, while BabyCakes sat inside, perched on the chair by the kitchen window.

Libby had examined the yard for the perfect spot and set out blocks for the future hive. Here, the bees would get morning sun to rouse them and afternoon shade to welcome them home. Here, they would be safe. Happy, safe, protected. Not threatened.

She caught herself adding that last, realizing that Apple Street, for all its city-life offerings of community—neighbors helping neighbors, the array of interesting people—it could also be a place of danger, far more so than she could have imagined three months ago.

Vandalism. The destruction of property for the pettiest of reasons.

Murder. The ultimate destruction of human life. Was there any reason that it was not a petty and horrific act?

Next door Major barked. Libby heard a sharp "Shut up!" from Nick and the barking stop.

But the world was not really a quiet place. August cicadas, siss-hissing in the trees; crickets chirping, burping tree frogs would not be silenced.

The bark again.

"Poor Major," Libby said out loud. "What is it that unsettles you so?"

On either side of the fireplaces that sat on the south walls of many of the houses on Apple Street were small windows overlooking a neighbor's side yard.

Or porch.

To the left of her fireplace, dark, with no warmth summer or winter, Mrs. Thorne stood at her small window and tapped.

Tap, tap, tap.

She couldn't see the dog but smiled when she heard him bark again.

Tap, tap, tap.

The End

Acknowledgments

For me, this second book was harder to complete. The first blush and rush of creativity was not the same, and while there were days of joy and triumph, rewriting, editing, and plowing through to the end were more the mode of operation. And so it is even more important for me to thank those who made such a difference along the way.

For honest input and helpful suggestions, thanks to my first readers: Anne Marie B., Renee K., Margaret K., Jennifer M., and Louise C.

For those who continued to express exuberant anticipation over the long haul, thanks to my family, literal and figurative: Mary Beth I., Mary S., Julie D., Joanie G., John I., Lisa A.

For those who made dark writings days bright just by asking, "How's the book coming?": Nancy W., Kathy W., Becky E., Robert K., Kathleen Ann C., Susan S., and Ann S.

For Andre M., who generously opened his forensic library to me.

For Charkiera Smith, for all her technical aid throughout the project; and for taking a pile of typed pages, formatting, and turning them into print.
To the same Charkiera Smith, for a most elegant and enticing cover.

Made in the USA
Monee, IL
22 June 2020